Death Wields a Henry .44

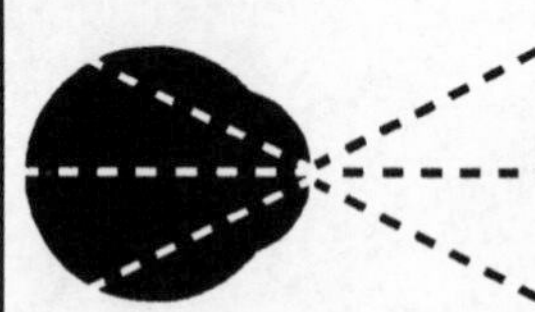

This Large Print Book carries the Seal of Approval of N.A.V.H.

MIKE SARTAIN, THE REVENGER

DEATH WIELDS A HENRY .44

A WESTERN DUO

FRANK LESLIE

THORNDIKE PRESS
A part of Gale, a Cengage Company

Thorndike Press, a part of Gale, a Cengage Company.

Thorndike Press® Large Print Western.
The text of this Large Print edition is unabridged.
Other aspects of the book may vary from the original edition.
Set in 16 pt. Plantin.

LIBRARY OF CONGRESS CIP DATA ON FILE.
CATALOGUING IN PUBLICATION FOR THIS BOOK
IS AVAILABLE FROM THE LIBRARY OF CONGRESS

ISBN-13: 978-1-4328-4883-5 (hardcover alk. paper)

Published in 2020 by arrangement with Peter Brandvold

Printed in Mexico
Print Number: 01 Print Year: 2020

CONTENTS

Savage Barranca

Chapter One

Mike Sartain, the Revenger, rode into the little mining supply camp of Low Range, Colorado Territory, just before midnight on a hopping Friday night in the late summer.

He found a feed barn on a side street just off the main drag, and gave the Irish proprietor, who was half-soused and had been bending a saucy *señorita* over a saddle tree when the Revenger had first encountered him, two dollars for water, feed, and a clean stable.

Leaving his prized buckskin stallion, Boss, in the Irishman's dubious care, the tall, broad-shouldered Cajun, his cobalt eyes staring hungrily out from beneath the broad brim of his sand-colored Stetson, and wearing a big, silver-plated LeMat revolver thonged on his right thigh, slipped his Henry repeating rifle from his saddle boot and headed for the Oriental Saloon & Gambling Parlor.

He strode purposefully through the crowd of rollicking miners, mule skinners, cattlemen, pleasure girls, and even a few blue-clad soldiers on furlough from a nearby cavalry outpost. Young Mexican boys were selling *tamales* wrapped in corn husks from handcarts. Horses whinnied, mules brayed; a couple of oxen harnessed to a stout ore wagon were locking horns, as though infected by the raucous atmosphere.

Dogs ran, grinning and barking, down the main street, which was identified as Arkansas Avenue by a crude wooden sign.

Several scantily clad girls stood on the balcony of a hurdy-gurdy house calling to the men in the street. One of them lifted her skimpy red wrap to show Sartain her breasts. The Revenger, who enjoyed the women as much as any man — in fact, even more than most, having been well-schooled in the intimate arts by the most talented sporting girls in the country while growing up in the French Quarter of New Orleans — merely gave the girl a cool, passing nod.

Later, the Cajun would find a girl, maybe this girl, to bleed off his loins. At the moment, he had more pressing matters.

The indignant whore scowled as she lowered the wrap and cursed him angrily while several onlookers laughed.

Sartain made his way to a mud-brick building identified by a wooden sign stretching into the street atop a crooked cottonwood pole as the establishment he was looking for. He mounted the broad front gallery, pushed through the batwings, and squinted against the heavy wood and tobacco smoke swirling in the sprawling room filled with men and painted ladies, assaulted by the frenetic pattering of a piano, and lit by a dozen smoky gas lamps.

Beneath the din, Sartain could hear the clattering of a roulette wheel and the clicking of craps dice. Men were clumped at various gambling layouts here and there about the room, while some were tramping arm in arm with colorful, albeit skimpily attired, *nymphs du pavé* up the carpeted stairs at the back of the room.

Sartain, taller than most of the other fifty or sixty men in the room, surveyed the crowd carefully until he found the man he was looking for. Shouldering the Henry once more, he made his way through the crowded room. He skirted a group of men standing around a faro layout and then pushed up to a large, round, baize-covered table around which seven or eight men were playing what appeared to be five-card stud.

A beautiful blonde, attired in a frilly

purple gown and smoking a slender cigarillo with a long, black wooden holder, moved slowly through the crowd gathered around the far side of the table from Sartain.

She was young despite the implacable coolness of her gaze and the matronly swells of her body. Her limbs were long. Her shoulders were bare, as were the high plains of her ample breasts. Her ivory skin was flawless, nearly translucent. Her eyes were a hard light-blue. They were the faintly jeering eyes of a stone-hearted siren.

Her full, blood-red lips glistened in the light from a near lamp.

Her hair was piled in creamy swirls atop her head and held in place with a jewel-encrusted comb. A jewel-encrusted black choker encircled her long, slender neck. The jewels in the comb and the choker sparkled like the glitter on a Christmas tree.

The blue-eyed beauty stopped near the man Sartain was scrutinizing with his shrewd, cobalt gaze. The impeccably dressed man would have been handsome but for his dark, narrow-set, mean little eyes.

He was maybe thirty, and he was having the time of his life, calling and raising and flinging his cards down with aplomb, pausing now and then to jeer at one of his opponents. He was drinking beer and shots of whiskey, swilling the stuff and slamming the glasses down on the table.

He had longish, dark-brown hair combed straight back off his forehead and curling onto the shoulders of his cream silk shirt, which was adorned with a celluloid collar and a brown four-in-hand tie. A thick brown mustache mantled his thin-lipped mouth. He wore two shoulder holsters containing two gold-plated derringers.

When the blue-eyed beauty in the purple gown drew near him, he grabbed her arm, pulled her brusquely down to him, and kissed her lips. She didn't seem to mind. In fact, she wrapped her arm around the man's neck and returned his kiss with passion while the men sitting or standing around the table cheered.

She straightened, winked winningly, puffed her cigarillo, and, blowing the smoke toward the ceiling, continued making her queenly way through the crowd. As she moved, all male eyes flicked to her, darkly, lustfully.

Sartain pushed his way toward the table. When he was six feet away from it, he stared hard at the man with the derringers. The man seemed to sense his gaze, and returned it, frowning incredulously, a long, slender cigar smoldering in the corner of his mouth.

Sartain raised his voice: "Clancy Coles?"

The men around the table fell silent as they turned their own skeptical gazes at the big, dark-haired Cajun in the pinto vest, the handsome Henry repeater resting on his shoulder, the pretty LeMat jutting from his holster.

The little eyes of the man across the table nearly crossed as, flaring his nostrils, he said, "Who, by god, wants to know?"

"Mike Sartain."

The low roar still emanating from the room beyond the table grew noticeably quieter. A few men hushed the others.

"Come again?" said the man across the table from Sartain.

"You heard me," the Revenger said.

Now the entire saloon was nearly as quiet as a barn at night.

Apprehension flickered in Coles's gaze.

"You killed innocent men, Coles. That's why you yourself are a dead man," Sartain said, reaching down with his right hand to free the keeper thong from over his LeMat's hammer. "You gonna just sit there and take one through your brisket, or do you want to stand up and take your chances with those derringers?"

There rose a rumbling like a cyclone sweeping through town as all the men at the table abandoned their cards, scrip, and specie and hustled away, cursing, tripping over each other and their chairs. The table was nudged. Coins clattered. Several chairs tumbled over. One man fell and grabbed his knee, and two others pulled him to his feet and dragged him out of the line of fire.

The blonde in the purple dress swept up to the table, near Coles, and stomped her foot on the carpeted floor. "What is the meaning of this? I am the proprietor of the Oriental, sir. You have no right to come in here and threaten my clients!"

"I'm not threatening one damn thing," said the Revenger, keeping his eyes on Coles. "I'm making a promise." Several beefy men in three-piece suits had started toward Sartain from several different points around the room. He glanced at the woman. "Call off the apes unless you want 'em bloodyin' up your floor."

She jerked around, throwing up her pale hands.

The apes stopped dead in their tracks.

While studying Coles, Sartain was pricking his ears to the rest of the crowd, listening for the telltale snick of a pistol being unsheathed and possibly leveled at his back. The back bar mirror flanked Coles, and the Cajun occasionally flicked his gaze that way, as well, unable to discern any other immediate threat beyond Coles himself.

"So," Coles said, "I've warranted me a visit from the Angel of Death himself, is it?" He smiled proudly at that. The smile slipped away quickly as he lowered his chin angrily and said, "Who sent you?"

"What does it matter? In less than a minute, you're gonna be too dead to do anything about it."

"Please," the blonde said, taking one more step toward Sartain. "Can't this be resolved in some other way?"

"Nope."

Coles chuckled. "Well, then." He set his cigar in an ashtray, slid his chair back, and slowly gained his feet. He hooked his thumbs in the black belt looped around his slightly bulging waist. "I reckon I'll take my chances with these purty ladies right *here*!"

With that last, he snarled and reached for the derringers.

Sartain palmed the big LeMat and sent Clancy Coles dancing backward, tripping over a chair, firing both his derringers into the floor, and then leaning back against the long, ornately scrolled mahogany bar.

The blonde sandwiched her face with her hands; it had now turned peach with shock. "Oh my god — *Clancy!*"

Coles winced, blinked, and stared at Sartain through the wafting powder smoke. He wobbled on his hips. As he gave a savage cry, he raised both his derringers once more and Sartain finished him with two more shots that punched through his chest — one about two inches right of the first.

Coles jerked back, stumbled forward, dropped to his knees, and raised his chin to the ceiling. "Go to hell," he said through a ragged sigh. "You killed me!"

He dropped the derringers and hit the floor on his knees. He fell forward and smashed his head against the seat of a chair, where it stayed as his arms dangled to the floor and his shoulders shook.

Sartain wheeled, clicking the LeMat's hammer back once more and cocking the Henry one-handed. He looked around the room. Several men had started reaching toward holsters, but they stayed the movement when they saw the Revenger's two guns aimed at them, smoke curling from the LeMat's maw. Their faces acquired sheepish expressions.

When Sartain thought he had the crowd relatively cowed to the point he wasn't assured a bullet in his back within the next few minutes, he holstered the LeMat. He off-cocked the Henry's hammer, plucked

Coles's cheroot from the ashtray, and puffed it as he walked around the table to the blonde glaring up at him.

She was a piece of work, all right. Her heavy, pale bosoms rose and fell sharply as she breathed. She backed up against the bar, staring up at the Cajun fearfully.

"You his woman?" Sartain asked, canting his head toward the body of Clancy Coles, which had fallen still now as his life had fled. His head remained on the chair.

"So what if I am?" the woman said.

Sartain grinned around the cheroot in his teeth and let his eyes flick again across her heaving bosom. "Spoils of war, honey."

He leaned down and threw her over his shoulder.

"No!" she cried, punching his back as he straightened, carrying the woman like a fifty-pound sack of feed corn. "Put me . . . put me down this *instant*!"

Sartain spun and leveled the Henry straight out from his hip, clicking the hammer back to full cock, again stopping the woman's bouncers in their tracks. One had drawn a pistol. He dropped it like a hot potato.

Sartain pivoted around and made his way through the crowd as the woman continued to curse him and punch his back with her fists.

"Damn you!" she cried as he climbed the stairs. "Goddamn you to *hell*!"

Several half-dressed men and pleasure girls had congregated on the stairs to observe the festivities in the main drinking hall. They made way for Sartain and the woman, who berated him all the way down the second-story hall to a room at the far end. The Revenger flung it open, stepped inside, and threw the woman on the bed.

"Goddamn me to hell?" said the Cajun, incredulous. He slammed the door, then turned the key in the lock. "That was a little strong — don't you think, June?"

She laughed as she sat up, peeled her dress down to her waist, and began unlacing her whalebone corset. "Shut up, you cad," she said, tittering. "Get over here and let me reward you for a hand well played!"

Chapter Two

"Oh, my dear Lord," June said in a Southern accent that Sartain had not detected before they'd started making love, at which point it became as pronounced as his own, "I thought you were going to kill me as dead as Clancy!"

Breathing hard and sweating, the Revenger rolled off the beauty and curled an arm behind his head, on one of June's pink silk pillows. "Same here, dear June. Same here."

He rolled toward her once more, nuzzling her left breast still mottled red from his previous ministrations. "I realize it's too late now," Sartain said, "but I was remiss in informing you, dear June, that I never require payment for my services." He kissed her sweet, full, sensuous lips. "I mean . . . payment of any *kind.*"

She blinked, staring up at him with feigned shock in her lustrous, catlike blue eyes. "Well, what a convenient time to inform me so late in the game, Mr. Revenger, sir."

Footsteps rose in the hall as chattering doxies and their Jakes sauntered past June's room.

June gasped. "Oh, you wretched beast!" she intoned, rolling around on the bed to make the springs cry out again. "Oh, the horrible things you're making me do. You're absolutely . . . *incorrigible,* Mr. Sartain!"

Sartain glanced at the door, chuckling.

When the doxies and their customers had drifted away, June pulled on the Cajun's ears, and pecked his lips. "I knew that you didn't require payment, dear Mike," she said. "Payment of *any* kind. I investigated you quite thoroughly before I sent for you . . . and *hired* you, so to speak."

"In your case, the satisfaction of killing that snake, Coles, was all the payment I could ever want or need." The Revenger had heard of Coles and his outlaw operation that, until this evening, had this part of the Colorado Rockies in a stranglehold of corruption. Coles, who'd started out as a small-time stage robber, had built up an influence that had even spread into local politics. He'd not only become rich off thievery, but he'd become powerful, as well, with the local law eating out of his hands, so to speak.

Until Sartain had been summoned by the

lovely June McCarthy, proprietor of the Oriental Saloon & Gambling Parlor here in Low Range, which was also the best hurdy-gurdy house in this neck of the Rockies, he'd never had good reason to kill the man.

He killed only for those who had good reason for wanting someone dead and couldn't do the deed themselves.

"Oh, my god — you want me to do *what*?" June cried out as voices and footsteps rose in the hall again. "After you killed the love of my *life*?" She flopped around, making the bedsprings groan and sigh. "Oh, what a *devil*!"

Sartain glanced at the door once more. When the voices and footsteps had dwindled to silence, and a near door had closed, the Revenger turned to June. "Miss June, I declare, you're gonna get me shot down in the street tomorrow, like a hydrophobic cur!"

June snickered. "I have a reputation to uphold," she said, smoothing his hair back from his handsome, ruddy face. "You'll be leaving tomorrow. But I have to stay here and run my business. If anyone should get any idea — any idea at all — that I directed you to kill Clancy Coles, my life would be in very grave danger."

"And what about my life?"

"After what I saw downstairs earlier, Mr. Revenger, sir," June said, slowly sliding her hand down his belly toward his nether regions, "you can take very good care of yourself. If not, you wouldn't be here."

Sartain closed his eyes and groaned. "You got me there, Miss June. I can, indeed." He groaned again. "But no man is immune to getting backshot from a dark alley."

Manipulating him, June said, "Not to worry. Most folks won't be sorry to see Clancy's corpse planted on Boot Hill. He'd gotten too big for his britches, and over the past several months, he'd made far more enemies than he had friends. This town — hell, the whole damn county — had outgrown him, but Clancy would have been the last to realize that."

"How'd you fall in with him, June?" Sartain asked, keeping his eyes closed.

Her hands were soft, her touch like warm water.

"He gave me little choice. You see, I once owned half of this place with a local businessman, Burt Donleavy. Burt got drunk one night and gambled his share of the Oriental away to none other than Clancy, who, it turned out, saw me as not only his business partner, but his . . ."

"Bed partner, as well."

"You got it," June said. "He was very convincing, that brigand. Not to mention threatening. I had little choice in the matter. The varmint even thought he was going to marry me. And, believe me, he made no bones about the fact that when we were married, my half of the Oriental would just naturally go to him. To Clancy's way of viewing the world, no woman —"

"Should own property," Sartain said in a slow, heavy voice. He was having trouble concentrating on what the woman was telling him. "I see, I see . . ."

"Are you sure you see, Mike?" June whispered in his ear. "Or . . . maybe you're only *feeling* at this point in the conversation . . ."

She tittered and nibbled his earlobe.

That, coupled with her deft touch south of his belly button, was almost too much for him.

"Oh, no," June admonished, pulling her hand away. "Don't you dare! Not without me!"

"But —"

"But, nothin'," June said, pulling him down on top of her and spreading her knees wide. She pressed her lips to his and squirmed around beneath him, her bosom heaving, nipples jutting. "I'm far from done showing my appreciation, Mike Sartain!"

As she reached down and slid him into her, more voices rose in the hall.

She pressed two fingers to his lips and whispered, "Don't worry, Mike. Most of the men in this town are probably far more grateful for your killing Clancy than they are worried about my honor." She dropped her head back onto her pillow. "Oh, you horrible man!" she cried, bucking up against him. "First you kill my beloved and now you ravage me just like some heathen Apache! You're a *barbarian*!"

As the din in the hall passed, she clamped her knees against the Cajun's hips and dug her fingers into his buttocks.

Sartain cursed. He was having a little trouble concentrating on the task at hand. Despite the woman's reassurances, he half expected a gun to blast him through the door.

Sartain woke the next morning to a mule braying in the street below the large bedroom's two windows. A freighting outfit must have been heading out for the gold camps higher in the San Juan Range. He rose quietly, so as not to disturb June, who slept spread-eagle on the bed, no sheet covering her. Her head was turned to one side, her hair a lovely mess across her pillow.

The Cajun admired her body — as fine as he'd seen since laying his life's one true love, his dear Jewel, to rest in a rocky grave beside her grandfather. He'd buried Jewel with their child, which she'd miscarried when the drunken, renegade federal soldiers had savaged her out on her grandfather's diggings south of Benson, in the Arizona Territory.

Sartain raked a hand down his face, pressing away those bitter memories, and turned once more to June. He leaned down, lightly kissed her left breast, and then drew the twisted sheet up from the foot of the bed, covering the pretty woman against the morning's chill. As the freight outfit began clomping and clattering north out of Low Range, Sartain closed the window, took a whore's bath from a basin of tepid water, and quietly dressed.

When he'd buckled his holstered LeMat and sheathed Bowie knife around his lean waist, shouldered his Henry rifle, and donned his hat, he glanced once more at June. He could hear her breathing deeply, regularly in the room's misty shadows, exhausted from their night of lovemaking.

The Cajun pinched his hat brim to the

woman, grinning at the memory of the previous night, and opened the door. As he stepped out into the hall, a shadowy figure stopped abruptly to his left, gasping and falling back against the wall on the hall's opposite side.

It was a dove with sleep-mussed brown hair wearing a man's wool shirt that hung halfway down her thighs. She dropped the bottle and two glasses she'd been carrying, and regarded the Revenger with wide-eyed terror. Her eyes flicked to the big LeMat, the Bowie knife on his left hip, and the Henry repeating rifle on his shoulder.

"Oh, Lord!" she said.

Sartain pressed two fingers to his lips and canted his head toward the door he'd just closed.

The girl pressed a hand to her breast, and swallowed. "You . . . you didn't hurt her too bad . . . did you?"

"Miss June?" the Revenger said. "Nah. She'll be back on her feet in a week or two . . . good as new."

He winked.

The dove frowned curiously, then slowly lowered her hand from her breast. She glanced around cautiously and then said just loudly enough for the Cajun to hear: "Most folks around, me included, ain't sore at all about you shootin' Clancy Coles, though I'd appreciate it if you kept that between you an' me, Mr. Sartain."

"You got yourself a deal," the Revenger said as he scooped up the bottle and the two glasses, and handed them to the girl.

As she stared at him through her thin screen of mussed hair, vaguely befuddled, he nodded his head cordially and then drifted on down the hall to the rear of the second story. There he found an outside door and descended the stairs to the alley flanking the place. He'd killed a man last night, and though most folks might not have given a hoot, or were even relieved to have ole Clancy Coles strumming a harp with the angels, there might be one or two of his gang around who felt otherwise.

They might be waiting for Sartain to step out the Oriental's front door.

The Revenger had not lived as long as he'd lived, riding the vigilante trail for those who couldn't ride it themselves, by being careless.

Digging a cheroot from his shirt pocket, he strode west along the alley, paralleling the main street past two buildings before swinging back south through a break between a harness shop and a feed store. He paused at the mouth of the break, looking out onto the main street the early morning light had painted smoky gray.

The sun was nearly over the eastern ridges, the sky over there growing brighter by the second. All of the stars had faded except one very faint one in the west, to Sartain's right.

The street jogged crookedly off to the east and the west, with here and there a cottonwood rattling its leaves in the morning breeze, the ponderosa standing by the Arkansas River Hotel dropping the occasional pine cone on the hotel's porch roof. The fresh, deep, overlaid furrows of the recently departed freight trains shone silver, brighter than the gray of the older wheel tracks.

Somewhere on the far side of town, a blacksmith was hammering an anvil — steady, regular, clanging beats.

That was the only sound.

Sartain cupped a flame to his cheroot. Lighting up and puffing smoke, he flicked the match into the dust and began crossing the main street, heading for the stable down the cross street ahead of him. He hadn't gained the center of the main street before the muffled drumming of hammering hooves rose in the west.

He turned to see what appeared to be an

army ambulance bearing down on him. The high-sided wagon was covered with a cream canvas tarpaulin stretched flat across its box. A soldier in cavalry blues and leather-billed forage cap was driving two shaggy horses, popping a whip over their backs. The horses and the wagon bouncing and clattering behind them seemed to turn slightly toward Sartain, who began moving backward, toward the side of the street he'd just come from.

Obviously, the army man was in a hurry. He also didn't have a firm rein on his team. Bad combination.

Sartain was about to yell out to the man, who wore a sergeant's chevrons on the sleeves of his dark-blue army tunic, but then when the team was maybe twenty yards away from the Revenger, the driver turned the team full around in the middle of the street, the rear wheels sliding and kicking up dust, and stopped.

Dust wafted, painted pink and salmon by the early sunlight.

The back of the canvas-colored wagon was now facing Sartain. The sergeant yelled to his team, holding the reins neck-high and turning to glance over his left shoulder. He was broad-shouldered, red-bearded.

The team smartly backed the wagon

several yards toward Sartain, and stopped. The Revenger pensively puffed his cheroot and studied the wagon cautiously, raking his thumb across the hammer of the Henry still resting on his shoulder.

The driver quickly set the wagon brake, grabbed the end of a rope, and jerked it toward him. The cream canvas rolled toward him, back along the high sides of the wagon toward the front, exposing two more soldiers, one crouched over the large, brass-canistered maw of a Gatling gun mounted on a wooden tripod. His hand was on the Gatling gun's wooden handle.

The other soldier was on one knee beside the first soldier, aiming a Henry repeater at Sartain's head.

Chapter Three

Sartain still studied the soldiers casually, slowly puffing the cigar, knowing he had a fair amount of trouble facing him but befuddled by its origin.

The Gatling gun was aimed directly at him. The soldier manning it had thrust a long, brass cartridge tube into its action. The soldier smiled along the brass maw at Sartain, eagerly tapping his thumb against the machine gun's wooden handle.

The Revenger had just started considering possible cover options, wondering if he could get the Henry off his shoulder before the grinning soldier cut him to shreds, when boots thudded on a porch across the street. Sartain slid his gaze slightly left to see a man in a crisp blue Hardee hat with the right-side brim pinned up, and a blue wool cape, step out of the narrow gap between two mud-brick buildings, still dark and silent at this early hour.

He was armed with a pistol in a black leather flap holster on his right hip, and a long, brass-hilted Solingen saber dangling down his left leg in a steel scabbard. The shoulders of his tunic bore the brass bars of a captain. His neatly trimmed, upswept mustache was pewter gray.

"Mr. Sartain." He did not have to yell in the early morning stillness, which seemed even more still and silent now after the thundering of the wagon had stopped. "Kindly throw down your weapons — even the double-barreled derringer you keep in your vest pocket — and lie belly down in the street for me, please. Do so slowly. If you make any sudden moves, I assure you that you will be carved up like a Thanksgiving turkey not only by that hiccupping cannon you see facing you, but by the good twenty-five rifles aimed at you from nearly every direction!"

Sartain cut his eyes around, studying the street through the cigar smoke billowing around his head.

A shutter opened in the second story of a drugstore just left of the captain. A soldier in a blue forage cap thrust a Spencer repeating carbine through the window, slanting it down toward Sartain. As the Revenger continued to slide his gaze around the street, he saw more rifles bristling toward him from second-story windows and from behind water barrels on street-level boardwalks and from alley mouths. Two were aimed at him from the far side of a wagon that had been parked for the night in front of the mercantile, hard to Sartain's left and a half a block away.

Sartain sighed.

Funny — he'd always wondered how it would feel when the soldiers finally ran him down, as he supposed they would eventually. He'd always figured to go down fighting, but he didn't see much point in fighting here, with all these rifles aimed at him. He didn't have a chance. The only reason he didn't go ahead and end it all right here, right now, by pulling the Henry off his shoulder and commencing to fire as many shots as he could, was because he didn't want to make it that easy for the federal bastards.

They'd have to try and hang him.

Meanwhile, he'd look for a way to escape and maybe take a few more federals with him. He'd killed all the bluebellies who'd ravaged and killed Jewel and her grandfather — even shot their mule — but he didn't mind killing a few more who meant to punish him for what he considered justified revenge.

Dying was the price you paid for piss-burning the Revenger.

"Your wish is my command, Captain."

Sartain slowly lowered the Henry, then laid it down gently in the dirt. Just as slowly, he slid the big LeMat from its holster with two fingers, held it up to show the captain that its barrel was pointed down, and set it beside the Henry. Finally, he reached into his pinto vest and slid out the brass-framed, pearl-gripped, double-barreled derringer, and set it in the street, as well.

The captain glanced toward the two men crouched behind the wagon to Sartain's left. The two men ran out from behind the wagon, holding their carbines at port arms — two young lieutenants with thin mustaches mantling their pink upper lips. One was also trying to grow a goatee without much success; his pale chin was mostly sporting red pimples.

Both soldiers' eyes were wide and glassy with anxiety.

"Hold it right there!" Pimples shouted, though he'd stopped only six feet away from Sartain. "Get those hands raised!"

Sartain glowered at the youth likely fresh from West Point — he couldn't have been much over twenty-one, if that — and slowly raised his hands, rolling his cheroot from one corner of his mouth to the other. As he did, the second young lieutenant crouched as he closed on Sartain, and, watching the big Revenger apprehensively, gathered up the Cajun's weapons, pocketing the derringer.

"Careful with that little popper there, sonny," the Cajun said in his slow, Louisiana drawl. "Both barrels are loaded and liable to blow your pecker off you don't handle it right."

"Shut up!" said Pimples, jutting his Spencer toward Sartain. "Flat on the ground! Now! Don't make me tell you again!"

"Hold your water, soldier," Sartain drawled, taking his time getting to his knees.

"Cuff him, Lieutenant Grodin," said the captain, who was moving out into the street, coolly keeping his hand away from his sidearm.

Lieutenant Grodin moved behind Sartain and slammed the flat of his boot against the Revenger's back, pushing him unceremoniously to the ground.

"I'm going to remember that one," Sartain said with a grunt as Grodin jerked his arms behind his back and pulled a set of steel handcuffs out from a leather pouch on his shell belt.

Sartain winced as the young lieutenant clicked one bracelet closed, then the other. They were so tight they pinched, making the Cajun's hands swell and tingle.

He cursed.

He cursed once more when he saw one of the soldiers from the ambulance hauling a set of heavy leg irons over from the wagon. Both irons were open, with about a foot and a half of heavy log chain drooping between them. The soldier from the wagon was also carrying a long-handled clamp, the head of which looked similar to a buzzard's beak.

When he had one manacle closed over Sartain's left ankle, he applied the clamp to it, his face turning red as he closed the jaws as well as the manacle. When the manacle was taut, the soldier applied the same treatment to the Revenger's other ankle.

The captain chuckled. "I've heard you're slippery. Well, you're not slipping out of those." He looked around at the soldiers still aiming carbines from here and there around the street, and cupped his hands around his mouth. "Fetch your horses, men. Time to ride!"

He looked at the nearer men still breathing hard and flushed with anxiety, as though they'd chained a particularly menacing mountain lion after a long, harrowing chase.

"Sergeant Case, fetch the man's horse from the livery barn."

"Here." It was a woman's voice.

Sartain looked up, incredulous, to see a comely, dark-haired woman riding toward him from the direction of the livery barn. She rode a fine, black thoroughbred gelding. She was trailing Boss by the buckskin's bridle reins. "I fetched him to save time, Captain."

Even in his compromised, utterly frustrating predicament, Sartain took the time to admire the filly atop the thoroughbred. She was probably twenty-five, with straight, chocolate hair tumbling down her back and secured in what appeared a loose braid. She wore a soft, doeskin jacket over a white silk blouse, and form-fitting, dark-green denim trousers stuffed into high, black, recently shined riding boots.

On her head was a man's broad-brimmed, cream Stetson with an Indian beaded band.

On her hips, two silver-plated, small-caliber pistols rode behind a wide brown belt that accentuated the narrowness of her waist and the fullness of her bosom. In her saddle scabbard rode a Winchester. As she rode slowly over to where the captain and several other soldiers were now gathered around Sartain, the Revenger saw that her eyes were nearly the same pearl color as the grips of his derringer.

Her creamy cheeks were lightly tanned to a dark peach by the sun. Her face overall was flawless, carefully crafted by an adoring god who knew his way around a bone mallet and a chisel. Her eyes were cool as she stared negligently at the Revenger, who was trussed up like a calf for branding.

"Is this him, Miss Gallant?" the captain asked her.

She studied Sartain a long moment, the corners of her wide, officious mouth lifting in a self-satisfied half-smile. "Oh, yes," she said, blinking slowly. "Oh, yes. It's him, all right."

She tossed Boss's reins to the sergeant who'd been driving the ambulance. He wasn't ready for them. They hit the sergeant in the head, nearly knocking his hat off.

The man grunted his displeasure as he scowled at the woman. Ignoring the soldier, she cast one more cool glance at Sartain, slightly curling her upper lip in victory, then booted her fine horse into a canter eastward along the street into which the other soldiers were now riding on their army bays.

"Now, who in the hell is that?" asked the Revenger, staring after her.

"None of your damn business," the captain said, scowling down at him. He turned to the sergeant. "Throw him into the wagon. Tie his horse behind. We'll be pulling out as soon as we've formed a column. I want your wagon in the middle."

"Where we goin'?" Sartain wanted to know.

The two lieutenants hauled the Cajun to his feet. He stood nearly a full head taller than both the lieutenants and the captain, who looked him up and down critically and then said, "I told you to hobble your mouth, mister. You'll know where you're going when we get there."

The two began leading Sartain, who tripped every time the chain between his ironclad ankles drew taut, over to the wagon. "Not even a hint?"

Ignoring him, the captain walked over to a private leading a bay gelding toward him, and swung up into the saddle.

Sartain hesitated before climbing up into the back of the wagon, beside the soldier who'd manned the Gatling gun and was now taking it apart and crating it. Pimples rammed the butt of his Spencer repeater against the Cajun's back, between his shoulder blades.

"Get in there like the captain said, *Revenger*!" Pimples laughed. "You done been de-fanged and de-clawed!" He laughed again.

Sartain whipped around automatically, forgetting for the moment that his ankles were hobbled. He swung both his manacles at the laughing, pimple-faced lieutenant, who jerked back with a start, his eyes and mouth wide in horror.

But before the Revenger's fists could connect with the young officer's bony jaw, he got his ankles tangled up. He fell sideways and backward, slamming his head against the end of the wagon bed. His last sensation was hitting the street like a stack of lumber.

Then an inky gauze of semi-consciousness settled over him, quelling the throbbing in his battered head, until he became aware he was riding in the wagon toward some unknown destination.

It would probably turn out to be some remote ravine where he'd face a hangman's noose or a firing squad.

And then the carrion eaters . . .

Chapter Four

"Hey, fellas — where we headed?" Sartain asked the two soldiers guarding him as the wagon continued rocking and clattering along a rough, shaggy, two-track trail.

High, rocky, copper-colored ridges sparsely populated with pines loomed over the canyon, their soaring crests sometimes appearing to converge and almost entirely close out the sky. The wide, shallow Arkansas River chuckled along the base of the ridge on the trail's west side.

Sartain rode with his back resting up against the wagon's front panel, beneath the driver's seat. The stench from the driver's sweat-soaked wool uniform occasionally wafted back to assault the Cajun's sensitive nose. The two soldiers guarding him — the same two privates who'd been riding in the back of the wagon when Sartain had first seen them and the Gatling gun — sat near the tailgate, one with his back to the left-side panel, the other with his back to the right-side panel.

The Gatling gun rested in its crate to Sartain's left, like a cobra slumbering in a basket.

The soldiers, rocking with the often-violent bounce and sway of the wagon, merely exchanged droll, weary looks. The one to Sartain's left was the one who'd borne down on him with the Gatling gun; he was now taking occasional drags of a loosely rolled cigarette.

"Come on, fellas," the Cajun urged. "I'm all trussed up like the fatted calf. What's it gonna hurt to tell me where we're headed?"

The soldiers glanced at each other once more, and then turned to look behind the wagon at half the column following from far enough back to not be eating the wagon's dust. The other half of the column rode just far enough ahead that the wagon was not eating *their* dust.

"Hey, lookee," said the soldier on the right to the one on the left, staring a short ways up the eastern ridge, where two elk cows grazed on a flat shelf just above a brushy wash. He raised his rifle and pretended to fire two shots, chuckling.

Chewing grass, the elk turned to stare at the convoy, nervously flapping their tails.

Obviously, the two soldiers had been told not to answer any of the Cajun's questions or converse with their prisoner at all. So far, they hadn't even told him to shut up, which, to his way of thinking, was just plain rude. On the other hand, he supposed he should count his blessings. He'd been fully expecting to have been hanged or shot by now, his body left for the coyotes and diamondbacks.

That he wasn't was a plus in his column, but it did make him damned curious.

But he obviously wasn't going to learn anything from the two wet-behind-the-ears federals riding guard on him, their Spencers resting across their thighs.

That he wasn't dead yet didn't really mean much. It probably meant that ole Uncle Sam was fixing to make a spectacle of him, maybe use him to set an example to all other would-be vigilantes roaming the frontier. He'd probably get a "fair" trial to which a dozen or so big-city newspaper scribblers would be invited, and, only after the government had squeezed everything they could get out of the man known as the Revenger, they'd make one last spectacle of him by hanging him before a crowd on a busy city street.

If that were the case, however, wouldn't they be heading for Denver? That was the closest federal courthouse. But the soldiers had turned off the trail that led to Denver and were now angling south, which led to nowhere or, possibly, to northwestern New Mexico.

But what in the hell was in northwestern New Mexico?

Damned befuddling.

Sartain craned his neck to peer over the driver's spring seat toward the front column. At the very head of the column, the captain, who'd never told Sartain his name, rode beside the chocolate-haired beauty. Her hair, even from this distance, shone in the brassy, high-altitude light as it hung down her back in its loose braid.

Sartain turned around to face the two soldiers guarding him. "How 'bout that purty little filly ridin' with the captain?" he said, curling half of his upper lip. "What the hell's she doin' out here?"

The soldiers glanced at each other speculatively.

"Ah, come on — I know you both seen her," Sartain probed, grinning. "Probably like to see what she looks like under all them neat clothes of hers." He whistled and pulled his shirt out away from his chest. "Tits out to here. Now, those, soldier boys, would be a sight to see!"

The soldier on the left snorted a laugh and said, "Shee-it," to his partner as he exhaled smoke into the breeze.

"Private, what did I tell you about conversing with the prisoner?" The captain was riding back to inspect the column. Sartain heard the thuds of his horse's cantering hooves. "Would you like to walk along behind the wagon, Private?"

"Sir, no, sir!" the private shouted, turning around to face the man riding toward him, and saluting.

As he cantered on past the wagon, the captain said, "And strip that cigarette! You're on guard duty, Private!"

The captain glanced back at the beefy sergeant riding behind him, both men now well past the wagon and heading toward the second half of the column. "Sergeant, place that man on report. I want to see him first thing in my office Monday morning!"

"You got it, Captain," said the sergeant, his voice dwindling away.

The private dropped his cigarette on his lap. "Shit, shit, shit!" he intoned, brushing the sparks away.

The other private snorted.

The admonished young soldier turned to Sartain and wrinkled his freckled nose, his eyes bright with fury.

"Uh . . . sorry there, sport," the Cajun said.

An hour later, they stopped for lunch and to rest and tend the horses.

Sitting in a patch of shade along a dry arroyo that fed into the Arkansas, Sartain sipped a tin cup of coffee he held in both his manacled hands, and looked around. There were several small fires around which most of the men dozed or conversed in desultory tones, washing down hardtack and army issue desiccated beef with coffee so weak it tasted like stale tea.

Some of the horses were splashing around in the river shallows behind Sartain. He could smell the smoke of the quirleys of the men tending them, hear the soldiers' occasional muffled jokes and ribald laughter.

As he raked his gaze around the various groupings of men and horses, Sartain saw the captain and the chocolate-haired young woman standing on a low ridge about sixty yards away. They were facing away from the Cajun, shoulder to shoulder, conversing.

After a time, as though she sensed the Revenger's stare, the woman turned sideways and looked at him. Wisps of hair that had strayed from the chignon blew around her cool face in the breeze.

"Who are you, pretty lady?" the Cajun drawled softly, speculatively. "And how in the hell do you know so much about my doin's?"

Sartain thought his bones were going to rattle apart before they stopped again, as he was sitting on the wagon's bare, hardwood bed. The two soldiers were, too, but they didn't have their wrists and ankles bound, so they could move around a bit, keep their blood flowing. The Cajun's hands were swollen and numb, but he knew it wouldn't do any good to ask the soldiers to loosen the cuffs, so he swallowed the pain.

The one who'd been caught smoking rode in brooding silence, injured by the captain's public chastising.

They stopped again just before sunset, and Sartain thought they'd set up camp for the night, but a mere fifteen minutes later, they were all mounted and rolling again. As the sun went down and a chill threaded the hot, dry air, Sartain slid into a front corner of the wagon, tipped his head back, pulled his hat brim down over his eyes, and willed himself to sleep despite the wagon's violent churning and the precariousness of his situation.

How in the hell had they found him

without his noticing anyone on his back trail?

Where were they taking him?

What were they going to do with him?

And who in the hell was the pretty, insouciant young woman with the chocolate hair? She looked as out of place out here amongst these soldiers as would a gold-crowned English princess amongst a tribe of red savages. Something told Sartain she had been key in the soldiers' running him down, though he had no idea what that something was.

He'd find out sooner or later.

Somehow, he slept.

He woke when the wagon stopped. Blinking, he looked around at the shadows of the milling soldiers silhouetted against several swinging lanterns and what appeared to be a small train combination stopped on tracks that glinted pearl in the moonlight. The light shone dark gray on surrounding mountains looming against the starry sky. There were only four or five cars sitting dark and silent behind the puffing locomotive, its nose aimed south.

The iron beast panted loudly, its pressure-release valves pinging noisily as great clouds of wet steam that smelled like copper billowed out from around the giant, iron wheels. Somewhere, a bell was ringing.

"Where . . . where in hell are we?" Sartain asked as his two chaperones manhandled him out of the wagon.

They chuckled as they dropped him down over the open tailgate. Unable to spread his feet far enough to catch himself when he hit the ground, he fell with a curse, and rolled.

Fury burned through him. Instinctively, he swung both bound legs toward one of the two laughing soldiers, knocking the soldier's feet out from under him.

The soldier screamed as his boots went one way, his shoulders the other way. He hit the ground with a resolute thud, cursing.

Snarling at Sartain, he started wrestling his army-issue .44 from the flap holster on his right hip. The beefy sergeant who'd been driving the wagon kicked the pistol out of the soldier's hand.

Again, the private screamed. He clutched his hand and glared up at the bearded, sack-bellied noncom.

"Go ahead and shoot the son of a bitch, Davey me darlin'," the sergeant said in a heavy Irish brogue. "See how many years that gets you in the guardhouse, ya bloody fool!"

"Sergeant, what's going on over there?" the captain called from some distance away.

"Oh, nothin', Captain, just nothin'!" the sergeant said, helping Sartain to his feet. "Our clumsy prisoner just took a little tumble out of the wagon, that's all. You'd think a man so renowned for his pistols would be a little lighter on his feet, now, wouldn't you, Cap?"

Chuckling, he brushed Sartain off and then turned him around and started leading him toward a stock car three cars down from the locomotive. The stock car's doors yawned wide. A loading ramp slanted from the open doors to the ground. Behind the stock car was another stock car up into which some of the soldiers were leading their horses, hooves thudding hollowly on the ash planks.

Behind the second stock car were a flat car and a caboose.

"Get on up there and be quick about it," the sergeant told Sartain. "It's late and I'm needing my beauty rest."

"Where we goin', Sergeant?" the Revenger asked as he entered the stock car.

"Wouldn't you like to know," the sergeant laughed from the bottom of the ramp. "Wouldn't you bloody well like to know . . ."

The Cajun's two chaperones tramped up the ramp behind him. The injured Davey flared his nostrils at him, and shoved him inside the stock car. Sartain tripped over the manacle chain and fell on his ass with another curse. Davey and the other soldier slid the doors closed, shutting out the dancing lights and jostling silhouettes.

Sartain sat in the musty darkness, hearing the clanks of the iron latch being closed and then the clinks of a chain securing the doors. He looked out through a gap between two boards in the wall before him. He'd seen a flash of something pale just before the doors had closed. Now he saw what that paleness was.

It was the chocolate-haired young woman in the white blouse and fawn-colored vest, sitting her thoroughbred, staring at Sartain from beneath the brim of her tan Stetson. The captain sat his army bay beside the girl. He said something to her, and then reined his horse toward the other stock car.

The woman held her gaze on Sartain until he wondered if she could see him staring out at her. She reined her fine mount away, clucking to the beast, and trotted off toward the other stock car.

The hollow clomps of shod hooves on wood told the Revenger that she and the captain were riding their horses up the other loading ramp.

"Who are you, pretty lady?" Sartain found

himself muttering again as he stared through the gaps in the stock car's wall. "And what's your business with me?"

Chapter Five

The train clicked along all the rest of the night and throughout the next day. It was only a little less rough than the wagon had been. Sartain had found that his grim, sparse surroundings were furnished with a horse blanket, a tin slop bucket, and a water pail with a gourd dipper.

Occasionally, when the train stopped to take on water, the doors were opened as wide as the locked chain would allow, and his benefactors would slide through the gap a Spartan plate of food — mostly crusty bread, a small pile of warm beans, a wedge of old cheese, and a wormy apple — and sometimes a cup of coffee.

Through the gaps between the boards, he watched the country roll by — mostly broad valleys carpeted in blond grass that smelled of summer curing, and pine-clad mountains. Sometimes the train ran slowly up through these mountains, chugging hard, the wheels grinding. Sometimes the mountains fell back to the west.

When they were far enough west, the Revenger could see the ermine of snow mantling their highest ridges.

They were either the Sangre de Cristos or the San Juans. Or maybe neither. He was too disoriented to know for sure. All he knew was that he was heading south, either through the heart of southern Colorado or northwestern New Mexico.

Night fell again. The air grew brisk. Sartain sat against a stout post and drew the blanket about his shoulders.

The car rocked and swayed around him. The cooling air sifting through the gaps in the boards occasionally carried glowing cinders from the locomotive, and the heavy smell of dank steam and pine smoke.

Sometime during the night, the train came to a screeching, shuddering halt, the iron couplings clanging loudly. Sartain woke and stared through the gaps in the car's wall.

Shadows were moving, men were talking. The captain barked orders, though Sartain couldn't hear what he was saying because of the horses being loudly led out of the second stock car. He could hear the wagon being unloaded, as well, its wheels clattering on the plank ramp.

Sartain sat against the post, waiting.

Something was happening. He knew the horses were being saddled; he heard the clanking of buckles and bridle bits, the squawks of saddle leather. Horses whinnied and stomped around while the soldiers conversed in businesslike tones.

Finally, the ramp was raised to the Revenger's car. Two men climbed the ramp. A key scratched in a padlock, the chain was removed from the door's iron handles, and the latching bar was freed. The door opened.

Davey and the other young private stood staring at Sartain.

"Up," Davey said.

"Nah, I don't think so — I like it right here," Sartain said, mostly to amuse himself, but also because he didn't like the kid. He didn't like any man in a blue uniform. In fact, they were all making him grind his molars and wish like hell he could get his hands on a gun.

He'd lay waste to as many as he could before they killed him.

Davey stomped forward and kicked the Cajun's left foot. "Up! I ain't gonna tell you again!"

"What's the matter, Davey boy?" asked the sergeant from the bottom of the ramp. "Did I send a pair of girls to do a man's work?" He chuckled.

"Sergeant, what's keeping those men?" the captain demanded from farther away.

"Private Wilson, Private Ellison — bring the prisoner *now*!" ordered the sergeant, stomping his boot.

Davey lunged forward, reaching for his pistol, threatening.

"Hold your water, kid," the Revenger said, pushing back against the post and heaving himself to his feet.

Several minutes later, he was back in the wagon. The wagon was back on a trail heading toward what Sartain, disoriented by the confined travel and the dark night, not to mention the surrounding mountains blocking out half the stars, thought was southwest.

The surrounding terrain was much the same as during his previous wagon ride. Cedars, *piñons,* junipers, and silver-green sage. Hills covered in grama grass rolled up toward bluffs, stony dykes, and tall mountains, though no mountains lay directly ahead along the two-track wagon trail.

As the wagon and the soldiers guiding it drifted away from the train, the locomotive chuffed back to life after taking on fresh water, and chugged off to the south, belching, sighing, and clattering away into gradual silence.

A little less than an hour later, the column rode into a ranch yard.

A big one with a large, two- or three-story, tile-roofed Spanish style house abutting the far southern end and set off from the main yard by an adobe fence and what appeared a yard of tended trees, shrubs, and vines. The place shone almost eerily in the moonlight, its long windows dark.

There were what appeared to be two low adobe bunkhouses, many corrals including a stone-walled breaking corral, several log barns, stables, and as many more small outbuildings. A windmill loomed in the yard's center, around a large stone stock tank, the mill's wooden blades tapping softly in an easy breeze.

Someone from the ranch had apparently been awaiting the procession, which stopped just after the wagon had entered the yard. Sartain heard voices. When the wagon continued forward as the soldiers spread out to both sides, the column dispersing, two men appeared in drover garb and *sombreros* astride horses. They watched the wagon pass, their faces dark though the crowns of their gaudy *sombreros* glowed in the moonlight.

The wagon stopped near the north wall of

the house. Only a few of the other soldiers, led by the captain, had followed it this far. The sergeant climbed over his seat and dropped into the box beside Sartain.

"Raise your wrists, bucko."

Sartain frowned up at the man, who had a face like seasoned cedar. "Huh?"

"I said raise your fuggin' wrists, an' be quick about it!"

Puzzled, the Cajun raised his wrists. The sergeant stuck a key in the lock. The cuffs fell away. The surge of blood felt like a swarm of bees stinging Sartain's hands.

Wincing, he rubbed them but didn't mind having been freed all that much. The sergeant had reached under his seat for a pair of steel jaws. After much grunting and cursing, he spread the ankle bracelets apart until they fell, one by one, away from Sartain's ankles.

Sartain shuttled his befuddled gaze from the sergeant to the captain, who was still mounted and staring at him grimly, and then back to the sergeant.

"You fellas, uh . . . have a change of heart?" the Revenger asked. "You lettin' me go?"

"Shut up," the captain snarled at him. "Come on — get him inside, Sergeant," the officer said, grimly. He sounded worn down and out of sorts. There was clearly something he hadn't liked about this job.

There was something Sartain hadn't liked about it, too. But now he was even more puzzled than troubled. Where was this place? *What* was this place? What was he doing here . . . ?

He was helped a little more gingerly out of the cabin this time, young Davey steering clear.

"This way," ordered the captain, who had dismounted.

He opened a wooden door in the wall. The soldiers, including the burly Irish sergeant, led Sartain through the opening and through a fragrant garden that smelled richly of citrus and sandalwood. The smell of wood smoke also hung in the air, and Sartain saw a large, adobe brazier sitting on an arbor-covered, fieldstone patio with several comfortable-looking wicker chairs. Someone had been sitting out here not all that long ago.

Ahead, a torch burned from a bracket in the adobe wall, near a stout oak door set deep in its frame. There was a small, grilled window in the door, closed from the inside.

The captain stopped in front of the door. He sighed, shook his head, then tapped on the door with the back of his hand. He clicked the door's latch. The door squawked free of the frame, opening a few inches on squeaky hinges.

Sartain looked at him.

"Sleep tight," the officer said through gritted teeth. "Don't let the bedbugs bite." He held up a key. "This door will be locked from the inside. You'll be let out tomorrow. If you try to leave before then, you'll be shot on sight. Got it?"

"I reckon," Sartain said, his befuddlement showing in his voice.

He pushed the door wide, stepped inside, and closed the door behind him. As the captain's key scraped in the lock, Sartain faced the room. He was vaguely aware of the scowl lines deepening across his forehead and at the corners of his eyes. He stood in a modest-sized but well-appointed room.

There was a full-sized bed to his right, a stout dresser and armoire to his left. A marble-topped washstand stood against the wall near the bed, under a crucifix set just above a one-foot square mirror.

A red lamp, its wick turned low, cast a watery umber light around the room, but mostly shadows. Though the room was dark, he could see a person in the bed. The sheets and blankets were lumped, and a mass of thick, curly, dark-brown hair was spilled across a pillow on the bed's right side. A delicate, brown, female foot poked out from under the blankets, near where Sartain stood, taking it all in — the long ride, his free hands and ankles, the room.

The girl.

She groaned, turned her head on the pillow, and stared straight off to her left. She swept her tangled hair away from her left cheek, turning her head more sharply until her brown eyes found the newcomer. She sat up suddenly, pulling the covers up over her breasts, the tops of which he'd glimpsed through the dancing locks of her hair. She obviously wasn't wearing a nightgown.

Or anything else, for that matter.

Her heart-shaped face was brown and pretty. She had three very small moles on her neck, another one off the right corner of her wide mouth. Sartain doubted she was twenty.

"You have come," she said, her voice raspy from sleep, and cleared her throat. She spoke with a thick Spanish accent. Judging by the darkness of her skin and eyes, he guessed she had some Indio blood. Apache or Yaqui, most likely.

"Who're you?"

"Sonja." She blinked, tossing her hair back

to reveal more of her round, cherubic face. "You are the *gringo* they call the Revenger."

She smiled warmly and patted the bed beside her.

Sartain walked up to the bed and stopped at the washstand. "What's going on? Where am I?" As he pulled a pitcher of water out from the stand's bottom shelf, he glanced at the girl. "Who're you, Sonja?"

"That last question is the only question I am allowed to answer, *Señor* Sartain." She smiled again. "I am your lover for the rest of the evening."

"Had a feelin' you weren't the housemaid."

Sartain poured water into the washbasin. He glanced at the door once more. No sounds rose beyond it, but the soldiers were likely out there, smoking, talking, killing time until their assignment — whatever that was — ended.

The Cajun shrugged out of his vest and hung it on a peg in the wall beside the washstand. As he did, he glimpsed a bottle on the dresser beside the smoky lantern. A bottle and two short, thick, green goblets. The bottle had a fancy label on it. He popped the cork, and sniffed the lip.

The aroma was akin to spring roses, old books, and leather.

Spanish brandy.

The Revenger chuckled, splashing some of the brandy into a glass. "All right — I'm easy. I can be chained and hauled halfway across the west and still be plied with good Taos Lightning and a pretty girl. Why not?" He raised the glass to the girl in mock salute, and threw back the entire shot.

The brandy burned pleasantly, leaving the taste of roses on his tongue.

"Forgive me, *señorita.*" Sartain splashed brandy into the second goblet, then handed it to her. Keeping the covers over her breasts, she leaned toward him to take the glass and then sat back against the headboard again. *"Gracias."*

"Oh, shit, don't mention it."

He didn't know why he was feeling owly toward the girl. She was pretty and obviously, inexplicably for him. But there wasn't anyone else around to take the brunt of his fury.

The girl had nothing to do with any of this, however. He doubted she even knew much more about what was happening than he did. He'd best mind his Southern manners.

He splashed more brandy into his glass, raised it to her, and dipped his chin. "To your beauty, Sonja."

She crinkled her brow skeptically, then raised her own glass and sipped the brandy.

"Ummm," she said. "Good, no?"

"Oh, very good."

Sartain set his glass on the small table beside the bed. He pulled his shirttails out of his pants, and unbuttoned the shirt. When he'd shrugged out of the shirt, he went ahead and continued undressing until all of his clothes lay in a pile on the braided hemp rug near the door.

Barefoot, he walked back to the washstand. The girl's eyes were on him, caressing his tall, broad, slim-hipped figure, a very faint, pensive smile stretching her pretty lips. He took up a cloth folded beside the basin, and soaked it. When he'd scrubbed himself thoroughly from head to toe, he dried himself with a towel.

When he was finished, he turned to see Sonja watching him, her chin propped on the heel of her hand. She was no longer bothering with the bed covers; her copper-colored, brown-tipped breasts sloped toward the sheet beneath her. Her eyes were low on him. A flame appeared to burn in them.

Slowly, her gaze climbed his torso to his eyes, and then she drew his side of the covers back, and patted the bed beside her.

Chapter Six

Sartain grabbed his glass and the bottle from the bureau, and sat down on the edge of the bed. The girl crawled over to him, wrapped an arm around his upper torso, and ran her hand through the thick hair on his chest. Her breasts felt full and supple against his back.

"You like me?"

"I like you just fine."

"You . . . don't seem happy to see me, *amigo.*" Sonja pressed her lips to his shoulder.

Sartain chuckled. "That's not it at all, *señorita.*" He held her hand and pressed his lips to her arm. "Just been a long trip."

"Come. Lie back."

She pulled him down onto the bed. He lifted his feet off the floor and stretched out. She kissed his lips very tenderly, then his chin.

He stared up at the heavy-beamed ceiling,

trying to let his thoughts surrender themselves to the girl's ministrations. It wasn't easy at first. He'd been hauled around like some zoo animal, and then his chains had been removed and he'd been locked in a room with a comfortable bed and a girl.

What in hell's name was going on?

Were they going to try him for murder in a federal court, kill him, or stud him?

But then Sonja's lips were working magically. He lowered his gaze to see her head rising and falling slowly, her breasts pressing against his thighs. She made very faint sucking sounds, cooing deep in her throat.

"Oh, hell," he said, and dug his hands into her thick, messy hair. "There's always tomorrow, isn't there?"

"Sí." She smiled up at him. "There is always tomorrow."

"Carpe diem."

"What's that?"

"Seize the day." Sartain chuckled. "Or . . . night, rather."

"Oh. Mmm-hmmm."

When morning came, a wash of salmon light through the curtained window to the right of the door, she plied him with her warm, soft hands, and then straddled him. Her full breasts jostled as she rose and fell on top of him, her groans growing louder and louder until she jerked her chin at the ceiling and loosed a she-cat's wail of carnal satisfaction.

If she was faking it, Sartain thought, she was a better actress than most whores he'd known. And he'd known a few . . .

With a deep, shuddering sigh, she rolled off of him. She lay on her side, facing him. She pressed her hands between her legs and raised her knees to her belly.

"Re-ven-ger." Sonja rubbed her face against his shoulder, catlike. "Why do they call you that?"

"Why do you think?"

"But it's we Mexicans who love revenge so much." She gave a wicked half-smile. "For us, it is an art. Like eating and love-making."

"Señorita," Sartain said, rolling toward her and nuzzling her breasts, "I don't mean to sound disrespectful to your race, but I could teach you folks a thing . . ."

A knock came at the door.

The captain's voice said, "Sartain."

That was all.

The Revenger sighed and gave the girl's left nipple a parting kiss before he crawled out of bed and took a slow, leisurely sponge bath at the washstand.

The knock came again. "Sartain?"

Leisurely scrubbing his privates: "Uh-huhh?"

"Breakfast."

"Be right out, Captain!" Sartain grinned at the girl, who returned it.

When he'd thoroughly dried himself, he took his own sweet time dressing.

"Come on, come on!" the captain said, pounding on the door.

Sartain whistled as he set his hat on his head, carefully adjusting the angle in the mirror over the washstand. He reached inside his shirt for a cigar, and Sonja rolled to the little table beside the bed, and scratched a match to life.

Crouching, the Revenger touched the cheroot to the flame. Puffing smoke, he said, *"Gracias, señorita."*

"Any time, *el largo*!"

Sartain winked at her and opened the door. Fists balled at his sides, the captain was staring off into the walled yard lit by the sun poking its lemon head above the eastern horizon. Orange trees grew amongst cacti, and wrens cheeped amongst the leaves. The captain swung toward the Cajun, his flushed face causing his pewter mustache to stand out starkly against it.

His light-blue eyes glinted angrily beneath

the brim of his Hardee hat. "Think you're pretty smart, don't you?"

Sartain rolled the cheroot from one corner of his mouth to the other. "That's an odd question, Captain. I don't rightly know how to answer it. Don't we all think we're smart?"

Davey and his young partner stood sneering up at Sartain, holding their rifles at port arms across their chests. The beefy sergeant flanked them, a boyish glint in his eye as he slid his gaze from the brown, naked body of Sonja on the bed behind Sartain to the Revenger himself.

The captain wheeled and said, "Come on, goddamnit. Let's get this miserable shit over with!"

"Took the words right out of my mouth," Sartain said, falling into step behind the man.

They walked through an inner courtyard and then into an inside hallway. Sartain followed the captain through a door off the hall's right side and then through a series of well-appointed rooms whose windows gave out onto the walled front yard.

The red tile roofs of the bunkhouses and the red wooden blades of the windmill shone vividly in the climbing morning sun. Dust rose from one of the corrals, around which men had gathered, their figures murky in the morning shadows.

As the small procession, flanked by the sergeant, tramped through a sitting room as large as many saloons but a whole lot better decorated, the Cajun's stomach began to groan. His mouth watered. Touching his nostrils teasingly were the aromas of a succulent breakfast that included bacon and rich, black coffee and something spicy — probably Mexican-spiced gravy — cooking on a range.

Two heavy, scrolled doors were thrown back against the stout, pink *adobe* wall that was cracked and pitted, showing its age. On the other side of the broad, arched doorway, the two privates separated and moved back against the wall, clicking their heels together in military attention.

Holy shit, Sartain thought, impressed.

He stepped into the dining room between the two privates, and stopped. The captain and the sergeant moved into the room behind him, the captain stepping to the Revenger's left, the sergeant to his right.

Sartain studied the pair before him. One was the chocolate-haired young woman, sitting in a high-backed, gold-and-wine upholstered chair on the far side of a twenty-foot-long dining table. The other was a middle-aged man with a thick head of salt-and-pepper hair with a matching mustache and muttonchop whiskers trailing down the sides of his overly fleshed face.

He stood near the woman, one high-topped, gold-buttoned, black boot propped on a chair between them. He was smoking a dynamite-sized cigar and leaning toward the beauty, his right arm resting on his corduroy-clad knee.

He'd been favoring the girl with the grin of a sycophant when Sartain had first seen him. Now he turned away from the girl, the grin fading quickly. It was replaced with a faintly annoyed look.

The annoyed look just as quickly switched to one of vague sheepishness as he lowered his boot from the chair beside the girl and squared his shoulders at the newcomers, jerking his black leather waistcoat down with his fleshy, beringed hands.

"Ah . . . Mr. Sartain, I take it?" He lifted the stogie to his lips, then took a few puffs as he studied the big man in the pinto vest through the smoke.

"Who did you think you had trussed up like a trapped mountain lion in that wagon? The pope?"

"Mr. Sartain," the captain snarled admonishingly, "show some respect. This is the governor of New Mexico Territory, Samuel L. McDougal."

"I don't give a shit who he is." Sartain massaged his backside. "My ass is still sore, and I don't think all the blood has run back into my hands yet." He glanced at the young woman — a real beauty even this early in the morning, and from closer up than Sartain had so far gotten — and winked.

Her peach-tan cheeks colored slightly but she did not look away from him. Her pearl eyes were vaguely defiant.

"Have we met?" the Revenger said.

The governor glanced from Sartain to the girl and then back to Sartain, scowling. "I don't much care what level of gutter talk you use in my presence, Mr. Sartain," McDougal said, "but as you can see, you are in the presence of a lady."

The Revenger grinned. "A man would have to be blind not to see that."

Now the girl's gaze flicked slightly away, and the nubs of her cheeks turned redder. Quickly, however, she shook her hair back away from her face, and met his cool gaze once more.

"No, we have not met, Mr. Sartain," she said. "At least, we have not been formally introduced."

Her voice, slightly husky and raspy, was

like a fist clenching the Cajun's nether regions.

"This is Miss Jasmine Gallant from the Pinkerton Agency. She is how we all came to be here . . . together . . . in this room here at my ranch." The governor had pronounced her last name with the accent over the final syllable, so that it sounded like "Gal-AUNT."

Sartain scowled through his tobacco smoke. "Could you explain that to me, Governor?"

Ignoring the question, McDougal turned to the room's third original occupant — a portly, double-chinned, gray-headed man in a three-piece suit and wearing a cloth napkin tucked into his shirt collar. He'd been working on devouring a plate spilling over with what appeared to be *huevos rancheros,* and had hardly slowed his work a notch when the soldiers and their prisoner had entered the dining room.

He had some yolk and beans on his spade beard and also on his makeshift bib. The eyes peering up at Sartain through small, round, silver-framed spectacles were sky blue and only perfunctorily interested in what was happening before him. He was far more interested in his plate.

"This," said the governor, gesturing toward the fat man with the hand holding his big cigar, "is Lieutenant Governor Foster Briggs."

Sartain didn't say anything. Neither did Briggs, who merely continued to chew and stare at Sartain like a cow chewing its cud. The fat man tore off a piece of corn tortilla and swabbed it with the rich, brown gravy flecked with red chili peppers on his plate, and stuffed it into his mouth.

The governor slid his gaze to the captain standing to Sartain's left. "You've met Captain Nelson, I take it . . . ?"

"He had the bad manners not to introduce himself." Sartain puffed on his own cheroot and said through the smoke billowing around his head, "Now that we've all gotten friendly, maybe you mucky-mucks could kindly tell me what in hell I'm doing here."

He glanced around. "Peculiar place for a court trial. Even more peculiar for a firing squad or a hangin'. I'd think you'd want the eastern scribblers here for that, get your name in black and white, maybe with a baby in your arms and a foot propped on my cold, dead ass."

He took another puff and blew it at the governor. "Isn't that how you politicians work it?"

The girl made a slight choking sound and

turned away, rubbing two fingers across her bee-stung mouth. Sartain looked at her. Her cheeks had reddened even more. Her expression was bland as she stared at an oil painting of the governor himself in full dress, military regalia sitting astride a fine, cream stallion, gold-crowned dress helmet resting on his thigh.

Just then it dawned on the Revenger that the girl had been stifling a chuckle. The governor seemed aware of it, too. He looked at her indignantly, as though he were a little injured by the stillborn outburst. He'd obviously been trying to impress the vixen, maybe lure her into his bedroom.

Manufacturing an over-bright smile, he turned back to the Revenger. "I trust, Mr. Sartain, that you enjoyed last night's . . . uh . . . shall we say, *accommodations*?"

"If you mean Sonja," Sartain said, "what man wouldn't? Especially after a long pull in the back of an army ambulance, trussed up like a tiger headed for a zoo."

He glanced at the woman again. She was back to studying him critically, wistfully, her rich lips ever so slightly parted so that they framed a small O in the middle.

"Yeah, she was fun. So was the brandy. Now, would you kindly tell me what the game is here?" The Cajun shuttled his gaze to Miss Gallant once more. "You said she's responsible for us all being here. Was Sonja her idea, too?"

"Whoever Sonja is," said the woman, Jasmine Gallant, with a bored, tolerant air, "no, she was not my idea, Mr. Sartain. Rest assured."

The lieutenant governor, Briggs, chuckled at that, spitting bits of egg and tortilla onto the table beyond his plate. That was the first indication the Cajun had had since entering the room that the man was paying attention to anything but his food.

"Please have a seat, Mr. Sartain," the governor said, gesturing at a chair nearly directly across the table from Jasmine Gallant. "You will dine with us, and by the end of the meal, the reason you were hauled here 'like a trussed up mountain lion,' as you so colorfully call it, will be crystal clear to you. You may not like it" — the governor chuckled wryly and glanced at his fat underling, who spat more egg on the table — "but you will have a complete understanding."

Chapter Seven

No mention was made why the portly lieutenant governor hadn't waited to dine with the others. The fat man merely sat sipping his coffee while two Mexican cooks rolled in a cloth-draped cart filled with steaming plates and mugs and glasses of chilled milk, and set them before each of the diners — the governor himself, Sartain, Jasmine Gallant, Captain Nelson, and the sergeant, who was introduced as Jamieson Fridley.

The two privates remained by the doors, rifles held at port arms. While Sartain dug into his own heaping plate of *huevos rancheros,* he thought he could hear the stomachs of Davey and the other soldier growling.

Inwardly, he smiled.

The food was delicious, and while the Revenger ate hungrily, the grub did nothing to assuage his indignation. He supposed he should be grateful that he wasn't dead or hadn't been thrown into some federal hoosegow; instead, he'd been entertained by a saucy whore and now fed a wondrous meal.

But he'd been toyed with, and he didn't like it. He didn't like the expression of smugness on the governor's overfed features, either. He knew he had only himself to blame for allowing himself to be captured, of having grown overconfident and careless in his abilities to stay ahead of the law.

Still, if he could in some way have gotten his hands on his LeMat, he'd likely have blown the self-satisfied look off the governor's face with one blast of the twelve-gauge wad beneath the pistol's main barrel. Of course, the soldiers who were likely surrounding the place would riddle him with lead before he could get away, but at least he'd take that satisfaction to his grave . . . or whatever draw they tossed him in.

While Sartain and the others ate, the lieutenant governor muffled belches with his hand, and sipped his coffee. The Mexican servers kept the diners' own coffee mugs filled. The privates' bellies continued to growl.

Finally, the meal was over. At least it was for Sartain, who sat back in his chair and ran his napkin across his mouth. He saw that while Jasmine Gallant had cleaned only half of her own plate, she appeared finished with her breakfast. She had one elbow on the edge of the table, and she was resting her chin on the heel of her hand, regarding Sartain with a furtive, speculative air, tucking her bottom lip fetchingly under her upper teeth.

When the Cajun caught her staring at him, she arched her brow and slid her own plate slightly toward him with two fingers. "Would you like to finish mine, as well, Mr. Sartain?"

Sartain smiled wolfishly. "I thank you for the offer, Miss Gallant. While I was indeed hungry, not having had a *proper* meal on the way here, I reckon I'd best let this wriggle down a bit. Soon, I'll no doubt be feelin' like a swelled-up tick fit to burst!" He chuckled, then frowned. "Gallant . . . is that a French name?"

"Yes, it is."

"What a coincidence. So is Sartain."

"Yes, I suppose it would be," she said tolerantly, with a frigid smile, her pearl eyes boring into his.

Why was it the chillier and more beautiful they came, the more he tended to imagine what they would look like sprawled naked on a bear rug before the flickering, homey light of a cold winter night's fire?

As though she were reading his thoughts, the nubs of her fine cheeks colored again, and she turned away.

The governor finished his own plate, and wiped his mouth and mustache. "Now, then, Mr. Sartain, shall we get down to business?"

Sartain was still staring at the fetching creature across from him. "I can't imagine anything better."

She whipped her cold eyes back to him, and they flashed angrily beneath beetled brows.

As one of the servants removed his plate, the governor tapped his coffee mug with a spoon. "I'm . . . uh . . . over *here,* Mr. Sartain. . . ."

The Cajun leaned back in his chair and folded his hands over his well-filled belly. "Let's hear it." He could feel the captain's reproving eyes on him, and added dryly out the side of his mouth, "Mr. Governor, sir."

He'd lost all respect for authority after the Union soldiers had murdered his girl. The way he saw things now, the governor and everyone else who faulted him for his actions were in league with the killers.

"I have brought you here, Mr. Sartain,"

the governor said, "to offer you a deal."

"A deal . . . ?"

"Yes. Your freedom in return for a job."

"A job."

"Yes, a job."

"A job doing what?"

The governor lifted his recently refilled mug, and looked across the table at the captain.

"Ah . . . oh, yes. Of course." Captain Nelson glanced behind him at the two privates, and said, "Wilson, Ellison — you're temporarily dismissed. Please go out and close the doors. Wait in the sitting room for orders."

He looked at the sergeant and canted his head toward the door.

The sergeant wiped his mouth once more with his napkin, gained his feet heavily, saluted the captain, and stepped through the open doorway.

Both privates saluted the captain, as well. They glanced hungrily at the captain's nearly empty plate, which a servant was carrying away, and then went out and closed the doors behind them.

The governor sipped his coffee and returned his gaze to Sartain. "I want you to hunt down a Mexican border bandit and kill him."

Sartain stared at the man. He wasn't sure he'd heard what he thought he'd heard. But as the governor stared back at him blandly, Sartain turned to the young woman, who regarded him seriously, as well. So was the lieutenant governor, as well as Captain Nelson. The portly Briggs hung his head low, as though it weighed too much to hold upright; his spectacles appeared about to slide down off the end of his nose.

Sartain slammed the ends of both his fists onto the table, and laughed loudly. "You're not joking!"

They all flushed somewhat, sheepishly. The lady Pinkerton even gave a slight, involuntary wince and then used her right index finger to flip her spoon in the air. She caught it before it could clatter back down on the table, and gave the governor a diffident smile.

Sartain laughed again, harder this time. He threw his head back and guffawed at the ceiling. His laughter echoed loudly around the room.

The governor merely looked down at his coffee. Miss Gallant did the same. The lieutenant governor kept his cow-eyed gaze on Sartain, a faint smile quirking the corners of his mouth. The captain glared angrily, nostrils flared.

As the heat of the Cajun's amusement at the irony of the governor's request — or was it an order? — began to lose some of its volume, Sartain said, "Why in the hell should I?"

"Because the governor is telling you to," said the captain through large, yellow, gritted teeth.

"Oh, well, in that case," the Cajun said, suddenly serious, "the governor can go straight to —"

"No, no, no!" McDougal said, shaking his head and glowering at Nelson. "That isn't how it is, at all. Captain Nelson, would you mind kindly keeping your mouth shut and allowing me to lay out the details of this . . . of this *opportunity* to Mr. Sartain?"

"Of course, Governor," the captain said, raking his angry gaze from the Revenger, his ruddy cheeks turning sunset red. "I beg your pardon, sir."

"Thank you, Captain." The governor turned to Sartain. "I am asking, *urging* your help in this matter of the *bandidos,* Mr. Sartain. You do not, of course, have to accept my request."

"And if I don't?"

As though it were a silly question, McDougal shrugged one shoulder and said, "You will be court-martialed, likely found guilty of mass murder, and shot by firing squad."

"And if I do?"

"You will be paid twenty-five thousand dollars and, of course, given back your freedom."

"You'll pay me and turn me loose." Sartain studied the governor, innately not trusting the man. The ludicrousness of such a request made him distrust him even more. "And what about the federal soldiers I killed?"

McDougal shrugged again. "I, of course, am in no position to forgive such crimes. I couldn't possibly offer you amnesty, but only a good chunk of *dinero,* your freedom, and, I hope, the opportunity to start over."

"Preferably in another country," the captain said again, adding out the side of his mouth, "Mexico, say . . ."

"Captain!" the governor said, almost showing his teeth at the underling, like a dog showing ownership of a bone. "What did I just tell you, sir?"

"Again, Governor," the captain said with what appeared genuine chagrin, "forgive me." Lowering his voice as though Sartain couldn't hear him, he leaned over the table, canted his head toward the Cajun, and said, "But, good Lord, Governor, this man is a cold-blooded killer! He's killed *soldiers*!"

"He killed the soldiers who murdered his young lady," the governor said.

"That is a matter under some dispute, Governor," the captain said indignantly, turning red again. "And one that requires further investigation!"

"Captain?" It was the first time that the lieutenant governor, Briggs, had spoken at the table. When the captain turned to face the man in surprise — as did the others, including Sartain — Briggs said quietly but firmly, "Shut up."

That appeared to cow Nelson even more than McDougal's own admonishments had.

All eyes then returned to Sartain, who said, "So after I've been paid and given my freedom, I'll still be hunted."

"Of course," the governor said again, as though the answer were obvious. "But you will be twenty-five thousand dollars richer, and" — he smiled shrewdly — "probably a whole lot more cautious. At least, cautious enough to make sure this lovely Pinkerton agent, Miss Gallant, is not shadowing your every move."

It was Sartain's turn to flush as he slid his gaze to the lady of topic: "Just how long were you doggin' me, anyway, and how come I never saw you back there?"

Miss Gallant smiled with one side of her mouth, flipped her spoon in the air, and caught it again.

Sartain muttered a curse under his breath as he turned back to the governor.

"How come you can't just send some federal boys after those *bandidos*? Or a posse of deputy U.S. marshals? Hell, if Miss Gallant is so damn good, why don't you just send *her*?"

The governor chuckled, pleased by the Revenger's displeasure at having been run down by a female. Leaning forward and planting an arm to each side of his smoking coffee mug, the governor's face acquired a deeply serious, even troubled expression.

"This is a special quarry. A tricky situation. In fact . . . it's a deeply *personal* situation for me, Mr. Sartain. One that no one outside of this room must ever know the full details of." He cleared his throat, adjusted his black foulard tie at his throat, and said, "You see, this young Mexican cutthroat has kidnapped my young daughter, Priscilla."

He looked at Sartain, his eyes grave. "He's taken her deep into Chihuahua."

Sartain nodded, absorbing the information. "Still, why not just send . . . ?"

"Because this young desperado is my

stepson, Maximilian San Xavier de Tejada." The governor lowered his gaze to the table in shame.

"He's your stepson?"

"Yes. His mother died three years ago, God rest her soul." McDougal crossed himself. "Young Maximilian loved her deeply. Her death drove him insane. Quite mad."

"And he *kidnapped* your daughter? He's holding her for *ransom*?"

"If there's a ransom, he's taking a long time to inform me. He and Priscilla have been missing for nearly three months." He waved a hand over his shoulder. "Gone with the wind!

"I'm thinking he might have joined one of his relatives down there — an old *bandido* named Hector Tejada. He is Maximilian's wayward uncle. I think they're in cahoots. What they're up to exactly, aside from stealing away my precious Priscilla, I'm not sure. They might be trying to regain their old *hacienda,* which became mine when my wife died. Her first husband is dead, as well, which is fitting since he's the one who ran the place into the ground. Fortunately, there had been an extraordinary provision in the late Angelica's father's will that when he died, all of his holdings went to her and not to her husband or her only brother, Hector."

"How did that happen?" Sartain asked. "Such a thing is practically unheard of in Mexico. Even up here . . ."

"Angelica's father was a good judge of men, though he didn't command them very well. He wasn't a good rancher, either. He lost much of my wife's family's land to poor management and a small revolution but managed to retain over twenty thousand acres. It is mine now. My own men work the holdings. It's my belief that Hector . . . and Maximilian . . . have decided they are going to build an army to regain their land in Chihuahua . . . by waging war on my cowpunchers."

He shook his head dismissively. "Common bandits is what they are. Cattle rustlers, stagecoach and train robbers. Desperadoes with delusions of grandeur." His nose colored as he glared at Sartain. "And kidnappers, probably rapists!"

He swallowed, then drew a calming breath. "I want Maximilian killed, Mr. Sartain. I don't care about old Hector, but if he's running with Maximilian, then you'll likely need to kill him, too. For your own sake. Please make sure that my Priscilla is unharmed. Return her to me. She's a hazel-eyed blonde. Very pretty. Very sweet. She's my only daughter, Mr. Sartain."

"Why don't you send some of your own men down there after 'em?"

"I have. They've come up with nothing. No trail sign, nothing. Maximilian is a sneaky devil and a formidable outdoorsman."

"I don't understand why Maximilian kidnapped his stepsister in the first place," Jasmine said. "Was he in love with her?"

"Probably." The governor tapped his temple. "Maximilian is quite insane. Insanely romantic and devilish. I don't bandy the word 'insane' about. Hector is also crazy. My dear wife, I'm afraid, suffered from the same disease, which eventually caused her to take her life. None of them has ever had both feet placed firmly in reality."

He glanced at the others as though uncertain whether he wanted to continue. Apparently deciding to go ahead, he added demurely, while absently stirring his coffee, "My dear Angelica hanged herself with one of my belts in our bedroom. Maximilian found her . . . and blamed me for her death. He tried to skewer me with a poker. Fortunately, one of my aides was there — a big man who was able to subdue the young man quite handily. He vowed he'd either kill me or ruin me. If I never see my daughter again, Mr. Sartain, he will most definitely have ruined me."

He pounded the table, causing the china and silver to jump noisily. "I will not allow him to ruin me!"

The governor waited for his blood to cool.

"You see, Mr. Sartain, I need you to do this task for me because there is no one else I can order . . . or ask . . . to perform it. It proved too much for my own cowpunchers. It would be against the law for me to order anyone assassinated, downright *unseemly* to order anyone in *my wife's* family assassinated. Furthermore, it would be against the law for me to send anyone across the border without the written permission of the Mexican authorities. Because of my position as a public figure with political as well as professional ambitions beyond this office, I'm sure you can understand how it all needs to be handled quite secretively and by someone outside my usual realm.

"You've killed before, Mr. Sartain — for people who've been unable to accomplish the task themselves. That's all I'm asking you to do for me. Ride down into Chihuahua. I'll give you detailed maps of the general area where I believe Maximilian is hiding. Find where Maximilian is hiding my daughter, kill him and old Hector, if need be, and return my dear Priscilla to me."

Sartain flipped his own spoon in the air, caught it, and cast Miss Gallant a victorious look. She regarded him blandly, unimpressed.

The Revenger turned to the governor, who eyed him speculatively, as though wondering what his answer would be. "My freedom and fifty thousand dollars."

The lieutenant governor and the captain grunted as though they'd been kicked in the gut.

"Half now," Sartain added, "half when Maximilian and his cohorts are snuggling with diamondbacks."

"Jesus Christ!" laughed the captain.

The governor waved him off.

He studied Sartain with what appeared admiration, approval. "You have a deal." He glanced at the lady Pinkerton. "Miss Gallant rides with you."

Sartain gave a caustic chuff. "Why in the hell would I need a woman to — ?"

"To make sure you perform the duties prescribed without running off with half of the fifty thousand," McDougal finished for him. "Miss Gallant will also verify that you've accomplished the task and that you have earned the second half of your pay."

Sartain shook his head vigorously. "No. No way."

The comely Pinkerton merely stared at him with that same bland look as before.

"She's quite a good tracker . . . obviously," the governor said.

The lieutenant governor snorted a laugh and thumbed his glasses up his nose.

"No," Sartain repeated. "Do you have any idea how hard it would be to travel in Mexico *unharassed* with a woman who looks like *that*?" He shook his head again. "No. Absolutely not, Governor. Pure suicide for both of us. If she goes, I stay. The deal is off. That's all I have to say on the subject. Call the guards and cart me off to my court-martial!"

Chapter Eight

Sartain turned the wheel of his field glasses slowly with his gloved right finger, squinting into the eyepieces.

There wasn't much out there in the sun-blasted badlands he'd just traversed, but a few minutes ago, before he'd hauled out his army-grade binoculars, he'd seen — or thought he'd seen — a telltale curl of dust along his back trail. This part of Chihuahua was haunted by desperadoes of every stripe, and there were still packs of bronco Apaches on the hunt for white blood, as well.

That dust could have belonged to anyone. Whoever it belonged to, the Cajun would have bet gold nuggets to horse apples that their intentions were not benign. There were few benign intentions in Mexico.

Cursing under his breath, Sartain gained his feet, returned his binoculars to their baize-lined leather case, and picked up his Henry repeater with the ivory diamondback carved into the rear walnut stock. He set the rifle on his shoulder and walked back toward the nest of rocks in which he'd set up camp for the night.

"Well, we got company," he groused, kicking a stone in frustration. "*Bandidos* most likely. *Bandidos* with a taste for . . ."

Sartain stopped walking abruptly, letting his voice trail off slowly with, "pretty female flesh . . ."

Before him stood a husky Mexican with a scar over and below his milky white left eye. He wore buckskins and coarse cotton and he had cartridge bandoliers strapped across his chest. He smelled bad. Real bad — like deer piss. If he smelled bad to Sartain, ten feet away, then he must have really reeked to Jasmine Gallant, because she was about as close to the man as she could be without copulating with him, though that seemed to be what the beefy *bandido* had in mind.

He was standing behind her, holding her back against him. He'd ripped the lady Pinkerton's blouse open, and he was holding her bare left breast in his thick, brown left hand, pinching the nipple. In his other hand, he held a rusty Bowie knife up close to Miss Gallant's creamy neck.

The knife looked especially barbaric against the woman's fine, delicate skin and the torn silk of her blouse.

If she was appalled by the *bandido's* rancid smell, she didn't let on. She seemed more concerned with the big Bowie knife whose savagely upturned tip was pressing ever so gently against her jugular vein. She shuttled her fear-bright gaze from the knife to Sartain and back again. She was groaning. Tears of terror and pain rolled down her cheeks.

Two other *bandidos* stood to the right of the big man and Jasmine, around the small fire the woman had obviously been building and erecting an iron tripod over when she'd been set upon by these trail wolves. Those two each had a pistol drawn. The pistols were cocked and aimed at Sartain.

"Amigo," said the big Mex holding Jasmine, giving her breast another squeeze and causing her to cry out in pain, "how much for the woman, huh? We'll give you a good price for her" — he glanced at the other two laughing men on his left — "won't we, *mis compadres*?"

"Hold on," Sartain said, slowly lowering his Henry from his shoulder, wincing when he saw the big Mex push the tip of his Bowie knife a little harder against the woman's neck. "Ease up a little, there, pards. You're hurting the lady."

"How much you want, *amigo*?" the Mex said, stretching his lips back from his large, cracked, crooked teeth. "How much you want for us to take her out into the bushes and have our ways with her? Huh? Name your price."

"She ain't for sale," Sartain said, glancing at the other two and wondering how much of a chance he had. Could he snap off a shot with his Henry before those two turned him into a human sieve?

"Oh, she is most definitely for sale, *amigo,*" intoned the Mex who held Jasmine. "Every woman has a price. But it is just out of politeness I offer to buy her from you when as you can see I could very easily just take her!" He laughed raucously, squeezing the woman's breast and causing her to scrunch up her face with pain. "On the other hand, I don't think you are the reasonable sort, *amigo,* so you know what I think I'm gonna do? Huh? Do you know what I have decided to do?"

He actually seemed to be awaiting an answer. The other two grinned and chuckled and kept their revolvers aimed at the Revenger.

"What's that?" Sartain asked, knowing he wasn't going to like the answer.

"I think I am just going to have my *com-*

padres kill you and be done with you, and then we will be free to have a very lovely afternoon and evening with your woman!"

He threw his head back, laughing loudly.

"Amigos!" he yelled at the other two. "Kindly give us some privacy!"

"No, wait!" Sartain shouted. "Let her go!"

The two pistols began bucking and blasting in the Mexicans' hands.

The men laughed as they fired.

"Let her go!" Sartain shouted as the bullets punched through him.

But then she was far closer to him than she'd been only a second ago. Only a few inches away, in fact.

"Mr. Sartain!" she said, staring down at him, shaking his shoulder. "Mr. Sartain! Wake up! You're dreaming!"

"Let her go!" he heard himself shout again before he'd fully come to his senses.

He'd heaved himself up onto his elbows. His heart was racing and his feet were still moving, like a dog trying to run in its sleep.

Now he stared at her. Embarrassment washed over him like a cold ocean wave. He let his legs relax. He ran a hand down his sweaty face, blinked, and looked around. There were only himself and Miss Gallant here in this isolated desert camp at the edge of a dry arroyo. It must have been after midnight. The sky was black velvet awash with floury swirls of glittering starlight.

The cold, dry night air chilled the sweat on his face and under his collar. Miss Gallant was on one knee beside him. She removed her hand from his shoulder, letting it fall to her thigh.

He shivered.

"Oh, shit . . ." he said as the dream finally cleared out, though he thought he could still hear the *bandidos'* dwindling laughter beneath the roaring of their pistols.

"Let who go?" the lady Pinkerton asked him. She had a blanket over her shoulders. Her hair was a pretty, tangled mess as it hung down around her shoulders. He couldn't help noticing that a couple more buttons than usual were undone on her blouse, exposing an alluring glimpse of flesh.

"Let who go?" she repeated.

"Just a dream."

"About what?"

Annoyed, he frowned at her. "Just a dream. What — you never dream?"

She studied him. It was hard to see her eyes in the darkness. The starlight glinted in her left one as it shone through a lock of her hair. She placed a hand on his forehead. "My god — you're sweating on this cold night."

His chagrin was not diminishing. "Like I said . . ." He lay back down, resting his head against the wool underside of his saddle, and drew his blankets up to his chin. "Just a dream. Good night, Miss Gallant." They'd been on the trail for five days, and they still were not on a first-name basis. She was as chilly as they came, as though she didn't much care for men in general.

Or was it him in particular?

In those five days, they'd probably not spoken more than twenty sentences.

She rose and, still holding the blanket around her shoulders, walked over to where her gear lay on the far side of the cold fire over which they'd roasted a good-sized jackrabbit he'd snared just after they'd set up camp for the night, and pulled a bottle out of her war bag. She grabbed a couple of tin cups and walked back over to him, sinking to her butt on the ground.

"Drink?"

Sartain looked at the bottle. It had a label on it. Frowning, he scrutinized it more closely. "Well, I'll be damned," he said, genuinely surprised. "That's ole Sam Clay. Ole Sam's my fav. . . ." He let his voice trail off, narrowing a suspicious eye at her. "You knew that, didn't you?"

"Of course. I've learned a lot of things

about you, Mr. Sartain. It's my job to learn things about my quarry."

"Quarry," he grunted, not liking the sound of the word when applied to himself.

"Yes, quarry."

She poured a couple fingers into one of the cups. He liked the tinny sound of the top-shelf firewater striking the bottom of the cup. Just the sound alone helped take the sharp edge off his humiliation about having been discovered in a nightmare.

As she handed him the cup, he couldn't help glancing at her bosom again, remembering her exposed breast in the dream. Would it look the same as the dream breast had? A fleeting speculation, no less provocative for being childish.

She followed his glance to her blouse, gave him a vaguely reproving look, and then splashed bourbon into her own cup. She sighed. "Yes, you're every bit the man my investigation indicated you were."

Sartain sipped the bourbon. It felt wonderful, sliding over his tongue and tingling down his throat to spread a gauzy warmth through his chest and belly. "And that is . . . ?"

"A lusty whoremonger."

"Hey, I was raised by whores. Let's not get personal — shall we, Miss Gallant?"

"Yes, of course. Your appraising my bosom isn't at all personal. Or lusty."

Sartain leaned back on an elbow, swirling the whiskey around in his cup. "I'm just a man, Miss Gallant. You can't blame me for wondering . . . you know . . . about . . ."

He didn't need to finish that. Even in the darkness, he could see that her cheeks turned darker.

"If you were so bothered by my character, why were you so persistent about followin' me down here? I gave you every opportunity to bow out. The governor would have let you back out of the deal. No man in his *right* mind would send a pretty woman, Pinkerton or not, down here with a known killer, to kill a man illegally."

"You're the one who'll be doing the killing, Mr. Sartain."

"Come, now, Miss Gallant. Let's not sift the dirt too fine. You're down here to make sure I kill a man."

Ignoring that, she sipped her bourbon and shook her hair back. "What you said about a man in his 'right mind.' Are you suggesting the governor is not in his right mind, Mr. Sartain?"

"Hell, yes." Sartain laughed. "Isn't that obvious? He's a territorial governor. His job is to see that I, a wanted man with several federal bounties on his head, is tried and hanged. Not sent down to Mexico to kill his own stepson and the stepson's uncle. Let me see — how many laws is he breaking?"

The Revenger laughed again. The ludicrousness, not to mention the hypocrisy, of the assignment actually tickled him. That's why he'd not been overly bothered to accept the chore. It confirmed what he already knew — he was no worse than most of the men who were after him, including some of the most powerful men in the government. He'd long heard that McDougal's prospects of winning the presidency were fair to good, and it was a target he had his sites on.

Sartain hadn't taken the job for money. He'd had no choice. Still, it wasn't all that bad. It amused him. And he wasn't about to turn the money down. He didn't normally charge for his services, but, then, he usually worked for people who couldn't have afforded him. McDougal could afford that and more.

And fifty thousand dollars would take him many miles; and for a good, long time it would prevent him from having to take on odd jobs when his larder needed restocking.

"I guess it doesn't matter to me," Miss Gallant said. "Any of that stuff about being right or wrong. All I know is that the governor hired the Pinkerton Agency to track you down. Mr. Pinkerton sent me." She shrugged.

"You're feeling pretty good, aren't you?"

She shrugged again, then tried to hide a grin by chomping down on her bottom lip.

"Why'd they send a woman?" Sartain asked her once he'd taken another sip of his drink.

"Think about it, Mr. Sartain."

The Cajun pooched out his lips. "All right, I'm thinking . . ." He frowned ironically, as though studying hard on a difficult subject, which it was.

"Don't strain yourself. Women are invisible to men like you. Even beautiful women."

She didn't appear at all chagrined to have complimented herself so frankly.

"Maybe even especially beautiful women," Miss Gallant said. "When you see a woman, beautiful or otherwise, you think about one thing. Don't worry. You're not unlike most men. At least most handsome men who've traditionally had an easy time in working your way into a woman's boudoir.

"You saw me several times during the time I was tracking you — once in Coffeyville, again in Denver. There was another time —

in a small supply camp on the trail into the mountains. I wasn't worried. I knew you wouldn't entertain the notion that I might be doing exactly what I was doing — stalking you, learning your habits in preparation for setting a trap. Because I'm a woman. A beautiful woman. If you'd given me any consideration at all, it would have been about how you'd go about trying to bed me."

Sartain studied her from beneath his rumpled brows. "Jesus — I did see you!"

"See?"

"Yeah, now I remember. You were pretty far away, but in the back of my mind I thought you were awful pretty to be alone on a horse on the rough and tumble frontier. I reckon I thought — if I gave any consideration to you at all beyond wondering what you'd look like in your birthday suit, or what pitch your voice would climb to during a tussle — you must have had a man around *somewhere.*"

"It's not going to work, Mr. Sartain."

"What's that?"

"You're not going to embarrass me." She set her cup down and crawled slowly toward him, smiling beguilingly.

Her long, wavy hair danced about her shoulders. Her plump lips were parted.

He couldn't have been more surprised when she slid her head up close and kissed him. Her lips had the texture of ripe plums.

"And you are not, under any circumstances," she added, then kissed him once more, intentionally getting his blood up, "ever, in your entire, miserable life going to see me naked."

She kissed him once more with agonizing tenderness, pulled her head away, and winked.

She scooped up her cup, rose, and walked over to her bedroll.

Sartain stared after her, hang-jawed. He felt as though he'd been poked with a stiletto in all the places it would hurt most.

"Oh, and . . . Mr. Sartain?" she said as she lay down and started drawing her blankets up.

He could see only her silhouette in the starlight.

"Yes, Miss Fancy Britches?"

"You won't be needing to shout for anyone to let me go. I'm perfectly capable of protecting myself."

"Miss Gallant?" the Cajun called, ironically.

"Yes, Mr. Sartain?"

"I got twenty dollars says I can seduce you by the time we fork paths."

Jasmine Gallant chuckled dryly. "You're on."

"Good night."

"Good night, Mr. Sartain."

Chapter Nine

Sartain woke relatively refreshed at dawn's first blush.

Sitting up, blinking and stretching, he saw that Pinkerton's princess, as he amused himself by silently referring to her, was still deeply slumbering. He could hear her soft, rattling snores as she lay curled on her side, her left cheek flat against the underside of her saddle. Two blankets and her striped blanket coat covered her.

Sartain rose quietly and started dressing. There was no point in waking her just yet.

He doubted that the young woman was accustomed to riding as far as they'd ridden over the past five days without more than a few hours' break. She hadn't complained, of course. That wasn't her way. She'd have walked ten miles with a snake-bit ankle swollen to the size of a wheel hub before she'd have asked for a ride in a buckboard wagon.

The Cajun had found himself admiring that about her. She was beautiful and tough, not unlike many of the doves who'd raised him.

Still, she was too beautiful, her skin too perfect, to have ridden as far as they'd ridden together over several consecutive days, under a merciless Mexican sun and with damned little water. He'd let her sleep another hour before rousing her.

He'd practiced the art of moving silently during the war, when he'd often led skirmishes behind enemy lines. Then, if you made a sound, sometimes even the most muffled sound imaginable, you died. It had often been as simple as that.

Now, in silence, he dressed and gathered his gear. Rifle on his shoulder, wincing against the steely morning chill, he drifted off away from the camp. He intended to scout around a bit, making sure he and the lady Pinkerton were alone out here.

Despite his embarrassment, the nightmare lingered. Also, he'd actually seen a faint upsweep of dust yesterday afternoon, when he'd scanned their back trail from a ridge not unlike the one in the dream. He'd passed it off as a mere dust devil, because that's probably what it had been.

But the dream had suggested the dust

might have been something else, and several of the more superstitious doves who'd raised him had taught him to heed his dreams. Sometimes the visions were trying to tell you something — about certain choices to make in life, say.

Sometimes they were warnings.

When he was a good distance from the camp, Sartain lowered the Henry from his shoulder, quietly pumped a cartridge into the chamber, off-cocked the hammer, and continued tramping off over gravelly desert knolls spiked with sage and cacti. He moved as quietly as during his war days, scrutinizing the shadowy features around him.

Dawn and dusk were the most challenging times of day for scouting, for the thin shadows seemed to move with the gradually fading or intensifying light. So he used his ears as much as his eyes. Picking up unnatural sounds wasn't so easy, either, for as the wash of silvery light grew in the west, and the shadows lightened, more and more desert birds began piping and chittering in the branches of the mesquites and flitting amongst the rocks and cactus plants, scrounging for seeds and beetles.

He circled the camp without finding any sign that he and Jasmine were being stalked. Still, he wasn't satisfied. He had an uneasy feeling. It was like the sensation you felt after drinking slightly sour milk. Some sense beyond the usual was trying to tell him something.

On the way back to the camp, he stopped and tended their horses, which he and the Pinkerton had tied in the arroyo just south of the bivouac, where they wouldn't be easily spotted, but from where they could give warning of possible interlopers.

Sartain's buckskin, Boss, was frisky, tossing his head and switching his tail. When the Cajun checked the horse's hooves, making sure the shoes were still properly seated, the stallion pressed his cold nose to the back of its rider's neck, and snorted loudly. Sartain laughed despite the added chill rippling along his spine. The mount had been on the trail for five days after his unceremonious train ride to the wilds of New Mexico with his rider, but the horse was still chomping at the bit to get moving.

The thoroughbred, too, pawed the ground and sharply switched its tail, snorting.

Finished checking both horses' shoes, Sartain draped a feed sack over their ears.

"All right, boy," the Cajun said, running a hand down the stallion's fine neck. "I'll go clatter some pans around Pinkerton's princess."

He looked around. The sun was on the rise behind distant mountains. It was splashing pink and salmon into the sky and against the bellies of high, ragged clouds. There was enough light to start riding even through rugged, unfamiliar terrain.

Sartain figured they still had at least another three days' ride to get to the general region, a vast, remote *sierra* where the governor believed his daughter was being held by his stepson, Maximilian. The stepson's lair lay in or near an old church in a forbidding mountain range known as *Las Montañas de Sombra,* or the Shadow Mountains.

Sartain climbed up out of the arroyo and started weaving through rocks and boulders, approaching the camp. He smelled smoke, which told him the princess was up. As he stepped between the last two boulders ringing their camp, he saw the small, leaping yellow flames as well as the coffee pot.

"Now, that's about the best smell a man can — *oh, shit . . . I do apologize!*"

He hadn't seen the woman standing on the far side of the fire, her slender, bare back to him, until she'd swung toward him and gasped. She had her camisole raised above her breasts. She was holding a sponge in her left hand, her canteen in her right hand, giving the lovely orbs a bath.

She turned away quickly, giving her back to him again. As she did, he caught a profile view of her lovely, pink-tipped breasts, and again he felt that stiletto poking him in several sensitive areas.

"Do you *mind,* Mr. Sartain?" she said, haughtily.

"Nope, not a bit," he said through a chuckle, leaning his rifle against a rock and moving toward the fire.

"Could you make a little noise?" she said, pulling her camisole down and reaching for her blouse, which lay on a nearby log.

"You make noise in this country, you're liable to end up slow-roasting over an Apache cook fire. Hell, just snapping a finger during the War of Northern Aggression would cost a man —"

"I just mean when you're approaching the camp," she said, swinging toward him and buttoning her blouse. Her eyes flashed angrily. "So that I know you're coming. How about a couple of quiet whistles? Surely, you can whistle!"

Sartain laid a couple of small *piñon* branches on the flames, and stared at her. "Good lord, you're a beautiful woman. What in the hell ever made you throw in with Pinkerton, anyway?"

She glared at him as she continued buttoning the blouse. "I would appreciate it if you would scour that image from your mind, Mr. Sartain. You and I are colleagues. In order to maintain a professional working relationship, we are both going to have to conduct ourselves in a professional manner!"

"Well, that's gonna be hard to do — I'm sorry." Sartain placed his hand on the coffee pot to see how far along the water was. "Especially now. Good lord . . ."

"Mr. Sartain!"

"I do apologize, Miss Gallant," he said, sitting on a rock near the fire. "If you're so damn worried about your privacy, next time you might wander a little farther away from camp to tend to your ablutions."

"It's chilly. The fire was warm."

"Again, I'm sorry," he said, reaching into a croaker sack for a canvas pouch of Arbuckle's. "But that's what you get when you come down here." He looked at her pointedly. "To make almighty sure a man kills another one."

She laughed as she reached back to throw her hair out from under collar. "Aren't you the voice of moral authority!"

After a quick breakfast of coffee, fatback,

and the baking powder biscuits she'd cooked the night before, they rode on down the arroyo, which generally angled south. The watercourse climbed into more rugged country than before. The mesquites and briars grew thick along the sides of the wash. Red stone outcroppings loomed.

Hawks gave their ratcheting hunting cries as the hot, late-summer sun beat down.

Sartain wasn't accustomed to partnering up with anyone, so he wasn't accustomed to talking much on the trail — aside from talking to his horse, that was. Now he glanced back at Miss Gallant, who was leaning out to sniff a flowering shrub as she passed it.

"Tell me about yourself, Miss Gallant. Or would you mind if I called you Jasmine? We have been on the trail nearly a week, and" — he grinned devilishly as he turned forward in the saddle — "I do know quite a bit about you . . ."

He chuckled.

"A gentleman wouldn't keep bringing that up, Mr. Sartain."

"Well, obviously . . ."

"You're not a gentleman. I gathered that."

"Answer my question."

"Do you think we should be yammering out here, Mr. Sartain?" Out of the corner of his eye, he saw her looking warily around. "We are in Apache country, aren't we? Don't bands of Chiricahuas still roam this area? Not to mention *bandidos*?"

"Yeah, it's a country fit only for rattlesnakes and Gila monsters." Sartain narrowed an eye at a column of striated rock rising steeply on his left. "But if there are any Apaches around . . . or *bandidos,* for that matter . . . they already know we're here. Besides, I'm not accustomed to enjoying a lady's company when I'm on a job. I'd like to take advantage of it. Most likely won't happen again." He frowned at her curiously. "Why are you so reluctant to talk about yourself, Miss Gallant?"

She gave him a bold, defiant look. "I have my reasons. Now, if you don't mind, I was enjoying the peace and quiet."

She clucked to her horse and touched spurs to its flanks, trotting around Sartain and continuing on up the wash. Brambles rustled loudly on the wash's right side. The Cajun turned to see a big man in a short *charro* jacket and deerskin leggings leap out from the arroyo's bank and into the wash, howling like a war-crazed Apache.

"Hey!" Sartain shouted, clawing his LeMat from its holster.

The big man grabbed the bit of Jasmine's

horse, raised his own pistol, and fired two shots at Sartain.

As the Cajun got his LeMat leveled, Boss rose off his front hooves, loosing a shrill whinny. Sartain hadn't been prepared for the sudden pitch. He slapped his left hand down toward the saddle horn but missed it.

"Ah, shit!" he cried, kicking free of his stirrups so he wouldn't break his ankles.

He was leaving the saddle no matter what.

As he slid back off Boss's rump, what sounded like a dozen or so pistols and rifles opened on him from both sides of the wash.

CHAPTER TEN

Somehow, Sartain managed to hold onto the LeMat.

When he landed on the sandy bottom of the wash, the relative yielding of which prevented his brains from being overly scrambled, he rolled onto his belly and commenced triggering lead into the briars on both sides of the arroyo.

Lead plunked and screeched around him. Some of it tore straight across the wash and into the shrubs and thorny vines on the other side, evoking screams, apparently from the shooters' own *compadres.*

The damned fools were shooting across the wash at each other!

With more lead spanging off the rocks around him, Sartain got up and ran at a slant back down the arroyo and then threw himself behind an escarpment bulging out in the wash like a giant beer belly. Amidst the crackling of the gunfire, he could hear

Boss's indignant whinnies as the horse galloped straight up the wash away from the lead storm.

Under the circumstances, that was fine with the Cajun. He wanted the stallion out of harm's way. Without a horse out here, he was a dead man. Of course, if the bushwhackers got their way, he'd likely be dead anyway, but there was no point in getting ahead of himself.

He clicked the twelve-gauge shotgun shell into action, and flung the buckshot into the briars on the other side of the wash. He'd seen part of a mustached face and a knotted red bandanna there.

Now the face jerked back while the man's pistol lapped smoke and flames into the air. There was a crunching thud as the shooter hit the ground.

At the same time, another pistol popped near where the wounded shooter had been standing. The slug tore into a large boulder to Sartain's right. It must have ricocheted off the rock, because the Cajun felt a hot fist of stabbing pain hammer his left temple.

He crouched and shook his head, as though to ward off an attacking horsefly. He felt the warmth of fresh blood oozing from the seam, trickling down the side of his head.

"Shit!" he grated out, swinging around and staggering away from the wash.

The pain felt like a bayonet rammed into that temple and probing around in his brain plate. He felt sick to his stomach and weak-kneed. He walked, dragging his boot toes, for several yards, not sure where he was heading, just knowing he had to get away from the wash. He pushed through some brambles, kicked a rock, tripped, and fell forward.

He didn't hit the ground as quickly as he'd thought.

Then he saw why.

He'd landed on an incline that dropped away into a canyon. He tried to keep from rolling down the slope by releasing the LeMat and reaching for a handhold. But there were none to be found. At least, no stable holds.

"Ah, *shiiiittttt*!" he heard himself cry as gravity, like the massive hand of an angry god, rolled him on down the slope that seemed to drop forever and ever before he finally landed on the canyon floor some hundred feet beyond.

But by that time he wasn't aware of anything but a vague, gnawing pain in his throbbing temple and elsewhere.

For a minute or two, he thought the

canyon was flooded with warm water. Then he rolled onto his back, digging his fingers into the arroyo's dry sand. No, not flooded. It had just seemed that way as he'd teetered on the edge of consciousness.

He lifted his aching head, blinking against the sunlight stabbing down on him like a thousand razor-edged bayonet blades.

A whimpering sound rose on his right. A coyote was studying him from between a creosote shrub and a palo verde.

The coyote's gray-brown eyes narrowed. The black nostrils opened and closed. A deep groan rose from the beast's throat. Sartain's right hand dropped automatically to his holster.

Empty.

It took him a few seconds to remember dropping the gun during his descent from the ridge.

Keeping his eyes on the coyote, whose hackles were raised and whose lips were lifting above the black gums and white canines, the Cajun touched his vest. He felt the hard lump of the derringer. He reached inside and pulled the wicked but pretty little popper from its pocket, the gold-washed chain trailing it from the old Waterbury watch stowed in the opposing pocket.

Sartain gritted his teeth and clicked both

hammers back, aiming the pearl-gripped piece at the coyote.

"No, I ain't dead," he raked out, his throat feeling as dry as parched leather. "But thanks for asking. Move along, now, friend. I'm sure you'll find something *dead* to eat soon . . ."

The coyote lowered its head slightly, sniffing.

It groaned again, even deeper in its chest, then, the very picture of disappointment, slowly backed away through the spidery branches before wheeling and soundlessly disappearing. As though to take its place, a small shadow flitted across the arroyo. A hawk's ratcheting cry followed.

Sartain sat up, wincing against sundry aches and pains, some sharper than others. He shaded his eyes with his forearm as he looked skyward. "You, too, hawk. Sorry to disappoint. I ain't dead. Not yet, anyways . . ."

His voice was deep and raspy. He needed water. He hadn't been in the arroyo more than twenty minutes or so, judging by the light, but he was all dried out. His canteen was with Boss, however.

Boss . . .

If the horse was badly injured, Sartain was a goner.

He chuckled dryly to himself. Obviously, he was more worried about his horse than Jasmine Gallant. He was so accustomed to traveling alone, he'd nearly forgotten about Pinkerton's princess. Now as he gained his feet and brushed himself off, he had a very clear image of the big Mexican in the deerskin leggings bounding into the wash and grabbing the bit of the woman's horse.

Sartain stuffed the derringer back into his vest pocket, ran his fingers along the chain stretching from pocket to pocket, and then looked around for his hat. No, it wasn't down here, he remembered as he mentally swatted at the cobwebs clouding his battered brain. He'd lost it back up near the arroyo.

He blinked against the trickle of blood running into his left eye. Then he remembered why that temple was thundering so damned hard. He used his neckerchief to give the wound, little more than a crease in his scalp but a bloody, painful one, a cursory cleaning. The blood had turned to half-dried jelly caked with dirt and sand. When he deemed it clean enough until he could get his hands on Jasmine's whiskey, he wiped the cloth around his head.

As the cobwebs continued to clear, he grew more and more concerned about the lady Pinkerton. The *bandidos* had obviously been tracking them for some time. They were what had been tolling the warning bells in the Revenger's ears, only having a partner — a comely partner, at that — had been novel to him and, thus, distracting. He made a mental note never to travel with a woman again, especially a beautiful one, and limped over to the base of the ridge down which the angry god had thrown him.

Water . . .

He started up the ridge, weaving around tufts of brush and rocks. He found his LeMat about halfway to the top, brushed it off, and slipped it back into its holster. He took a deep breath and continued climbing until he'd gained the ridge crest, breathing hard, head pounding. He unholstered the LeMat, in case any more attackers lingered in the area, and moved through the brush and boulders until he stood at the edge of the arroyo.

Nothing moved except for small birds flitting about the branches overhanging the sandy bed. As he carefully raked his gaze up and down the dry watercourse, Sartain saw what appeared a man hanging out from the far bank about forty yards up the draw from him. The Cajun looked around once more, listening carefully, and then stepped into the arroyo, the LeMat cocked in his fist.

He stopped near what was indeed a man lying with his head and shoulders on the arroyo floor, his legs hung up in the brush of the bank. A dead Mexican with a round face and a star-shaped scar on his temple. His lower jaw sagged, giving his face a slack, stupid look, brown eyes staring at nothing. He had two bullets in him — one in his left elbow, the other in his upper left chest.

A lung shot. The frothy blood on his lips said that he'd died hard. Probably shot by one of his own men from the opposite bank. Sartain doubted any of his own hasty shots had hit their mark.

He wrinkled his nostrils against the smell of blood mixed with the sour stench of alcohol. The man was — or had been — drunk. They all probably had been.

Fools, all. Probably a wandering band of raggedy-heeled *bandidos* who mostly robbed prospectors and remote-traveling stagecoaches for their meager living. They'd likely spied Sartain traveling with the beautiful Pinkerton, and allowed their goatish compulsions to lead them here.

The Revenger dropped to a knee near the dead man, and looked around.

Now, where were they? Most likely, they had Miss Gallant, because they'd obviously been too distracted to care for their dead. Distracted by their comely plunder.

Sartain walked up the arroyo a ways, and found one more dead man — another who'd probably been killed by one of his own. He had a bullet in one cheek, another in his forehead. He also smelled like raw tequila; a half-filled bottle stood on the ground nearby, at the base of a palo verde.

An ambush affected by drunkards.

Sartain cursed.

Drunkards who'd taken the woman.

Never, under any circumstances, travel with a beautiful woman in Mexico, he reminded himself. That should be written somewhere. Sartain had tried to tell the governor and the rest of them that. But they hadn't listened. Now he had to find her, and most likely he'd be burying what was left of her.

He cursed again and started looking around for his horse. Fifteen minutes later, he heard a low whicker. He followed the sound to a slight clearing on the south side of the arroyo. Boss stood near some Mormon tea, reins hanging, saddle angled down over his right side, staring at Sartain with a faint look of incredulity.

Boss didn't like gunfire. He never had and, despite how much of it he'd heard over the last several years, he likely never would. That was all right. Sartain didn't like it much, either. But it came with the job, so . . .

He walked up to the horse, gave him a handful of grain and some water from the canteen still hanging from the saddle horn, and then reset the saddle and tightened the latigo.

Leading Boss by his reins, the Cajun dropped back down into the arroyo, scouring the eroded sand and gravel for tracks. They weren't hard to find; it wasn't hard to see that the gang of bushwhackers had headed on up the cut, in the same direction that Sartain and Pinkerton's princess had been heading.

He mounted up and followed the wash. He thought that the gang was around an hour ahead of him. He put Boss into a canter, following the wash's meandering course through the rocky desert but keeping an eye skinned for another possible ambush. His anxiety over the young woman was a hard knot in his belly, but he had to take his time. For once this trip, he had to keep his wits about him. His getting shot out of his saddle wasn't going to do either of them any good.

As the old saw went — *Fool him once,*

shame on them. Fool him twice, shame on him . . .

Since they hadn't pursued him after he'd been clipped by the ricochet, they probably thought he was dead. If they were giving him any thought at all, that was, and they weren't too distracted by their trophy . . .

He decided the latter was probably the case, for the tracks he was following had been made by seven or eight shod horses riding fast. They were riding so fast that some of the catclaw angling into the wash from the banks glistened with blood and bits of horsehide. The ambushers were in a hurry to get to their destination, wherever that was, and get down to business with the girl.

There was a good chance that their loins were so heavy, they hadn't ridden far.

Easy, the Cajun warned himself, over and over, when he felt himself loosening his grip on the reins and half-consciously urging more speed from the stallion.

Easy. They could be anywhere in here . . .

An hour passed. Then another.

Sartain paused to water himself and his horse. He swabbed the bullet crease again, cleaned the bandanna, and retied it around his head. As he rode, he reached into his saddlebags for a few bits of jerky, and chewed the salty beef slowly, working up enough saliva to keep him from thinking too much about the water he was growing short on.

The arroyo broadened gradually until it was a vast river bottom stretching between low banks peppered with the lime colors of desert shrubs, including mesquites, creosote, and palo verde. The ancient *barranca,* as such winding river courses were called down here, was peppered with boulders and cactus.

It appeared to lead into jagged-crested mountains humping darkly on the distant horizon, straight ahead of the Cajun. Very gradually as he rode, the mountains grew taller and broader. The black color of the massive ramparts turned to a furry green, which later in the afternoon became streaked with peach.

The green had not been from foliage, but only a trick of the light for an hour or two. The closer the Cajun rode toward the *sierra,* the more clearly he saw that there didn't appear to be any green on them whatever. They looked nothing more than a massive, inhospitable hump of bald rock.

A massive clump of forbidding stone ramparts that the *barranca,* the floor of which rose gradually, appeared to cleave right down their middle.

The Shadow Mountains, most likely. Sartain knew they were the only range out here.

The tracks he followed had spread out across the *barranca,* and, judging by the stride they depicted, the riders had slowed down considerably from the gallops they'd started out in. As he rode, the Cajun noted where they paused to water their horses, where they walked them, and where they increased their speed.

They were obviously following the ancient watercourse into the mountains.

Just as obviously, they hadn't been in the all-fired hurry the Revenger had thought. He continued to ride cautiously, however. He also scoured the terrain for the woman's clothes and, possibly, for her body. Most likely they'd kill her after they'd sated their hunger. Once she'd satisfied a man's desires, a woman wasn't much good out here.

The sun sank behind Sartain. The air chilled as the night came down.

Chapter Eleven

The Revenger followed the *barranca* as it rose steadily into the mountains, continuing to curve between steep, dark mountain walls. The wide course narrowed dramatically; it was littered with driftwood, and, in some cases, entire trees and cracked boulders, probably washed down from the higher reaches during the monsoon rains.

The moon rose, shedding an ethereal light into the chasm. If not for the light, the Cajun would have had to stop or risk serious injury to the stallion. But the moon lit his winding way into the *sierra.*

Finally, he came to a plateau where the mountain wall on his left dropped gradually away to little more than a slope. The ambushers' trail swerved out of the *barranca,* which was little more than a narrow wash at this point, hugging the base of the right-side ridge, and rose up through a jog of low, dark hills in the northeast.

Widely scattered pines and stunted aspens thrust their branches toward the lilac sky in which the stars glittered dully.

Ten minutes after he'd ridden up out of the *barranca,* the Revenger jerked back on the stallion's reins and slipped the LeMat from its holster. He clicked the hammer back as he scowled into the moon-relieved darkness off the trail's right side.

A chilly mountain wind had picked up. It was blowing several dark shapes hanging from a large deciduous tree. Large shapes. Not the sort of thing you'd normally see hanging from a tree.

Man-shaped figures . . .

Sartain looked around. Spying no movement, he clucked to the stallion and rode toward the tree. The branches creaked in the cold wind. There was the whining sound of stretched and straining hemp, as well.

Sartain checked Boss near one of the shapes. The moonlight angling over the canyon's southern ridge pooled in the eyes staring down at him, and he flinched. Sensing his rider's unease, Boss jerked beneath him.

The boots of the hanging man hung down to the level of the Revenger's hat crown. They were soft and brown, so worn in one place that Sartain could make out the dead man's stocking-clad foot.

Sartain appraised the long figure attired in worn, Mexican-style trail clothes. He wore a short vest and a red neckerchief. His hair was black, his face long and angular, a black mustache mantling his small mouth. He'd been hanging here awhile; his clothes had been badly pecked and torn by birds. Part of one eyeball had been chewed out of the socket.

The wind jostled the body, making the branch and the rope creak.

Sartain kept a firm hand on Boss's reins so the stallion, unsettled by the sour stench of death heavy in the Revenger's own nostrils, wouldn't bolt as he circled the tree. He counted five dead men hanging from three separate branches. Four appeared Mex. One looked like a sandy-haired *gringo* with one eye hanging by a bloody thread down his badly bird-pecked cheek, his swollen tongue poking out a corner of his mouth.

The five bodies pitched and swayed in the wind.

They didn't call this part of Mexican *Las Tierras Baldias* for nothing.

The Wastelands . . .

These men were likely *bandidos* who'd run afoul of some other band of desperadoes. Or maybe they'd double-crossed their own. For such a breed of men, revenge was swift. Even swifter than it was for Sartain's breed of man, which was saying something.

The Revenger looked around and then rode on, following the ambushers' trail up a gradual rise. As he rode, he sniffed wood smoke on the wind. Wood smoke laced with the aroma of roasting meat. It grew stronger as he rode. Ahead, another odd silhouette revealed itself, off the trail's left side this time and up a rocky knoll.

It wasn't a tree but was more in the shape of a cross.

Sartain dismounted, ground-reined Boss, and slipped the LeMat from its holster. Holding the big pistol low by his side, he pushed through low, gnarled cedars and climbed the knoll. A minute later he found himself staring up in awe at the naked body of a man who appeared to have been crucified on a stout cross made of unpeeled pine poles. The moonlight revealed a thick, gray beard and tufts of gray, curly hair running around the edges of an otherwise bald pate.

In the pearly light, the man's body was the color of bleached bones. Bleached bones liberally stained with the darkness of dried blood.

His lower jaw hung slack, chin almost resting on his bony chest. Around his neck hung a wooden crucifix — the kind Sartain had seen Catholic priests wear. His eyes were gone, and birds had torn away a good bit of his flesh. Judging by the stench, he'd been there a good four or five days.

Sartain backed away from the crucifixion, giving a shudder and looking around cautiously. Crucifixion was a nasty way to die. Maybe not as creative as Apache methods, but nasty, just the same.

Sartain made his way back down to Boss, and heaved himself back into the saddle. Apprehension was a handful of caterpillars crawling along his spine as he continued up the rise. As he rode, he watched what appeared to be firelight growing before him. He was nearing the ambushers' camp. About ten feet from the crest of the rise, he slipped off the trail and tied Boss to a stout cedar.

Shucking his Henry repeater, he climbed to the top of the rise, right of the trail and in a nest of small boulders and shrubs, and dropped to a knee.

A broad fold in some pale bluffs lay below. The white objects that lay in willy-nilly fashion about the fold, like dice on black velvet, were most likely the small adobe *casas* of an ancient *pueblito.* They were strewn around a bluff rising just ahead of Sartain, maybe a quarter-mile away.

A large building topped the rise. It was so well lit by torches and the two small fires that had been built near it, Sartain could see it was an old *adobe* church — a simple, crude affair in the shape of a large stone block, its broad open doors thrown wide to reveal flickering, umber lamplight within. A two-story *adobe casa* sat about fifty feet to the left. The *casa* had a crude stone wall around it, stone pens to the left, some with small woven-ocotillo corrals attached.

No sounds, light, or movement issued from the dark folds between the rolling buttes in which the old *pueblito* lay. Either the town had been abandoned or the townsfolk were lying low.

The top of the bluff was a noisy, fire- and moonlit contrast to the darkness surrounding it. A few men were moving around atop the bluff, about the churchyard, silhouetted by the dancing firelight. Between wind gusts, Sartain could hear them talking and laughing.

They sounded drunk. Their horses milled in one of the corrals, though the Cajun could only make out their silhouettes. Some of the men were sitting on the stoop of the *casa;* others lounged around the two fires fronting it. They were too far away for Sartain to be sure, but they appeared to be passing a bottle.

Sartain raked a thumb through his several-day growth of beard stubble.

Where was the girl?

Only one way to find out.

He retreated several yards back down the hill and then swung to the south. He ran, crouching, over the shoulder of the hill, worried the moonlight might reveal him to the men by the church. He dropped down into the dark fold encompassing the *adobes.* He could see only the very top of the church from this vantage, which meant the men probably couldn't see him unless they'd posted a lookout.

He moved carefully through the broad crease between the buttes, weaving around the *adobes,* which, he could see now, were likely all abandoned. They were old ruins, possibly damaged in an earthquake or one of the many Apache and Yaqui battles that had ravaged this part of northern Mexico, just as they'd been a blight for so many years on the American Southwest. The *adobes* were cracked and crumbling vestiges of former homes, some with attached stone corrals now grown up with briars, *piñons,* and cedars.

The wind swept through the crease from the south, sawing and moaning through the hollow caverns, whistling through windows that gaped like the empty sockets of bleached skulls, and caused the brush to dance eerily in the moonlight.

As Sartain moved across the floor of the crease and started up the hill atop which the church loomed, he heard the whine of a cat amongst the ruins. Judging by the whine's pitch, it was either a small bobcat or a wild domestic cat, nothing to be worried about. As he kept moving, he could hear other beasts running through the brush away from him. They left their wild, sour stench on the moaning wind.

They were coyotes or foxes, most likely, keeping an eye on the churchyard in which the desperadoes were roasting meat. Later, when the men had gone to bed and the fires had died, the carrion eaters would move in to carry off the leavings.

The ruined *casas* thinned out about halfway atop the steep hill. There was little cover here. Sartain crouched low and doffed his hat as he moved slowly, quietly, though the wind would likely cover his approach. When he reached the top of the hill, breathing hard, he crouched behind one of the few boulders at the edge of the yard, and peered out around its right side.

The church was about a hundred yards away across the relatively flat top of the hill, the *casa* to the left. The men were no longer strolling around between the church and the two-story, brush-roofed hovel. They were all gathered around one of the two fires, some eating and drinking, a couple standing and facing the *casa* from which firelight or lamplight spilled from deep-set windows.

One of the men facing the church, holding a carbine in one hand, appeared to grab his crotch with his other hand as he said in unaccented English, "Hurry it up in there. Give the rest of us a turn!"

"Sí," said one of the others, laughing. He continued half in English and half in Spanish with: "I have gone to church and said my prayers, *jefe,* and the great *Jesus* has vowed to forgive me for my forthcoming sins!"

One of the men threw something — maybe a meat bone — at the man who'd last spoken, hissing, "Stop taking the name of *Jesus* in vain, fool, or he will laugh in your face and send you packing to *el diablo*!"

The *gringo* yelled toward the house, "For Christ sakes, if you can't —"

He was cut off by a Spanish-accented voice yelling from somewhere in the second story, "Come in, gentlemen! The lady yearns for a party!"

The voice had sounded raspy, stilted, distant.

The others looked around at each other, stunned. Then one of the Mexicans laughed, whooped, and bolted for the front door.

The *gringo* grabbed his arm and jerked him back, growling, "Hold on — I'm next in line, goddamnit. We flipped for it!"

"Diddle yourself, Decker!" said the Mexican, swinging around and bringing up a right-handed roundhouse, slamming his fist in the *gringo*'s face.

The *gringo* hit the ground with a shrill curse. The other seven or so dashed past him and into the house.

Sartain gave a curse of his own as he stepped out from behind the boulder and began making his way toward the *casa.* The wind lifted dust around him, and blew the flames of the two fires, sending cinders showering over the *gringo* called Decker, who gained his feet heavily and stumbled into the *casa.*

Sartain could hear the men's running footsteps, their eager shouts and yowls. The Cajun broke into a run, gritting his teeth and racking a cartridge into the Henry's breech. Amidst the din inside the *casa,* a gun barked.

It barked again.

A man screamed.

Sartain stopped, frowning through the *casa's* door, which had been propped open with a chair from the back of which a black shirt and bolo tie hung.

The shouting had stopped for about three seconds. Now it resumed louder than before. Above it, the gun barked again . . . again . . . and again.

There was the thunder of bodies falling. Through the open door, Sartain saw several men tumbling down a crude stone stairs that rose beyond a small monkey stove and a round wooden eating table. They hit the floor hard at the bottom of the stairs, a couple piling up together while a third one bounced off the two-man pile and rolled toward Sartain, blood gushing from a hole in the man's red-shirted chest.

The gun's barking continued. As did the men's screaming and the thunder of the dead and dying tumbling down the stairs, until all seven who'd run into the house lay in a ragged semicircle around the bottom of the stairs.

The gun or guns fell silent.

Two of the desperadoes were still moving, writhing.

As Sartain stared incredulously into the *casa,* lit by a fire in a beehive hearth and a lamp hanging over the table, the spindly wooden stair rail sagged out away from the stairs. There was a snapping sound, and then the rail fell to the short, dim hall running along the outside of the stairs.

Silence.

Fog-like gun smoke rolled down the stairs, growing brighter as it reached the rusty lamp sagging from a wire over the table. The rotten-egg odor of the smoke pushed through the open door to tickle the Revenger's nostrils.

"*Puta* bitch!" a man shouted in the *casa's* second story. "Oh, you are a she-devil for sure!"

Sartain climbed the three steps to the *galleria* and stopped again as a pair of slender legs clad in tight slacks appeared at the top of the stairs. The black boots descended until Sartain could see a cotton blouse and doeskin vest and then twin cascades of dark-brown hair dropping down over the breasts pushing against the blouse from behind.

Halfway down the stairs, Jasmine Gallant stopped and lifted her chin, the brim of her cream Stetson rising to reveal her pearl eyes glistening in the lamplight. The eyes narrowed, and one of the two pistols she was holding came up, smoke curling from the barrel.

"Sartain?" she called.

He moved into the *casa* and stopped near the loose pile of bloody bodies. Only one man — the lone *gringo* in the bunch, a tall man with a hangdog look and buckteeth — was moving. Decker had a black eye from the earlier punch. He rolled from side to side, clamping both hands over the hole in the lower middle of his chest.

"No, no, no!" he wailed. "No, no, no! Ohhhh . . . you miserable woman!"

"What'd you expect?" Sartain asked him, mildly. "When you tangle with a she-lion, you're bound to get bit."

Jasmine continued down the stairs. She stopped near the bottom, aimed one of her Colts at the howling *gringo,* and fired. The bullet slammed into the side of his head, causing the entire top of his head to explode like a ripe cantaloupe.

Lowering the pistol, the Pinkerton looked at Sartain.

"What kept you?"

"I had some errands to run." The Cajun shrugged as he looked at the bloody carcasses slumped in one widening pool of dark-red blood. "I see I could have run a couple more."

"Come upstairs," she said, heading back up the steps.

"Need comforting, do you? It'll cost you twenty bucks."

"There's someone I'd like you to meet."

Chapter Twelve

Sartain followed the woman up the stairs that literally dripped blood.

The second story had such a low ceiling, the Cajun had to remove his hat and crouch as he moved down a short hall. He followed Jasmine into a small room with a brass-framed bed on which a big Mexican, who, naked as the day he was born but a whole lot hairier, lay spread-eagle on his back.

The man's wrists and ankles had been tied with strips of rawhide to the bed frame. He was in his late middle age. His large, olive-skinned, fleshy body nearly covered the entire bed. The top of his head was almost bald, with long, salt-and-pepper hair falling from the sides onto his shoulders. His cheekbones were high, but his face was just about perfectly round.

He wore long, mare's tail mustaches. The rest of his fleshy, pitted face with close-set, fear-bright, chocolate-brown eyes was carpeted in three-day beard stubble.

His clothes were strewn around the room. There was a bottle on a small dresser by the bed. It was Jasmine's Sam Clay. Over the bed, nailed to the *adobe*-brick whitewashed wall hung an oil painting of the Virgin Mary with a halo over her head. It was a crude painting even to Sartain's untrained eyes.

Obviously, the room had been the priest's quarters, though his quarters now were with the saints.

Sartain ducked into the room and said, "You two been bein' bad together?"

"Mr. Sartain," Jasmine said, "meet Uncle Hector San Xavier de Tejada. He has a couple of other names in front of 'Tejada' but suffice it to say he's Maximilian's bad uncle."

Tejada pulled at the straps tying his wrists to the brass frame, and gritted his teeth. "Oh, you are a devil! Release me! I demand you release me! You may know my name, but you do not know who I am!" He gritted his teeth and cast a wary look past his chest and soft, bulging belly. His voice rose several octaves as he said, "Oh, you are a miserable beast to do such an indignity to a man of my position . . ." His watery eyes found Sartain. "*Por favor, señor.* One man to another. Please remove the knife!"

Sartain had followed the man's eyes to the knife whose handle had been embedded in the tightly woven corn-shuck mattress between the man's spread thighs. The blade was pointed up, the curved tip snugged firmly against the man's wrinkled brown scrotum. Blood was smeared on the leathery sack.

Sartain scowled, impressed and repelled. "That's gotta hurt, *señor.*"

"It does, *señor. Please* . . . one man to another . . . !"

"What's this gent done to deserve such an indignity, Miss Gallant?"

"He brought me up here to rape me. Then he was going to throw me to his savages. Only the fool left his knife and guns lying around. He didn't have enough respect for me to think I might fight back."

Sartain turned to the man on the bed. "Guess you been taken to the woodshed, Uncle Hector."

Jasmine narrowed her eyes threateningly at Sartain. "Let that be a lesson to you, too."

"One I've already learned," the Cajun said, grinning. Then he frowned, curious. "Say, where's Maximilian been keeping himself these days?"

"Oh, go to hell, both of you!"

"I had a hunch I'd learn something from

this bunch of morons. That's why I didn't try to get away . . . until this old bastard dragged me up here to, uh, *entertain* me, as he called it. He is . . . *was,* I should say . . . their fearless leader."

"Where's Maximilian?" the Revenger asked again.

"We haven't gotten that far yet. I wanted some peace and quiet, so I threatened to geld him unless he called his men up here."

Sartain winced again as the tip of the knife nipped the underside of Uncle Hector's scrotum. Blood beaded on the razor-edged tip of the blade. "Old son," the Cajun said in a hushed voice, "I wouldn't move around too much if I was you."

Sweat dribbled down Hector's pocked and pitted cheeks. "*Señor,* please . . . one man to another."

"One man to another," Sartain said, "you've tangled with the wrong wildcat." He moved to the side of the bed and crouched over the sweating Mexican, his hat in his hand. He said as though conspiratorially, "I might be able to see about making you a little more comfortable if, one man to another, you tell me where your nephew, Maximilian, is keeping himself these days. Himself and his half-sister, Miss Priscilla McDougal."

"Ha! Your guess is as good as mine, *señor.*"

"That's not a very good answer," said Jasmine. "That knife isn't going anywhere until you've given one more to our satisfaction." She looked at Sartain. "Shall we go downstairs and have a drink, while *Señor* Tejada thinks about your proposal? This squirrel rummaged around in my saddlebags until he found my bourbon."

"*Señorita — por favor,* I beg of you to release me!" Uncle Hector jerked his wrists again violently. As the tip of the blade disappeared into his scrotum, he threw his head back on the pillow, and screamed. "This is no way to treat a man. Especially a man who is telling the *truth*!"

Suddenly, the painting hanging above the bed swung sharply to the left, where it dangled by that corner before falling down the wall. It smacked the top of the headboard and then tumbled forward onto the howling Hector.

The canvas was large enough that it covered him from his neck to below his knees.

He stopped howling and stared up at the ceiling, mouth drawn wide in shock.

Sartain felt his own lower jaw hang as he stared up at the wall from which the painting had fallen. The painting had covered an arched, recessed area in the whitewashed stone wall — the sort of niche that normally held a shrine in a Mexican church or *casa.*

Only this niche did not hold a shrine. It held a cache of what appeared to be two solid gold candleholders with several small, gold statues surrounding it, with three or four gold crucifixes hanging from the candleholders by gold chains with links as large as the tips of the Cajun's little fingers.

"Well, I'll be," Jasmine said, breathlessly, as she moved slowly toward the niche.

Sartain was moving toward the display, as well. But it was no display. It had been covered by the painting to hide the secret cache of valuables.

Sartain peered into the niche from the right side while Jasmine peered in from the left side. The cavity was about a foot deep. Beside the candleholders were two gold vases, each standing about a foot tall. From behind each vase rose a gold flower molded into the shape of a rose.

Solid gold vases outfitted with solid gold roses.

At the base of each vase was a gold apple a little smaller than Sartain's clenched fist. Gold snakes were wrapped around each apple, the heads of the vipers rising above the fruit with what appeared enticing expressions in their flat, golden eyes. Near the snake-wrapped apples were two small statues of Adam and Eve, both holding leaves over their private parts.

Eve held a small gold apple a little larger than a pebble up to her expressionless face, as though about to take a bite.

"Mierda — Maximilian, pequeño bastardo," said Uncle Hector in a hushed voice, turning his head awkwardly to stare up at the cache. "For the love of all the saints in Heaven, it's true! *Dios mio!*"

Sartain picked up one of the apples, and glanced at Jasmine. "Has to weigh a good six, seven pounds." He hefted it again, his mind swirling, his head feeling light. "Solid gold. Good grade of gold, too, I'll bet."

Jasmine picked up a candleholder, pulled it out of the niche, and nodded. "My God," she whispered, hefting the solid gold object in her hand. Her face was flushed.

"Por el amor de todos los santos en el cielo!" raked out Uncle Hector. *"Es cietro!"* His eyes fairly glowed in the light flickering from the room's single lamp. "It's true! It's true! *No es sólo una leyenda, después de todo!*"

Jasmine frowned at him, then flung the canvas onto the floor. "What did you say, you depraved old fool?"

Sartain said, "He's saying it's not just a legend, after all." He looked at Hector Tejada. "What's not a legend?"

The older man studied him warily, then shrewdly. "Nothing, señor. My, uh, discomfort has clouded my brain. What is that up there, anyway? Gold? Imagine that. The old priest must have been squirreling it away for years. Where do you suppose he came upon it, huh?"

Sartain sat down on the edge of the bed, causing the bed to lurch and the knife to prick the older man's balls. Uncle Hector sucked a sharp breath through his teeth.

"What does it have to do with Maximilian?" the Revenger asked him.

"Huh?" Uncle Hector said. *"No lo se, señor."*

Jasmine dropped down on her side of the bed, shaking it. Uncle Hector screamed.

"Does that make it clearer?" asked the Cajun.

"Por favor," Uncle Hector said, glancing pleadingly, miserably, at each of his tormentors in turn. "*Señorita, señor* — I know not what you are talking about."

Sartain grinned devilishly as he shook the bed.

Uncle Hector screamed more shrilly than before, squeezing his eyes closed. More sweat trickled down the sides of his face. It glistened in his mustache and ragged goatee.

"What does the gold have to do with Maximilian?" the Revenger asked him.

"Por que?" Uncle Hector squeezed his eyes closed again and bit his lower lip, knowing what was coming.

He screamed as Jasmine shook the bed.

"Enough!" the older man yelled. "You are both an insult to Mother Mary and her beloved Jesus. You are depraved to treat one of God's children so poorly!"

Sartain shook the bed. Again, Uncle Hector squeezed his eyes shut and screamed.

"I don't know what you're trying to buy time for," the Cajun said. "Your gang is dead. Every one of 'em. They're all lyin' piled up at the foot of the stairs. Miss Gallant here made sure of that." The Revenger chuckled. "Me an' her — we got all the time in the world . . . to sit here and shake this bed until you got nothin' left between your legs but cherry jam."

"No!" Uncle Hector shouted, eyes now wide with horror. "Not again! *Por favor!* Maximilian is after the gold. He brings it here from time to time, and the old priest was hiding it for him. I knew that much. I just didn't know where the old devil was squirreling it away."

"That why you crucified him?" Sartain asked, sneering.

"*Sí*. I mean no! *Señor, por favor,* I would never do such a thing to a man of the church. Oh, *dios mio.* What a sacrilege. That was my men who committed that atrocity. They are . . . were . . . animals. Common border *bandidos* — vile, mean as bobcats but with brains the size of raisins. Thus they shot more of each other at the *barranca* than . . . well . . . than of you."

"Quit stallin'!" Sartain warned.

"No! Please! Don't shake the bed again, *señor. Sí,* that is why they crucified the old priest. He would not tell us where he was hiding the gold for Maximilian. For some reason, old *Padre* Sandia threw in with my evil nephew, Maximilian Alfredo San Javier de Tejada. Probably out of greed. Maximilian probably promised the priest a cut of the gold. A stubborn devil, that old fool.

"He would not tell even those demon men of my gang — a nasty bunch if I ever saw one, and I never would have ridden with them if I could have found others who would ride with me, and take my orders. But me, an old man who fell so far from grace and privilege — what honorable, self-respecting band of desperadoes would ride with me?

"They crucified him, thinking the agony would be so terrible that he would tell them where the gold was, where Maximilian was finding it on the Tejada family's grant, but the old man outsmarted them. I think he was ready to die. Truly. He was very old. Long ago, the Apaches had burned out one of his eyes and cut off one of his testicles for mere entertainment — the red devils! No, he was ready to go."

Jasmine glanced at Sartain.

Then she shuttled her glance back to Uncle Hector. "But Maximilian rides with you, no? What kind of bullshit are you shoveling us, old man?" She nudged the bed slightly.

"No!" the old man cried. "What I have told you is the truth. What man would lie in such a situation — with his *cojones* half cut off at their roots?"

"That's right," Sartain said. "What do you have to lose?"

"No! *Por favor, señor,* I am telling the truth. Maximilian does not ride with me. He is a bad one, that one. I don't know where he is. Most likely, he is out looking for more of the gold you see there in the wall." He frowned at Sartain. "Say, why are you two looking for him, anyway?"

"We have our reasons," Jasmine said.

Sartain narrowed a suspicious eye at Uncle Hector. "You sure you and your nephew aren't riding together? That you both don't have Priscilla McDougal stowed away out here, somewhere?"

"Maybe you're attempting to reclaim your family's *hacienda* from McDougal," Jasmine added. "Since after your sister's death, it went to him, though you'd been kicked off the place long before, because of your *bandido* ways."

"No, no, *señorita.*" Uncle Hector shook his head. "You have it all wrong. I know nothing about *Señorita* McDougal. I am a desperado — that is true. I am an old outlaw. But one who cannot even put together an honorable gang anymore, but only a cavvy of bone-headed cutthroats who shoot each other in a cross fire and crucify old priests! Oh, the sacrilege!"

He sobbed loudly, closing his mouth, lips quivering while tears ran down his cheeks.

Jasmine said tightly, her nostrils flared, "You forgot about your old man's penchant for rape. Or, at least, for *attempted* rape."

"Sí," said Uncle Hector, nodding again. "I am even a failure at that. You got the upper hand easily enough." Again, he howled a sob. "Why don't you just finish me? Go ahead — put an old desperado out of his

misery!"

Jasmine gritted her teeth.

"Sure, why not?" she said, raising her pistols and clicking their hammers back.

Chapter Thirteen

"I can understand why you'd want to send this useless slob to *el diablo,*" Sartain said, "but it might be counterproductive."

Jasmine held her pistols on the old Mexican, who lay with his eyes squeezed shut. "It wasn't you he tried to shove his leathery old noddle into, was it?" she said.

"No, it wasn't. And I see your point. You go ahead and do what you want."

Uncle Hector moved his lips, praying quietly, quickly in Spanish.

Jasmine glanced at the Cajun, who was standing on the other side of the bed from her. "What're you thinking?"

"I'm thinking he knows this country better than we do. Hell, even with McDougal's maps, we don't know it at all."

"Go on."

"If Maximilian is somewhere in these mountains, looking for more gold like that there in the niche, Uncle Hector could probably lead us to him. And, hopefully, to Priscilla. Or at least guide us in the right direction."

"I think we're close enough," Jasmine said. "I think we can sniff out his trail on our own. You're not much for sniffing out an ambush, Sartain, but I know you can track."

The Revenger's ears warmed a little with embarrassment. "Yeah, well, I can usually stay ahead of an ambush . . . when I'm not riding with a pretty *señorita* in the wilds of Old Mexico."

"Sorry," she said. "I didn't mean to insult you."

"Yes, you did."

"Okay, I —"

Uncle Hector broke in with: "*Señor, señorita — por favor.* I think I can lead you to Maximilian."

"How come you didn't just go root him out of these mountains yourself, then?" Jasmine wanted to know.

"I didn't think I would need to. You see, I know an old desert rat, Tio, who has been prowling these mountains for the past thirty years or more. Tio has been looking for the same hidden treasure as Maximilian, which I thought until now was mere legend. I ran into Tio a month ago in a little watering hole, and learned from him while drunk —

sober, he is as silent as stone; drunk, he blabbers like a schoolgirl — that he believed someone was hauling treasure out of the mountains. He had seen the signs — overlaid tracks, meaning several trips had been made — and concealed campfires. But no one can conceal anything from old Tio. The tracks lead in the direction in which Tio believes can be found the *Catedral de Nuestra Señora de Guadalupe de las Montañas de Sombra.*"

"The Cathedral of Our Lady of Guadalupe in the Shadow Mountains," Sartain translated, thoughtfully. "Never heard of it."

"That's because it has been lost for over two hundred years. It is believed that an earthquake destroyed it. It is believed to reside somewhere on the Tejada family's old Spanish grant, though for generations our people looked for it without success. It was built by the Indio slaves of the Franciscan monks, who, so the legends say, decorated the cathedral in gold from their own mines. Millions and millions of *pesos* worth!

"Old Tio is the bastard son of my grandfather, though he was never considered part of the family. He's is one-quarter Yaqui, which means, to most *Mejicanos,* he is part devil."

He chuckled. "Old Tio likes that about

himself. Not being accepted by others, and for others to see him as a devil. That is Tio. But he knows this country better than most. And he has always believed in the lost cathedral, always believed that one day he, a devil banished from the Tejada family, would be richer than all of us put together. Than all of the Tejada generations put together! And that he would lord it over us from a *casa grande* on a high hill!"

"Did he tell you where the trail was?" Jasmine asked. "The one he thinks leads to the cathedral?"

Uncle Hector made an incredulous face. "Of course not, *señorita.* Even drunk, Tio is not in the business of giving away any secrets at all, much less the route that might lead to Guadalupe!"

Sartain said, "How does he know the trail he stumbled on was blazed by Maximilian?"

"Because he saw Maximilian out there in that area, from a distance, earlier that same week he found the trail."

"How many were with the kid?" Sartain asked.

"Only one other."

Sartain and Jasmine shared a look.

Sartain turned back to the older man. "If you don't know where the trail is, why shouldn't I let the *señorita* blow you to *el*

Diablo?"

Uncle Hector glanced at Jasmine scowling down at him.

He smiled, lips twitching nervously. "I may not know where to find the trail, but I know where in these mountains you are most likely to find Tio, if he is not out scouting the trail for the treasure himself. When I saw him last, he was suffering from the gout, so he might be holing up until the illness passes. His big toe" — the old Mexican shook his head slowly — "was swollen up to the size of a pistol handle!"

"Ouch," Sartain said.

"*Sí.* He was in much pain. He said only mescal helped."

Jasmine looked at the Cajun. "Even if this old pervert is telling the truth about any of this, and not just making up stories to save his life . . . or at least prolong it . . . I doubt that a man like old Tio would give away the trail to the treasure he's spent most of his life searching for."

"No, *señorita,*" Uncle Hector answered for Sartain. "But Tio is as deaf as a post and as blind as a deer. You could easily follow him from his little stone shack to the trail made by Maximilian." He added with a whisper, as though the old desert rat were right outside the door, "He wouldn't even know you were there."

He smiled with satisfaction, pressing his thick lips together beneath his mustache.

Jasmine arched a brow at Sartain.

"All right," the Cajun said. He leveled a threatening look at Uncle Hector. "First thing tomorrow, we'll start out for old Tio's camp. If you try anything, old man, or if I get the fantods over your story, suspecting you might be leading us into another trap of some kind, I'm turning you back over to *Señorita* Jasmine for swift and decisive punishment."

"Sí, señor." Uncle Hector gave another brittle half-smile. "I would never lie to such a man . . . with such a weapon. Now, if you will be so kind, would you mind please removing the knife from . . . down there? I am most, uh, uncomfortable."

"No," Jasmine said, resolutely. "The knife stays right where it is." She headed for the door.

Sartain followed her, glancing over his shoulder at Uncle Hector. "Sleep tight."

He pulled the door closed and followed Jasmine downstairs.

While the lady Pinkerton admired her handiwork at the bottom of the stairs, Sartain stepped over and around the bodies as well as the blood, and went outside into the cool mountain night. His breath frosted in the thin air around his head.

Both fires were nearly out. A pot of what appeared bean stew was still smoking on the fire nearest the priest's shack that had suddenly been turned into a morgue as well as torture chamber. Two rabbits had been roasting over the fire several yards from the church, but they'd turned to black ashes on the sticks upon which they'd been roasting.

Sartain looked around carefully. He didn't think there was anyone else around, but it never hurt to play it cautious, which is what he should have been doing in the arroyo just before they'd been ambushed and Jasmine had been kidnapped.

Never travel in Mexico with a pretty girl . . .

He scouted the area carefully and then returned to the front of the shack. Jasmine sat on the shack's front step. She placed a long, black cigarillo between her full lips and scratched a match to life on a roof support post.

"Didn't know you smoked," Sartain remarked as she touched the flame to the long cheroot, which she must have found on one of the dead men.

She inhaled deeply, blew out the smoke, and stared at the coal. "There's a lot of things you don't know about me, Mr. Sartain."

"I'll say." Her efficient, cold-blooded killing of her would-be rapists, as well as her handling of Uncle Hector, had made him more curious about the woman than ever.

Sartain placed two fingers in his mouth and whistled. He stared toward the northwest where, beyond the hill on which the church and *casa* perched, about all he could see were the silhouettes of low hills capped in winking starlight.

The moon had angled off behind a western ridge.

Presently, the thuds of galloping hooves rose. They continued to grow louder, as did the bellow-like chuffing of the horses' lungs. Finally, a shadow materialized at the edge of the bluff, and Boss leaped off the incline and stood at the edge of the yard, shaking his head and blowing.

He whickered softly, likely smelling the blood on the night breeze.

Sartain whistled again, softly. "Come on, boy — it's all right."

When Boss had made his way over to Sartain, the Cajun began to unsaddle the mount.

"You've trained your horse well, Mr. Sartain," Jasmine said, blowing out another plume of smoke. "I bet you'd like to have a woman who'd come when you whistled."

As he set his saddle on the ground near the fire, Sartain glanced at her. He could see only her dark silhouette against the flickering light of the open doorway behind her. "Miss Gallant, are you proposing to me?"

"Hardly!" she said, turning her head away. "I just know the kind of man you are, that's all." Her voice was, as usual, pitched with disdain.

Sartain set the rest of his gear, including his rifle and bedroll, near his saddle, and began wiping Boss down with a swatch of old burlap. "I'm sorry about the ambush," he said after a while. "I should have been more careful."

"The ambush was my fault, remember? It happened because I'm a beautiful woman, and beautiful women just naturally attract trouble in Mexico."

"I'm glad *you* said it this time."

"I could have gotten away from those fools, you know."

Sartain looked at her. Her head was turned toward him now. She lifted the cheroot to her lips. The coal glowed as she inhaled.

"Why didn't you do it? I mean, earlier

than you did . . ?"

"Because I sensed I'd learn something when we got to where we were going. And I was right. We have learned something."

"Maybe."

"Do you think he was lying?"

"I reckon we'll find out."

When he finished rubbing the horse down thoroughly, Sartain led the stallion over to the corral in which the dead men's horses milled, most regarding the new horse and the man warily, a few nickering, one breaking into a contentious run around the corral, the rising dust catching the starlight. Boss whinnied as though to alert the others he wasn't to be trifled with. Another horse whinnied in kind, ran to the far side of the corral, and ran back to stand about six feet away from Boss.

It was Jasmine's thoroughbred recognizing an old friend. The fine horse stretched his head out, sniffing the air between him and Boss.

Boss whickered and turned away proudly but gave his tail a single affable switch.

Sartain retrieved a couple of buckets of water from the well behind the casa, and set both inside the corral, near another that had been placed there by the men who were now dead. That one was empty. He carried it back to the well, refilled it, and hauled it over to the fire, which Jasmine was building up with mesquite sticks from a nearby pile of wood and brush.

Sartain filled his coffee pot and set it on the fire to boil. Then he knelt beside the water bucket, doffed his hat, and dunked his head. The water had come from a deep well — it was so cold, it made his jaws tighten and his ears ring. It dribbled into his ears, feeling like little spikes penetrating his brain plate.

He pulled his head out of the bucket and gave a whoop.

"That's cold!"

"Well, it's a cold night, you fool," Jasmine said, stirring her kidnapper's stew with a stick. "You're likely to catch your death of cold and die in Mexico."

"Would that bother you?" he asked, squeezing the excess water from his thick, curly hair. His heart was fluttering from the chill bath. He felt as though he'd left five pounds of trail grit in the bucket. He felt refreshed.

"It would bother me if you're unable to fulfill your duties."

"Duty. I just have one, right? Kill Maximilian." Sartain scowled at the woman, speculatively. "But hell, you could do that yourself. In fact, I'm not sure why McDougal didn't just send you. Or . . . maybe he doesn't know how handy you are with a pair of pistols."

Until tonight, he hadn't seen her brandish a weapon. She'd worn her two .38-caliber, five-shot Smith & Wessons with polished rosewood grips wedged behind the belt on her slender waist, but so far she hadn't used the fancy weapons.

They had fluted cylinders and sleek bird's-head profiles. He'd begun to think they were just for show. He saw now he was wrong.

The two pistols she'd taken from Uncle Hector sat on the same gallery step on which she rested her feet, one pistol to each side of her spurred boots, barrels pointing straight into the yard.

She didn't respond to his comment about her shooting, but only continued to sit back, knees drawn to her breasts, smoke, and wait for the coffee and stew to boil.

"According to the pervert upstairs," she said finally, when the coffee water began to bubble, "Maximilian has someone with him. I guess we should assume that person is Miss Priscilla."

"I guess we should hope so, anyway. If he's as poison-mean as everyone's been telling us, he might have had his fill of the girl and killed her. If so, I don't envy you relaying that bit of news to McDougal."

Jasmine said, "Chicken."

Sartain frowned as he tossed a handful of Arbuckle's into his coffee pot and set the pot back on the coals. He kept the puzzled scowl on his face as he cast another look at the woman. "Where did you learn to shoot like that, Jasmine? Where did you learn to kill like that?"

She drew another lungful of smoke and blew it toward the stars. "Maybe I came from the same school you did, Mr. Sartain."

That was all she said. Sartain could only study her, baffled.

She tossed the cheroot into the fire and pulled the stewpot off the tripod.

Chapter Fourteen

As usual, Sartain was up at first cockcrow, though if there was a cock crowing anywhere in the *Montañas de Sombra,* he didn't hear it. What he did hear was the morning breeze nudging the clapper against the bell in the tower looming atop the church.

It sounded like the intermittent sounds of a wind chime, though one with very deep but sonorous notes.

He sat up and listened to the quiet sounds as the cool breeze ushered leaves across the yard around him and the curled-up figure of his comely partner. The sounds reminded him of the *padre.* He should probably take the time to bury the man, but what was the point? The Revenger was not, nor had he ever been, a religious man. Still, he would have taken the time if he'd had it, but he didn't have it.

He had a job to do and, while it was one he hadn't chosen, he'd see it to its end and get the hell out from under the shadow of the federal government. Not only that, but he'd resume mocking it by doing what he did best — breaking the law for his own good reasons.

He rose, dressed, took a drink of water, and, as he usually did before he did much of anything else as he started his day, checked on his horse. He was happy that, despite yesterday's ambush, Boss looked fit as a fiddle and ready to hit the trail. To prove it, as Sartain slipped through the corral fence fashioned from woven coachwhip or ocotillo branches, the horse plopped down and rolled, kicking up a large cloud of dust that smelled like horse and manure, and which the breeze blew against the Cajun.

The thoroughbred watched Boss dubiously.

"Thanks, Boss," the Cajun choked, as the other horses stared as though in fascination at the stallion's antics, " 'preciate that."

He fed and watered all the horses with fresh water from the *padre*'s well, and grained them from his own and the dead outlaws' stores. That first major task accomplished, he returned to the front of the shack where Jasmine was rebuilding the fire in moody silence, her hair tangled, her blankets draped around her shoulders.

She didn't seem like a morning person and she didn't much care for him, anyway, so he didn't bother speaking. He just went on into the *casa,* stepped over the dead men, who appeared rigid shadows in the house's dimness, and climbed the stairs to where Uncle Hector remained sprawled spread-eagle on the bed.

"La alabanza a Maria!" the Mexican intoned raspily as Sartain entered the room. "That was the worst night's sleep I have ever endured, *señor.* Please tell me you are here to free me — free me from that nasty blade!"

"Shut up, you old rapist," Sartain snarled, and dug the knife out of the mattress. He used the blade to free the man from his rawhide ties.

Later, after he, Uncle Hector, and Jasmine had eaten a quick breakfast of biscuits, leftover stew, and coffee, they went over to the corral to saddle their horses. Once they'd led their own mounts out of the corral, Sartain opened the creaky gate so the other horses could leave when they felt the urge. They all appeared desert-bred and able to survive on the mountains' slim pickings, though naturally mountain lions would probably get a few.

For the time being, however, the lions and any other carrion eaters in the area would have enough to dine on inside the *casa* itself.

Sartain ordered Uncle Hector onto his horse — a skewbald paint with a white ring around its right eye. An odd-looking mustang, it was a sinewy, wild-eyed beast with one ragged ear and short, muscular legs made for fast travel over rugged terrain. Jasmine used her handcuffs to secure Uncle Hector's ankles to his stirrups. As another precaution against his attempting to flee, Sartain had made him remove his boots and socks and didn't allow any more gear on his horse but his saddle and bridle.

No saddlebags or bedroll and, of course, no weapons of any kind. Nothing he could even use in place of a weapon. He could steer his horse with its reins, but if he knew what was good for him, he wouldn't try to flee.

"Perhaps a . . . a cushion, *señor*?" Uncle Hector asked, staring down at Sartain from beneath the brim of his wagon-wheel *sombrero*.

"A cushion?" Jasmine said with a caustic chuff.

Uncle Hector kept his eyes on Sartain. Knowing the woman had no reason to go easy on him, the Mexican spoke only to the Cajun. *"Por favor?"* He stretched his lips back from his large, yellow teeth, wincing and rising up slightly in the stirrups to ease the pressure on his backside. "I am, as you could understand, a little sore in my unmentionable regions."

"That's just too bad," Jasmine said. "You're damn lucky I didn't cut anything off, Tejada. Now just shut up and ride. If you lead us to anywhere but this fellow Tio, I'm going to be very quick to finish the job I only *started* last night. Let's call you a work in progress, shall we?"

With that, she swung up onto her gelding's back and shook her hair back from her pretty face with its hard, pearl eyes.

"Sí, sí," the old man said, melodramatically. "Whatever you wish, *señorita.* I deserve nothing better, I know."

"Good," Jasmine said firmly, adjusting her pistols behind her belt. To Sartain, she said, "Let's get a move on. Sun's on the rise."

"Sí, sí," said the Revenger, grabbing Boss's reins. "Whatever you wish, *señorita . . .*"

They followed an old horse trail back to the *barranca,* which Uncle Hector told Sartain and Jasmine was called *Barranca Salvaje,* Savage Barranca, for good reason. When he didn't bother explaining, Jasmine prodded him with, "Why?"

His only response as they headed on up the *Barranca Salvaje* was a headshake and a sigh.

The ancient watercourse followed the steep southern ridge, which turned colors almost by the minute as the sun slid across its face, for many miles. The ridge was still on their right by the late afternoon, when they stopped to wash some jerky and biscuits down with water. They were in a deep canyon formed by another tall, imposing outcropping jutting high in the southeast, beyond another brush- and boulder-choked wash.

The shade was deep and cool.

Sartain walked down into the wash with three preset rope snares and triggers made of carved cottonwood spikes. He used the snares when he needed food but didn't want to give his position away with a rifle shot. When the snares were set in brush that looked like good rabbit graze, he returned to the wash.

Tejada sat on the ground with his back to a boulder, cuffed hands resting in his lap. Jasmine had hobbled his ankles with a two-foot length of rope. He was barefoot. He wore a filthy chambray shirt with a torn pocket, and worn buckskins with whang strings down the outsides of the legs.

A wide, black belt with a sheath for holding a knife was wrapped around his thick waist. Sartain had confiscated his knife. The man's two pistols — conversion Remington .44's — had been stowed in Jasmine's saddlebags.

Tejada was snoring softly behind his *sombrero,* which he'd pulled down over his face and long, broad nose. Jasmine sat on the other side of the wash from him, against the base of the towering southern ridge. She was also sleeping behind her hat, hands resting on her lap below her fancy twin pistols. Her long legs clad in black denim were crossed at the ankles.

Sartain squatted over the fire to pour himself a cup of the coffee simmering on a rock near the short, wavering flames that wrinkled the air above them. He'd built the fire with the nearly smokeless wood of the catclaw shrub.

Tejada raised his cuffed hands and poked the brim of his *sombrero* off his forehead with both thumbs. *"Señor,"* he whispered.

"What is it?"

Uncle Hector glanced at the pot.

Sartain gave a quiet chuff of disgust and then poured the older man a cup of coffee.

He took it over to him and then sat down beside him, leaning his back against the same large rock. He set the coffee down beside him to cool and then reached into his shirt pocket for his makings sack.

"She makes a good cup of coffee," Uncle Hector said, keeping his voice low, after he'd sipped the potent brew. "It is good to have a woman around who can make a good cup of coffee."

"Yeah, she's right handy."

"Beautiful, isn't she?"

"Pretty as a speckled pup."

Uncle Hector chuckled deep in his chest as he smiled admiringly at Jasmine, still sleeping under her hat. "Pretty as a coral snake would be a more appropriate description," he said with cunning. He glanced at Sartain. "I would tread carefully around her."

"You would, would you?" Sartain snorted ruefully as he sprinkled chopped tobacco onto the wheat paper he troughed between his fingers. "I guess you learned your lesson, then, didn't you — you old pervert?"

"*Sí,* I have learned."

"Not to resort to rape?"

"Rape can be fun in its way. To take a beautiful woman by force is one of the pleasures of a man. It has been done for thousands of years. Quite intoxicating. There is sex and there is rape." He slowly shook his head, grinning lasciviously, sweat dribbling down his cheeks as he stared at Jasmine's rising and falling chest. "Fornication is meat and potatoes. But rape is a delicacy."

"We should have left it in the caves."

Uncle Hector glanced at Sartain again, narrowing an eye. "You might want to take a turn. You are much stronger than I, an old man. But you are a large, vigorous *hombre.* You could manage it. I would like to see that."

He made a groan-like grunting sound in his chest, narrowing his eyes slightly.

Sartain scowled at the old, depraved Mexican. "Hard to believe you were ever a man of honor, Uncle Hector. From a supposedly good family."

"Oh, my family was always half savage, *señor.* Just because we had money didn't mean we weren't depraved." Uncle Hector grinned, chuckling. "Ask the *campesinos* who worked for us."

Sartain regarded him askance as he snapped a match to life on his thumbnail. "Mister, I'm almost hoping you're leading us on a wild goose chase, so I can put a bullet in you."

"To have one such as that moaning and writhing beneath you," Uncle Hector said, as though he hadn't heard the Revenger's threat. "Now, that would be something, would it not? To cup those lovely breasts . . ."

He let his voice trail off when Jasmine grunted and turned onto her side, curling her legs under her right hip, snugging her shoulder up tight against the stone wall, facing down the ravine. Her hat tumbled off her hip and onto the ground. She didn't retrieve it. Her thick hair hung in a pretty mess down her back and shoulders.

"Ahh," Tejada said luxuriously.

Sartain found himself regarding the woman with a male admiration akin to the depraved Mexican's, his heart thudding, loins heavy. Annoyed, he said, "Do me a favor and hobble your lips from now on, Uncle Hector, or I'll hobble them for you. With the butt of my pistol."

Tejada only chuckled as he kept his slitted eyes on the woman.

"Be careful of her, *señor,*" he warned in a soft, lilting singsong. "Tread very carefully. That one there — she is up to no good. I will guarantee you of that."

The Revenger didn't want to encourage conversation, but he couldn't help asking,

"What makes you say so?"

Uncle Hector hiked a shoulder. "The way she looks at you at times. You haven't noticed because she makes sure you aren't looking at her before she looks at *you.* It is a strange, dark look. *Sí, Señor.* I don't know what darkness women carry in their hearts — no man can ever know for sure — but I assure you with my old man's experience it is a darkness very much like that we carry in our own. It just plays out a little differently, that is all."

He grinned with menace and enunciated the rest very precisely: "Hard-edged."

There was the crunching whip of a snare being sprung. A rabbit gave a high, clipped shriek.

Uncle Hector stretched his lips back from his teeth in a grin. "And almost always more surprising."

He lifted his coffee in both cuffed hands, and sipped.

Chapter Fifteen

They camped that night along the base of the same southern ridge, about five miles as the crow flies from where Sartain had set his traps. They roasted the two large jacks he'd taken. They drank coffee spiced with whiskey, and then Jasmine and their captive turned in while there was still a little spruce-green light left in the sky beyond the jutting, black ridge.

Sartain took the first watch from the top of a near outcropping.

The next day they rode through spectacularly red country that was a tormented landscape of jutting mesas, fluted pinnacles, wind-blasted pediments, and distant *sierras* that seemed to float above a gauzy, dark-blue horizon. They skirted the edges of several canyons. The only sign they saw of other humans were the remains of old fires, probably Indian fires, and a single rusted food tin lying near a seep from which they filled their canteens, a process that took nearly an hour due to the slowness of the trickle.

That night they camped in higher country, where a smattering of pines grew here and there against crumbling escarpments. There was more grass, too, which meant feed for the horses.

That night they dined on a wild turkey that Jasmine took down with a slingshot, further fueling Sartain's admiration of the woman and wondering where in hell she came from. But she was as tight-lipped about her past — and pretty much everything else — as ever. The only complete sentence she'd uttered all day was to Uncle Hector: "If you keep ogling me, you old bastard, you're going to be dancing in hell."

"I will be dancing in hell soon, anyway, *chiquita,*" was the old man's response. "Forgive an old man his wanting to wring out all of life's sweet juices."

Sartain again took the first watch. He sat on the rocky crest of an ancient volcano, under a sky awash with stars. A large sycamore stood behind him, growing crooked from a large crack in the upper wall of the cone — a massive, beautiful ruin of a tree that had probably lived for a hundred years or more. In its top, an owl hooted from time to time before taking flight and winging off with a great rush of its wings, probably sweeping the lower slope for mice or rabbits.

There would be another such rush of wings and feathered body again in a few minutes, and then the hoots would commence from the top branches of the ancient tree.

Wolves gave their mournful cries from distant ridges. Coyotes yammered maniacally in surrounding canyons.

Around midnight, Sartain heard the crunch of boots climbing the mountain.

"It's me," Jasmine said in her customarily toneless voice, subtly announcing her disdain as if the Revenger might forget how she felt about him.

"Did you bring the bottle?" he asked as her silhouette gathered shape before him, against the dark backdrop of the canyon in which the coals of their fire glowed umber.

"Why would I bring a bottle?"

"So you and me could have a few drinks and bury the hatchet," Sartain said. "Though why we need to is beyond me."

"It likely always will be."

She stood facing him, hands on her hips, her left foot planted out to the side and a little forward. Her hair blew in the night wind. The stars shone in it. Her shoulders were back, breasts forward. He could see the cone of each one as her blouse stretched taut against and around them.

She scowled down at him with an almost feral look on her face.

Sartain's blood ran hot. He'd never felt so challenged before by any woman. He gained his feet, leaving the Henry leaning against the tree. He stared into her eyes. She didn't blink. He stepped forward.

She took one step backward, smiling mockingly, shaking her head.

"Yes," he said, and took another quick step forward.

He planted his right hand on the back of her head, and kissed her. She did not respond at first. Neither did she fight. Her breasts swelled against his chest.

Gradually, she opened her lips. Her saliva was warm against his own lips and his tongue. Her mouth relaxed. Her body relaxed, as well. He let his right hand roam down her back and then he placed it on her right breast, feeling the fullness of the orb beneath it.

She groaned, and tried to step back. He grabbed her around the waist, held her taut against him, and kissed her harder, with more passion. She returned the kiss in kind, but her body struggled in his grip. She tried to step back, but he was far stronger than she was. He placed his right hand on her butt, drawing her crotch hard against his.

She continued to return his kiss with a passionate one of her own, relaxing once more, caressing his probing tongue with her own. She reached down between them and placed her hand on his stiffening member through his denims, rubbing it in a slow, hard up and down motion, groaning as she did so, her hair blowing around in the wind to slither against his cheeks.

Each strand felt like a miniature lightning bolt, causing his face to tingle.

She lowered her head to one side, and placed her free hand on the back of his neck. He lowered his own head, keeping his mouth locked on hers. She groaned. He grunted as her hand plied him almost savagely until he came close to the verge of his passion.

He grunted again when she pulled her hand away. He thought she was going to open his pants but then he felt something small, round, and hard press against his ribs. He pulled his mouth off of hers and looked down between them to see her right hand holding one of her fancy pistols against him. She broke free of his grip and stepped back away from him.

She clicked the pistol's hammer back and smiled devilishly, her hair and her eyes shimmering like those of some black-hearted succubus in the starlight.

She waved the pistol toward the canyon in which the fire glowed. "Get the hell out of here."

Sartain stood staring at her, wide-eyed, heart thudding. His crotch throbbed. His knees felt like warm mud.

"You heard me," she said, running the back of her hand across her mouth. He could see her nipples jutting against her blouse. "Get out of here. And if you ever try that again, I'll put one in you."

Sartain turned around and picked up his Henry. "All right."

He stepped toward her. She stepped back and to his right, raising the cocked pistol higher.

He chuckled as he set the rifle on his shoulder.

"Whatever you wish, *señorita,*" he said as he started down the slope, cold sweat trickling down his back.

Midafternoon of the next day, Sartain swung down from his saddle. He moved off the trail and knelt beside a mesquite.

"What is it?" Jasmine asked as she rode up behind him, beside Uncle Hector, who still rode barefoot, ankles tied to his stirrups.

Sartain picked up the horse apple he'd spied as his gaze had raked the terrain around the ancient horse trail they'd been following along the *barranca,* which was once again sheathed by steep, red cliffs. He sniffed, then crumbled the manure between his gloved fingers, letting it dribble to the ground.

"Fresh," he said. "Sort of, anyways. Not more than a day old."

He studied the *barranca* whose north ridge was shoving out purple shadows that angled eastward. Cactus wrens and finches peeped in the sparse mesquites and palo verdes. Scanning the ground around him, he frowned, straightened, and walked over to run his gloved finger along the outline of an unshod horse hoof. He'd done enough tracking both during and after the war to glean several bits of information from a single horse print.

The unshod mount that had made this print was light but probably not young, because the hoof had a slight crack in it. Probably a middle-aged, desert-bred mustang carrying a relatively light rider and little gear, for the impression was not overly deep. Sniffing the apple had told him the horse had not been grained recently, only grass fed. And he'd recognized several half-digested mesquite beans.

All together, those details told him the horse most likely belonged to a desert native. Most likely a Yaqui or an Apache.

"What is it?" Jasmine asked again, rising up slightly in her stirrups and leaning forward.

"Unshod hoof print."

"So?"

Uncle Hector, sitting his horse to her left, frowned at her. His cheeks had turned pasty beneath the brim of his *sombrero*. "*Señorita,* I believe you do not understand the significance of such a thing. What *Señor* Sartain has likely found is the print of an Indio horse. And if there is one Indio, there are most likely more Indios. And I, for one, would like to hold onto what little hair I have left."

The old Mexican shook his head. "No — this is bad. Very bad."

"What?" Sartain said. "You actually thought we'd travel through these mountains in the heart of Apacheria and not run into Apaches?"

"No, no, no. I warned you of this, *Señor*

Sartain. I knew we would. I *hoped* we wouldn't, but I *knew* there was a very good chance we would enter these mountains and fall prey to one of the many things that haunts them — wild animals of particularly bellicose dispositions, for instance. Rattle-snakes of similar ill temperaments. Spiders, scorpions, gila monsters, *bandidos, revolucionarios, rurales, federales,* thirst, the possibility of being stranded on foot by a dead or injured horse. Rock slides, volcanoes — oh, yes, these mountains have been known to blow their tops like angry wives from time to time! — and, of course, the ever-present and always blood-thirsty Apache."

"When I was learning all I could about this part of Chihuahua," Jasmine said, "I believe I read that the Yaqui also call this part of Mexico home. From here to the Yaqui River, I believe."

Uncle Hector sighed deeply, wagged his head fatefully, and shuddered. "*Sí, señorita.* Thank you for amending my list. The Yaqui dwell in this *sierra,* as well. And they are no spring maidens, either. I assure you. That is why I warned you that rational men not on the run *from* something do not venture into these mountains. *Las Montañas de Sombra* are known for swallowing men . . . and women, forgive me, *señorita* . . . and leaving their bones to the javelinas."

Uncle Hector gave another sigh. This one was not as throaty as the one that had preceded it. It was mostly air. Looking down, Tejada opened his mouth wide. His eyes sharpened with shock. Sartain followed the man's gaze to the arrow bristling from Tejada's left calf.

"Oh!" Jasmine cried.

"Go!" Sartain shouted, spying movement on a knoll behind Uncle Hector. "Get outta here!"

He waved his left arm furiously, and raised the Henry. The Apache stood about halfway down the knoll, beyond a palo verde and several ragged mesquites. He was pulling another arrow from the quiver hanging down his back.

Jasmine reached over and grabbed Uncle Hector's reins out of the shocked man's hands. She ground her spurs into her horse's flanks and shot off up the trail, jerking Tejada's horse along behind her. Sartain began pumping lead at the Apache, a stocky youngster wearing only the traditional red-felt bandanna, a deerskin breechclout, and moccasins. His skin was as dark as worn saddle leather.

Two of the Revenger's bullets plumed dust around the brave, who shot another arrow wide and then wheeled and dashed back up the knoll.

Sartain's third bullet punched into the kid's left shoulder blade, flinging him violently forward with a clipped, animal-like wail. He dropped his bow. As he rolled down the side of the knoll, his deerskin quiver spilled arrows.

Sartain lowered the Henry and reached for Boss's reins, the big stallion backing away from him, his eyes looking wild. When the Cajun got the reins, he saw several horseback riders plunging down the steep side of the ridge beyond the knoll from which the brave had flung his arrow into Uncle Hector's leg.

They were too far away to see clearly — a couple of hundred yards — but Sartain didn't bother to scrutinize the riders. Only Apaches could put their horses down a cliff that steep and not break their own and their horses' necks.

The Revenger swung up into the saddle, whipped his rein ends against Boss's left hip, yelling, "Hi-yahhh! Hi-yahhh, boy — let's *go*!"

Without needing further encouragement, Boss chewed up the ground in front of him. Jasmine and Uncle Hector were about sixty yards away and riding hard, the Mexican slumped in his saddle, *sombrero*-clad head bobbing and wobbling from side to side. Behind Sartain, rifles belched. The Indians lifted their ululating cries that never failed to turn his spine to cold jelly.

CHAPTER SIXTEEN

Glancing back over his left shoulder, the Cajun could not see the warriors, but judging by the loudening of their rifle shots and coyote-like yells, they were galloping toward him. As he started to turn his head forward, he glimpsed movement out of the corner of his left eye, and turned back.

Sure enough — they were coming hard and fast. Several paint ponies showed themselves galloping through the chaparral, white spots glowing in the sunshine. There were flashes of red or green bandannas and the riders' leathery brown skin. Dust rose from the chaparral.

Ahead, the *barranca*'s walls began dropping in places, so that the ridge crest appeared a saw blade with teeth of vastly different lengths. The ridges also began leaning away, so that the *barranca* floor widened. Sartain saw little cover straight ahead. He glanced behind once more.

The Indians had broken out of the brush and were riding hell for leather, yammering and hunkering low in their saddles, a couple triggering carbines.

There were a half-dozen. That wasn't so many. But then the Revenger cursed again when he saw that he'd made a hasty count. There'd been a gap between the first six and the others that were just now galloping out of the brush. Six more, at least. No, ten . . . twelve . . . maybe fifteen to twenty!

No point in keeping track. Sartain, Jasmine, and their prisoner were in trouble. That was all they needed to know.

He whipped his rein ends against Boss's hip again and dropped his head low over the galloping mount's neck. The stallion was blowing hard, lungs sounding like a bellows, pinning his ears back against his head. Jasmine was slowing her mount, looking back at Sartain and the Apaches thundering down the *barranca* behind him, quickly closing the gap with the fittest ponies anywhere on the continent.

As the Revenger closed on the woman and their prisoner, he saw she had a question in her eyes. He knew what she was wondering.

What in hell were they going to do?

He looked ahead and right, where the ridge on that side of the *barranca,* now a good hundred yards away, had lowered appreciably. It looked downright surmountable in one place that was maybe fifty yards wide — an inclining stretch of boulders and open ground between two steeper monoliths of solid sandstone. It probably rose a hundred and fifty yards to its crest, leaning away from the broad canyon.

Sartain pointed to the gap in the ridge wall. "There! Go there!"

Jasmine swung her horse to the right, angling toward the sloping belly of the ridge, tugging Uncle Hector's mount along behind her.

The yowling of the Apaches grew louder behind Sartain. So did the cracks of their carbines. He could hear the thudding of their horses now, as well. They sounded like an earth tremor. Several bullets landed close, whining shrilly off rocks to each side of the Cajun, who steered his own mount toward the ridge.

Ahead of him, Jasmine gained the base of the ridge and put her mount up the slope that was partly shaded by the steeper ridge to the right of it. Shade also bled out from the large and small boulders peppering it. Jasmine's thoroughbred zigzagged around the rocks, the woman glancing back at Tejada's horse, tugging its bridle reins.

The Mexican slumped miserably forward in his saddle, the arrow protruding from his left calf.

Sartain got to the base of the ridge and began climbing. The horse's breathing grew harsher, deeper, the bit rattling in its teeth. As Boss turned sharply left to steer around a cabin-sized boulder throwing out a trapezoid of purple shade around its base, Sartain glanced behind. The Apaches were less than fifty yards from the base of the slope and galloping hard, like a herd of wildcats smelling blood.

Sartain slipped his Henry from its sheath and swung down from Boss's back. He slapped the horse's rump, shouting, "Go on, boy!" He wanted the horse to continue up the slope. If the mount caught a bullet or an arrow, the Cajun's goose would be cooked, not to mention he was rather fond of the surly buckskin.

As he stepped behind the cabin-sized boulder, Sartain pumped a cartridge into the rifle's action and glanced upslope. Jasmine had reached a talus slide and was swinging down from her mount to lead it as well as the Mexican's steel dust across the loose patch of sharp-edged gravel. Her right boot slipped, and she dropped to a knee but quickly gained both feet again and resumed tramping on up the slope, pulling on the reins of both horses.

A bullet slammed against the side of the boulder near Sartain, flecking his cheeks with rock shards and dust. He glanced out behind the boulder to see the Apaches now approaching the base of the slope, not slowing their mounts a bit.

Sartain stepped out from behind the boulder and commenced firing the Henry from his hip. He unseated one rider with his first shot. He thought he winged another with the second one. When he'd fired two more rounds, he'd accomplished his task of slowing the braves' pursuit, several dismounting and starting up the slope on foot, with either a rifle or a bow and arrow in their hands. Some had steel-bladed war hatchets wedged behind red sashes.

As one brave ran out from behind a flat boulder near the base of the slope, Sartain raised his Henry, carefully planted a bead on the brave's chest, and squeezed the trigger. The Indian jerked back, screaming. The Cajun stepped back behind the boulder and then started running up the slope directly behind it, using the large obelisk for cover.

His shots had been like beating a hornet's nest with a broom. That really piss-burned the Apaches. Their yips and howls rose to a cacophony. The rifle fire picked up, and several arrows whistled through the air around Sartain, one glancing off a rock as he dashed up the slope. A bullet blew up the talus just as he hit the slide-rock. Breathing hard, pumping his arms and legs, he increased his pace, silently chastising himself for overindulging in cheroots.

He was low on wind, his lungs straining.

Another bullet sizzled across the right side of his neck. It was like being raked by the frigid tip of a witch's finger. He winced against it and kept running as more bullets and arrows ricocheted off the rocks around him.

As he ran, he allowed himself another backward glance.

Most of the Apaches were on foot now, running up the slope behind him, weaving around boulders and scattered cedars and *piñons.* One of the braves jerked back and sideways, wincing and slapping a hand to his bloody left shoulder. He sagged back against the flat boulder from which Sartain had flung lead.

Upslope, a rifle cracked.

A bullet blew a dark hole in the Apache's forehead, just above his right eye. The Indian's head whipped back, bouncing off the boulder. Blood bubbled up out of the hole as the Apache dropped to his knees, twisting around and rolling back down the slope, another brave leaping over him and then howling and clutching his left knee a half-second after the rifle cracked again on the upslope.

Hunkered down in a gap between two rocks at the crest of the ridge, Jasmine pumped another cartridge into the action of her Winchester, and pressed her cheek up against the neck of the stock.

"What's taking you?" she yelled a half-second before smoke and flames lapped from the Winchester's barrel.

Sartain bounded up the last several yards and hunkered down behind a rock to her left.

He took a few seconds to catch his breath, then, still raking deep draughts of air into his burning lungs, he said, "Didn't know you were handy with a long gun."

"There are a lot of things you don't know about me, Mr. Sartain." Jasmine triggered another shot, levering another round into the Winchester's chamber.

"Yes, there are, Miss Galla . . ." Sartain let his voice trail off as he racked a round into the Henry's action and rested the barrel of the rifle on the lip of the ridge before him. ". . . Gallant," he continued, picking out a weaving, long-haired target, and taking the shot.

The Apache he'd hit dropped his bow and arrow, grabbed his belly, and howled. He flopped backward and rolled.

"Gallant," Sartain said, picking out another target and firing. "It just now occurred to me — I've heard that name before." Again, he racked a fresh round into the Henry's breech. He glanced toward where he couldn't see Jasmine herself but only the smoke and flames stabbing from her Winchester's barrel.

"Have you?" she said, thumbing fresh cartridges from Tejada's belt into the Winchester.

"I'm sure I have." Sartain ducked when a bullet blew up dust and gravel about three feet in front of him. "But I'll be damned if I can remember where."

He picked out another target and fired, evoking a muffled grunt and sending another Apache rolling down the rocky decline.

He cursed and was forced to focus all his attention on the Apaches when it became clear they were going to keep coming despite the half-dozen or so he and Jasmine had sent to the Happy Hunting Ground. When he'd snapped off all sixteen of the Henry's rounds, he slid the loading tube out from beneath the main barrel and refilled it with fresh brass from his cartridge belt.

In ten minutes, he'd spent all that ammo, as well, with little to show for it.

The Indians were still coming but more cautiously now, holding up behind covering rocks and clumps of brush before bounding out, fleet as wildcats, to another rock or brush clump. They howled and hooted, jeering at Sartain's and Jasmine's missed shots.

"Shit," Jasmine said, from the other side of her covering rock. "This isn't looking so good."

Sartain didn't say anything, but his throat was dry. That meant he was thinking the same thing she was. They were badly outnumbered, and they were low on ammunition.

"Help me!" Uncle Hector said from a fringe of mesquites down the slope behind Sartain. Jasmine had cut him free of his saddle, allowing him to dismount. He lay folded up on the ground, clutching his bloody calf. "I need some assistance here, *amigos*. I'm bleeding quite profusely!"

"Shut up," Sartain raked out, planting his LeMat's sites on the dark-brown blur of a dashing Apache and squeezing the trigger. He couldn't tell for sure, but he thought it was another miss.

Again, he cursed.

Then the LeMat's hammer clicked on an empty chamber.

He cursed again and reached for the Henry, forgetting in the direness of the situation that it was empty. He set it down, and pulled the loading tube from beneath the barrel. To his right he heard one of Jasmine's own guns, probably one of her pistols, clapping benignly down its firing pin.

"I'm out!" she yelled. "All three guns!"

"Goddamnit!" Sartain said. "Don't tell 'em that!"

He hadn't gotten the admonishment entirely out when a wiry young Apache came storming up the ten-foot gap between Sartain and the boulder the brave had been hunkered behind. Another was close on his heels, both holding only war hatchets. They were whooping wildly, grinning, their sense of honor and challenge making them resort to the oldest tools of their trade. They must have known enough of the white man's tongue to understand the Pinkerton's pronouncement.

The first brave bounded toward Jasmine while the second one came running up the slope toward Sartain, who set his Henry aside and rose from behind his rock, sliding his Bowie knife from its belt sheath. He crouched as the Apache approached, whooping and hollering so loudly, Sartain's eardrums rattled.

The brave thrust the war hatchet down at an arc toward the Revenger's head. Sartain jerked his head back. As he heard Jasmine scream, he gritted his teeth and sliced the blade of the Bowie across the Apache's belly, opening him up like a field-dressed deer.

The brave screamed shrilly, digging his hands into the blood pudding spilling from his belly and dropping to his knees. Jasmine groaned. Sartain turned to see the other Apache holding her taut against him, on the other side of her rock. The grinning brave started to thrust the war hatchet down toward her head.

Sartain sent the Bowie careening through the air end-over-end until its wickedly hooked tip crunched into the brave's left eye. The war hatchet dealt Jasmine's left shoulder a glancing blow as she twisted around and away from the brave, who staggered backward, howling and swatting both hands at the knife handle as though it were a pesky fly.

His arms dropped and he fell straight

backward without trying to break his fall. He lay silently jerking, as though the ground were bounding around beneath him, the hide-wrapped handle of the Bowie quivering, as well.

Jasmine dropped to a knee, clamping her right hand to her left shoulder.

She gasped and widened her eyes as two more braves came charging up the slope, howling and slicing the air with war hatchets and knives.

Chapter Seventeen

Sartain bolted off his heels, slamming his head and shoulders into the chest of the first Apache. He bulled the howling brave over onto the Indian's back so hard that the brave's eyes rolled back into his head. The Cajun jerked the war hatchet from the Apache's slack hand, smashing it across the brave's head.

There was the sound of cracking bone. One of the brave's eyes popped out of its socket to hang by a ragged thread.

The other brave kicked Sartain in the ribs, throwing the Revenger onto his back. His side screamed out in misery. He felt as though he'd been impaled with a dull sword. Gasping for air, he looked up and saw the brave diving toward him, clenching the Bowie in his right fist, the curved tip of the rusty brown blade driving down toward the Cajun's throat.

Sartain reached up and grabbed the

brave's wrist, stopping the blade six inches from his jugular and slowly driving the squirming brave, whose sweat and raw-meat stench almost made the Revenger's eyes water, onto his back. When Sartain had gained a knee over the brave, he smashed his left fist hard against the Indian's right cheek.

The brave stiffened, brown eyes glazing. The Bowie clattered onto the rocks.

Sartain delivered three more punishing blows, until the brave's body had fallen slack. He looked downslope. The bottom dropped out of his belly as he saw more braves lunging up the incline toward him, howling, all dropping carbines and bows and arrows and unsheathing knives and hatchets to cut the Cajun to bloody ribbons.

Sartain glanced at Jasmine. She knelt ten feet to his right, holding the Bowie down low by her right thigh, blood dripping from the blade onto the rocks beneath her.

She stared in slack-jawed shock at the Indians storming up the slope, the first three within thirty yards and closing fast, eyes bright with the promise of a satisfying kill. They were racing, shoving each other back as they ran, laughing.

Back when he was soldiering in Arizona, Sartain had come to learn how Apache warriors thought. These young men had seen him kill three of their own virtually barehanded; each was eager to wear the trophy of having killed such a formidable warrior himself.

Not only would such an honor garner them esteem from their *compadres* but the veneration of the prettiest girls in the band, who would vie to be the one or ones to bear his children.

"Run!" he shouted to Jasmine, throwing an arm out to indicate the backside of the ridge. "Get your horse and ride the hell out of here! I'll distract them for as long as I can!"

He squared his shoulders and balled his fists, ready to challenge the Indians' assault. He had enough ammo on his cartridge belt to reload the Henry, and he had two more boxes of shells in his saddlebags, but not enough time to put any of it to use.

He glanced again at Jasmine. She just knelt there as if frozen, staring in shock at the braves charging toward her.

"I said run, goddamnit!" he bellowed.

That caused the young Pinkerton to jerk with a start. She'd just begun to straighten when what sounded like a cannon blast rose somewhere above and to Sartain's left. The echo of the heavy explosion danced around the slope, dwindling.

Sartain blinked, his mind slow to comprehend what his eyes had just told him.

The head of one of the charging braves had exploded. White bone and brain and red blood and black hair sprayed in all directions. The braves looked around, shocked. Another head exploded, and the Indians wheeled and scattered across the slope, diving for cover.

Again, the heavy gun's explosion-like report vaulted across the ridge.

Sartain didn't see where this slug landed.

"Take cover!" he yelled at Jasmine.

He grabbed his Henry and dropped down on the other side of the ridge crest, pulling out the loading tube to begin reloading.

Soon there was another rocketing blast. Again, the Revenger didn't see where the bullet had gone.

The Indians had fallen eerily silent.

When Sartain had reloaded the Henry, he rested it on the gravelly crest of the ridge and gazed down the slope toward where the Indians had been dashing toward him only a minute before. Now he saw only swatches of black hair and the occasional glimpse of a dark-brown face as the Indians remained behind boulders and brush clumps and low hummocks of rock and cactus, looking around, trying to discern the shooter's location.

Sartain looked up hard on his left. Smoke puffed from a niche of high rocks maybe fifty yards away. As the dark smoke ribboned on the breeze, another heavy blast flatted off across the slope. There was the crashing *whunk!* of the large-caliber bullet smashing rock.

Sartain scowled up at the shooter. He had no idea who the man was. He was wielding what sounded like a Sharps "Big Fifty," as the .50-caliber buffalo-hunting rifle was known, and he no longer seemed to be shooting at the Apaches. He was shooting at the higher ridge on the slope's north side, where there appeared an outcropping of loose rock.

Sure enough, on the heels of the next blast, rock dust puffed from near the top of the outcropping.

After the shot's last echo, silence.

A low rumbling started, building.

Sartain frowned, staring up at the outcropping. Then he grinned as the large thumb of rock set against the north ridge wall began shaking. He grinned wider when the highest rocks, roughly the size of small farm wagons, began tilting toward the slope across which the Indians were hunkered.

They tilted farther and farther. Several began to fall. They appeared to spend a long time in the air, turning slowly end-over-end. When they landed, Sartain felt the ground lurch beneath him.

Then more rocks fell.

More and more, cracking together as they plunged to explode on the slope like the rounds of mountain howitzers, the ground now moving beneath the Revenger as the rocks hammered the slope as though to crush it into submission. The rocks and boulders bounced, dancing across the slope. Now the Indians were lighting out down the incline, back in the direction from which they'd come.

They resembled black-tailed deer, leaping rocks and cacti and weaving around boulders, the rocks from the outcropping giving chase as though with a vengeance. One Apache screamed and disappeared as a large, pale boulder crushed him. Two more screamed and disappeared.

Then there were so many rocks and so much dust that Sartain's view of the declivity was nearly totally blocked. Beneath the explosions of the rocks on the slope, he occasionally made out the muted screams of another soon-to-be-crushed Apache.

After several minutes, the rocks stopped

falling. A couple shifted position and tumbled a few times, but the brunt of the slide was finished. Dust roiled up from the slope like smoke from a hard-fought battle.

"There," the Cajun said, blinking dust from his eyes, "that'll teach ya."

He could hear Jasmine coughing on the dust. Then she rose from the far side of her boulder, blinking and batting her hat against her thigh.

"What . . . was . . . that . . . ?" she asked, turning her incredulous gaze to Sartain.

The Revenger had straightened, as well, coughing and running his shirtsleeve over his eyes. "Your guess is as good as mine, my dear."

He gazed up the southern ridge from which the shots had been fired, seeing nothing. Then he heard the crunch of gravel and saw an old Mexican man, skin as dark or darker than any Apache's, step around a pinnacle of rock about three-quarters of the way down from where the big rifle's smoke had been puffing a few moments earlier.

A straw *sombrero* hung down his back, flopping to and fro as the oldster moved carefully down the rocks. He wore high-topped, mule-eared boots and baggy deerskin breeches. A tobacco pouch hung down his spindly chest, which was clad in a grimy red-and-black calico shirt. A Schofield revolver sagged in a worn leather holster on his left thigh. Attached to the same belt was a leather cap box for holding the Sharps's long brass cartridges. A hide-wrapped waterskin dangled from his right shoulder.

His face was long and bony, upturned nose cleaving it in two. His rheumy brown eyes regarded Sartain curiously as he kept coming down the rocks, moving purposefully, one step at a time. He held a Sharps rifle in his right hand. As he approached, the Cajun could see a thin ribbon of smoke skeining from the barrel.

He dropped off the last rock and came along the lip of the ridge, swerving from Sartain to walk down the back slope where Uncle Hector was still down and crouched over his arrow-pierced calf. The old reprobate was smiling in spite of the pain blanching his cheeks and watering his eyes.

"Tio," he said. "Old Tio. Still handy with a buffalo rifle, I see . . ."

The old Mexican's face turned into a mask of badly cracked leather as he grinned, stretching his lips back far enough that Sartain could see he had no front teeth. In Spanish almost too fast for the Revenger to keep up with, old Tio said, "Those Chiricahuas have been hound-dogging my trail for days. I am much grateful and amused that you led them into my trap!"

He stood smiling proudly, cradling the rifle, which appeared to weigh more than he did, in his sinewy arms. He canted his head toward Sartain and Jasmine. "Who are the *norteamericanos*?"

"Friends of Señor Tejada," said Sartain.

Old Tio scowled at the Revenger. "No friend of *Señor* Tejada is a friend of mine!"

"Well, shit, then," the Cajun said.

"I thought you two were related," Jasmine said.

"We are! We are!" Uncle Hector said, ingratiatingly, in Spanish. "Family means much to the Tejadas . . . does it not, old Tio, my uncle?"

"I should finish what the Apaches started," old Tio said, grinning devilishly down at the wounded Tejada. Anger turned his near-black face even darker. "Why do you bring them here? Did I not tell you that I would kill you if I ever saw you in these mountains again?"

"Perhaps . . ." Uncle Hector glanced down at the arrow bristling from his calf. ". . . we could continue the conversation after this arrow has been removed from my flesh . . . ? It is gravely uncomfortable, I assure you."

"Yours is the devil's flesh." Old Tio

glanced at Jasmine and then at Sartain. His shrewd, washed-out eyes returned to the young Pinkerton, his gaze flicking down slightly to admire the woman's well-filled blouse. "That, however, is the flesh of an angel."

Jasmine flushed slightly.

Old Tio grinned, then narrowed one eye suspiciously at the female Pinkerton. "Are you really a friend of this thief and killer?"

Despite his ragged, soiled attire and small stature, the old man had a regal air about him. He'd lived the life of an outcast, but there was something in his eyes and his bearing that reminded the Revenger of a fallen *hacendado* — a man of wealth and respect who had been badly defeated but had still retained his dignity and formal bearing.

"When you put it that way," Jasmine said, cutting her eyes at Sartain, "no. No we're not friends at all. Let's just say business associates. We're here looking for you, *Señor* Tio. We were hoping you could help us find someone."

"And who might that someone be?" asked another voice from somewhere behind the wizened Tio.

Sartain winced when he saw a young Mexican man step out from behind a rock flanking old Tio. He was dressed nearly all in leather, a knotted red neckerchief fluttering in the wind. He wore a broad-brimmed black *sombrero* low over his eyes. A dust-smudge mustache trimmed his upper lip. He was maybe twenty, with long, straight, dark-brown hair hanging to his shoulders.

"Maximilian San Javier de Tejada?" The young man hardened his voice and pulled a Colt from its holster positioned for a cross draw on his left hip. "If so, you've come to the right place. The right place to die, my friend!"

"Stop!" said another voice — this one a girl's. A petite, hazel-eyed blonde, she moved out from behind a rock to place a hand on the young man's cocked revolver. "Let's find out what they want first, *mi amor.*"

Chapter Eighteen

Sartain stared down at the fire over which a haunch of javelina roasted on an iron spit. Uncle Hector turned the spit slowly, wincing against the pain in his calf, which old Tio had wrapped in a whiskey-soaked cloth after breaking and pulling out the Apache shaft.

"Turn it, old man," growled the young man, Maximilian San Javier de Tejada, as he basted the meat with grease, tequila, and wild onions and herbs he'd placed in a cast-iron skillet and sautéed over low coals. "Turn it, fool!"

"I am turning it! I am turning it, Maximilian! I apologize if I am not turning it fast enough for you, on your order, but in case you have forgotten, my health has been compromised by an arrow of the devilish Apache! A *Chiricahua* Apache!"

Maximilian tossed a spoon into the cup of seasoned liquid, and cursed in Spanish. "I don't know why he shot you." He turned to old Tio sitting back in the shadows of their camp amongst dark rocks, roughly a mile from the scene of the Indian attack, smoking his pipe. Only the upper right third of his Indian-dark face was lit by the dancing, umber firelight. The rest of its pits and crags were in watery shadow.

Cold night had fallen quickly. Stars shimmered across the arching vault of the velvet sky.

"He is family," old Tio said with a bored, tired air, staring at the roasting meat. Maximilian was following Tio's directions for roasting and basting. "If one Tejada kills another, a hundred years of bad luck will come to all the rest of the living family. I learned this not from my father, a Tejada, but from my mother, an India. A very wise India."

Maximilian stared at the wizened old-timer incredulously. Sartain knew he was wondering how Tio could care about killing a Tejada when none of the Tejadas except Maximilian himself had ever accepted him as one of their own.

"Well, this big *hombre* isn't family." Priscilla McDougal came around from the far side of the fire to aim a pistol at Sartain, clicking back the hammer and scrunching up her pretty, fire-lit face distastefully. "Let's get down to business. Who are you? Who sent you? To do what? Hurry, or I'll kill you now" — she canted her head at Jasmine — "and then her."

Sartain stared up at her. He'd been trying to free his hands, tied behind his back with rawhide, but he wasn't having much luck. He stopped the attempt now with the girl's flashing eyes on him.

"I will repeat the questions only one more time," she said.

"Don't get your panties in a twist," the Cajun drawled, crestfallen. "The name's Sartain." He hadn't bothered to come up with a fake name, as it was doubtful many in Mexico had heard of him. Especially anyone in this remote Mexican backwater.

"Ah, the Revenger." Maximilian snickered girlishly. "Your father sends only the best, Priss."

She glanced over her shoulder at the boy, who was sitting by the fire now, legs crossed Indian-style. Maximilian looked up at her. "The Revenger's reputation is known down here. We *Mejicanos* respect a man who exacts revenge for those who can't do it themselves." He lowered his smoldering, threatening gaze to Sartain. "Only, my respect for such a man will not prevent me from killing him, since he was sent here to kill me."

He snickered, again girlishly, which was a habit with him. He had several feminine traits, including a higher voice than was usual for a young man.

"Nah," Sartain said. "The governor only wants his daughter back, that's all."

"Hah!" said Maximilian.

Priscilla still aimed the gun at Sartain, bunching her lips malignantly.

Sartain canted his head toward Jasmine, tied up to his right. "Let her go. I'm the one he sent to kill you, Maximilian. She's just a tagalong sent to keep me from whoring and drinking when I have more pressing matters to attend to."

He thought he heard Jasmine draw a deep breath of bridled anger.

"Who're you?" Priscilla asked the woman.

"Pinkerton agent."

"Is what he said true?"

"Sure." Jasmine offered the Revenger a wan smile.

He returned it.

"What are you after out here, Maximilian?" he asked the boy.

Maximilian studied Sartain sidelong and then glanced at old Tio, who merely continued to puff his pipe pensively while Tejada turned the pig every minute or two, desperately trying to keep it from burning, as were his orders. Maximilian looked at his wayward uncle, who looked quickly down, sheepish.

"Treasure," Maximilian said.

"Hush!" admonished Priscilla angrily.

"What difference does it make if he knows?" Maximilian glanced at his impoverished, *bandido* uncle. "If they all know. They all must die, even the Pinkerton." Then the boy turned to Jasmine and added sincerely, "I'm sorry."

Indignant, Hector said, "You would not kill your blood uncle!"

"You have been no uncle to me!" Maximilian scolded the older man. "Gold! It's always been the gold you have been after — ever since my mother, your sister, married Priscilla's father and ruined us. Only the gold."

"How did the governor ruin the Tejada family?" Sartain was curious to know.

"Our land was a grant from the King of Spain. There was what had always been considered a *legend* of treasure on it — gold milled by priests and their Indio slaves. After generations of Tejadas had looked for the gold, no one ever found it. So, it was believed to be a fable. One of many these mountains are known for. When my father died and my mother married our family friend, Governor McDougal" — he smiled icily — "she turned the grant over to McDougal, though he assured us the land would remain part of the Tejada domain.

"But when mother died after losing her memory and her wits, McDougal moved in with his own men, rushing the Tejada *vaqueros* and *campesinos* off the land some had worked for generations. Now, the Tejada *hacienda* is owned by McDougal, and run by McDougal's men — all *gringos.*"

"That won't be for much longer," Priscilla said tightly. She'd lowered the gun and gone over and taken a seat beside her stepbrother, throwing one arm around his neck and kissing his cheek. "We found the gold, thanks to the help of *Padre* Sandia, who put us on the right track after reading some of his old church documents. He'd never been able to explore this deep in the mountains himself . . . and saw little need, him being a pious man of the cloth, and this being part of the old Tejada grant."

"*Sí,* I knew you found it!" wheezed Uncle Hector as he gave the javelina another turn. He was nearly breathless, eyes gleaming, voice wheedling. "Where? You must share a little bit, if only a tiny bit, with your uncle whom you must never kill and thus save the family from the wretched curse!"

"We are already cursed, you old fool," said Maximilian, curling his lip.

Sartain gathered that Maximilian knew nothing of Uncle Hector's men having crucified the priest back at the little cathedral. He decided to keep the nasty news under his hat for now. No need to set off any explosions just yet, when he himself and the lady Pinkerton might get caught in the blast.

"What're you going to do with the gold?" Jasmine asked.

Maximilian reached toward the fire and daintily pulled bits of meat from the succulent, golden brown carcass. He blew on the chunks and handed them chivalrously to Priss before tearing some of the meat off for himself, and blowing on it. "We are going to hire a gang of the best *pistoleros* in Mexico — an entire army — and run McDougal's men off of the Tejada grant, or kill them all."

"And ruin the governor," Priss said, sucking grease from her thumb. "Most of his own money is now tied up in the *hacienda*." She let a satisfied smile tug at her mouth corners.

Sartain gave her an ironic smile. "Not a

very nice thing to do to your father."

"My father is a guttersnipe," Priss said matter of factly. "He was never a father to me. Only a politician. He killed my mother. Maybe not outright, but with all his orders and restrictions about how a politician's wife should behave — all the formalities about how to keep a house, throw parties, and be seen in public — it drove her to suicide. She ate a handful of wild mushrooms and died on our dining room table." She glanced at her young lover. "Pretty much the same thing happened to Max's mother. He drove her quite mad, though a vein of madness tends to run through the Tejada family."

She smiled again, this time with faint irony at her lover, who gave a vague, devilish grin.

"So you ran off together," Jasmine said. "After falling in love."

"That's right," Priscilla said saucily, keeping her arm around Maximilian. "We fell madly in love, utterly in love, and journeyed down here to find the treasure with help from Uncle Tio and *Padre* Sandia. Pure luck helped us find it after an earthquake exposed part of it."

There was a hoarse wheezing sound. Old Tio removed his pipe from between his leathery lips, and said, "I searched for that treasure for thirty years — me and the *padre* — and these two lovebirds found it within two months after coming down here." He chuckled again fatefully, and tapped the dottle from his pipe into his hand. "It was practically right under my nose . . . all those years . . ."

He sighed.

Maximilian reached over and squeezed the old man's forearm. "You'll be rich now, Tio. Richer than your wildest dreams."

Even with his missing teeth, the old man's smile was beatific.

"And I will get the *hacienda* back," Maximilian said, looking at Priscilla. "And we will raise our family on it."

Priscilla pecked his cheek and ran her hand through his hair. She turned toward Sartain and Jasmine. "What about them?"

Maximilian regarded them dubiously. *"Sí,"* he said, nodding. "What about them?" He turned to Tio. "Kill them?"

Old Tio regarded the pair with faint, ironic humor in his old eyes, in which the firelight flickered dully. He hiked a bony shoulder.

"And him?" Maximilian said, turning toward Uncle Hector.

Tejada smiled deviously, wincing as he gave the pig another turn. "You cannot kill one of your own, my nephew." He clucked.

"You must not kill one of your own. Listen to Tio!"

"I told you, you old killer — you are not one of my own. You are a filthy, cowardly killer and rapist. If you had found the treasure first, you would not have hesitated to kill us so that it all could be yours."

"Enough talking," Priscilla said. "I say we kill them all now." She turned her determined gaze to her young lover. "Why wait?"

Maximilian gazed at Sartain, at Jasmine, and then at his outlaw uncle, who returned his gaze with a fearful one of his own. Maximilian's throat worked as he swallowed. He rubbed his hands on his leather pants and turned to Priscilla.

"Would you like the honor, *mi amor*?"

Priscilla smiled. "Sure." She stood and held her hand out. Maximilian set his Colt pistol in it.

She closed her hand around the gun and turned toward Sartain. She looked at the other two prisoners, brow beetling. She shifted her weight from one foot to the other. Even in the dim light, Sartain could see some of the color leech out of her cheeks.

She turned to Maximilian. "Maybe tomorrow. Shots tonight might draw trouble."

"All right," Maximilian said, looking

relieved. "Tomorrow."

Priscilla gave the pistol back to him.

Tejada gave a long sigh. *"Por favor,"* he said. "If you must kill me, you must. But first, you must show me the treasure. I want to see it with my own eyes before I die."

Maximilian looked at old Tio, who said nothing but just kept staring into the fire with that beguiling, sage-like smile lifting his mouth corners.

"We will see," said Maximilian. "It is more than you deserve, you old *bastardo.* We will talk about it tomorrow."

Sartain glanced at Jasmine, who returned the look. She was nervous. He had to admit he was relieved to hear that his demise would be postponed for a few more hours.

He also had to admit that he felt sorry about the quandary the young lovers were in. He had been sent down here to kill Maximilian, after all. Of course, he'd been told the situation was much different than it had turned out to be.

Still, he'd been sent down here to kill the boy . . .

He wasn't sure if it was just wishful thinking, but something told him Maximilian didn't have cold-blooded murder in his blood. Priscilla acted tough, likely knowing it was the best way to live in such a tough land. But Sartain didn't think she had it in her, either.

Nevertheless, he wasn't going to tempt fate. Somehow, he had to get himself and Jasmine out of here. He had no intention of killing Maximilian now, even if he got the chance. All he wanted now was to get himself and Jasmine back across the border. They'd been sent on a wild goose chase, and McDougal could go to hell.

Learning he wouldn't be meeting his Maker in the next couple of hours caused him to remember his hollow belly.

"Kind of hard to sit here and look at all that meat without eating some of it," he said. "How 'bout you untie me and my colleague here, and throw us a bite or two?"

Priscilla wrinkled her nose at him. "The dead don't need to eat."

CHAPTER NINETEEN

Sartain didn't fall asleep after the fire had been kicked out and the others had rolled up in their blankets. He pretended to sleep, but instead he lay on his side, on the blanket Priscilla had grudgingly allowed him — he'd thought she was going to tell him that "dead men don't need blankets . . ." — and worked on trying to loosen the rawhide strips binding his wrists together behind his back.

He was glad for the loud, semi-measured snores of the two older Mexicans drowning out any sounds he might be making.

He worked quietly but with a grim, desperate determination. The bindings were tight. As he twisted his wrists against them, he felt the chill wetness of blood oozing beneath them. That was all right. If the rawhide got wet, it was more liable to stretch.

He'd been working on stretching the bindings for a good two hours when he heard the young lovers whispering on the other side of the cold fire from where he and Jasmine lay. He stopped working and lay still, tense.

Had they seen him?

There was more low talking. He heard the faint, furtive rustling of blankets. There was the clink of a belt buckle. A muffled girl's laugh.

"Shhh!" said Maximilian.

The old men's snores continued.

"They can't hear us, Max," said Priscilla in a voice just barely audible above the snores and the crickets, the occasional scratching of creosote branches in the breeze. "They're all asleep. Come on — hurry!"

Maximilian grunted. More rustling of cloth.

Silence.

Priscilla gave a faint groan.

Facing away from the fire, Sartain slowly lifted his head and turned to gaze over his right shoulder. The two lovers lay together, about five feet on the other side of the fire, old Tio about ten feet away on their left, the *bandido* uncle ten feet on their right, tied to a tree.

A blanket half-covered Maximilian and

Priscilla. They both lay on their sides, spooned against each other. The blanket had fallen to the girl's waist, exposing her breasts.

The pale orbs sloped toward the ground, jostling as Maximilian took the girl from behind, thrusting his hips ever so slowly and quietly up against her rump.

Maximilian grunted softly as he worked, holding her right hip with his hand. Priscilla breathed raspily. Her blond hair quivered as she rocked forward and back.

"Oh," Priscilla whispered, placing both hands on the ground and thrusting her rump up higher to receive her lover's mast. "Oh, oh, oh . . ."

"Shh!"

"I *am*!"

"Shhh!"

Priscilla giggled, showing her teeth in the darkness, squeezing her eyes closed as Maximilian continued to thrust against her.

"Oh," Priscilla said again, after a time, throatily. She dropped her head forward, hair spilling toward the ground.

Maximilian levered himself up higher with his left knee, pushing against her more forcefully, his long, dark-brown hair tumbling down his right shoulder. Priscilla turned her head to one side, and Maximilian kissed her. They kissed for a long time as the boy continued to thrash against her. Priscilla pulled her lips from his and reached back to place her right hand against his cheek, a celestial smile of carnal pleasure showing on her face in the starlight.

Then she jerked her head forward, and placed both hands on the ground, whispering, "Oh, Lord!"

Maximilian grunted and thrust himself against her hard, and held her fast against him by both her hips. He quivered. Priscilla had fallen silent as the boy spent his seed and she quietly enjoyed her pleasure.

Maximilian sighed throatily. He kissed the girl's right shoulder and sank down onto the ground. Sartain lay his head back down on his saddle, ashamed of himself for having watched and noting a frustrating tightness in his own trousers.

He glanced at where Jasmine lay five feet away from him, facing him. Her eyes were open. He thought he could see her chest rising and falling sharply as she breathed. As though suddenly realizing he was watching her, she closed her eyes and rolled abruptly away from him.

Sartain grinned.

Then he went back to work on the rawhide.

■ ■ ■ ■

Old Tio sniffed the wind and then lifted his head abruptly from the underside of his saddle. He turned toward Sartain and widened his eyes in shock. Sartain had the morning fire going, smoke skeining into the air over this niche in the rocky hills.

"*Ay, caramba,* I'm an old fool!" intoned the Mexican. "No wonder I never found the treasure. My senses are as dull as my prick."

Now both exhausted lovers, Maximilian and Priscilla, lifted their own heads from their saddles. When they saw Sartain sitting on a rock and poking a stick into the fire, Jasmine sitting beside him and pouring water from a canteen into a speckled blue coffee pot, they both cursed — one in Spanish, the other in English.

Automatically, Maximilian reached for his Winchester '73.

"Don't be an idiot," Sartain warned him through a growl. He raised his hands to reveal the bloody swatches of skin below his sleeve cuffs. "Rope works better."

"No!" Priscilla cried, throwing herself into her lover's arms, as though to shield him from a bullet. "If you kill Max, you'll have to kill me, too!"

"Don't be so damned dramatic," Sartain said, poking the fire again with his stick.

"He's not going to shoot Max," Jasmine said. "When we were sent down here, we didn't realize the situation. Apparently, you hid your love for each other very well from your father."

"Oh, he knows," Priscilla said, pulling away from Maximilian. "That's why we ran away — Max and me. When my father caught us together, he had Max horse-whipped and threatened to kill him if he ever saw us so much as looking at each other. And he told me next time I would get the whip, too . . . after I was forced to watch my lover die!"

"Figures," the Cajun said. "I had a real bad feeling about that coot. Now I know why." He sighed and tossed his stick into the fire. The coffee pot had started whooshing on the glowing coals. "As soon as we've had a cup of coffee, maybe a few bites of your javelina, if you don't mind sharing, we'll be saying *vaya con dios*."

"You're just going to ride out of here?" Maximilian asked with a skeptical frown.

"That's right," said the Revenger.

"Without fulfilling your job?"

"It'll be a first for me, but I'll get over it."

He glanced at Jasmine, who turned her

mouth corners down at him as she continued to clean her rifle.

"Pssst!" It was the old reprobate, Uncle Hector, sitting up and holding his arms out toward Sartain, as though beseeching the Cajun to cut his ties. He chuckled through his teeth.

Sartain gave a mirthless chuff. "You're their problem now, Hector."

"Please, *señor,*" Hector urged, canting his head toward his shoulder. "They'll kill me."

"And that'll be too good for you," Jasmine told him, removing the pot from the flames and tossing a couple of handfuls of coffee into the water.

"Do not worry, you cur," said old Tio. "We'll make sure you get a good, long look at the treasure before we kill you. We might even allow you to assist us in hauling a wagonload back to the church."

Sartain felt it was time to break the news; he couldn't very well not tell them that their friend the *padre* was dead.

"About the church," he said, speaking in low, dark tones. "If you head back there, you're not going to like what you find."

Priscilla gasped.

"What?" said Maximilian, awfully, his eyes wide and horror-stricken.

"That's where we met up with Uncle Hector," Jasmine said, scowling at the old killer.

Slowly, Maximilian, Priscilla, and old Tio turned their heads toward Uncle Hector, as well. Hector grimaced, sweat trickling down his cheeks.

Old Tio bellowed Spanish epithets as he pulled his pistol and pumped three rounds into Uncle Hector's chest.

After two weeks of hard, hot, dusty riding, Sartain and Jasmine crossed the Rio Grande and rode into the little village of San Rafael shaded by poplars and tamarisks. They checked into the only hotel in town.

Each ordered baths sent to their rooms.

They met down in the hotel's brush-covered *galleria* in time to enjoy the cooling night breeze scratching in off the desert.

They hadn't spoken much about what had happened down in Mexico, but now Jasmine sipped her tequila and turned to the Revenger. "Where will you go now?"

Sartain sipped his own shot, and chuckled, running his hands back through his still damp hair. "Good question. Here's a better one. What're you going to tell the governor?"

Jasmine held her shot glass up close to her cheek. Pooching her ripe lips out pensively, she turned the glass slowly in her hand. "The truth." She turned to Sartain. "That's best — don't you think?"

"Might get you fired."

She regarded him strangely, wrinkling the skin above the bridge of her fine nose.

"You were supposed to kill me down there," he said, leaning back in his chair. "After I'd killed Maximilian."

He waited.

She continued to gaze at him strangely.

"Am I right?"

Jasmine took another sip of the tequila and set the glass on the table. "How did you know?"

"Why else would he have sent you? Just to confirm that his stepson was dead?" The Cajun shook his head. "Nah. He wouldn't have sent a beautiful woman for that menial task. He sent a beautiful woman to kill me, knowing I got a powerful weakness for beautiful women. I'd give you my back sooner than I would some dude from McDougal's office. He sure as hell wouldn't have sent a soldier. That's why you've been so cold, this entire ride. You knew you were going to have to shoot me."

"All right," she said, mildly. "There you have it. I was going to kill you."

"But you didn't. Why not?"

Her gaze wavered. She looked off across the town's little, cobbled square where an old lady in a black dress and *reboso* was filling a clay pot from the stone fountain fronting the obligatory, copper-colored adobe church. A brown mongrel pup was rising onto its back legs to sniff the pot.

A brown-robed priest came out of the church, smiling and gesturing to the old woman to let him help her with such a heavy pot. The pup barked at the man and backed off warily.

The priest laughed.

Jasmine smiled at the scene in the square and then she turned her head back quickly to the Revenger, tossing her hair as she did and resting her chin on the heel of her hand. She looked fresh and rosy after her bath. Her thick hair was only slightly damp. She must have brushed it dry on her room's small balcony.

"I don't do everything a man asks of me, Mr. Sartain."

"Even the governor of New Mexico Territory?"

"Not when it goes against my conscience. The governor overestimated me, I'm afraid. It will all be in my report. If Mr. Pinkerton doesn't like what he reads, then he and I will fork paths. I've been considering going into business for myself, anyway." She narrowed her eyes, causing them to crease at the corners. Both pearl orbs fairly smoldered. "Know this, Mr. Sartain. I didn't not shoot you because I thought you didn't deserve a bullet. While I discovered down in Mexico that you are human, after all, you're still a killer."

"I didn't kill your father, Jasmine."

She snapped a surprised look at him.

"Jasmine Gallant. Daughter of Jim Gallant, United States marshal out of Denver." Sartain nodded slowly. "I finally remembered where I'd heard the name before. Jim Gallant was shot down coming out of the Denver Federal Building with his young daughter. The man's wife, the girl's mother, had died earlier that winter, and he took his daughter out for lunch nearly every day. Three men seeking revenge on the marshal, because he'd tracked down one of the men's brothers —"

"Cousins," she corrected.

". . . because he'd tracked down one of the men's *cousins* and brought him to trial, after which he was promptly, rightfully hanged."

Jasmine sighed as she sat back in her chair. "My, you have a good memory."

"Wasn't all that long ago. It was a big story. Ran in all the papers." Sartain dug a half-smoked cheroot from his shirt pocket.

"I wasn't one of them, Jasmine."

"No," she said, shaking her head and staring down at the table, tears glazing her eyes. "No — you weren't one of *them.* But you are of their sort."

Sartain scratched a match to life on the table. Again, he shook his head. "Not even close. You learned that down in Mexico. That's why you didn't turn one of your pretty little pistols on me." He lit the cheroot, blowing smoke and tossing the match out into the courtyard. "And killing me won't bring him back."

"Killing doesn't bring anyone back," she said, tears rolling down her cheeks. She sniffed, brushed her hand across her face, and gave him a pointed look. "Does it, Mike?"

She sobbed and turned away as though ashamed of the emotion.

"No," he said, taking a long drag on the cheroot, feeling a dull knife of old misery prick his heart. "No, it don't."

She hung her head, weeping. Sartain scraped his chair back, rose, and knelt beside her. He wrapped his arm around her, and held her as she cried.

Later, after a few more drinks and *carnitas tacos* for supper, they went upstairs. Sartain turned to his door, expecting to see her turn to her own room across the hall. Instead, she sidled up to him and placed her hand in his. Her eyes sparkled in the light from a single near candle.

He felt something cold in the palm of his hand. He opened it.

A twenty-dollar gold piece glinted up at him.

San Juan Bushwhackers

Chapter One

Mike Sartain, the Revenger, heard the clipped screech of the bullet half a blink before the shot tore into the roof of the well from which he'd been winching up a bucket of fresh water. It hammered the moldering wood only six inches from his head.

As the bark of the bushwhacker's bullet reached his ears and bits of wood from the well's roof flew in all directions, the big Cajun released the winch handle.

He threw himself hard right to hit the ground behind the well's stone coping. The filled bucket hit the water with a hollow thud and a splash. Behind Sartain, his big buckskin stallion, Boss, whinnied his disdain for the rifle's bark.

The Revenger knew how he felt.

The buckskin wheeled and ran, trailing his bridle reins, kicking up dust in the street of this remote and somewhat eerie mountain ghost town somewhere on the southwestern flank of Colorado's San Juan Mountains.

Another bullet smashed the far side of the well, followed close on its heels by the rifle's echoing blast.

Sartain rose to a knee, flicking the keeper thong free from over the hammer of his big LeMat revolver outfitted with a twelve-gauge shotgun shell in a stout barrel beneath the main .44-caliber barrel, and took hasty aim at the first man-shape he saw. He triggered three quick rounds, the heavy pistol leaping and roaring in his hand, smoke billowing over the top of the well to be trapped by the pitched roof, peppering the Cajun's nose.

Between Sartain's second and third shots, he'd heard a muffled grunt. As he'd triggered his third shot, he saw the man facing him from a gap between two weathered log buildings. The shooter twisted around and stumbled sideways into the gap. The rifle in the man's hands sagged and finally dropped as the son of a bitch turned full around and stumbled away from the man he'd tried to beef from bushwhack.

Sartain considered a fourth round, then thought better of it.

Holding the smoking LeMat in front of him, he straightened and walked out from behind the well. He strode quickly across the street, keeping the big popper aimed at the man who continued stumbling down the ten-foot gap between the two buildings, both of which sagged on their short stone pylons with forlorn abandonment.

The man was dragging his boot toes. As he stumbled out of the gap, the watery sunlight revealed the bloodstains on the back of his tan leather vest. He took two more halting steps and then gave a groan and dropped to his knees.

Sartain stepped over the ambusher's rifle, a .38-40 Winchester, and walked down through the gap littered with bits of ancient trash. He moved around the bushwhacker to face him. The man, still on his knees, stared straight ahead, lower jaw sagging. His black, low-crowned Stetson lay on the ground beside him. A pair of steel-framed spectacles with one cracked lens drooped from one ear.

The man's eyes were light blue. He had a ginger, soup-strainer mustache and thick muttonchops. His thin hair of the same color was carefully trimmed. His skin was soft and on the pale side, though his nose was sunburned. A gold watch chain sagged from a vest pocket. There was something of a dude about him, the Cajun silently opined.

He might have been thirty-five, forty. He

wasn't going to see fifty.

"Why?" Sartain said, keeping the LeMat aimed at the man's head, though he'd obviously taken the venom out of him.

The man continued to stare straight ahead, as though he didn't know Sartain was standing nearly in front of him. Blood issued from the two rounds in his chest, soaking the ends of his string tie and the pinstriped cotton pullover shirt he wore beneath the vest. Two cartridge belts were cinched around his waist; two holsters bristled with Remington revolvers.

"Why?" Sartain said again, louder this time, gritting his teeth.

He felt an odd amalgam of fury at nearly having gotten his head blown off, and sympathy for a dying man. A man who was likely just then sifting through all the meaningful moments in his fast-fading life, taking one more look before the long night closed over him.

The man turned to Sartain. He gritted his teeth, flared his nostrils, enraged. He had a chipped eyetooth.

He appeared to try to say something, stretching his lips back, trying to get his vocal cords to work. But then his eyelids fluttered closed. He dropped straight forward, not breaking his fall in the least. He hit the ground with a resolute thud and sighed out his last breath, jerking slightly.

He lay flat against the ground, arms close against his sides.

Sartain stared down at him. "Come on, you son of a bitch — why'd you try to grease me?" He kicked the dead man's side. "Who *are* you?"

The man lay inert. His head was turned toward Sartain, his eyes half-open and glassy. A blood pool grew beneath him.

The Revenger looked around. If there was one bushwhacker, there could be more, though he thought he'd probably know by now if this man had been riding with anyone. Then he had a strange sensation, his spine turning chill, as though someone were watching him, maybe planting a pair of rifle sights on him.

Presently, hooves thudded somewhere to his left. He jogged through a stand of dusty pines and cedars, crossed a wash and then ran through more pines and cedars, and stopped. A horse was just then cresting a rocky ridge about two hundred yards away, heading northeast.

The rider was a blur from this distance. All Sartain could see of the horse was a black patch on its left flank, which glinted briefly in the high-altitude sunlight just before horse and rider plunged down the opposite side of the ridge.

Sartain raised his hand holding the LeMat and ran his blue chambray shirtsleeve across his forehead. Still staring after the rider, he cursed and said, "Now . . . who in the hell are *you* . . . ?"

Sartain found his would-be killer's horse in a corral with a lean-to stable a short walk from where the man lay dead.

The horse was a sleek sorrel gelding, well cared for and both saddled and bridled, though its bit had been slipped and its saddle cinch had been loosened. The horse didn't seem overly spooked to see someone other than its own rider entering the corral, which flanked what had once been a three-story mud-brick hotel. The corral was a bit tumbledown, and brush had grown against its weathered rails.

The horse whickered a few times as the Cajun went through the dead man's saddlebags and blanket roll, looking for anything that identified the rider. He'd already gone through the dead man's pockets and found nothing more than a few coins, a single playing card with the name Elvira Houston penciled on one corner, and a broken comb.

There wasn't much more in the saddlebags but cooking gear and some coffee, flour, and fatback. There was nothing in the man's possibles that identified him. Not even a bill of sale for the groceries. All he could find that might remotely hint at his identity was a spare, holstered revolver wrapped up in his bedroll.

The initials J.L.F. had been scratched into the worn walnut grip. The initials probably didn't mean much. The gun looked old, and the initials could have been scratched there by a previous owner.

Still, the initials gave the Revenger *something* to go on.

And then there was the woman's name — Elvira Houston. Like the initials on the gun, the name might or might not mean anything, but it was all the Cajun had. What he'd do with the bits of information, he had no idea.

He wasn't sure what to do with the horse, either. No point in leaving it alone here in this ghost town. Deciding he'd take it with him and turn the sorrel over to the first livery he came to, he led the mount out of the stable and onto the deserted main street, tying it to a worn hitching post near the well. The horse blew and switched its tail, now a little uneasy about the turn of events.

It seemed a trusting beast, however, and took the stranger in stride.

The Cajun patted the horse's neck, and talked to it a little, letting it get used to him; he had no grudge against the horse, only the horse's rider. He walked back out to the well and stared off in the direction his own mount had run after the first rifle shot.

He placed two fingers between his lips, and whistled. After about thirty seconds, hoof thuds rose. Then Boss appeared, moving tentatively around a dogleg in the deserted street, head down, ears twitching, occasionally stepping on his drooping reins.

The big buckskin wasn't taking any chances.

"Come on, you old cayuse," Sartain urged, beckoning. "It's all clear." He glanced around at the abandoned buildings nearly surrounding him, narrowing one dubious eye. "I think . . ."

As the horse continued forward, taking its time, a cautious cast to its copper eyes, Sartain returned to the job he'd started when he'd been so rudely interrupted. He winched up a bucket of water, set it on the ground by the well, and cupped several dripping handfuls of the cold, refreshing liquid to his lips.

When he'd slaked his thirst, he plunged

his head into the water, corkscrewing it, giving his face and scalp and the back of his neck a good scrubbing with his fingers, ridding himself of three days' worth of trail grime.

He'd ridden down from Deadwood in the Black Hills, where he'd been sent to kill a man for an older gent out of Denver whom the other man had shot and paralyzed. The older gent, Mike McCarthy, was a liveryman, and he'd been innocently waiting in line at the bank when the owlhoot, Bob Norman Thomas, an outlaw out of the Dakota Territory, had held up the teller and shot him dead.

Mike McCarthy, raising his hands above his head along with the bank's half-dozen other customers, had simply said, "Now, wha'd you have to go and do that for?"

It had been an automatic response to the pointless killing of a young man whom McCarthy had known. Bob Norman Thomas's response had been to turn around, laughing, and shoot McCarthy from nearly point blank range, shredding his guts and severely injuring his spine.

For that, Mike Sartain had ridden up to Deadwood on the trail of Thomas, and shot not only Thomas but the brother he'd been riding with. He'd left their bodies to cool near their coffee fire in a fringe of Douglas firs not far from Pheeter's Station, just south of the diggings and hurdy-gurdy houses of Deadwood.

Then he rode away, satisfied with another job well done.

Because that's who he was — Mike Sartain, the man who exacted revenge for those who could not.

The newspaper scribblers called him the Revenger.

Scribblers with a sense of humor had dubbed him "the Ragin' Cajun."

Now the big, handsome, curly-headed man from New Orleans slipped Boss's bit from his mouth. He intended to bury the man he'd shot, so he'd likely be here a while. Since the sun was edging behind the high, fir-clad western ridges, he might have to spend the night, though he didn't relish the idea.

He wasn't too proud to admit that the old ghost town, an abandoned mining camp whose heyday had long since come and gone, gave him the fantods. There was an unsettling sound to the wind blowing through the town, raking across empty window frames and fluttering over loose roofing shakes, occasionally giving a rusty shingle chain a chilling squawk.

Dust rose now and then, and an ancient, yellowed newspaper fluttered just above the ground to paste itself to the stone pylons of a small cabin that boasted a sign over its porch announcing in badly faded letters: AUNT JENNY'S HOUSE OF FORBIDDEN DELIGHTS.

Aunt Jenny's empty windows stared blackly out at Sartain, like the empty eye sockets of a dead man's skull. Tattered, filthy curtains jostled in the rising breeze, casting shadows, some of which almost looked like phantoms skulking around the windows to peer out at the stranger by the well.

In the darkening mountains around the town, a coyote lifted a long, mournful wail.

Sartain shuddered as he winched up another bucket of water. He wasn't usually the spooky sort, but this town had hiked his short hairs even as he'd first ridden into it. Hard Winter, a beaten-up sign had pronounced it. Likely a right fitting handle. Maybe the hard winters were why it was dead.

But the hard winters weren't why the place made him shiver. There was something sinister about the defunct settlement. Sartain wasn't normally the superstitious sort, though he was from a superstitious place —

the whores who'd raised him in the New Orleans French Quarter were some of the most superstitious folks he'd ever run in to, and he'd been all over Appalachia during the war — but he could feel a foreboding deep in his Cajun bones.

There was something off-kilter about this place. He'd be glad to get shed of it. He would have hightailed it straightaway if he hadn't felt compelled to dig the dead bushwhacker a shallow grave. The man sure as hell didn't deserve it, and Sartain wasn't one to shed any tears or even bury men who came that close to trimming his wick. But there'd been something about this gent that had compelled him to give him at least a slightly better send-off than he deserved.

He wasn't sure what that was.

Maybe it was just the fact that he hadn't *looked* like a cold-blooded killer. Maybe he thought it was possible the man had made an honest mistake, though plenty of men had come gunning for the Revenger in the past. He'd had a bounty on his head after he'd killed the soldiers who'd raped and murdered his girl and her grandfather.

Sartain filled his canteen from the bucket and watered both horses. He unstrapped his folding shovel from his saddle, walked back to where he'd left the dead man . . .

and stopped dead in his tracks.

The expired bushwhacker was not where he'd left him.

CHAPTER TWO

Under his breath, Sartain said, "Holy shit."

He looked around. He must have made a mistake, become disoriented by the moving of the late-day shadows. But then he saw the blood pool in the sand and gravel where the body had obviously been.

The Cajun's heart raced, skipping beats.

He dropped the shovel and palmed his LeMat, clicking back the trigger. He turned full around, slowly, probing every nook and cranny around him for another would-be ambusher. Seeing nothing out of sorts — except for a missing body, that was — he moved slowly toward the bloodstain that had turned brown now as the blood had soaked into the ground and semi-dried.

The blood was there. But the body was not.

Someone had carted it off.

Sartain inspected the ground around the stain. He couldn't find the direction in which the man had been dragged. The ground was broken up around the stain, so it didn't leave much of a sign. He thought he saw what could have been scuffmarks possibly made by the heels and spurs of the dead man's boots.

On the other hand, those marks could have been natural, or made a long time ago. This back alley had been worn hard by the folks who'd once populated the boomtown.

One thing was for sure — the dead man was gone. *Someone* had carted him off.

Who? And was the man or men still around?

Could it have been the man he'd seen fleeing on horseback?

Just then the sun slipped down behind the western peaks. Instant dusk, thick, purple shadows stretching flat and wrapping around the Revenger like a gloved hand. He holstered the LeMat but did not secure the keeper thong over the hammer.

He picked up the shovel and returned to where the horses milled by the well, facing each other over the empty water bucket. They could have been having a stare-down.

Sartain took a careful look around once more. The town was small, maybe three city blocks long with shacks, stock pens, and privies forming the ragged edges in all directions. There were eight- to twenty-foot gaps between most of the buildings.

Breaks where a man or men could be lurking, waiting for a clear shot.

The Cajun dropped the bucket back into the well, and took stock. It was getting too dark to ride far, but he'd rather ride a ways into the mountains before setting up camp for the night. The pines and firs beckoned. These empty buildings seemed to be chuckling silently, malevolently at him.

Besides, there were too many places where more bushwhackers could lurk out of sight here. He'd feel safer amongst the forested slopes beyond.

He walked over to shove the sorrel's bit back into its mouth, and stopped.

Frowning, he turned to stare east down the vacant street that had turned vanilla now as the buildings had turned the color of old saddle leather to either side of it. He spied movement out there, just beyond the town.

Then he heard again what he'd heard a moment ago, the faint clink of a bridle chain.

A horse and rider were approaching the town. They were a dark-brown blur until a fleeting ray of last light touched the crown of the rider's hat with gauzy salmon. The rider appeared to be slumped forward in his saddle. The horse loped with its head raised tensely, and half turned to one side. As it approached the well, Sartain could hear the thudding of its hooves growing louder.

"Now what in the hell . . . ?" the Cajun heard himself mutter, his stomach beginning to churn, adding to his overall unease about this ghostly place.

Horse and rider rode on into the town, almost disappearing in the thick shadows pushing into the street. They emerged again when the horse came to within fifty yards, and slowed. The horse gave a nervous whinny. Boss returned the cry, rippling his withers. The sorrel turned toward the newcomer, gave its tail a single, incredulous switch, and whickered.

Sartain placed his right hand on his LeMat but left the gun in its holster. As the horse and rider continued toward him, walking now, he looked around. This newcomer could be trying to distract him so another bushwhacker could take a shot at him.

Or maybe, slumped forward like he was, he was playing possum. Feigning injury.

Sartain went ahead and slid the LeMat from its holster, clicking the hammer back. He looked around again and then faced the newcomer as the horse drew to a stop about twenty feet away, lowering its head and blowing. Tan dust sifted around it.

It was a broad-chested, short-legged skewbald paint — a fine-looking animal, mostly pale dun lightly sprinkled with white. Likely not the horse he'd seen fleeing earlier. The rider was young and thin. He was slumped entirely forward against the paint's neck, his hat mashed against his forehead. Sartain could smell sweat lather on the horse. It had come far at a hard pace.

The rider's narrow shoulders rose and fell sharply. The young man was grunting and groaning softly, miserably.

"Who're you, kid?" the Cajun asked, stepping wide around the horse and casting another quick glance to his flank, half-expecting another would-be bushwhacker to step out from a break between buildings and throw down on him.

From the side, he could see blood trickling down from the kid's upper chest to form a narrow stream across the paint's wither. He was wounded, all right. Not faking it.

"What happened, kid?" Sartain said, stepping forward and reluctantly sliding the LeMat back into its holster. Again, he wouldn't secure the keeper thong over the hammer. He wanted the gun free for a quick, easy draw if needed.

The kid's face was turned toward Sartain. He had his eyes squeezed shut in misery. Now, as he lifted his head slightly from the pole of his horse, his hat tumbled to the ground. He was sandy-haired, sharp-chinned, with a lean, narrow face turned copper by the sun. He had a thumb-sized birthmark on his left cheek, slightly darker than the rest of his face.

A Schofield .44 rode in a soft leather holster up high on his left hip, on a cartridge belt half-filled with brass. Hide had been wrapped around the handle. An old-model Winchester carbine was sheathed on the left side of his horse.

"Help me, mister," the kid said. "Too . . . took a bullet about two miles back."

Sartain looked at the young man's bloody blue work shirt. He'd taken a bullet through his right suspender, it appeared. Up high on that side of his chest. Probably not a lung or heart shot, unless the bullet had danced around inside him after entering.

"Who shot you?"

The kid swallowed, grunted, and shook his head. "I don't know. Didn't see the bastard . . . uh . . . pardon my French. I don't usually cuss, but, holy cow, I sure didn't deserve that bullet! I'm just passin' through!"

He opened his watery, light-blue eyes to regard the Revenger pleadingly. "Can you help me down from my horse? I'm hurt miserable, and if I'm gonna die, I'd just as soon do it on the ground as up here on ole Taz."

Sartain took another careful look around. Not seeing anyone bearing down on him, though it was getting harder and harder to see anything out here now, he reached up and wrapped a hand around the young man's left forearm. The kid swung his right boot over the paint's rump. Sartain wrapped his hands around the kid's lean waist, easing him down to the ground.

The kid slumped forward against his horse, breathing hard.

Sartain kept a hand on the boy's shoulder, wondering what in hell he was going to do about this undesirable change of situation. He couldn't very well ride off and leave a wounded, possibly dying, young man behind to expire alone. Not without trying to lend a hand in some way. What he could do for the lad, however, he had no idea.

He supposed he could at least try to make him comfortable and see how bad the wound was, maybe give him a shot or two of whiskey to help ease the pain.

"Got a handle?"

"Dewey," the kid said, resting his arm on his saddle and leaning his forehead against his arm. "Dewey Dade from Alamogordo." He hadn't quite gotten that last out before his knees buckled. As he dropped, his horse sidestepped away from him, and Sartain had to grab him around the waist to keep him from falling belly down in the street.

He picked the kid up in his arms. The Cajun didn't figure he weighed over a hundred and forty. He looked around for somewhere to take the kid.

He considered the stable in which he'd found the bushwhacker's horse. Then he remembered seeing an old saloon and hotel that had two or three stories and that had also looked reasonably intact — at least, intact relative to the rest of the town.

There might still be a bed in the place.

He peered to the east, and saw the building on the street's north side roughly a block away. Starting to walk toward it with the kid in his arms, he whistled for Boss. The horse came trotting up behind him, following like a loyal dog. He wanted to keep near the horse and the Henry repeater sheathed on his saddle, in case he needed both.

He mounted the saloon's porch steps. It

was too dark to read the large wooden sign stretched across the second story, just above the broad front gallery, but he remembered that it read: MELVIN PEPPER'S KICKING HORSE SALOON & HOTEL, in letters that probably could have been seen from a quarter-mile away in the saloon's and the town's prime.

Now, however, the letters were ghostly representations of their former selves, barely discernible against the rotting, sun-blistered wood.

Sartain wasn't surprised to find the front door boarded over — several planks nailed at angles across it. Several more were stretched over the front window. The gallery itself was in poor shape, missing several boards in the floor, so that the Cajun had to watch his step if he didn't want to fall through to the ground beneath it.

Tumbleweeds, dust, sand, and old trash littered the place.

Not seeing an easy way in the front door, and figuring he'd probably end up taking the kid to the stable, after all, he dropped down off the gallery and walked around to the saloon's rear.

There was a small door back there, atop a few stone steps. He gave a half-hearted nudge to the metal and leather latch and was surprised to hear it click.

The hinges groaned as the door gave a shudder and swung inward.

"Well, I'll be damned."

Sartain moved on into the earthen-floored room before him. It must have been a storeroom. There was enough light pushing through a dusty, cobwebbed window to his right to show him the way to another door on the other side of the room.

This one opened, as well. Now he found himself at the rear of what appeared the main saloon, with a stairs angling up over his left shoulder.

He walked haltingly down the short, narrow hall abutted by the stairs on one side and a wall on his right from which a moose head stared dubiously down at him through the misty shadows. He stopped near the newel post at the bottom of the stairs, and stared into the room before him.

From what he could see in the dusky light, the saloon was still outfitted with a fancy bar, back bar, and a half-dozen or so tables onto which chairs were still overturned. So far, so good, the Revenger thought, starting up the stairs with the groaning kid in his arms. If the downstairs was still reasonably intact, there was a good chance the upstairs would be, as well.

It was.

At least, as far as the Cajun could tell. He stopped at the first door he came to, turned the knob, and nudged the door with his boot toe. The door groaned open. Sartain saw the outline of a bed before him. He gentled the kid onto it and then stepped back, looking around the room.

Surprisingly well appointed for a ghost town, he thought.

He dug a match out of his shirt pocket, scraped it to life on his thumbnail, and held it high. The watery light revealed a bracket lamp near the door. He lit the lamp and looked around again. He'd be damned if the room didn't look lived in. There was a dresser, a green-painted armoire, a room divider, and a washstand complete with porcelain bowl and water pitcher. A towel even hung from a rail, and a good-sized mirror hung above the towel.

He turned to the bed. It looked not only well kempt but freshly made.

Either the ghosts in this town were damned neat and tidy and preferred all the comforts of home, or someone living and breathing was haunting Hard Winter.

On the bed, the kid groaned.

Sartain turned to him. The kid writhed from side to side, moaning.

"Kid, you hang tough," the Cajun said. "I'm gonna go out and fetch my bottle. I'll be right back."

"Mister?" the kid said as Sartain started for the door.

The Revenger turned back to him.

"You ain't gonna go off and leave me to die here alone, are ya?"

"No, I'm not."

"I'm awful scared. I'm hurtin' bad and I'm just plain scared. I don't wanna die!"

"Don't blame you a bit, son," Sartain said. "I'll be right back."

He started again toward the room's open door but stopped when Boss lifted a long, warning whinny from the street fronting the place.

"Ah, shit," Sartain groused. "Now what?"

Chapter Three

Sartain went back downstairs, the LeMat again in his hand.

Strange sounds were coming from the front of the saloon. Thudding and squawking sounds. As he walked through the saloon, the bar on his left, the tables on his right, he could tell someone was on the front gallery. They were removing the planks from over the front door — which was actually two doors with beveled and colored glass still in their top panels.

The squawking and thudding continued. The Cajun stood near the doors, waiting, the LeMat in his hand, an incredulous scowl on his face. He could feel the reverberations of the toil of the man or men through the floorboards.

Finally, the last board was removed from over the door, and tossed onto the gallery floor.

"Ouch!" said a voice.

The Revenger's scowl deepened. Had that been a young woman's voice?

"Shit!" she said, as though to herself. She must have injured herself on a nail.

Sartain could see her silhouette through the colored glass, the top glass squares showing the single word "Saloon" from the backside. One of the doors opened halfway. The girl's shadow moved toward Sartain. She wore a hat and a coat, and he could see long hair hanging down past her shoulders. She half-turned as she closed the door.

As she started to turn back toward the drinking hall, Sartain scratched another match to life on his thumbnail, and held it high.

The girl screamed, stumbled back against the doors, stretching her arms out to both sides, and fell to her rump on the floor.

Sartain stepped forward, the match sputtering between his thumb and index finger.

The young woman's battered Stetson tumbled off her left shoulder to reveal a rich, messy spill of chocolate-colored curls framing a clean-lined face with a straight nose and resolute jaw.

"Who're you?" Sartain asked.

"Who'm I?" she said, dark eyes sparking in the match light. "Who're *you,* you son of a bitch?"

"Sartain."

Just then, the match burned down to his fingers. He dropped it. Darkness closed over him and the girl once more. He heard her give an angry grunt. There was the scuffing of boots and then she was on him in two-fisted fury, bulling into him while smashing her fists against his face.

"Hold on!" he said, dropping the LeMat to get hold of her.

Before he could grab her flailing arms, which he could barely make out in the darkness before him, she'd shoved him back onto a table. Her supple body pressed against his. Her coat fell open, and he could feel the yielding curves of her breasts loosely restrained behind a blouse.

Sartain got hold of her right hand and was surprised to feel the cold, hard, irregular bulk of a pistol in it.

"No!" she cried through gritted teeth.

Sartain jerked the pistol free of the girl's surprisingly strong grip. As he did, he fell back and sideways, rolled off the table, and hit the floor with a *bang!* The girl came with him, landing on top of him, getting to her knees, straddling him, and going back to work on his face with her fists.

Sartain tossed her gun away, then heard it hit the floor and slide.

"I wasn't open, you son of a bitch!" she railed. "No one comes in here when I'm not *open*! I saw the horses, but I didn't think whoever belonged to 'em would be ill-mannered enough to break into my *place*!"

Sartain cursed when one of her fists split his upper lip, and the coppery taste of blood touched his tongue. Her silky hair raked him as her fists battered him. None of the punches did any real damage. She was a small girl, though tough and as resolute as her jawline. His biggest problem was trying to restrain her without hurting her.

If this place belonged to her, he was the interloper here, after all.

Finally, he managed to grab both her wrists again, instantly stopping the onslaught. He pushed up to a half-sitting position and rolled the girl onto her back. He straddled her, holding her wrists taut against the floor above her head.

"Now, hold on!" he grunted, pressing his pelvis taut against hers.

She bucked up against him, evoking an involuntary male response in his loins.

"Hold on!" he said. "I'm not your enemy, miss. I just needed a bed for a younker who rode into your fair town with a bullet in his shoulder. He's upstairs. He needs tendin' by someone who knows what they're doin' — which I don't. My name is Mike Sartain, and I was just passin' through."

When he felt her go somewhat slack beneath him, he climbed off of her and lit a lamp bracketed to a ceiling support post. Turning up the wick and spreading a dull, yellow glow around the room, he glanced at her. She'd pushed up onto her elbows. Her hair was in her face. She shook it back.

"Why didn't you say so?" she said.

The Cajun chuckled.

She started climbing to her feet. He went over and gave her his hand, which she accepted. "How did you get in here?" she said when she was standing before him, looking him up and down, critically, as though seeing him for the first time.

"Back door."

She turned her mouth corners down. "Yeah, it doesn't lock. Last time I left for the week, I must've forgot to slide the sideboard in front of it. I only open up on weekends."

"I'm glad you forgot about the sideboard. Like I said Miss . . ."

"McKee. Dixie McKee."

"Like I said, Miss McKee, I got a young man upstairs with a bullet in his shoulder."

She tucked her hair behind one ear and

narrowed a suspicious eye at him. "He ride with you?"

"No. Why?"

"Because you got trouble written all over you."

"You're not the first to tell me that."

"Are you?"

Sartain poked his hat up off his forehead. "Not tonight. Not here. Unless somebody tries to bushwhack me again."

"Huh?"

"Never mind." Sartain shook his head. "Is there a sawbones around, Miss McKee?"

"Does this place look like it still has a sawbones, Mr. Sartain?" She had a salty, frank air about her. It mixed well with her feminine attractiveness.

"Well, it doesn't *look* from outside that it still has a saloon and a hotel. You do a damn good job of disguising that fact."

"Best way to keep scavengers out."

Dixie McKee wrinkled her nose at him snidely. It had a few small freckles on it, standing out against her tan in the lamplight.

"Let me get a pan of water and some cloths and some whiskey," she said. "I'll go up and take a look at him. I was raised with two brothers twelve miles from here. There weren't any sawbones close around. Leastways, no good ones. So Ma and I did all the doctoring in the family. I keep a kit up in my room."

Sartain had been trying to keep his eyes off her cleavage, which was revealed when her blouse had come partly open during their tussle atop the table. His eyes had strayed on their own, however. She followed his gaze and then turned away, pulling the top of her blue blouse closed and reprimanding him with a stern look.

"You said you weren't trouble," she said as she headed for the bar.

"I said I wasn't trouble here tonight, Miss McKee," the Cajun said, giving her a wink. "I didn't say I wasn't a man."

She gave him another critical up-and-down, as though she were appraising a dangerous animal. "Yes, I know what men are all about." She'd said it like she knew, all right, and didn't like it.

She walked around behind the bar, reached down, and then set a rusty porcelain pan atop the varnished oak. "How about if you go out back and fill this pan with water from the rain barrel? I'm going to need plenty of water to clean that wound. You can bring in some wood, too, and get that potbelly stove fired up good and hot. Gonna be a cold night, and I'm gonna need some hot water."

Sartain grabbed the pan off the bar. "You got it."

"Then you can get those chairs down off those tables and light my lamps down here. I have a handful of regular weekend customers. More on Saturdays than Fridays, but there'll be a few in tonight, most likely. There's a few prospectors and ten-cow cattlemen around here, and they like to come in and have a few drinks on the weekends. Mine is the only place around."

"Whatever I can do to help out."

"That's good enough for starters," Dixie said, heading upstairs with a bottle and a couple of rags. "Now, let's go see how bad off your friend is."

Sartain didn't see the point in reminding her that the wounded younker was not his friend. Dixie McKee was a headstrong girl. Once she got something in her head, you'd need a crowbar to lever it back out again.

And that might not even work.

Sartain fetched water from the well and brought a pan up to Dixie, who was busily tending the boy. The kid was out of his head now with shock, warning someone named Roamer that lightning struck in high places, "and they best get these beeves to lower ground or get lit up like firecrackers!"

"Why, he's just a boy," Dixie said to Sartain scoldingly, as she mopped up the blood around the young man's wound. "Nothing but a child."

The implication was that Sartain had corrupted him, somehow caused him to take that bullet.

"I know that, Miss McKee," the Cajun said. "But, like I said . . ." He let his voice trail off. She wasn't listening, and he didn't have a crowbar near big enough. "Never mind."

He went back downstairs, brought in several washtubs full of split aspen and pine, and started a roaring fire in the potbelly stove, which sat in the dead center of the saloon's main drinking hall. He filled a couple of iron kettles from the rain barrel, and set them on the stove. When he'd pulled all the chairs down off the tables, he went around the room to make sure all the lamps were lit.

Because the stove was heating the place up like a washhouse in mid-July, he opened the front door.

That's when he saw Boss, the kid's paint, and the dead bushwhacker's sorrel. All three horses were limned by the lamplight spilling out of the saloon behind him. They stood in the street, still saddled and in need of tending.

Sartain led the trio over to the stable in which he'd found the bushwhacker's mount. What he took to be the girl's mount was there — a handsome cream touched with dun speckles across its hindquarters. He saw no black on this horse, either, which made it unlikely that Dixie McKee had been the fleeing rider he'd seen earlier.

He also found a bin filled with oats, and another rain barrel.

He rubbed all three horses down carefully, then fed and watered them and shut them up in the stable. When he got back to the saloon, the water in both pots was boiling, and two men were sitting at one of the tables, regarding the big Cajun incredulously.

"Who're you?" one of them asked — a tall, hawk-nosed, horse-faced man in dusty trail garb. He wore a bowler hat. A red bandanna was knotted around his scrawny neck. Apparently, he couldn't find pants long enough to fit him, so he'd sewn otter skin to the cuffs.

"Sartain."

"Where's Dixie, Sartain?"

"Upstairs."

"What the hell's she doing upstairs?"

asked the other man, a beefy, red-faced, middle-aged gent in dusty trail garb similar to the string bean's. He had silver hair beneath his sweat-stained Stetson, and he wore a red-and-white checked shirt under a brown leather vest.

He grinned lasciviously. "She tryin' to earn a few more *pesos* on her back up there, is she?"

He slapped his thigh.

The string bean clouded up, rose tensely from his chair, and turned his fiery eyes on the beefy gent. "Don't you talk about Dixie like that, Slater! You hear me?" He slammed the end of his fist on the table. "Or you'll have *me* to answer to!"

Just then the wounded younker screamed in the room above Sartain's head, "Don't kill me! Oh, God — please don't kill me!" The plea was followed by a strangled, *"Noooooooooooo!"*

Chapter Four

"Holy Christ — what's happenin' up there?" said Slater as Sartain wheeled and ran to the stairs at the back of the room.

He took the steps three at a time. As he gained the second floor, he pulled the LeMat, cocked it, and thrust the kid's door open.

He stopped in the doorway, peering into the room lit by two lamps — one on the wall, another on a small table near the kid's bed. The kid lay back on his pillow, eyes shut, mouth half-open. Dixie McKee was crouched over him, half-sitting on a chair beside the bed, probing around in the kid's wound with long, bone-handled tweezers.

She glanced at Sartain, lowering her eyes to the LeMat in his hand. "Holster that hog-leg and give me a hand here." She made a face as she continued probing the wound. "I've almost got it."

As he moved slowly into the room, the

Cajun said, "I thought . . . heard him cry out . . ."

"He's out of his head. He woke up to find me about to probe around in his shoulder, and he went *loco* on me. He's out now." She glanced again, testily, at the Revenger, who holstered the revolver as he approached the bed. "Hurry — I need you to hold the wound open while I reach inside. I just about had the bullet but it slipped away."

Sartain crouched over the bed and took the handle of the tweezers in his right hand.

"Hold it tight. Good and tight," Dixie said. "Maybe use both hands. Pull down on the wound to give me some room to get my finger in there."

"What the hell's goin' on in here?" the thick man, Slater, asked over Sartain's right shoulder. The Revenger had been vaguely aware of Slater and the string bean following him up the stairs. Now they were both in the room, gazing inquisitively at the doings.

"Shut up," Dixie said. "Can't you see I'm busy?"

"Yeah, shut up, Slater — or I'll clean your clock, you cork-headed fool," admonished the tall string bean. "Can't you see Dixie's busy?"

Sartain did as the girl told him. She poked

an already bloody finger into the wound, leaning far forward and turning her head to stare at the big Cajun with grave concentration, wincing and chewing her rich bottom lip.

She toiled, moving her finger around in the wound for nearly a half a minute before, keeping that finger about halfway in the wound, she took the tweezers back from Sartain and used it to help her finger guide the bullet to the opening.

"Got it!" she said, holding the bloody chunk of lead up between her thumb and index finger. "Told you I could doctor a wound."

Sartain sighed with relief. "That you did, miss."

She grabbed an uncorked bottle off the table by the lamp, and splashed whiskey over the wound. The kid gave a long, ragged sigh, his eyelids fluttering, as the busthead turned the wound to fire.

"That's about all I can do." Dixie turned to the string bean. "Lonnie, run downstairs and stick the stove's poker into the flames. Get it good and hot. Glowing. Then fetch it back here *pronto.*"

"You got it, Miss Dixie," said Lonnie, wheeling.

He was a good head taller than the doorway, and he didn't duck enough. He smacked the top of his head hard, grunted, slapped a hand to his forehead, and continued running with a little less vigor than before.

"Who's he?" asked Slater, nodding at the wounded kid.

Dixie was dabbing up some of the blood around the wound with a whiskey-soaked cloth.

"Said his name's Dewey Dade from Alamogordo," Sartain said. "You ever see him in these parts?"

"Can't say as I have," Slater said. "Who shot him?"

"That was my next question for you," Sartain said.

Slater chuffed. "What — you think I shot him?"

"All I know is I was just passin' through here a few hours ago, and someone bushwhacked me. Damn near hit his target. And then this kid here rode into town with that chunk of lead in his shoulder."

"Who bushwhacked you?" Dixie McKee wanted to know, looking up at him from her work on the kid.

"I don't know. But he'll never bushwhack me or anyone else again."

"You shoot him?" asked Slater, closing

one eye.

"Yes, I did. Dudish sort of gent in trail garb. Didn't look like your regular cowpuncher. Had a trimmed beard and spectacles. Rode the sorrel I stabled with mine and the kid's horse out back."

Slater rubbed his jaw. "Dudish sort, huh? With glasses?" He and the girl shared a fleeting glance.

Sartain frowned. "You think you know him?"

Slater colored slightly. "Nah."

Sartain looked at Dixie. She turned her head away sharply and resumed mopping blood from around the kid's wound.

"What about you, Miss McKee?"

"I wouldn't know your dude from Adam's off ox, Mr. Sartain," Dixie said crisply but none too convincingly.

Lonnie returned with the glowing poker, interrupting the conversation. Sartain left the room and headed downstairs, scowling his consternation at the recent turn of events that had made his life a whole lot more complicated than it had been when he'd ridden into Hard Winter a few hours ago, merely wanting a cold drink of water for himself and his horse.

"If you had the sense of a stupid mule," he told himself, "you'd ride hell for leather out of here right now." He knew what trouble smelled like it. And he smelled it here.

But it wouldn't be wise to ride out in the mountain dark, which was the darkest kind of dark. Besides, he thought he'd heard distant thunder a while ago, when he'd been fetching wood for the stove.

He wasn't sure that he'd have ridden out of here even if there'd been a few hours of good light left and no storm on the way. He smelled trouble, all right. And he was curious about where it was coming from.

Who was the man who'd bushwhacked him and died for his sins? Who'd carted his body away? Who'd bushwhacked the kid, Dewey Dade from Alamogordo?

A new customer had entered Dixie's place while he'd been upstairs. A small Mexican man with thick, salt-and-pepper hair in elkskin leggings and a short, wool vest over a yellow and green plaid shirt. He'd draped a quilted elkskin mackinaw over his chair back.

Like the other two customers, Slater and Lonnie, the Mexican had served himself. He was sitting alone at a table near the front door, against the far right wall, facing Sartain but not making eye contact. He sat hunched over a tin cup. A brown paper cigarette smoldered in his right hand, which he lifted now to take a deep drag from the quirley, narrowing his eyes and gazing out the window beside him.

Sartain could do with a drink and a smoke himself.

Again hearing thunder rumbling, but from much closer this time, he went over to the woodstove and gave it a good stoking. Dixie had been right. The night had turned cold. He added several chunks of pine and then fetched more from outside, where it was beginning to rain — large, quarter-sized raindrops falling at an angle. He was good and damp by the time he got back inside.

When he'd filled the wood box near the stove, the little Mexican was helping himself from a bottle on the bar. The Mexican tossed a dime onto the counter, near where several others lay around the bottle, turned to Sartain, grinned broadly, and raised his tin cup in salute.

Wiry and bandy-legged from a life on horseback, he had large, vanilla-colored teeth edged with brown. Limping slightly, as though he had one bad knee, as did most cowpunchers his age, he returned to his chair and began building another cigarette from a small, burlap makings sack.

He seemed almost mesmerized by the rote

endeavor.

Sartain walked around the bar, hearing the rain hammer the front of the saloon. Through the open window, it looked like a gauzy curtain had been thrown over the front door, just beyond the gallery. Thunder peeled, and the floor leaped beneath the Cajun's boots. Dust sifted from cracks in the ceiling beams.

As Sartain poured himself a glass of whiskey, he noticed that neither the stout Slater nor the tall, horse-faced Lonnie had returned from the kid's room upstairs. He could understand why Dixie would still be up there — tending the kid — but why were the other two still up there? They must have had something private to talk about.

Something private regarding the bushwhacker whom Sartain had beefed?

As if reading his thoughts, they appeared on the stairs — Lonnie ahead of Slater. They were both cutting dubious looks toward the Cajun but otherwise doing their best, which wasn't good, at looking nonchalant. When they'd each retaken their seats at their table, Slater hauled a deck of playing cards from his shirt pocket, and started laying out a hand.

The Mexican smoked his new quirley as though it were the best tobacco he'd ever tasted and he wouldn't likely taste it again.

Sartain took his drink over to a table by the bar. He'd just started building his own quirley, hoping he'd enjoy his as much as the Mexican was enjoying his own, when Dixie came down the stairs, carrying the basin of bloody water. She walked over to the front door, and threw the bloody water out into the storm. She stood there, staring out for a time, shoulders tense.

She stepped backward as a man mounted the gallery deliberately, not like a man in a hurry to get out of the rain. As he stepped into the saloon, two more men came in behind him.

Dixie stood before them, eyeing the men skeptically, as the man who'd first entered, a tall man with a handlebar mustache and clad in a yellow rain slicker, doffed his gray *sombrero* and batted it against his thigh.

"I'll be damned if it don't pour in these mountains like someone up there's working up a sweat on the ole pump handle!" he intoned, adding a jovial whoop, as though he enjoyed nothing more than a good storm.

The other two were similarly dressed. They were all pretty close to the same height — lean, tall, hard-faced men. They all had considerable hair on their faces. They were each holding a rifle. Sartain could see holsters bulging under their dripping rain slickers. When they unbuttoned the slickers, he could see well-filled cartridge belts cinched around their waists.

"Look at you," the first man said, grinning at Dixie, who stood regarding him and the others testily. "Ain't you a sight for sore eyes!" She had her arms crossed on her breasts, and she had one boot cocked forward. She was tapping the toe of that boot on the floor.

"What're you doing here, Chick?" she asked the man.

He'd moved toward her, spreading one arm out as though to give her a hug. Now he frowned and let the arm drop to his side. "What're you talking about, honey? What am I doing here? What're you doing here?"

"I own this place," Dixie said. "Paid the back taxes on it, so I own it. You might have owned it once with Melvin Pepper, but Pepper's dead, and you let it go under."

"That's fine, that's fine," Chick said, grinning again and spreading his arms out again. "That ain't what I meant. I just meant that ain't no way to greet your best pal, Chick Beacham, sugar-bunny! Come here and give me a hug! Boy, do I need a hug!"

"Don't call me that," Dixie said, swinging

away from the man — who had outlaw written in every line carving the hard planes of his face — and walked toward the bar, setting the pan on top of it as she strode past.

She walked behind the bar, flushed with anger. She took the pan down the bar and tossed it onto the floor with a clang.

Outside, the rain continued hammering. Thunder peeled. Slater and Lonnie held their cards in their hands, but they weren't playing. They had their eyes on the three rain-soaked newcomers.

The Mexican didn't seem interested, however. He sat at his table, his eyes glazed with contemplation, staring straight ahead, slowly smoking his quirley and drinking his whiskey. He might have been in a different place altogether.

"Is that any way to treat your best pal?" Chick asked Dixie, who crossed her arms on her breasts and did not return his gaze. She stared straight across the room.

"I for one would like a drink," said one of Chick's partners, shrugging out of his rain slicker. He tossed the slicker onto the bar and leaned forward. "Set me up — will you, Dix?"

"Tell him to get out of here first," Dixie said tightly.

"Ah, shit," said Chick. "Is that how it's

gonna be?"

"Get him out of here, Earl," Dixie told the man leaning against the bar, "and I'll set you and Johnny both up. You'll be drinking on the house tonight. But you have to get him out of my place. I told him I'd never let him step foot in here again after what he did to the Pierson boy, and I mean it."

Chick strode angrily up to the bar and slammed his fist on top of it. "You shut up about that, goddamnit!" He pointed an angry finger across the bar at Dixie, who backed up a step and crossed her arms on her chest once more. "I told you to never mention it again, or you knew what I'd do to you!"

"Get out of my place, Chick!" Dixie screamed, clamping her hands over her ears and wildly shaking her head.

"Goddamnit!" Chick turned and began striding past Sartain, heading for the end of the bar with the intention of getting behind it.

Sartain put his left boot out. Chick's own left boot snagged it. Sartain whipped the man's foot up high. Chick dropped face-first on the floor with a loud, indignant grunt and a *boom!*

Chapter Five

Save for the storm outside, the room fell silent.

Chick lay belly down on the floor. He stared up at Sartain, wide-eyed, his ruddy, scarred face flushed with exasperation. It took him a few seconds to understand what had just happened. He'd probably never been treated so poorly; he was having trouble comprehending someone interfering in his nefarious affairs.

The other two outlaws, Earl and Johnny, stared at the Revenger with similar expressions. Johnny, slightly shorter than the other two, was still standing near the open door. He laughed once, suddenly, incredulously, girlishly.

Then his eyes widened as he stared down at Chick.

"I'll be damned!" He glanced at Earl standing by the bar, now facing Sartain. "Did he just do what I *think* he done?"

Earl didn't say anything. His lower jaw hung loose.

Chick continued to glare up at Sartain, who gazed mildly back at him. Slowly, his cheeks blazing red with humiliation, Chick gained his feet to stand over the Cajun, his broad chest rising and falling slowly as he breathed through flared nostrils.

"Mister," he said with mock concern, wrinkling the skin above the bridge of his nose, several veins showing in his leathery forehead, "you just made one *terrible* mistake."

Sartain said, "Nope. You did."

The LeMat was almost instantly in his hand. The others in the room probably only saw him twitch slightly, and then a blur of motion before the big popper was in his right hand and leveled steadily at Chick Beacham. He clicked the hammer back.

"You see," Sartain said, "telling me I made a big mistake was in fact *your* big mistake. I took it as a threat. Now, whether or not you aimed to follow up on said threat don't matter." He lowered the LeMat's barrel slightly.

Boom!

The LeMat hurled a .44 caliber bullet into the top of Chick Beacham's left boot, curling back the shredded leather around the hole. Smoke wafted. The loud report was absorbed by the building's stout walls, so that Beacham's shrill scream was nearly drowned by the storm.

He rose up off that foot so high that his head hit the ceiling, squashing the crown of his *sombrero* against the top of his head. He fell back against the bar, lost his footing, and again hit the floor with another loud *bang!*

"Goddamn!" said Earl.

He automatically reached for one of the two long-barreled pistols holstered on his hips. He didn't have it even half raised before the LeMat spoke again.

"Oh!" the outlaw cried, dropping the pistol and looking down at his belly.

Sartain had got to his feet and now he swung the smoking LeMat toward the outlaw standing by the door. Johnny had grabbed the handle of one of his own pistols, but now he released the weapon as though it were too hot to handle and thrust both arms in the air.

"Okay!" he shouted. "Okay, okay . . . ohh-*kayyy*!"

He reached so high that his fingers brushed the underside of the ceiling beam above his head.

Dixie stared slack-jawed at Sartain. She moved slowly forward to peer over the bar at Chick Beacham, who lay on one side, holding his bullet-torn right foot in both hands. Blood bubbled up out of the hole in the boot. Beacham writhed and cursed through gritted teeth, the veins in his forehead now appearing as though they were about to burst.

"You son of a bitch," he said tightly, with menacing softness. He rocked on his right hip. "Oh . . . you son of a bitch!"

Dixie closed her hand over her mouth in shock at what she was seeing. She laughed and lowered her hand as she said, "Careful he don't take that as a threat, Chick." She laughed again and looked at Sartain, her eyes bright with astonishment and humor. "Whether you mean to try and follow up on it or not."

Earl had now dropped to his knees. He was holding both hands over the hole in his belly from which blood oozed like oil from a fresh well. "Oh, no," he said in a strained, uncomprehending voice. "Oh, no. I don't . . . I don't think I'm gonna make it, Chick."

He lowered his head and fell face forward to the floor and lay still.

Sartain stood over Beacham. He held the big, smoking LeMat low by his side. It was about even with Beacham's head. The outlaw glanced at the impressive, deadly weapon and then glared darkly up at the man holding it.

Sartain said, "Who are you, Beacham?"

"I don't know," Beacham said tightly, through gritted teeth. "Who're you?"

"I'm a fella who was bushwhacked out by the well earlier. One of your boys wouldn't have done that, would they?" Sartain didn't think so. The bushwhacker hadn't looked like a man who'd ride with a rawhider like Beacham. But Sartain had nothing else to go on.

"My boys don't need to bushwhack nobody. Here, you got the drop on us, understand? If you'd fight fair, 'stead of trippin' folks like a girl, then you'd see just how much we don't need to bushwhack nobody!"

Sartain glanced at Johnny, still holding his hands above his head. "Best fetch your pard here, *amigo.* Get him on his horse and ride out. Leave your other friend. I'll tend to him when the storm dies. If I see either one of you ever again in this life, I'm going to do more than shoot Chick here in the foot, though I might go ahead and shoot the other one to amuse myself." He glared hard at the outlaw writhing before him. "But you won't feel the pain long, Chick — if you get my drift."

Chick shook his head. "This ain't over."

"You'd better hope it is."

"Oh, it's not!" Beacham said through a caustic laugh.

"Come on, Chick," Johnny said, helping Chick to his one good foot.

As Chick hobbled out with the help of his friend, Chick swung another searing glare over his shoulder at Sartain, "Oh, this is *far* from over!"

As he hopped, he accidentally rammed his injured foot against a chair. He stopped, stood balanced on one foot, and stared straight down at the floor, shoulders taut. His friend looked at him.

"You all right, Chick?"

Beacham drew a breath. His voice was pitched high as he said, "Goddamnit, will you look where you're goin', Johnny?"

"Sorry, Chick."

Beacham shook his head and then continued hopping until he and Johnny were outside in the rain and Sartain could hear the regular thumps of Chick Beacham hopping across the gallery on one foot. He stared at the open doorway until he saw the silhouettes of both men riding off to the west in the silvery rain.

Sartain looked around the room. The

Mexican was gone. He must have slipped out sometime during the dustup. The other two card-players, Slater and Lonnie, just then rose from their chairs. Slater was tucking his pasteboards back into a vest pocket and straightening his hat on his gray head.

"Reckon we'll be pullin' foot," he said.

"You ain't gonna stay the night?" Dixie asked. "Wet night, Slater. And it's a long ride back to your sawmill."

As he and Lonnie made for the door, Slater winked at Dixie and said, "That ride just seemed a whole lot drier and shorter. Much obliged, though, Miss Dixie. And good luck to you."

He glanced darkly at Sartain, and gave his head a quick shake. "Good luck to you, too, mister. I sure hope you got someone around who'll toss some daisies on your grave. Hell, every man deserves that."

And then he was out the door and crossing the gallery toward wherever he'd stowed his horse.

Lonnie stopped just inside the door and held his hat in his hands, looking sheepish, frustrated. "Good night, Miss Dixie."

"Good night, Lonnie."

"Maybe see you next weekend."

"All right. Thanks for comin' in."

Lonnie smiled bashfully, set his hat on his

head, and ducked through the doorway, knocking his hat askew as he did.

Sartain turned to Dixie. She was staring at him pensively.

"Sorry about business," he said.

She frowned, canting her head slightly to one side. "Who are you, Mr. Sartain?"

Sartain sighed and looked at the dead man lying belly down on the floor before him. "I reckon I'm the man who went and bloodied up your nice place. Let me get him out of here, and then I'll buy you a drink." He smiled. "By way of apology."

She just stared at him dubiously, as though she thought she might know him from somewhere but was having trouble recollecting his name.

"I reckon I'd best go check on your friend," she said quietly.

She turned slowly, still frowning thoughtfully, and headed for the stairs.

Sartain dragged the dead man out into the rain and left him in a break between the saloon and the next building, an old barbershop, to the west. The rain had let up, but the ground was too wet to dig a grave. He'd bury the body when he could. If the coyotes got to him first — well, they had to eat, too.

Or maybe whoever had taken the first

body would take this one, too . . .

He checked on the horses, making sure they had plenty of water and that the stable roof wasn't leaking overmuch, and then returned to the saloon. Dixie McKee stood in the open doorway, smoking a long, thin cigar and sipping tequila from a shot glass.

"How's the younker?" Sartain asked as he climbed up onto the gallery.

"Hard to tell. He might make it if I can keep his fever down. I've placed cold cloths on his forehead. This cold spell helps." She stepped back and indicated a table on which an open bottle stood. "Drink?"

"Don't mind if I do." Sartain slacked into a chair at the table. "Join me? I'm buyin'."

She straddled a chair across from him, crossing her arms on the chair back and regarding him with that same wistful look as before. He splashed tequila into her glass and she lifted it, turning the glass between her fingers.

"I got no complaints about what you did to Chick Beacham, but you've piled up some trouble for yourself, Mr. Sartain."

"I tend to do that." Sartain threw back the shot and then refilled his glass.

She threw back hers, as well, and he refilled her glass, too. She had a smoky look in her eyes. Her hair was slightly disheveled, hanging along the sides of her face. One lock was curled up against her left cheek.

"He'd been a friend of yours, I take it?" he prodded her.

"At one time. Not much of one. But it's hard to find good friends around here."

"Who'd you say he killed? A Pierson boy?"

"He was hired to kill the Pierson boy's father. That's what Chick does, when he doesn't have anything else going. He hires out his guns. The Pierson boy got in the way of the bullet. It was the boy he killed. An eleven-year-old boy. Chick won't own up to it, but everyone knows he did it. I think it unnerved him. That's why he took to bank robbing instead."

"What do you think he has to do with me or the kid upstairs getting ambushed?"

Dixie sighed as she leveled an inscrutable gaze on the Cajun, turning her mouth corners down. She let the question hang in the air a long time, staring at the man who'd asked it. Then she threw her tequila back, took a deep drag off her cigarillo, and blew the smoke at the rafters.

"I'm going to bed."

"Is that how you're gonna answer that question?"

"I don't know who you are."

"Just a drifter who rode into town looking

for water and almost got a bullet for my trouble. The kid got one for his, too, and that's why I'm here. The only reason why I'm here."

"That's not good enough."

"You're saying I should leave?"

"That's what I'm saying." Dixie rose from her chair and stood staring down at him with that smoky look in her eyes again. Her cheeks were slightly flushed. "But you can spend the night upstairs, if you've a mind." She blinked. "Third door down the hall on the right."

"What do I owe you for the drinks and the room?"

She'd started walking to the stairs. Now she stopped and glanced over her left shoulder at him. Her hair partly shaded her face. "Not a damn thing. In fact, I'm the one owin' you."

She continued walking toward the stairs. She had a proud, languid, lovely walk. The seat of her jeans was like two hands caressing her. Her hair jostled down her back as she gained the stairs and started up the steps.

"Lock up before you come to bed, will you?" she said and then disappeared into the second story.

Sartain poured himself another drink and

started building a quirley. His fingers stopped working. He glanced thoughtfully up from the wheat paper troughed between his fingers.

The third door on the right was her room.

CHAPTER SIX

Sartain stopped at the third door on the right. He canted his head toward the panel, pricking his ears to listen.

Nothing.

He turned the knob. The latch clicked. He pushed the door open and stepped inside.

She sat in a brocade-upholstered armchair with her back to him, one long bare leg crossed on the other. Her bare foot was nearly buried in a thick, wine-red Oriental rug trimmed with long, gilt wheat stems. A fire snapped in a small hearth to Sartain's left, pushing a soothing heat into the room, pressing back the chill of the dark mountain night.

Dixie sat facing an oval-shaped floor mirror in a swivel frame. She was brushing her hair, which she'd pulled over her left shoulder. It shimmered in the light from the fire and from several candles guttering around the crudely but comfortably furnished room. It ran down over her bare left breast, partly concealing it. The other breast, reflected in the mirror, was pale and full and tipped with a pink nipple jutting from a large areola.

The breasts were almost perfectly shaped. They were ripe, cream-colored melons.

Her back was long and slender, tapering to broadening pale hips and long, creamy legs. Sartain could see the crease between her buttocks where her rump met the chair.

Her eyes found him in the mirror. She smiled coyly, sensing the desire that had begun instantly tugging at his loins the moment he'd stepped into the room. As he closed the door and turned the key in the lock, she said, "I know who you are. It just came to me a moment ago."

She'd paused in brushing her hair, but now she resumed the slow, even strokes, the soft raking sounds mixing with the hissing of candles whose flames were licking wax.

The room was touched with a light, subtle female musk — a cross between cherry blossoms and sage on a damp, late-summer breeze. The aroma nibbled at the edges of Sartain's consciousness, increasing his desire for the erotic creature in the mirror.

"All right," was all he said, hanging his hat on a peg.

He ran his hands through his thick, curly hair and moved forward. She stopped brushing her hair to look up at him in the mirror. He stopped just behind her, leaned forward, wrapped his arms around her, and cupped her tender breasts in his hands.

He nuzzled her neck, then nibbled her right ear.

In the mirror, she closed her eyes and leaned her head to one side, groaning softly.

Her nipples came to life beneath his thumbs and index fingers.

He squeezed her breasts harder, lifting them up high against her chest. He kneaded them softly as he ran his tongue along the top of her right shoulder and then back to her neck, which he nuzzled some more.

Into her ear, he whispered, "Want me to go bed down with the horses?"

Keeping her eyes closed, head canted to one side, she said in a soft singsong, "Don't . . . you . . . dare . . ."

He ran his right hand down across her belly, then poked two fingers into her crease, where her pelvis met the chair.

He could feel her heart quicken, body temperature rise.

"Oh," she whispered after a time, giving a little shudder. "Oh . . ."

He withdrew his damp fingers, straightened, and then stepped away from her. She turned her head, frowning, as though to discourage his departure.

He unknotted his red neckerchief, dropping it onto a chair. He removed his old Waterbury timepiece and double-barreled derringer, which were connected by a silver chain, from the pockets of his pinto vest. He set the accoutrements on a table, then shrugged out of the vest itself and hung it on a peg by the door.

Slowly, keeping his eyes on the young woman, letting his desire build, he continued to methodically undress and set each article of clothing on the chair. She watched him over the back of her chair for a time, then rose and, keeping her hair trailing over her left breast, moved to the canopied, four-poster bed, walking with catlike grace.

She'd already drawn the covers back. Now she folded into them and lay on her side, breasts sloping toward the cambric sheets, watching him. She curled her knees slightly toward her belly, grinding one delicate foot against the other. She blinked slowly, her cheeks coloring, her nipples stiffening as she watched the big man lean forward to peel his longhandles down his legs.

When he straightened, he was naked, manhood jutting.

He walked to the bed. She crawled to the edge of it, pressing her belly flat against the mattress, the tips of her breasts brushing the sheets. She petted him, stroked him for a time before she shook her hair back over her shoulder, looked up at him, and blinked her long, brown eyes.

She gave him a coy smile and then opened her mouth and closed her ripe lips around him.

"Oh," Sartain groaned, rocking back on his heels. "Oh, yeah . . ."

"Just what I needed — I'm obliged, Miss Dixie," he said after he'd caught his breath, leaning his back against the tarnished brass frame of the bed.

She rolled toward him, hooked a leg over his, and pressed her lips to his belly.

"The least I could do for a dying man," she said, kissing him.

The Cajun ran a big hand through his hair, luxuriously scrubbing his scalp. "I feel just fine."

She kissed him again, her hair fluttering around her face pressed to his belly, caressing him softly. "You should have killed him, Mike."

"I thought I got the point across."

"There's no getting your point across to a

man like Chick Beacham. He thinks he owns these mountains. He'll be back."

Sartain slid her hair back from her face. "I dig you a deeper hole, did I?"

"No deeper than before." Dixie looked up at him, stretching her lips back as she laughed huskily. "Besides, I doubt he'll be feelin' plucky enough to come back here any time soon, strutting around demanding free drinks and hugs from the proprietor."

"That's kind of what I was thinking," Sartain said. "Thought the bed rest might give him time to ruminate, maybe make some adjustments to the path he's on."

"Where did you learn how to do that, Mike?"

"Hmm?"

She looked up at him again as she ran her hand down his thigh. Her cheeks were beautifully flushed, eyelids heavy. "To do the things you did to me just now?" She frowned as though deeply befuddled. "To make me feel the way I just did . . . so many times . . . ?"

Sartain reached for his makings sack, which, during a breather, he'd fetched from his pants pocket. He'd also draped his cartridge belt over a front bedpost, so that his sheathed LeMat and Bowie knife were within easy reach.

"I was taught by the best pleasure girls in the country, maybe in the world." Sartain troughed a wheat paper between his index finger and thumb and slowly dribbled the chopped tobacco into the fold. "French Quarter, New Orleans. Those whores not only raised me — I was an orphan, alone on the streets and docks — but they raised me to appreciate the *finer* things in life."

He grunted as Dixie gently hefted his scrotum and planted another warm, wet kiss on his belly button.

"I'm mighty beholdin' to those ladies." Dixie lifted her head to regard him once more as she fondled him. "Only problem is . . . who's going to pleasure me like that when you're gone — one way or another?"

Sartain poked the quirley into his mouth and rolled it, sealing it. "How come you're alone out here, Dixie? Where's that family you mentioned?"

"I was the youngest. Ma and Pa are dead. The boys long ago ran away from Pa's diggings, never to be seen or heard from again. I doctored Pa until just last year. He was out of his head, turned back into a child. I even had to put rubber pants on him. Had to tie a rope around him to keep him around the cabin while I did chores, or he'd wander off.

"I made enough sewing for folks and digging up some good color from an old creek bed to pay the taxes on this place. The town died, but there's still enough folks around who require a shot of whiskey now and then. Drifters like yourself pull through, needin' a pillow to rest their heads on for a night or two, a stable for their horses. I get by."

"But you don't have a man. A girl like you, hot-blooded and alive in all the best ways, needs a man. Same as a man needs a woman." Sartain always drifted back into his slow, Cajun drawl at such slow, luxurious times, and he did so now.

"Don't I know it!"

"You keep doin' what you're doin' down there, Miss Dixie, you ain't gonna go to sleep any time soon."

She giggled and did not stop what she was doing.

A half hour later, he eased both her legs down from his right shoulder, rolled her over onto her belly, kissed both her butt cheeks, and dropped down beside her again.

"Good heavens," she said through a long sigh, blowing hair out from her face. "Good . . . good heavens . . ."

She snapped her head up suddenly. "Good heavens — I'd best check on your partner!"

"Uh . . . he's not my partner," Sartain said half-heartedly, not really caring about correcting her when he saw the comely figure she made, dashing out of bed naked and fumbling around in an armoire for a night wrap.

She paused at the door, blew him a kiss, and went out.

Sartain lay back on the bed. He sighed. He was exhausted. A hell of a lot had happened in one day. And he'd only stopped here for water.

He'd been pondering the missing bushwhacker for a good twenty minutes, when he heard voices through the wall to his left. Dixie was speaking quietly but urgently. Sometimes her voice rose sharply and then, as though catching herself, she lowered it but resumed speaking.

Who was she speaking to so covertly?

The boy?

Suspicion edged away the tendrils of sleep that had started to nibble at the edges of the Revenger's consciousness. He rose from the bed. Not bothering with clothes but sliding the LeMat from its holster, he moved to the door, opened it quietly, and stepped down the hall on the balls of his bare feet.

He stopped at the boy's door, and shoved

an ear up close until he could hear the young man moaning. His bed squawked as he thrashed.

". . . told ya," the kid said. "Told ya . . . I'd be rich someday . . . sure enough. You never believed me, Homer . . ."

"Where?" Dixie said in a low, urgent tone. "Where is it, Dewey?"

"That whiskey . . . I never tasted such as that. I'd best go easy, or my pa . . . he'll strap me good if he smells it on my breath . . ."

"Dewey," Dixie said. "The gold. Where is the gold, Dewey?" She pitched her voice with sweetness. "I'll help you find it, Dewey. And then we can be friends."

"You'll know I found it when I come back wearin' a new pair of boots an' . . . an' one of them beaver hats!" The kid chuckled through a groan as he continued to thrash around on the bed.

"Goddamnit!" Dixie said.

Bare footsteps sounded on the other side of the door from Sartain. She was moving toward him. He started to turn away and retreat back to Dixie's room when Dixie said, "What was that, Dewey?"

A floorboard squawked. She must have been returning to the bed.

"Dewey, honey?" she said sweetly. Sartain

imagined her caressing the hair back from the young man's forehead, and he stifled the urge to chuckle. "What did you just say?"

More thrashing.

"The Mexican," the kid said.

"What Mexican, honey?" Dixie said.

Silence, save for the light squawking of the leather springs on the kid's bed.

"Oh, lordy, look at the lightnin'! We'd best get these beeves to lower pastures, Homer, or we're gonna be poppin' like Mexican firecrackers!"

"Shit!" Dixie hissed under her breath.

A floorboard squawked again as she padded toward the door.

Sartain cursed under his own breath and, gritting his teeth, retreated to her room. He managed to get her door closed and latched as he heard the kid's door groan open and then click shut. When she came into the room, the Cajun lay on his back under the bedcovers, eyes closed, hands folded on his belly.

"Mike?" She called to him quietly from the door.

He opened his eyes, blinking as though he'd been asleep. He raked a hand down his face and feigned a yawn. "How's the kid?"

She stared at him, one eyebrow arched

suspiciously.

"You all right?" he asked her, smacking his lips.

Finally, she smiled and shrugged out of her wrap. Naked, she crawled into the bed and spooned her cool, supple body against his, cupping his privates in her hand and pressing her lips to his shoulder.

"He'll be fine," she said. "I'll see to that."

Chapter Seven

Dixie was up at first light, wanting another go-round.

Sartain could have slept a little longer, but he felt obliged to the gal. She'd given him a room and a corral for his horse, and she was doctoring the younker on his behalf, though after last night, he suspected it was more on her own behalf.

On behalf of whatever gold the kid had been talking about in his fever dream. Likely, there wasn't any gold except in said dream, but Dixie was a lonely girl and likely as desperate for wealth as she was for human affection.

The affection the big Cajun could give her.

Gold was another thing altogether.

When they were through with another bout of gentle, soothing, early-morning coupling, Dixie kissed Sartain tenderly, tugged his ears, and gave herself a quick sponge bath while the Cajun watched. He'd always enjoyed watching a woman bathe. It reminded him of his not-so-innocent childhood when his foster "mothers" had bathed casually before him, sometimes two or three together.

He supposed that until the day he left this earth, there would always be something special and homey and nostalgic about the sounds of dripping water accompanied by a woman's soft humming.

When Dixie went out to check on the kid and then to start her day, preparing for Saturday night, the saloon's busiest night of the few nights it was open, Sartain took a quick sponge bath of his own, using her water. That was another thing that made him nostalgic — bathing in a woman's used bathwater. There was something profoundly intimate about that, and somehow reassuring, though he supposed his brain wasn't quite glued together the way most men's were — most men with traditional upbringings, that was.

He dressed leisurely, taking his time knotting his neckerchief, brushing the dust from his pinto vest before shrugging into it. He checked his weapons — the pearl-gripped, gold-plated over-and-under derringer, his Bowie knife, and the big LeMat — making sure all were sound and clean and loaded and ready for action. If he'd learned one thing after riding into Hard Winter, he'd learned he needed to be ready for action as long as he cared to stay.

He thought he'd stay at least the weekend. There were a few things he felt he needed to get to the bottom of before leaving.

By way of doing that, he thought he'd saddle Boss and take a ride around the outlying countryside. He knew from having ridden through this neck of the San Juans in the past that these mountains were rich in history. He was curious about their recent history. Namely, recent trouble that might have compelled a total stranger to try to blow his head off with a .38-40 Winchester while he'd innocently winched water up from a well.

Maybe while riding through these forested slopes, he'd kick something up. Possibly lure out whomever had dragged the dead bushwhacker's body away.

When he went downstairs, lighting a half-smoked cheroot, Dixie offered to cook him breakfast, but he declined. He thought that while riding through the mountains, where the creeks teemed with trout, he'd take a break, drown a few worms, and maybe, if he was lucky, fry himself a couple of Rocky

Mountain cutthroat he'd wash down with Arbuckle's.

He hadn't had a fresh, pan-fried trout in a month of Sundays, and trout was one of his favorite meals. Also, the smell of wood smoke and food had been known to lure in answers to pressing questions . . .

It was still dawn when he walked outside, leisurely smoking the cheroot, enjoying the peppery smoke in his lungs, the lightness in his head. Like a cup of coffee, there was nothing like that first cheroot of the day. The coffee would have to wait until he'd gotten some riding in, but by damn, he was enjoying his cigar.

He'd spent a night with a comely lass in a comfortable bed, and he was enjoying a Mexican cigar. Despite nearly meeting his maker yesterday afternoon, life was good.

But then he remembered the dead man he'd cached between the hotel and the barbershop. He was half-hoping Earl would be gone, and thus save him some digging.

Nope.

He was there, all right, just as Sartain had left him, pudgy hands crossed on his bulging belly. He was grinning as though in mockery of the work he was causing the man who'd shot him.

Sartain had a mind to drag Earl into the

nearest ravine. He would have if it had been later or earlier in the year. Earlier, the carcass would have decomposed quickly in the summer heat. Later, it would have frozen up solid, giving off little stench while the carrion eaters picked at it. This time of the year, late September, it wasn't hot or cold enough to do either job. It would likely molder slowly, and send the stench back to town and pester Dixie for the next several weekends.

Of course, he could drag it a good, long ways into the mountains, but it was easier to dig a shallow grave and throw some dirt and rocks over it. So that's what the Cajun did, making short work of the job amongst the pines flanking the hotel, where several ancient trash heaps were gradually being overgrown with brush and saplings.

As he worked, he thought that the fact this gent had been left in town probably meant that whoever had bushwhacked him yesterday hadn't been one of the outlaws riding with Beacham. At least, he'd learned that one thing. It wasn't much, but it was something, though it still left the nagging question of the bushwhacker's identity and the identity of the man or men who'd dragged him off.

As Sartain strapped his folding shovel to

his saddle and mounted up, he looked around carefully. Since the bushwhacker had had a friend or friends loyal enough to haul off his body, ostensibly for proper burial, that same friend might want to avenge his killing.

The Cajun slid his Henry repeater from his saddle sheath, racked a round into the action, off-cocked the hammer, and rested the barrel across the pommel of his saddle. His breath frosted in the chill air. He touched spurs to Boss's flanks, and rode off through the pines, heading straight up the gradual slope northeast of Hard Winter, where the pines, firs, and aspens gradually grew taller and thicker, the slope steeper.

The sun took a long time to climb above the steep eastern ridges. When it did, steam rose from the cool ground still wet from last night's rain. After another half hour, the Cajun stopped to remove his mackinaw, which he'd donned before heading out, as he'd judged the temperature around freezing when he'd first lit out of Hard Winter.

He rolled the coat in his hot roll, which he lashed behind his saddle, and continued riding along a valley floor just over the northern ridge from the ghost town.

It was higher here, the air thinner, the sun brighter.

To each side, timbered slopes rolled up to high, steep, stony ridges dusted with snow that had likely fallen yesterday, when it had only rained in Hard Winter. The gauzy greens of the conifer forest were spotted here and there with the golden hues of occasional changing aspens.

He followed a creek through a beaver meadow, the creek snaking and glinting through stirrup-high grama grass and mountain sage. He left the beaver meadow for a thick forest and then out again into rocky country, generally following the creek and continuing to climb toward a bulwark of gray granite looming high ahead — so high, in fact, that he was beginning to get a knot in his neck when he stared at the impressive formation mantled in bright, clean snow.

The Cajun wasn't sure where he was going. He wasn't sure why he turned away from the main creek and followed a feeder creek up a narrower valley than the last. But that's what he did . . . and found himself at a place so pretty, he decided to stop and hunt for grubs with which to bait a line.

The creek threading this canyon was virtually a falls. It *was* a falls in many places, the roar of the plunging water echoing off the steep, rocky ridges spiked with hardy pines, spruce, birch, Douglas firs, and tamaracks. At the bottom of a particularly steep, narrow falls was a swirling pool with a back eddy bridged by a blowdown pine and ringed with overhanging granite outcroppings.

Prime water for mountain cutthroat.

Sartain tied Boss to another blowdown spiked with broken branches and then, wielding his Henry, climbed the rocks to where the heavy forest began. He took a careful look down his back trail, which he'd been doing occasionally since leaving Hard Winter. He hadn't spied any telltale shadows on his trail so far, but that didn't mean he hadn't been followed.

In fact, something — maybe a special sense hunted men acquired — told him he had been shadowed. That was all right. Maybe soon he'd get some answers to a few nagging questions.

He found some grubs under a moldering log, and threaded a couple of fat ones onto a hook he carried in a leather case along with some fishing line. He tied the line to a six-foot-long aspen branch, and tossed the bait into the pool.

He rested the pole against a rock and fetched a fresh long-nine cigar from his store of cigars, recently replenished in a

Denver tobacco shop, and smoked while he built a small fire. He kept an eye on his line, which didn't move much for nearly a half hour.

He had a few strikes, got his grubs stolen twice by his cunning quarry, and then, just when he was beginning to think luck was not with him, he answered a quick, hard jerk on the line by pulling a fat, glistening trout up out of the pool and onto the uneven surface of the mossy outcrop he'd made noon camp on.

He fried the fish gently in lard in his cast-iron fry pan and ate it out of the pan with some wild mint he found growing around the rocks. He hadn't tasted anything so delicate, sweet, and delicious since the last time he'd pulled a fat trout out of a near-freezing mountain stream.

It didn't take him long to eat the fish. He followed it up with a cup of hot coffee to which he added a shot of his favored Sam Clay bourbon, and sat on a thumb of rock fifty feet above his camp, looking around. Again, he had the feeling someone had shadowed him out from Hard Winter.

He drank some more of the spiked coffee, enjoying the heat and headiness it touched him with here in the thin, cool mountain air rife with the tang of pine resin and loam and the steely smell of the cascading water.

He stared down along the twisting canyon, back in the direction of the main valley he could not see from here because of the high, rocky, pine-studded ridges. He sipped the coffee, sliding his gaze slowly across the canyon. He sipped again, and slid his gaze back to the other side of the canyon.

Then he saw it.

A brief flicker of movement along the canyon floor. Little more than a smudge of light brown moving out from trees on his right to an escarpment on his left. The movement had covered no more than a thumbnail from this distance, but it was a rider, all right. Heading slowly toward Sartain along the trail he'd taken into the canyon.

He looked down at his camp at the rocky lip of the stream. Boss stood staring into the creek as though he were looking for fish, reins drooping toward the dead tree he was tied to. The Cajun had chosen the camp because it was pretty, but also because it offered good cover from the trail snaking up from below and beyond.

"All right, then," he said, and threw back the last of his mud.

He rose and made his way back down the rocks to his breakfast camp. He built up his fire, gave Boss a reassuring pat on the rump, and then crossed the roiling creek on the makeshift bridge of a fallen pine. He climbed an angling crevice up the opposite side, having to climb with one hand while holding the Henry with the other.

It wasn't a hard climb. There were plenty of hand- and footholds.

When he gained the edge of the forest above the creek, he slipped in amongst the trees and dropped to one knee behind a wedge-shaped chunk of rock sitting precariously over the canyon, nestled in firs.

He waited, catching glimpses of the horse and rider coming up the canyon, the man wending his way between the cliffs.

Behind Sartain, a throaty voice pitched low with menace said, "Hold it right where you are, you son of a bitch, or I'll blast you to Kingdom Come!"

Chapter Eight

Sartain cursed as he held himself still, as he'd been warned to do.

The only problem with his choice of bivouac was that, while it was indeed well concealed, the creek was loud enough to cover anyone else's stealthy advancement. That's why the man coming up behind him — he could see his shadow in the periphery of his vision — had been able to steal up on him unheard.

Only now, when the shadow was nearly merging with his own, did he hear a branch snap under the bastard's boot.

The cold, round maw of a pistol was pressed against his spine. The man's voice said, "Hand me back that purty Henry of yours . . . real slow and butt first."

Sartain reached back with the Henry. The man took it.

Keeping his pistol pressed taut to the Revenger's back, the man behind him said,

"Now the purty LeMat . . . real slow and butt first."

Sartain slid the LeMat from its holster, and handed it back.

His assailant took that, too. Then the man snatched the Bowie knife from his belt sheath.

"Purty knife. You got all kinds of purty weapons. You got any more purty weapons?"

"That's it."

The man patted him down. When he patted the right flap of his vest, the man said, "Let's have it."

Sartain removed the derringer from his watch chain, and handed it over his shoulder.

"All right — you can turn around."

Sartain turned around to see one of the men, Johnny, who'd been with Beacham — the only one who'd walked out of the saloon unmarred — standing before him, aiming a horn-gripped Bisley .44 at him from six feet back. He was a stocky gent with a full cinnamon beard speckled with gray, and a mustache with upturned, ragged ends. His face was rife with freckles, and he had a mole at the corner of his chapped mouth.

His light-brown eyes were set too close together, and they were slightly slanted. They gave him a stupid, devilish look, but maybe he had that look because he was genuinely stupid and devilish.

Yesterday, he'd mostly looked cowed and sheepish.

Now, he was grinning like the cat that ate the canary, showing his large, yellow-edged teeth.

"You ain't so tough now, are ya?" he said. "Now that I took your guns away."

"You just took my guns away."

"What the hell's that supposed to mean?"

"It means, you simple fool, that if you put your guns down and fought me with your fists, I'd still be tough enough to smash your teeth down your throat and have you whimpering like a gutshot coyote."

Johnny scowled and chewed his lip, his freckled cheeks turning deep pink. Taking a halting step back, he said, "You think so, do you?"

"I think so."

"Well, we might just see about that. Right now, however, there's an *hombre* who wants to have a talk with you."

Sartain chuckled. "Oh? What *hombre* could that be? One with a sore foot, maybe?"

"Hah! — you can laugh now. But in a few minutes, you ain't gonna be doin' no laughin'. Only howlin'."

"I reckon we'll see about that. If you're done blowin' steam, you simple, ugly bastard, why don't we go visit this poor fella with the injured foot?"

He knew he was taking a risk, trying to get Johnny's dander up. Johnny might just go ahead and gutshoot him. But Johnny looked stupid enough that if he got mad enough, he might make a mistake and give Sartain an opening for making a move on him.

Johnny lowered his head and flared his nostrils. "You got a mighty big mouth on you for a man who could die right here and now. Mighty big!"

"Same to you, you simple fool."

A voice shouted from down in the canyon behind Sartain, "Johnny — what the hell you two doin' over there — discussin' the price of chaw? Get him over here, goddamnit!"

Sartain glanced behind him into the canyon. Two riders sat their horses near Boss, who faced them with his tail arched angrily. They were both hard-faced men like Johnny — likely two more of Beacham's bunch assigned to bringing Sartain to the outlaw leader with the bloody boot. One was leading a riderless horse. That was likely Johnny's mount. He must have slipped across the canyon on foot to circle around Sartain.

"You heard him." Johnny wagged the Bisley at the Cajun. "Get a move on. Nice and slow. You try any tricks, you'll pay hard."

Sartain started down the slope. When he glanced behind to see if Johnny was close enough for him to try jumping him, he gave a silent curse. Johnny stood at the lip of the canyon, aiming his pistol threateningly at Sartain.

"Just keep goin', mister. You head anywhere but the bottom of the canyon, I'll drill ya, an' so will my pards over there." When Sartain was nearly to the floor of the canyon, Johnny started down.

The other two were covering Sartain with their carbines.

"Howdy fella," the Cajun said, grinning affably as he approached his horse.

The man riding a claybank gelding narrowed his eyes beneath the brim of his black hat, and snarled, "Shut up and get mounted, you Cajun son of a bitch! You killed my cousin yesterday. What Beacham don't do to you to get even for a ruined boot, I *am*!"

Sartain gave a weary sigh as he swung up into the leather. "You ain't friendly at all."

Well, here he'd outsmarted himself, the

Cajun thought as he rode back down the canyon, in the direction from which he'd come. He was fourth in a group of three now. His hands were tied to his saddle horn, and Johnny was leading Boss by the bridle reins.

Johnny had the Revenger's LeMat and Bowie, while the man called Dominguez had cadged his Henry repeater; the third gent, Hagan, had so admired the Cajun's gold-plated derringer that he'd slipped the little popper into the pocket of his long, spruce-green duster, which he wore over deerskin breeches.

Dominguez looked part Mexican, while Hagan was an outlaw from Nebraska Territory. Sartain had heard his name before, and had seen his visage on wanted posters a few years back after the man had killed two deputy sheriffs while escaping a county jail in Wichita.

Of course, the three hadn't shaken hands and introduced themselves to Sartain. The Revenger had picked up their names from general conversation, most of which hadn't even been directed at him. Hagan was a long-nosed killer with what appeared a perpetual purple beard shadow on his fair-skinned face that didn't take the sun well. His nose was as red as a Rocky Mountain sunset, and badly peeling. As they rode, he kept looking grimly over his shoulder at Sartain, narrowing his dark eyes at the prisoner and then spitting chaw on rocks or plants along the trail. He'd look back again as he ran a grimy checked sleeve across his mouth, and then turn his head forward.

Obviously, he was in love with his reputation and aimed to prove he was worth every penny of the thousand-dollar bounty on his head. Sartain had been more impressed by dancing bears in opera houses. He was going to enjoy killing Hagan.

If he ever got the opportunity, that was, and he hadn't outsmarted himself into an early grave. He'd already decided these bad boys had had nothing to do with his bushwhacking, so here he was amongst them and likely with no better result than that he'd be eating lead for his efforts.

To pass the time and lighten his mood, he whistled to himself an old tune he'd learned long ago in the French Quarter — a Cajun tune about a happy young whore who became an old and lonely whore feeding her alligator friends out on the bayou . . . until she fell into the bayou, one cold winter morn . . .

"Shut up," said Hagan.

"You boys ain't gonna shoot me for whistlin'," the Cajun said, and continued whistling.

It turned out that Sartain had passed Beacham's camp when he'd ridden up the main canyon. He hadn't seen it because it looked like an old prospector's or fur trapper's shack tucked away in a fringe of yellow-leafed aspens poking out from the northern ridge.

As they followed a well-worn path through the trees, their horses' hooves crunching the leaves that skittered about the trail, Sartain sniffed pine smoke. Then he saw the smoke lifting from the sloping pole roof of the low-slung stone cabin that boasted two deep-set windows in the front wall, and an opening for a door, though there appeared no actual door. Just as there were no shutters on the windows. The shutters and door had likely rotted away long ago.

Sartain stopped whistling.

Hagan glanced back and chuckled darkly as he said, "End of the trail, *amigo.*"

"Jump yourself, *amigo.*"

As Dominguez, Hagan, and Johnny pulled their horses up to a large aspen fronting the shack, where one other horse was tied, a figure moved inside the dark shack. Chick Beacham limped up to the open doorway, using an aspen branch for a cane, and leaned against the casing. He wore a wool coat and a blanket over the coat, hanging off his shoulders.

His left foot was wrapped up in a thick, makeshift bandage of old rags.

He wasn't wearing his hat. His dark hair stood up in spikes around his head, as though he'd been lying down, which he probably had been. The bandages on his bullet-torn foot were bloody. He probably wasn't feeling very well.

"I'll be damned if you didn't find him," Beacham said as his three partners swung down from their saddles. In his free hand, he held a bottle. Now he lifted the bottle and took a long pull, several bubbles plunging to the bottom.

He lowered the bottle and smacked his lips.

Johnny said, "We rode into town to fetch him, like you said, Chick. But then we saw him pullin' out of town. Figured we'd follow him. You know — in case he led us to the cache. Instead, he just found himself a little trout pool up Old Grand Dad Canyon, and fished!"

Johnny wagged his head and chuckled, glancing at Sartain as though they'd caught him playing with himself. He reached up and cut the ropes binding Sartain's wrists to his saddle horn, and then he stepped back quickly, as though he'd just opened a wildcat's cage.

"Caught a nice one," Sartain said. "If you fellas would have showed up a little sooner, I'd have shared."

"Shut the hell up and come down off there," Hagan said, cocking his carbine one-handed, dramatically.

"Why didn't you say so?" Sartain swung down from the saddle.

Beacham smiled without humor, turned sideways, and beckoned. Then he drifted off into the shack's thick shadows.

While the taciturn Dominguez tied the horses, Hagan and Johnny held their carbines on Sartain, keeping themselves clear of a quick, slashing assault, which is exactly what the Revenger had in mind.

"You heard the man," Johnny said, wagging his rifle barrel.

"You fellas just move in? I feel like I should have brought a bottle of wine or something," Sartain said, striding toward the door, wishing like hell Johnny hadn't found the hideout gun in his vest pocket.

Sartain stepped into the doorway, and stopped, looking around. He couldn't see much, for his eyes were accustomed to the bright mountain light outdoors.

"Get in there!" Hagan snarled, ramming his rifle's butt against Sartain's back.

The Cajun went stumbling into the shack, blinking as his eyes adjusted to the dingy shadows. Beacham lay on a lone cot against the far wall, back propped against his saddle. His good foot was on the floor. The one Sartain had pumped a round through rested on a pillow at the end of the cot.

Several empty bottles were strewn around the cot, and some odds and ends of gear. Otherwise, the shack was empty, save for a dilapidated eating table and a sheet-iron stove that ticked and let blue smoke escape through cracks around its doors.

"Did you diddle that bitch?" Beacham wanted to know, poking an angry finger at his visitor.

Sartain laughed silently to himself. He'd blown a hole through the man's foot, but what Beacham seemed the most concerned about was whether he'd been cuckolded, if you could call cuckolding making love to a woman who considered herself unattached.

Sartain doffed his hat, then twirled it on his finger. "Out of respect for the lady's honor, that ain't a question I feel at liberty to answer."

"You did, didn't you?"

"My answer stands."

Beacham's face darkened in the shadows as he leaned forward, jerking his arm and extended finger furiously at the big man before him. "Goddamnit, I'm gonna blow both your feet off, you son of a bitch! I'm gonna blow both of 'em off, so's you know how it feels. And when your screams start dyin', I'm gonna pump one through your belly and leave you to die slow and hard!"

Chapter Nine

The Cajun felt the burn of fury spread up from his bowels. "You just gonna whistle Dixie or dance? I can't stand a man who's all talk!"

Flanking Sartain on his left, Hagan shook his head. "Boy, he's really got it comin', Chick."

Beacham sank back against his saddle. "Yeah, he does. And he'll get it, just as soon as we get our loot back." He glowered at Sartain. "You know where it's at, don't you?"

The Cajun didn't say anything. That was the second or third time since he'd ridden into Hard Winter that someone had alluded to hidden treasure.

"He does," Chick said. "I know he does. Hadley told you, didn't he? That's why you're here. You musta been out after it this mornin' but seen us trailing you, so you decided to do some fishin' instead." Beacham slapped his thigh and then winced slightly at the pain it evoked in his tender foot. "I knew it! You got a look about you. Owlhoot. Somehow, you've done thrown in with Hadley, and he sent you out here to get the loot for a cut of it!"

"Where is it, goddamnit?" That was the first time Sartain had heard the Mexican, Dominguez, speak. He was crouched in the doorway behind the Cajun, Johnny, and Hagan. "Maybe if we gutshoot him, he'll spill it."

"Where is it?" Beacham demanded. "That money belongs to us. Where is it, goddamnit?"

Sartain turned his mouth corners down, feigning chagrin. "You fellas done put me in a bad spot."

Johnny stomped up beside Sartain and thrust his broad, freckled face at the Cajun. "You're gonna be in a hell of a worse spot if you don't tell us where the loot's at!"

"I can't tell you," Sartain said. "I can only show you."

"He didn't draw you a map?" asked Hagan skeptically.

"No, he didn't draw no map. He didn't want it fallin' into the wrong hands."

Beacham drew the Colt on his hip, aimed, and cocked it. "You tell us or I'll gutshoot you right here and now!"

"You're not gonna get your loot back that way."

"Shit," Hagan snarled. "He ain't gonna tell us. He ain't gonna show us, neither. He knows what Hadley'll do to him if he lets us get the loot back."

"He'll show us," Beacham said. "He'll show us or he'll die slow." He jerked his chin toward the door. "Get him out of here. You fellas ride with him. If you don't have the loot in the next couple of hours, if he sends you off on a wild goose chase, bring him back here so I can blow holes in his feet and pop one in his belly."

"You ain't comin'?" Johnny asked the outlaw leader.

Beacham blinked slowly, then pointed at his foot wrapped in blood-speckled bandages. "Do I *look* like I'm comin'? Do I *look* like I can ride?"

"Sorry, Chick," Johnny said.

"You're always sorry."

"You feel better, now, ya hear?" Johnny said, truckling.

"I'll feel a whole lot better once I got my hands on that loot again."

"Out!" Hagan bellowed at Sartain, pointing toward the doorway.

The Revenger swung around. "I ain't

deaf," he said as he ducked through the door. "You don't have to yell."

"He's leadin' us on a goddamn wild goose chase," Hagan said to Johnny and Dominguez. "Hell, we're ridin' in circles!"

"Don't get your neck in a hump," Sartain said. "We're not riding in circles."

No, they weren't riding in circles, but for the past hour they had been riding aimlessly. Of course, the Cajun had no idea where the loot was. He was just trying to buy himself time.

For what, he had no idea. While his hands were no longer tied to his saddle horn, and he had command of his own horse, the three men flanking him all held their carbines on him. If he tried to make a break for it, they'd gun him down before he'd ridden more than twenty yards.

Tension was drawing the muscles between his shoulder blades taut as piano wire.

"By God, he's hornswogglin' us," Hagan said as they followed a winding horse trail along the crest of a windy ridge. "That's what he's doin', boys. He's hornswogglin' us!"

"Yeah, I agree," Johnny said. "I say we take him back to Beacham, let Chick get his satisfaction."

"Shit," said Dominguez. "I say we hang the sonofabitch right here. No point in takin' him all the way back to —"

"Fellas, it's right over this ridge," Sartain said, nerve sweat trickling down his back. "We got about a hundred yards more. So hold your water, and you'll all be richer than your wildest dreams."

The Cajun reined Boss up and over the crest of the ridge. The cool wind blew against him, whipping the ends of his neckerchief. He placed a hand on his hat to keep it from blowing off and then released it as he rode down into the shelter below the ridge.

There were rocks and fire-charred pines all around, and the thin, wiry grass that grew at higher elevations. Picas peeped and darted amongst the rocks and charred, fallen timber. He rode to the base of a granite outcropping protruding from the mountain slope and jutting two hundred feet in the air. There appeared a hollow area inside the outcropping, which probably made some wildcat a home.

"Well?" Hagan asked doubtfully. "Where is it?"

"See that little cave in the rock up there?"

"I see it," Johnny said.

"It's in there."

Dominguez rode his dappled gray up close to Sartain and grinned with menace, showing his yellow teeth beneath his black mustache. He aimed the carbine at the Cajun's heart. "Fetch it."

Sartain glanced at each man in turn. They were boring holes in him with their stares as well as with the barrels of their rifles, all of which were aimed at the Revenger's heart.

"All right," Sartain said, swinging down from the saddle. "Hadley sure ain't gonna like this, and I reckon I'm not gonna get the cut he promised me, neither, for fetching it."

The Cajun walked slowly up the steep slope, his boots slipping on the short grass. He glanced behind him. The three men remained on their horses, rifles trained on his back.

He glanced around, looking for possible escape routes. There were none. He was boxed in against the outcropping. Of course, he could try to run, but it wouldn't do him much good. There was nowhere to go where the outlaws' bullets wouldn't shred him before he got there.

He was sweating hard by the time he reached the cavern that had been carved into the outcrop. It was about two feet wide and five feet deep. Its sandy floor was littered with rabbit bones to which a few tufts of bloody fur clung. Sure enough, a wildcat called the place home.

That was all that was in there.

Just the rabbit bones.

Heart thudding heavily, Sartain grinned sheepishly as he turned back to the three mounted gunmen. Dominguez's head exploded like a ripe melon, blood and brains spraying across his dappled gray's mane. A quarter-second later, the rifle report flatted out across the hollow.

Sartain saw smoke billow from atop the ridge behind the three outlaws.

Another gun flashed from near the same spot. Johnny screamed and grabbed his shoulder. As his horse reared and half-turned, loosing a shrill whinny, another bullet plunged into Johnny's chest. Johnny screamed again and flew off his horse's right hip, the horse kicking his head before he landed.

Sartain had been so taken aback by the sudden gunfire, he'd stumbled back against the outcropping, watching in shock as all three outlaws were blown out of their saddles.

As Hagan flew ass over teakettle off his lunging grullo's rump, Sartain regained his wits and bounded down the slope. He saw his Henry repeater lying on the ground between the nearly headless Dominguez and Johnny. He grabbed the rifle and then ran toward Boss.

Too late.

The screaming stallion galloped off down the slope toward a fringe of pines at the bottom, shaking his head in disdain at the flying lead.

"Goddamnit, you son of a bitch!" Sartain shouted, though he couldn't really blame the horse. He'd have done the same thing if he could.

Two bullets blew up dirt and grass around him. Another barked off the escarpment behind him.

Confused by the ambuscade, Dominguez's dappled gray was wheeling right and left as though trying to find a safe direction to flee. Fortunately, it then bounded straight toward Sartain, who managed to grab the reins with one hand. Unfortunately, while reaching for the apple, he dropped the Henry.

Before he was fully mounted, the dappled gray took off at a dead run up the slope along the left side of the outcropping. Sartain hadn't been prepared for the uphill lunge. That was likely just as well. Because as he fell back down the side of the horse, he heard the tooth-gnashing zing of a bullet slicing the air where his head had been a moment before.

"Get him!" someone shouted from the opposite ridge, the voice not completely drowned by the gunfire. "For Christ's sakes, *get* that son of a bitch!"

The Revenger cursed loudly as his left boot got hung up in the stirrup, and the dapple dragged him up the slope, the Cajun's head and shoulders bouncing along the uneven ground, each blow feeling as though he were being slammed with an anvil covered in sandpaper.

More shouts from the ridge where the shooters were desperately trying to beef him. Several bullets plumed dust around him, but then the horse crested the ridge above the escarpment and bounded down the other side, the Cajun's boot wedged so firmly in the stirrup that he couldn't jerk it free, though he wasn't in the best position to do so even if he could.

At least he now had the outcropping between him and the shooters, which meant they, at least, wouldn't kill him. But the wildly fleeing gray seemed bound and determined to finish the job they'd started.

Halfway down the slope, Sartain felt the back of his shirt rip.

He struggled to free his boot.

The ground kept hammering him though the decline was relatively grassy and not as gravelly as the slope around the escarpment. Gritting his teeth against his misery, he glanced up and around the stirrup, which held his foot like a bear trap, to see the forest at the bottom of the gulch growing closer.

The horse would likely kill him when it hit the trees. It would bash his head against a bole . . .

He gritted his teeth and thought momentarily of his dead lover, Jewel.

"Here I come, honey!" he bellowed.

There was a sharp pain in his left ankle.

Then he was in the timber and rolling, and darkness snatched him from the jaws of agony.

CHAPTER TEN

"Mike?"

It was Jewel's voice. She was calling to him from far away.

"Honey?" he called back to her. "I'm here. Can you see me?"

"Mike?" Someone was shaking him.

"Jewel, honey — I'm here." Oh, God — what if we couldn't recognize each other in Heaven, because we were just spirits? He heard his voice pitched with hysteria. *"Can't you see me?"*

He'd been waiting for this day. He'd been anticipating their reunion for so long — but what if he couldn't see her or hold her?

His heart lurched in horror at such a vile cosmic joke. He opened his eyes to find himself staring up at Dixie McKee. She stared down at him, frowning, puzzled. She wore a red bandanna around the top of her head, beneath her Stetson, and a red and white checked shirt under a black vest. Her wavy, chocolate hair was splayed across her shoulders.

Sartain's head was propped on her thigh. She had one arm wrapped around him. In the other, gloved hand she held a canteen.

Sartain blinked. Tears oozed out of his eyes to dribble down his cheeks.

"It's Dixie," she said. "Here — take a drink, Mike."

She shook the canteen, causing water to slosh over the rim.

He looked around, his heart slowing. His dream about Jewel, about possibly not being able to see her and hold her, had been so real and horrifying that he thought he could smell her remembered aroma. Fear had been a wild animal in him, only now taking its leave. He looked around again, half-expecting to see her pushing through the pines surrounding him.

But she wasn't here, of course. As the cobwebs cleared from his aching head, he realized that, judging by the play of the light and the shadows, not much time had passed since the horse had dragged him into the gulch. Maybe a half hour at the most.

He heard what sounded like a switching tail, and he could smell horse. He glanced over his shoulder.

Boss stood at the edge of the trees, maybe

ten feet away, with Dixie's cream. Both horses stared toward the pair in the woods as though wondering what in hell they were doing in there.

"Mike?" Dixie said softly but firmly. "You'd best take a drink. Looks like you could use it."

"I could use somethin' stronger than water, but it'll do for now." Sartain took the canteen. His arm felt heavy. The back of it was burning. Then it occurred to him that his back, especially up around his shoulders, was burning, as well. He could feel blood oozing from scrapes and abrasions. He felt as though his left hip had been pulled out of its socket.

Maybe it had.

He winced at the various burning, throbbing pains, and took a long drink. The water was cold. Almost too cold. It aggravated the throbbing in his head.

"What the hell happened, Mike? I thought you'd been shot, but I couldn't find any bullet wounds." She looked down his back. "It looks like you were dragged."

Dixie added, "I heard the shooting. From the ridge yonder, I saw Chick's three boys lying dead."

"You got any idea who them ambushers were?"

"I didn't see 'em. Just heard 'em. By the time I got to the ridge, they were gone."

"How'd you find me?"

"I started kicking around up there, looking for you, and then I saw Boss standing right where he is now."

Sartain glanced again at the stallion, and drawled, "Better late than never, old son."

The horse shook his head, rattling the bit.

"Anything broken?" Dixie asked.

"Feels like everything," he said with a grunt, sitting up.

Dixie sucked air through her teeth. "Your back looks like freshly ground beef, Mike. At least, the upper half does."

"Feels like it."

"Looks like I have another patient. You think you can ride?"

Sartain turned to her, frowning. "What're you doing here, anyway?"

"I saw those three ride into town earlier, just after you left. They saw you riding to the north and headed in the same direction. I decided to ride out and try to warn you, but I lost your trail. I can pan for gold with the best prospectors in the business, but I'm not much for tracking, I'm afraid."

"Takes practice," he said, heaving himself to his feet.

He felt his bones grinding and barking, as

were the muscles in his left leg. But he didn't think he'd broken anything.

"Let me take a look."

Dixie walked up behind him. "Well, you're missing most of your shirt, and those cuts need a good cleaning, but I reckon that can wait till we get back to the saloon."

"Sorry to be a bother. I know you got a busy night ahead."

"After last night, Mike," she said, wrapping an arm around his waist and rising up on the toes of her boots to peck his cheek, "you could never be a bother. But I might require payment of more of the same." She winked. "Just so you know."

"Just what the doctor ordered," the Cajun said, walking stiffly toward his horse. "I need to make a side trip and fetch my guns. Those bastards sure aren't going to be needing them."

As he climbed heavily onto Boss's back, Dixie stepped up onto her own horse. "Where's Chick?"

"His foot was hurting," Sartain said when he'd gotten seated and was rolling his shoulders around, trying to ease the kinks in his sinew. "So he sat this one out."

Sartain and Dixie got back to town about an hour after setting out from the gulch. As he rode, the Cajun realized he'd gotten off lucky. A Dutch ride over rocks, as cowpunchers called being dragged, could easily kill a man or stove him up for life.

He was a tough bastard. He'd give himself that.

He might have been a fool to let Johnny get the drop on him, but he was tough. And, fortunately, he was a quick mender.

As he and Dixie rode side by side, taking it slow, he considered who the other three bushwhackers were. At least, he thought there'd been three. Maybe four. Anyway, the San Juans seemed to have a whole lot of bushwhackers.

Dixie didn't say much as they rode back toward Hard Winter. Sartain wondered why. She didn't seem curious about the bushwhackers, and she didn't seem to think that it was damned curious how the Cajun, a stranger to this country, had been bushwhacked and hound-dogged like a Smoky Mountain coon ever since he'd gotten here.

He glanced at her several times, puzzled. He wanted to ask her the questions weighing on him, but he decided to wait her out. Maybe she'd show her hand on her own, if she didn't think he was suspicious of her.

If she had a hand to show, that was. After hearing her probing Dewey Dade the night before about the gold, he believed she did.

The gold . . .

What gold?

And why had Beacham's boys thought he knew where it was?

And who on God's green earth was Hadley?

When he was back on his feet, which would likely be tomorrow, he'd track Beacham down and get some answers straight from the horse's mouth if from nobody else.

They rode into Hard Winter as the afternoon shadows were growing long and velvety. Sartain didn't bother with his horse; Dixie said she'd see to his care. Instead, the Cajun dismounted and went on inside. He was mildly surprised to see the Mexican, who'd been smoking his quirleys the night before as though he'd been making love to them, running the place for Dixie.

There wasn't much work to do, as the only customer was a grizzled, gray-bearded old mountain man nursing a whiskey and nibbling a cheese sandwich at the same table the Mexican had been sitting at the night before.

But at least he'd been able to keep the place open while Dixie scrounged the mountains for Sartain's battered hide.

"Miguel, would you set some water on the

stove for me, please?" Dixie asked the short Mexican, who had a quirley drooping from a corner of his mouth.

He seemed a strange, quiet little man. He only nodded and hustled out the back door to fetch a bucket of water from the rain barrel.

As Sartain climbed the stairs, he remembered that last night the kid, Dewey Dade, had mentioned something about "the Mexican." But there was probably more than one Mexican in the San Juans.

Sartain's head was thoroughly spinning by the time he reached Dixie's room and collapsed belly down on her bed. It wasn't spinning from the Dutch ride. It was spinning from all the questions swirling around in it.

He reached over to the table by the bed, and poured himself a tall drink of Sam Clay. He downed half in a single swallow and then lay belly down again, holding the glass in his right hand beside him. Instantly, the tangle-leg doused some of the fire licking up from between his shoulder blades and into the crown of his skull.

He heard Dixie on the stairs.

She came in carrying a basin of steaming water, a tin of salve, and some bandages.

"Gonna get you all fixed up, Mike. You

just relax, and I'll get those cuts all cleaned up and bandaged. Make you good as new."

"How's the kid?" Sartain asked.

"He's on the mend. I just looked in on him and he's getting restless, but I told him to stay in bed. Rest will help him get his strength back up." She grabbed what was left of Sartain's shirt, and ripped it off him. She pulled it out from under him, tossing it onto the floor. Then she cut away what remained of his longhandle top, thoroughly exposing his back.

"I just bought those longhandles in Denver, too," Sartain grunted.

Dixie chuckled. "You're lucky the shirt and the longhandles are all you lost."

"You're a damn fine sawbones, Dixie," Sartain said, taking another sip of the whiskey as she went to work, cleaning the burning cuts.

"Why, thank you, sir." She set the steaming pan aside and climbed off the bed. "Tell you what I'll do," she said, shrugging out of her vest and unbuttoning her blouse. "I'll give you something to look at while I work on that back of yours."

She smiled, nibbling her bottom lip, dimpling her smooth, lightly tanned cheeks. "Hmmm? Would you like that?"

"You don't get that kind of service from

every pill-roller you run into."

She laughed, tossed her shirt onto a chair, and then pulled her thin, cambric chemise up and over her head. Her breasts jostled, her long hair spilling around them.

Sartain sighed as he admired the young woman's succulent attributes. "You're makin' me damned uncomfortable."

Crawling back onto the bed, she giggled and rubbed the pale, cherry-tipped orbs against his shoulder. "You can play with 'em, if you want. I enjoyed you playin' with 'em last night. I liked your big, ole paws on 'em. Made me feel right fine. You know, Mike — you might wanna consider stayin' here in Hard Winter."

She was back to gently cleaning his wounds again.

Sartain took another sip of the bourbon. "Dixie?"

"Yes, Mike?"

"I don't know where it is."

She frowned, her breasts sliding around behind the light screen of her hair as she worked on him. "Where what is?"

"The loot. The stolen money or gold or whatever in hell it is. I have no idea."

He felt her pause in her work. Glancing up over his left shoulder, he saw her frowning down at him. "What stolen money?" She gave a weak chuckle. "I don't know what you're talking about."

"Yes, you do, honey. I'm just giving it to you honestly. I don't know where it is. I just happened into this town for water for me an' my horse. I was going to ride on toward Durango before that bushwhacker tore down on me, and then the kid came riding into town with a bullet in his shoulder. That's what held me up. Not the loot . . . or whatever in hell it is that's got everybody's drawers in a twist around here."

Dixie tucked her hair behind her ear and studied him, befuddled. "You're not working for Hadley?"

"Who's Hadley?"

Her gaze wavered from his. She glanced around the room as though to reorganize her thoughts. Then she went to work again on his back, cleaning the cuts. "Well . . . I'll be damned."

"Dixie, I think after all I been through, I deserve to know what in hell is going on here — don't you?"

She lifted the bloody cloth from his back and gazed down at him again, worriedly this time.

"Mike, if you've got no part in the loot, you'd best light a shuck. Just as soon as I get these wounds cleaned and bandaged. I mean right now — tonight!"

Chapter Eleven

"I'm not goin' anywhere," Sartain said, and drained his glass.

Dixie leaned close to him, and ran a hand through his curly hair. "Mike, someone's gonna kill you. Word's gotten out that you're here for the loot. Everyone thinks Hadley sent you. They assume that's why you shot Beacham. They think . . . and *I* thought . . . that you wanted him out of the way so you could get the loot back to Hadley, and you'd split it up. Everyone knows who you are. You get revenge on folks. Well, everyone thinks Hadley sent you here to get revenge on Beacham for double-crossing him."

Dixie kissed his cheek, and pressed her breasts against his arm. "I know you're tough. I know about your girl. The one them soldiers killed. I heard the story told around. But, Mike, there's lots of men in these mountains looking for that gold. If it's not found soon, there's gonna be more bloodshed."

"Dixie, tell me who Hadley is. Tell me about the gold."

She sighed as though frustrated by a stubborn child, and returned to doctoring his back. "Pour me a drink. My nerves are all jangled. Dang it, I like you, you big ole Brahma bull. And I'll admit I liked you some better when I thought you knew where the gold was, but I like you too much to want to see you turned into a human sieve by the rannies honeycombing these mountains. Word is spreading about the gold. More and more men will be coming to look for it."

Sartain refilled his glass, then handed it up over his shoulder. Dixie took a long drink and handed it back to him. "Oh, Beacham thought he was in good when he threw in with Rench Hadley. Hadley's a big *hombre* in these parts. Big physically and by reputation. The law's even afraid of him. He rode with some of the meanest dozen or so killers you'd ever like to meet.

"Somehow, Beacham and his small, raggedy-heeled bunch threw in with Hadley — probably because Hadley got short-handed when his group was bushwhacked by the army down in Arizona. Anyway, Hadley decided to rob the San Juan Mining

Company payroll last month, as it rolled down out of Denver. Close to a hundred thousand dollars in gold coins. Just after they did, Beacham decided to double-cross the biggest, meanest owlhoot in all of Colorado Territory. You see, Chick's been known to get too big for his britches.

"Only, it didn't work the way he planned. His men ambushed Hadley and his men. Terrible firefight. Chick lost three men. Hadley lost most of his. A few rode away with him wounded. Hadley himself took a bullet. He managed to hold onto the loot. But since he and his wounded riders were in no condition to ride far with a strongbox that heavy, and there was a chance Chick would catch up to 'em again, they buried it in these mountains somewhere. Then Hadley rode on up to Salida, where last I heard he's in jail."

"Jail?"

"Sure. As soon as he started askin' around for a sawbones, everyone in town recognized him. A sawbones came for him, all right. And so did the town marshal, the county sheriff, and three deputies. So he's in jail. And only he knows where the loot is buried. Apparently, he's not sharing that news with the law. Stubborn *hombre,* Rench Hadley. But everyone around here figured that if he survived his bullet wound, he'd bust out of that hoosegow and come looking for the gold. Or he'd send someone to look for it."

Sartain took another sip of the bourbon and handed the glass up to Dixie, smacking his lips. "Well, I'll be damned. Who'd I shoot yesterday? The *hombre* with the spectacles."

"Your guess is as good as mine. Probably someone who figured you were here to crowd the search for the gold."

"What about the kid?"

"Who?"

"Come on, Dixie. I heard you talking to Dewey Dade last night. When he was out of his head and talkin' out of school, so to speak."

"Ah, shit."

"Yeah, well, I got big ears to go along with the rest of me."

"Well, someone shot him for a reason. I got to wondering if *he* somehow got word about where the loot was, and when I walked into his room last night as he was muttering about the loot . . . well, I thought maybe Hadley had sent him, too. Or maybe he'd found out somehow and came to dig it up."

Dixie sighed as she started rubbing arnica on the Revenger's back. "It is not to my credit that I've joined the quest for stolen gold — money that is far from rightly mine — but there it is."

"Ah, hell — I don't blame you for that, Dixie. You're a beautiful girl living alone out here, working like a dog." Sartain splashed another couple of fingers of bourbon into his glass. "Hell, I'd even hope you're the one who finds it if I didn't think it would get you killed."

Sartain handed the glass back to Dixie. She waved it off. "I best stay clear. I'll have business tonight. Quite a few come in out of the mountains on a Saturday. And there's even more now." She sighed darkly. "You stay up here and keep the door locked. If anyone asks, Mike, I'll tell 'em you rode on."

"Is Miguel gonna help you down there?"

"Miguel's old. I'll give him a bottle, some food, and a room soon, and he can come up here and kick his boots up. He just likes to get away from his ranch every now and then, give his daughter some peace and quiet out there."

"Yeah, you'd best be good to him. Since the kid might've mentioned him last night."

"Boy, you do have big ears!"

"What do you suppose his part in this is?"

"Who knows?" Dixie said with a sigh.

"But Miguel has spent all his life in these mountains. There isn't much that happens in 'em he doesn't know about."

When she'd thoroughly bandaged the cuts on his back, Sartain rolled over and cupped her breasts in his hands, gently massaging them. She threw her head back, closing her eyes.

"You keep your head down, Dixie," he warned. "This neck of the San Juans is a powder keg primed to explode."

She smiled and placed her hands on his, atop her breasts. "If I find it, I'll share it with you. I might not be Jewel, but I'll make you happy, Mike." She leaned down and lightly pressed her lips to his. "I'll make you happy for the rest of your life."

She crawled lower on him, straddling him, and opened his pants.

He'd been ready since she'd skinned out of her shirt.

"I promise I will," she said in a hushed, sexy singsong.

As she closed her warm mouth over him, he clenched his fists at his sides. "I know you would, damnit."

In more ways than one, Sartain felt far better after Dixie had left him than before she'd come to him.

He was tired and sore, but the girl's ministrations as well as the whiskey had him feeling like he could go downstairs and hold his own in a poker game. He thought better of it, however. He didn't want to stir up any trouble. If the men after the gold thought he was gone, all the better.

He'd be gone first thing tomorrow. He had to admit that Dixie's offer had been tempting. At least the part about him staying with her for a while. No one could replace his beloved Jewel, of course, but it would be nice to settle down with a woman. It wasn't in the cards for him. However attractive such a life appeared to him now, there was just too much water under the bridge for him to ever settle down and live a peaceful life.

He was convinced he hadn't been fated a peaceful existence.

Besides, he wanted nothing to do with stolen gold.

He lay back on the bed, built a quirley, refilled his whiskey glass, and fished from his saddlebags an old *Rocky Mountain News* he'd picked up in Denver. He could tell a small crowd was growing down in the main drinking hall, for the din grew gradually louder. It also grew more raucous as the spirits flowed and the poker stakes climbed higher.

Around ten-thirty, when the whiskey was causing his eyes to grow heavy and he was pondering crawling under the covers, a couple of men's voices rose higher than the others. They were also pitched with anger. Dixie responded in kind, though because of the generalized din, Sartain couldn't tell exactly what she said in response to her disgruntled clientele.

But the next voice was raised loudly enough that the Revenger could hear exactly what the man said: "Come on, Dixie — we know he's up there! We seen his horse out in the corral!"

"Goddamnit, Slater — stand down or I'll get my shotgun!"

Sartain cursed and rose from the bed. Admonishing himself for not hiding his stallion, he dressed quickly, listening to the argument between Dixie, Slater, and what sounded like a few others grow in volume.

He strapped his LeMat around his waist and left the room.

He was halfway downstairs when the din dwindled quickly. Faces turned toward him. Men's faces. Dixie stood with her back to the staircase, facing the group of a dozen or so of all shapes and sizes and manner of garb.

The stocky, gray-headed Slater stood before Dixie, red-faced with anger. Three others, including the stupid-looking string bean, Lonnie, flanked him with their arms crossed belligerently. Now, however, as they turned toward Sartain, they slowly lowered their arms, hands moving toward their guns.

"I knew she had him up there." Lonnie turned enraged eyes on Dixie. "I *knew* you had him up there!"

"Or course we knew," said Slater. "We seen his horse in the corral!"

"Shame on you, Miss Dixie!" said Lonnie, hardening his jaws. "It is beneath you, cavortin' with a known killer such as him! If your pa only knew what you've become!"

Dixie said, "Oh, shut the hell up, Lonnie, you cork-headed fool! So, we been makin' time together. Finally, I found a *man* around here with some *balls*!"

Oh, shit, Sartain thought. This was going even farther south than before he'd shown himself.

He moved slowly, unthreateningly down to stand one step up from Dixie, holding up his arms to quiet the eruption on the heels of the girl's last proclamation.

"Hold on! Hold on!" he yelled.

When the men had piped down again, Sartain said, "I know you all know who I am, so there's no point in making introductions. I'm here by chance. I am not here because I was sent here by Rench Hadley or anyone else. I rode into Hard Winter looking for water. That's all. I know nothing about the goddamn gold. And what's more, I don't care about it. It's all yours."

He placed his hands on Dixie's shoulders. "But if one thing happens to this young lady, and if everyone ain't on their best behavior while you're enjoying her whiskey, you'll have me to answer to."

A man at the back of the room shouted, "Maybe you can't count, Sartain. But you're a little outnumbered here!"

Sartain's gaze found the man sitting near the back of the room with two others, far back of the crowd gathered near the stairs. They were the only ones sitting. Playing cards, coins, and silver certificates lay strewn around their table spiked with bottles and glasses.

They were dressed better than most of the others in the room — with some city style. One wore a bowler hat. They were attired similarly to the man whom Sartain had beefed when he'd first ridden into town. Though they were sitting down, he could see well-oiled revolvers strapped to their thighs.

Behind Sartain rose the ratcheting scrape of a rifle being cocked. "Now there's two, and I'm ready to cut loose with this carbine here," yelled Dewey Dade from the top of the stairs, extending a Spencer repeater straight out from his left hip. "So go ahead and start fiddlin', boys, and we'll dance!"

The kid wore only his longhandles and socks. His coarse, wavy blond hair, shaved above the ears, was badly mussed. His right arm hung down by his side.

"Thanks, kid," Sartain said. "But there's no need."

"I'll back anything you do, Mr. Sartain." Dewey kept his bright, angry eyes on the room. "You saved my bacon yesterday. If it hadn't been for you, I'm like to have bled to death."

Sartain turned back to the room. "No one's gonna make any trouble here tonight — are you, fellas?"

The man who'd made the last threat said "Shit," in disgust, and he and his friends resumed their card game.

The others in the room backed off, muttering.

Sartain turned and winked at Dewey Dade. The kid smiled, depressed his rifle's hammer, and walked back off down the second-floor hall.

"I could have handled it, Mike," Dixie said.

"I didn't want you to have to handle it by yourself."

"They probably don't believe you, anyway."

"No, but they're not as sure as they were. And they know I'm not afraid of 'em." Sartain squeezed the back of her neck reassuringly. "If you need anything, give a yell. I'm gonna go check on my horse, make sure he's ready to ride first thing in the morning."

Dixie turned her mouth corners down in a pout. "Goshdarnit, Mike. Did you even consider my offer?"

"More than I've ever considered any other but one."

The Cajun kissed her cheek and headed for the rear door.

The three well-dressed card players all turned their heads to watch him leave. They rose from their chairs, hitched their pistols higher on their hips, shared conspiratorial glances, and sauntered out the front door.

Chapter Twelve

Sartain removed the feedbag from Boss's nose.

"That's enough oats, old son," he told the horse, folding the bag and laying it over his saddle in the lean-to stable. "Don't want you getting the green heaves. We'll be pullin' out tomorrow."

He'd already checked the stallion's hooves, making sure all the shoes were set right and the frogs hadn't picked up any burrs. Now he gave the horse one more pat. As he turned away, the stallion brushed his head against the Cajun's shoulder.

Sartain chuckled. "You like that idea, do you?" He scratched the underside of Boss's snout. "Get some sleep. Mornin' will be here before . . ."

He let his voice trail off. He'd heard something. The crunch of gravel beneath a boot. It seemed to originate from behind the stable.

Scowling, he moved to the stable door that led out behind the corral. As he flicked the door latch, he released the keeper thong from over the hammer of his pistol. He stepped outside, scanning the darkness relieved by starlight and a moon rising over the Sangre de Cristos in the east.

He smelled the alcohol stench just before he saw a shadow move on his left. Something glinted brassily in the darkness, and then a long object slashed down toward his head. He smelled the lurker in time and managed to raise his arm and duck his head, so that the shell belt filled with brass gave his forehead only a glancing blow.

A stinging blow. But a full-on blow likely would have laid him out.

Fury threatened to blow the top of his head off. He lashed out at the shadow before him first with his left fist and then with his right. The left landed solidly on a jaw. The right caught the nub of the man's chin.

His attacker grunted and stumbled backward. Another figure moved up behind him — the Revenger could hear the footsteps — and wrapped two arms around his neck. He was thrust backward, the man's arms pinching off his wind.

"Hold him, Ray," said a third man tightly,

coming in from Sartain's right.

In the moonlight, he recognized the face of one of the three card players. The man bolted toward him, throwing a haymaker toward the Revenger's face.

Sartain stomped down on the toe of the boot of the man holding him. Ray instantly released him. Sartain leaned right, and the haymaker skinned off the side of his face to catch the man behind him in the throat.

Ray made a gurgling, strangling sound.

Sartain head-butted the man who'd thrown the haymaker, knocking his hat off. The man grunted as he rocked back on the heels of his boots, legs wobbling. Sartain punched him twice quickly, stepping into him as he stumbled backward.

The man who'd swung the cartridge belt came up on his left, cussing. His teeth flashed white in the purple darkness. The moonlight skimmed off the bald dome of his head. He buried his right fist in Sartain's belly, then jabbed his left against the Cajun's jaw.

Sartain stumbled backward, fury really dancing a jig in him now.

As the man came at him again, bringing up his fist from his heels, Sartain ducked. The man's fist whistled through the air over his head. The man grunted. Sartain straightened and slammed his attacker's left jaw with his right fist.

He slammed him again and again in the same place until he had him on the ground. He punched him two more times in the nose.

With the second punch, the man's nose exploded like a ripe tomato. The blood was warm against the Cajun's fist.

A shadow moved to his left. Something glinted in the moonlight.

"No guns, Clement!" Ray yelled hoarsely. "Keep it quiet."

"I ain't gonna shoot him. I'm just gonna — *ach*!"

As Clement whipped the pearl handle of the pistol toward Sartain's head, the Cajun bounded off his heels and thrust his head into the man's belly. The pistol slammed against Sartain's back without heat. The man's feet left the ground. The Cajun bulled him to the ground so hard, he heard what sounded like every bone in the man's back crack.

The Revenger gained his feet and whipped around, crouching, ready for another onslaught. Ray came at him again, weakly swinging his right fist. It was an ill-considered, half-hearted move. Again, the Cajun ducked the blow. He buried his fist twice into Ray's solar plexus. The man's lungs almost literally exploded as he jackknifed.

As his head went down, Sartain brought his knee up to meet Ray's head with a solid blow.

That finished him. He lay still.

Sartain wheeled, ready for yet another assault. None came. The other two men were down where they'd last fallen, writhing and groaning.

Something silvery lay on the ground, catching the moonlight. Sartain walked over and picked up the badge and tipped it to the light, brushing his finger across the letters engraved in the nickel-plated star and moon badge.

DEPUTY U.S. MARSHAL.

He chuckled caustically, tossing the badge into the darkness.

Then he drew his LeMat and ratcheted back the hammer.

"Which one of you lame-brained, badge-totin' sonso'bitches want it first?"

"Don't shoot," said the one lying straight out away from Sartain, pushing up heavily onto his elbows. It was dark where his nose should have been in the center of his otherwise pale face. He clamped a hand over the appendage in question. "Don't shoot us.

For Christ's sake, Sartain."

"Give me a reason. Better be a big one."

"We're after the gold — same as you," said Clement, sitting up and flexing his right arm. "We ain't here on business."

"Oh? Then what was this all about?"

Dixie's voice rose from the shadows at the rear of the saloon. "Mike?" The back door was open, spilling wan light from inside. Running footsteps sounded. Her shadow was limned by the moonlight. "What the hell is going on out here?"

"Hoedown," Sartain said. "Kind of unexpected, but the best ones always are."

Dixie slowed as she stepped around the three men on the ground. The third, Ray, was groaning now. Damn. Sartain had hoped he'd killed him. He had no use for federal badge-toters. He saw them as little better than the federal soldiers who'd raped and murdered Jewel and shot her grandfather out in the desert south of Benson.

Not that he'd known any marshals who'd done anything like that, but they were out to stop him from performing what he considered his destiny to further avenge Jewel and the old man: To avenge those who were unable to avenge themselves.

"What's this all about?" Dixie wanted to know, her voice brittle with anger.

"Very same question I just posed," Sartain said.

The man with the broken nose spat blood and said in a comically nasal voice. "That was our man you shot yesterday, you son of a bitch."

"The bastard who bushwhacked me?"

They didn't respond to that.

Clement rolled over onto his side and tried to get up but fell back. "Oh, mercy — I think my back is broken."

"Shut up or I'll give you more of the same," the Cajun warned him. He turned to the other two. "I didn't see no badge on him."

"You blew his badge off when you shot him!" Ray intoned.

"Why'd he bushwhack me?"

Clement got to a knee, breathing hard and grunting. "I don't know." He gained his feet, limped over, and scooped his hat up off the ground. He batted it against his leg, which was so covered in dirt it looked brown. "We'd split up. He was alone. Maybe he recognized you. There's a kill order out on you, Sartain. Shoot first and ask questions later. Unofficial, but there it is."

"Jesus Christ!" said Dixie.

The information didn't surprise the Revenger.

"Who rode out of here like a bat out of hell, just after I shot your pal?"

"Didn't see him," Clement said, shrugging. "Lots of folks been keeping an eye on the town of late. Thinkin' the gold's around here somewhere."

"We heard the shooting," said Ray. "I rode over and dragged Gleason off. We weren't sure what it was all about . . . till we glassed you over at the well."

Sartain stepped back, wagging his gun at the man who'd risen to his feet behind him. "What're you doing around here?"

"Federal business." The lawman with the broken nose, whose name Sartain had not caught, stumbled slowly over to join the others brushing off dust and working the knots out of their muscles, easing bones back into place. "And it don't involve you."

"This did."

"This was unofficial," said the broken-nosed man, tenderly touching his nose, blood dribbling over his lips. His voice was nasal, almost inaudible. "This was for Gleason."

"Way to go!" laughed Dixie.

Broken Nose glowered at her. "Miss, if you'd kindly shut the hell up, I'd really —"

"Uh-uh," Sartain said, wagging the LeMat once more. "You talk nice to the lady. I'm still debating whether I want to plug you three uglies right here and be done with you."

"No need," said Ray, holding his hands out in supplication. "We're out of here."

"Yes, you are," Dixie said.

"One more question," Sartain said, narrowing an eye. "Was that you three who bushwhacked me and Beacham's men yesterday?"

The three looked at each other, frowning. "Hell, no!" said Clement.

Sartain was skeptical, but he let it go.

When they'd mounted up and ridden out, Dixie turned to Sartain. "You've had quite a time in my fair city, haven't you, Mike?"

"It's a red-letter kind of place."

"You sure you're all right?"

"Fine as frog hair."

"The night's windin' down. Come on inside. We'll go up and curl each other's toes after I check to make sure you haven't opened your back up again." Dixie hiked a shoulder. "I guess this will be our last night."

Sartain kissed her cheek. "You go on inside. I'll be a minute. I'm gonna stay out here and have a smoke and make sure those three federals don't swing back in this direction. I don't trust any of 'em farther than I could throw all three uphill against a Dakota cyclone."

"Don't blame you."

Dixie walked off toward the saloon's open rear door. Sartain climbed the corral fence, sat on the top rail, and hooked his boot heels over the bottom rail. Deep in thought, he built a smoke and touched a match to it.

Just after he'd fired the quirley, another match scratched to life nearby. He looked to his right to see the slender, short shadow of a man in a *sombrero* cupping a lucifer to the cigarette drooping from his mouth. Sartain's right hand had started to slide toward the LeMat, but he stayed the movement when he recognized the Mexican, who walked toward him slowly.

The little man's quirley glowed in the darkness. Smoke billowed around his head, turning pearl in the moonlight.

"There is much trouble here now." They were the first words he'd heard Miguel Otero speak. He'd started to think maybe he was mute or didn't have a handle on English.

"You can say that again, *señor.*"

Otero leaned back against the corral to Sartain's right. He stretched one arm out atop the rail and lifted his round face to the moonlight. "*Sí,* much trouble. Gold trouble. The only other trouble similar to it is woman trouble. 'Gold and love affairs are difficult to hide.' It is an old Spanish saying. Very old . . . and very true."

Sartain drew a lungful of smoke and blew it at the moon growing smaller as it rose, touching the velvety darkness around it with lilac. Somewhere, a night bird screeched.

Sartain turned to the little man. "*Señor,* I got a feeling you know all about this gold trouble, don't you?"

Otero lifted a shoulder and looked away. When he turned his head forward again, he took another draw from his quirley and tapped ashes into the dust.

As he expelled the smoke from his lungs, he said, *"Sí."*

CHAPTER THIRTEEN

"You gonna tell me about it?" Sartain asked Miguel Otero.

Otero had a long pocket sewn into his elk-skin breeches. From the pocket he extracted a clear, unlabeled bottle. "First a drink, *señor*?"

"Don't mind if I do, *señor.*" The Revenger accepted the bottle, pried out the cork, and tipped it back.

The mescal burned going down, but chilled his belly, leaving a pleasant aftertaste akin to grapefruit. Suddenly, the night had softer edges, and the moonlight was pretty. The fire in his back had kicked up during the skirmish with the three lawmen. Now, it was nearly doused.

"Gracias," he rasped, his vocal chords momentarily paralyzed.

"De nada." The Mexican tipped the bottle back and then set it down on the ground between them. "I will leave it here. *Por favor,*

help yourself."

"All right, I will."

Otero took a long drag off his quirley and held it up close to his face as he studied the moon for a time. Exhaling the smoke through his nostrils, he said, "I know where the gold is hidden, *Señor* Sartain. I also know that you, being who you are, have little use for it. Your life is about other things, no?"

He didn't wait for a reply. "I would request that you take it and return it to its rightful owners. It is a sacrilege and a curse. It has brought evil to these mountains. Men have died looking for it. Many more will die until it is gone far away from here."

"How do you know where it is?"

"*Señor* Hadley rode wounded out to my *rancho.* He had the strongbox on a pack mule. He told me to hide the gold and hide it well, that he would be back for it. He told me that if it was not with me when he came for it, that if any of it was missing, he would cut my throat and the throat of my daughter, Celina. She lives with me. She is my only family, her mother having passed."

"Hadley's in jail, *Señor* Ortega. That gold could all be yours, if you wanted it to be."

"*Sí.* I am aware of that. But, like you, my life is about other things than getting rich on the sweat of others. Besides, I have penance to pay. The boy upstairs, Dewey Dade, worked for me last summer, cutting and chopping wood, wrangling my cattle — work that has become very difficult for me."

The wiry Mexican held up a brown hand gnarled with arthritis and shaking slightly. "He became my friend. A good boy, but a boy with little luck. A boy with a difficult past. When I ran out of work for him, he rode on to Taos. I sent word to him there about the gold. I thought that if anyone should have it, he should. And then it would be gone from these mountains. He rode back here, heading for my *rancho.* He was shot because of the gold."

"Who shot him?"

"I don't know. One of the men whose horns you filed here tonight, maybe."

"The lawmen?"

"*Sí.* But they are not here as lawmen." Otero reached down for the bottle, and handed it up to Sartain. "They are here for the gold. One of them keeps an eye on the town constantly, knowing that anyone looking for it will be drawn here to the well and to *Señorita* Dixie's saloon. I think they will kill anyone they think might be closer to it than they are."

"How do you know?"

"They have been too long in these mountains, riding and riding, searching and searching." Otero shook his head. "Like everyone else here now, they are here for the gold."

Sartain took another pull of the raw mescal.

More sharp edges were filed off the night, despite his consternation about the gold.

"If anyone can get the gold out of here before it can cause more bad things to happen, it is you, *Señor* Sartain. Will you do this for me? I know I am not a friend. But we have shared a bottle here tonight, and we both live for something besides wealth."

"What do you live for, *Señor* Otero?"

"My daughter, Celina. You see, she is blind from birth." Otero shrugged. "She has only me. All the gold in the world will not fix her eyes. It would only destroy her soul . . . and mine."

Sartain held out his hand. Otero gave a half-smile as he shook it.

"Just tell me where and when, and I'll come for it, *Señor* Otero." Sartain handed the bottle back to the Mexican. "And I'll make sure it's taken back to its rightful owners. Then, maybe, peace will return to your mountains. And to you and Celina."

Otero squeezed the Revenger's hand hard,

his smile brightening. *"Gracias, Señor."*

Sartain slipped the strap of Dixie's chemise off her shoulders.

The garment dropped to her waist. He leaned down to nuzzle her breasts.

"Oh, Mike," she said, running a hand through his hair. "I wish you didn't have to leave."

"Me, too, darlin'. It's time, though."

"You feel so good."

"You, too."

They were sitting on the edge of her bed. Sartain was naked. Dixie had been wearing only the chemise. It was around midnight, and the Cajun had helped her clean up around the saloon after the last customers had left or drifted off to their rooms on the second floor.

Sartain wrapped his arms around her tenderly and kissed her. She returned the kiss, flicking her tongue into his mouth, entangling hers with his and licking his teeth.

"Where will you go?" she said at last when they'd come up for air.

"I think I'm just gonna give ole Boss his head and see where he takes me."

"I thought you were heading for Durango."

"Was I? Well, hell, then. Maybe I'll head to Durango. If I give old Boss his head, he's liable to ride me right into a whole stable full of fillies."

Dixie tugged on his ears as she kissed him. "You'd both enjoy that, you cad."

"Got me there, gal." Sartain caressed her cheek with his thumb, brushing away a tear that had dribbled down from her eye. "But you ain't gonna be one I'll ever forget, Dixie."

"I'm not going to forget you, either, Mike."

She lay back on the bed. Sartain followed her down, planting kisses on her bare belly. She ran both hands through his hair. Her belly rose and fell as she breathed and writhed luxuriously beneath his ministrations.

Dixie looked down at him. "Was that Miguel Otero you were talking with outside?"

"Uh-huh."

"I thought he'd taken his bottle and a bowl of beans up to bed. He comes in once every few weekends, gives Celina a little time by herself, which she enjoys despite being blind. What were you two talking about?"

"Just them three suits I was dancin' with out by the corral. They're lawmen. But

Otero thinks they're here looking for the gold along with everybody else."

"Miguel would know. He knows pretty much everything that goes on in these mountains."

Sartain had drifted lower on her body.

Dixie squirmed.

"Oh," she said, gasping. "Oh . . . oh, my *God . . .!*"

The next morning, Sartain stopped Boss in an aspen copse and shucked his Henry from its saddle sheath. He led the horse deeper into the trees, tied him to a branch, and then drifted back out to the edge of the copse.

Now he saw the riders following the same trail he'd followed down from the northern ridge, on the other side of the deep, narrow valley. One, two, and then three of them appeared, riding Indian-file down the fir-carpeted slope and spilling down onto the canyon floor. The autumn-cured brome grass was high enough to brush their stirrups.

The Revenger could tell by the way they were dressed — wool coats, well-shaped Stetsons, or, in one case, a brown bowler hat — that they were the three lawmen from the night before. That they were following him, there was no doubt. Why, he had no idea.

Maybe they had circled back last night, after all, and heard him and Otero talking . . .

If they had, they'd made a big mistake. A bigger mistake than the one they'd made last night. He would not, could not, allow them to follow him to Otero's *rancho.*

The Cajun stepped farther back into the trees before swinging around and returning to his horse. He slid the rifle into its sheath, mounted up, and rode on through the copse, the new-fallen leaves crunching under the horse's hooves. Leaves danced in the air around Sartain, bouncing off his hat brim, sparkling in the sunshine like large burning cinders.

At the far end of the copse, a creek chuckled along the base of the ridge, over a stony bed that was also littered with fallen aspen leaves. Beyond the creek a trail wound up the bank and into the pines — probably an old Indian trail later used by prospectors crisscrossing these mountains looking for their El Dorados.

Sartain splashed across the creek and followed the trail, knowing his wet hoof prints were leaving a hell of a mark. Soon the pines shaded him as Boss lurched up the steep incline, and the heady pine resin filled his nostrils. He continued to follow the meandering trail, noting occasional old campsites here and there marked by scorched stones and rusty airtight tins.

Soon the trail crested the ridge and dropped down the other side where few trees grew. At the bottom of the next valley, the trail hooked around an old prospector's cabin.

The place didn't appear to be in current use. Weeds, brush, and pine saplings had grown up around it, and no smoke issued from the chimney. It was a cool day, and anyone living there would likely have a fire going, if only to keep a pot of coffee warm.

Sartain pulled Boss off the trail and around behind the cabin. He tied the horse to an aspen near a small creek gurgling between muddy banks over mossy stones. He unbuckled the horse's latigo, slipped his bit, and walked around to the front of the cabin.

There was a small, rotting boardwalk fronting the door. The door itself was gray with age but otherwise in good shape. It sagged open when the Revenger tripped the latch.

The cabin was a humble abode with an earthen floor, a sheet-iron stove, and a simple pine table. Split logs were stacked neatly by the stove, with a small tomato crate containing pine cones and needles and feather sticks for kindling. Apparently, the place was a common stopover for travelers; as was the custom of the country, wood was always left in good supply. There were even some airtight tins of canned vegetables stacked on a shelf over a small food preparation table.

Sartain opened the cabin's four shutters to let in some light and fresh air, then built a fire in the stove, hoping no birds had built a nest in the pipe since the last traveler had stopped here, and set a pot of coffee to boil. He went outside and looked at the stovepipe slanting up out of the moss-spotted shake roof. Smoke appeared to be issuing freely.

He looked toward the trail snaking through the columnar pines, firs, and spruces.

So far, he couldn't see the lawmen. That was good. Maybe they weren't following him. Maybe they were smarter than he'd given them credit for. No. Fools they were — all three. Sartain was convinced it had been they who'd ambushed Beacham's bunch. If not them, then three or four others looking for the gold and hound-dogging anyone they thought might know where it was.

It was hard to tell just whom the rumors of hidden gold had lured to this neck of the San Juans.

He had to make damned sure he wasn't trailed to the Otero *rancho* . . .

He'd know soon if they were coming, for they'd likely smell the wood smoke from a hundred, two hundred yards away.

When the coffee came to a boil, he dumped in a handful of Arbuckle's. When it boiled again, he poured in some cold water from his canteen to settle the grounds, and filled his tin coffee cup, dented and pitted and scorched by the flames of many fires.

He sat at the table, gazing through the open window before him, one boot hiked on a knee. He built a quirley and smoked and sipped the coffee, filling the cabin with tobacco smoke that mingled with the smoke from the leaky stove door.

Outside, chickadees cheeped in the pines. Nearby, he could see a nuthatch scuttling along the underside of a dead aspen branch, probing for aphids. There were all kinds of sounds in the forest around the cabin — the scuttling of rabbits and squirrels, the quiet chuckling of the creek, the scratching of branches stirred by a breeze.

He picked through the sounds, searching for the thud of a horse hoof or the squawk of saddle leather. Maybe the muffled scrape of a rifle being cocked somewhere.

So far, nothing.

Then a shadow moved in the forest beyond the open door, maybe fifty yards away. The shadow had slipped behind a red pine trunk. Now an arm reached out from the left side of the pine. It rose and fell slowly.

A signal.

Above Sartain, the ceiling creaked ever so gently.

He glanced up, frowning. Then he realized that his eyes were burning. There was more smoke in the cabin than he'd realized. It was boiling, thick and white, from around the stove door.

They were trying to smoke him out.

Chapter Fourteen

The Revenger grabbed his rifle from the table and pumped a round into the chamber.

Rising from the chair so suddenly that the chair flew back behind him, hitting the floor, he aimed at the ceiling and pumped three rounds through the gray herringbone-patterned wood around where he'd glimpsed dust sifting toward the floor.

There was a shrill scream and a loud thump on the roof. More dust sifted.

Behind the cabin, Boss whinnied.

Something buzzed in the air around Sartain's head and clanged off the chimney pipe. It was followed a quarter-second later by the hiccupping blast of a rifle in front of the cabin.

The smoke was still issuing from the stove door, but it had thinned considerably. Apparently whatever the man on the ceiling had placed over the chimney pipe had fallen off the pipe when Sartain had fired up through the ceiling.

Now more rifles barked from what seemed to be three directions around the cabin. The Cajun pumped another round into the Henry's breech and threw himself to the floor as more lead stitched the air around him, blowing chunks of wood from the table and the fallen chair and pluming ancient dust from the log walls. Smoke from the stove was ripped and torn by the careening lead.

There was a dull clank as a bullet clipped his coffee cup and set it bounding across the cabin, spewing what remained of his coffee.

He crawled across the floor beneath the swarm of bullets buzzing above his head. He wedged himself into a corner between the front window and the side window facing northeast. He'd counted three rifles hammering away at the cabin. Counting the man who'd been on the roof and whom he was relatively certain he'd put out of commission, the number was puzzling.

There were only three lawmen.

The Cajun doffed his hat, ran his sleeve over his eyes burning from the smoke, and edged a quick look out the side window. A rifle was lapping flames from some brush about forty feet from the cabin. When the shooter raised the barrel to lever another cartridge into the action, Sartain slid the Henry over the window ledge and triggered three shots as fast as he could, hearing a howl from the shrubs.

He pumped another round into the breech.

The man who'd been shooting from the shrubs was up and staggering away from the brush, sort of stumbling to his left. He glanced over his shoulder and Sartain saw the soft, round, red face and paunch of Slater. The gray-haired gent bellowed a curse as he levered his rifle, then swung around to face Sartain, who triggered two more rounds into the man's gut bulging his canvas coat and sagging over his belt buckle.

Slater fell straight back, dropping his rifle and throwing his arms out from his sides.

"Gone to hell, you bushwhackin' bastard," the Revenger grated out, racking another round.

"Slater?" called a familiar voice. "Slater, you hit?"

Sartain shouted, "He's gone to meet his Maker, Lonnie, you stupid bastard!" Quickly, he whipped around toward the front window, aimed, and fired four rounds in quick succession.

After the second round, he'd heard a yelp and saw a hat fly as bark spewed from the bole of the tree the string bean hunkered behind.

"You're gonna die, you son of a bitch!" Lonnie bellowed.

Sartain pulled his head below the window as the horse-faced string bean cut loose with a Spencer repeating rifle, chewing up wood from the window casing. Spying a shadow flick across the floor on his far right, Sartain whipped his head in that direction. A man was running toward the cabin from the west — an old, gray-bearded man in a wool coat and battered wool hat.

The man raised a rifle and aimed through the window . . . but not before Sartain flung a .44-caliber chunk of lead into his chest.

The oldster screamed, showing his teeth as he twisted around and backward.

Sartain remembered the old man from the saloon, though he'd not learned his name. Most likely a local prospector. One who was tired of prospecting and had turned his prospecting sites on minted gold instead of the stuff you broke your back for.

The Revenger raked out a curse. He didn't like killing old men, but this dunderhead had given him no choice.

Only one rifle was barking now. The string

bean had fallen nearly silent, flinging only the occasional shot through the window.

"You can't hold up in there forever, Sartain!" the kid shouted now in his grating, wheedling tone.

"It's just you and me, kid," the Cajun shouted. "Those are long odds for you! Why not give it up and go on back to the hole you crawled out of?"

"I didn't crawl out of no hole!" The kid sounded miffed. "*You* did!"

Sartain chuckled.

"You were keepin' time with my girl! You're gonna pay for that, too! I don't cotton to folks encroachin' on my territory, and Miss Dixie is *my* territory!"

The string bean's rifle belched again.

The bullet screeched through the window and thudded into the opposite wall.

Sartain chuckled again, snaked his Henry over the window, and fired five, then six, rounds at where he'd seen the kid poking his head out from behind the tree. He fired once more, but the hammer pinged, empty.

The kid's rifle dropped straight down onto the end of its barrel, flipped, and lay flat on the ground. Sartain couldn't see the kid himself, only the rifle.

He frowned. He hadn't thought he'd hit him. Maybe he had. Unless he was playing possum. The string bean probably wasn't bright or bold enough for that ploy, but there was only one way to find out.

Sartain quickly reloaded the Henry, racked a round into the chamber, and moved slowly out of the shack. The thinning smoke billowed around him like fog. He wiped his eyes with his neckerchief and, holding the rifle straight out from his right hip, he strode out toward the tree.

From ten feet away, he could see the kid's arms flung around the sides of the tree as though he were hugging it. Sartain walked slowly around the tree. The kid was slumped against it, pressing his left cheek against the bark. Blood trickled out a corner of his half-open mouth. His eyes were open and staring groundward.

Blood also oozed from the hole in nearly the middle of his back.

Sartain frowned, puzzled. That must be the exit wound.

The Cajun kicked the kid out away from the tree and inspected the front of his body. There was one more wound low down on his right side near his rib cage. It was a large, ugly hole issuing blood and viscera.

That was the exit wound.

But Sartain had shot him from the front.

A grasshopper of dread leaped up his

spine. From the corner of his right eye he watched three men walk toward him. He turned his head slowly.

The newcomers were the three lawmen whose clocks he'd cleaned last night. Two were grinning. The one with the busted nose wasn't grinning. His nose was three times its normal size. The nose and his eyes were blue, with the edges of the blue touched with copper. Understandably, he looked jaundiced and sullen.

All three lawmen were aiming rifles at him.

They hadn't learned a thing from last night.

"Throw it down, Sartain," Ray ordered, looking especially self-satisfied. A yellow aspen leaf was pasted to the crown of his bowler hat. "Then you and me and my compatriots are gonna have us a little talk."

"Well, shit," said the Cajun.

He turned his mouth corners down and began to lower the Henry.

He didn't lower it far before he whipped it back up, swung around to square his shoulders and hips at the three lawmen, and commenced firing the repeater from his side.

The rifle roared, flames and smoke lapping from the barrel.

Brass cartridge casings winked in vagrant

rays of sunlight angling through the forest canopy. They arced over the Cajun's right shoulder to clink to the ground behind him.

The sudden move had taken the three badge-toters by surprise. None got off a single shot.

They screamed as they danced wildly, and died bloody.

Sartain set the Henry on his shoulder. He sighed.

"All I wanted was some water for me an' my horse," he said. "Was that too damn much to ask?"

Sartain dragged the bodies off away from the cabin, so the stench of rot wouldn't pester future sojourners. The first four attackers had all been men whom Sartain had seen in the saloon. Regulars. He didn't feel bad about turning them toe-down, except for the fact that he was also whittling down Dixie McKee's clientele.

He set the cabin back the way he'd found it — aside from the bullet holes, that was — and then swung up onto Boss's back and continued his journey toward Miguel Otero's *rancho.* He followed the old Mexican's direction along the floor of the main canyon and then started climbing through sparse forest toward a stony pass that was already showing a thin mantling of snow.

As he climbed, following a two-track wagon trail up the steady rise peppered with pines, birches, and aspens, clouds moved in over the peaks and dropped. They were the color of dirty wool. A chill wind kicked up.

The clouds dropped lower, gauzy and gray. Snow began falling — hard, little flakes at first, before the flakes grew larger and softer.

"Oh, shit," the Cajun drawled as he paused to shrug into his mackinaw.

A late summer snow was all he needed. This high in the mountains — at least ten thousand feet, he should have expected it.

He continued riding. The sparse forest grew sparser near the base of the bald, craggy ridge jutting two thousand feet into the sky, though the low clouds and blowing snow had now obliterated the crest. He'd caught glimpses of what he assumed was the Otero — a brown smudge near the ridge base — though now the snow had obliterated that, too.

Hunched low in the saddle, he followed the trail through a portal with the name Otero blazed into the crossbar, and into the ranch yard. It was now as dark as dusk. The two-story stone- and wood-frame cabin sat hunched on the far side of a hard-packed yard, several log buildings including a large hay barn and several corrals outlying it.

A large cottonwood stood on the cabin's east side, shedding its leaves onto the roof.

A rifle barked.

Sartain drew back sharply on Boss's reins. He leaned forward to place his hand on the Henry's stock and peered straight ahead toward the cabin. A slender, black-haired young woman in a red wool shirt and denim trousers stood on the wooden gallery that ran along the front of the lodge.

The rifle flashed and barked in the young woman's hands. The bullet plumed mud and snow about twenty feet to Sartain's right. Boss lurched and sidestepped, whickering uneasily.

"Hold on, *Señorita* Otero!" the Cajun shouted. "It's Mike Sartain!"

The woman cocked the rifle and aimed it from her right shoulder.

"Ride in slow!" she shouted angrily with a Spanish accent.

He raised his hand from the Henry's stock, leaving the long gun in its sheath, and clucked Boss ahead through the slanting snow falling and melting, looking like thin slush in the dirt of the yard. Dirt that was fast turning to mud.

The Cajun kept his cautious gaze on the

slender, long-haired figure aiming the rifle at him, as he put Boss up to the cabin and halted about ten feet away. She was her father's size, but better filled out. She appeared in her mid to late twenties. Round-faced. Good-looking, but not pretty, though few girls looked pretty when they were aiming a rifle at you. The tails of her red wool shirt hung out of her jeans. Her long, straight black hair blew around in the chill wind.

"Better not try anything, *amigo*!" the girl said in a low voice pitched with menace. "You understand? I got the sights right on your heart, and I'll blow you in two if you try anything!"

But she didn't appear to have her sights lined up on the Cajun's heart. The gun appeared to be aimed more at his right knee.

He remembered that Otero's daughter was blind.

"I'm not going to try anything, Miss. I'm Mike Sartain. I'm here to see your father. I was invited."

She must have used Sartain's voice to recalculate the location of his heart, because she put her rifle's sights on it now. Sartain winced slightly. He felt Boss tense his back through the saddle.

"I'm here to see your father, Miss Otero,"

the Cajun repeated. "Is he around? Like I said, he's expect—"

She lowered the rifle and, sobbing, pressed a hand to her forehead and yelled, "He's not here! Somebody came for him earlier today and took him *away*!"

Chapter Fifteen

Sartain swung down from Boss's back. He quickly tossed the reins over the hitchrack fronting the ranch house, and mounted the gallery.

As he did, the young woman sank back into a chair of woven aspen branches. She too hastily leaned the rifle against the shack's stone front wall. It slid against the stones and clattered to the floor.

She kept a hand over her forehead as she bawled.

Sartain dropped to a knee beside her. "Who took your father, Miss Otero?"

She shook her head, sniffing and sobbing. "He didn't say his name. He rode into the *rancho* this morning. Papa was in the breaking corral, working with a colt. I heard them arguing. I ran out to the corral to see what the trouble was about, and Papa told me he had to leave with that man."

She hardened her voice, flaring her nostrils

and curling her upper lip angrily. "The man said, 'Don't worry, sweetie, I'll send this old chili-chomper back to you just as soon as he gives me what I want.' "

"You didn't catch his name? Anything about him that might identify him?"

"Not his name. But he smelled like blood, and I heard him dragging one foot."

Sartain said half to himself: "Beacham. I knew I should have gone back to that cabin and finished that simple bastard."

"Who is Beacham?" Celina wanted to know. Reaching tentatively for Sartain, she placed her small, brown hand around Sartain's left wrist, and squeezed it tightly. "What does he want with my father? What does he want Papa to give him?"

Sartain studied the young woman, hesitating. Obviously, Otero had told her nothing about the gold. He probably hadn't wanted to worry her. She was no child, but a full-grown woman; still, there was a childlike innocence and vulnerability about her likely due to the fact she'd been blind since birth.

The Cajun wasn't about to keep the old man's secret. Celina was worried sick about him, and not knowing why Beacham had come for him would only worry her more. Sartain wrapped an arm around the sobbing woman's shoulders. She felt so slender and delicate as he drew her against him that his heart ached for her.

Blind and terrified that she would end up alone out here without the father she obviously loved more than anything, not to mention depended on . . .

"It's about loot stolen from a mine. One of the robbers had your father hide it for him. One of the other robbers is Beacham. He came for it."

Celina gasped and pulled away from Sartain. *"Robbers?"* She placed a hand on his face. It was not an intimate gesture, he instantly realized. It was her way of communicating with him more deeply than words, because she couldn't read with her eyes the expression on his face.

Her hand was small and warm as she slid her fingertips across his cheek, as though she were reading an inscription in stone.

"He'll be all right, Celina," Sartain said, taking the girl's hand in his own, and squeezing it. "Your father will give the man what he wants, and he'll be fine. Beacham won't hurt him."

He hoped his voice hadn't betrayed any of the doubt in his mind. Maybe it had. The childlike young woman's smooth, brown, round face looked even more frightened than before. *"Dios mio!"* she cried. *"Papa!"*

"Where did they go, Celina? Do you have any idea?"

She held her face in her hands, shoulders quivering as she cried. She shook her head.

"Do you have any idea where your father would hide something important in these mountains? It's probably not far away."

Celina lifted her head and turned her flat, sightless eyes to Sartain. "There is an old stone sheepherder's shack in High Canyon. That is the only place I can think of. There are plenty of places to hide amongst the rocks in that canyon. Papa and I used to play there together when I was just a child, and he still takes me walking up there."

"*Up* there?" Sartain glanced out at the yard. The snow was falling harder, blocking out the forest beyond the ranch portal. Boss wore a furry, ermine mantling of the stuff, and the ground was now covered. "How high is High Canyon?"

"It's high. Another thousand feet." She flung an arm out, pointing across the yard. "To the east."

Slowly, she lowered her arm. Rising from her chair with a look of dire consternation on her face, she walked out to the edge of the gallery, and held her hand out to let the snowflakes flutter into her palm.

"Goddamnit," she bit out, hardening her

jaws and shaking her head. The curse word sounded especially hard, spoken by a woman-child who on first impression had seemed so fragile. "Goddamnit to hell. The gods are against us. There is a wide creek between here and the shack. It's been raining all day up there. I've heard it and smelled it. *Shit!*"

She turned to Sartain. "There will be no way across it until the snow quits."

Suddenly, she seemed less fragile. But no less frightened.

"You sure?" Sartain asked her.

"*Sí.* I am sure." She stomped her foot clad in a riding boot. *"Mierda de cabra!"*

"Goat dung," was how Sartain roughly, silently translated the epithet.

He straightened and walked over to Celina Otero, placing a hand on her slender back. "The snow will likely quit by morning. I'll ride up there then. They'll have to stay put, too. Don't worry, Celina. I'll find them and make sure Beacham doesn't lay one hand on your father."

"*Sí. Gracias.* Thank you, Mr. Sartain. You can put your horse up in the barn. There is fresh hay and corn."

"I'll hole up out there myself."

"Don't be silly. It is cold and will only get colder. You'll stay inside."

"Would that be proper?"

"Who would know . . . way out here?" It seemed a genuine question. Celina hugged herself tightly, shivering. "I'll build a fire and make some coffee. It is cold out here. Inside, we will be warm."

She didn't wait for a response. She stooped to retrieve her rifle, then went inside and closed the door.

The Revenger finished tending his horse and stabling him, and started back to the Otero cabin. He drew his coat collar up high against the chill breeze and the icy fingers of the snow seeking his bare flesh. It was probably only around four o'clock in the afternoon, but it was nearly dark.

The snow fell steadily. Half an inch already lay on the ground, covering the leaves that had fallen from the cottonwood standing just off the lodge's east wall. Dim light flickered softly in a couple of the first-story windows.

He tapped on the door.

"Come."

He moved inside, stamping snow from his boots on the hemp rug fronting the door. Celina sat at a table to his right. The range was behind her. Steam ribboned from the spout of the large, black coffee pot gurgling softly on a stove lid.

"Take your coat off, Mr. Sartain. I will get you some coffee. Are you hungry? I can warm some beans. I will make supper soon. Papa shot an elk earlier in the week. It is hanging in the keeper shed out back."

Sartain shrugged out of his coat and opened the door to shake the snow outside. The cabin was neat and tidy and warmly furnished with hand-hewn furniture, bright rugs, and striped-blanket room dividers. Tintypes and game trophies decorated the walls.

A fire popped in the fieldstone hearth to Sartain's left. Above it hung a wooden crucifix and an oil painting of the Virgin Mary.

"You don't need to tend me, Celina. I can pour my own coffee."

She was already filling a heavy, white mug. "I am blind, Mr. Sartain. I am not helpless. Papa did not raise me to be helpless. I can do everything everyone else does, within reason, except see. I've worked with our horses every day since I was six years old, and in the summer I raise chickens and goats. We butchered two weeks ago. Papa goes to town now and then to make me feel more independent. But also because he likes to drink in a saloon now and then," she added with a fond smile.

She set the mug on the halved-log table and glanced out the window behind Sartain. "Winter is on its way." She wrung her hands together. "And Papa is out in the first storm of the season. With a man who might kill him."

"He'll be all right. Beacham just wants the gold."

Celina reached behind her to adjust her chair and then sank slowly into it. "He did not tell me about any gold. Why didn't he tell me?"

"Didn't want to worry you, I suppose."

Sartain didn't tell her that the renegade, Rench Hadley, had threatened to cut her throat if her father did not adequately protect the gold, which was likely another good reason her father hadn't told her about the loot. He picked up the mug and blew ripples on the coffee. The aroma was intoxicating after the long day he'd had — killing seven men and enduring the start of a mountain snowstorm.

The cabin felt good and warm after the damp chill of outside.

They sat as the night slowly closed down just beyond the windows and the snow began piling up on the windowsills. Sartain and Celina Otero sat quietly at the table, drinking coffee and staying warm.

Celina was nervous. She sat with her head cocked slightly, as though listening intently — for what, the Cajun didn't know.

A distant rifle shot?

Finally, she rose from her chair and said, "How about some brandy, Mr. Sartain?"

Again, she'd surprised him. First the cursing and now the tangle-leg. He knew he was foolish to be surprised that a blind woman would have a proclivity for either.

"Why not?"

She retrieved a bottle and two cut-glass goblets from a cabinet near a ticking cabinet clock. She set the glasses on the table and stuck a finger into each glass as she filled it as high as her finger. She set the glasses on the table and set the bottle there, as well.

"I'll start supper," she said when she'd taken a sip of her brandy.

As she prepared the meal, moving with surprising ease about the large, well-appointed kitchen, she asked him to tell her about himself.

They had some time to kill, and she seemed to need to be distracted from the peril her father was in, so he told her about his life, starting with his orphaned childhood roaming the docks of the New Orleans French Quarter. He told her about being raised by whores, mucking out saloons, whorehouses, stables, and jails for pennies and nickels and then heading off to war on the side of the Confederacy.

He told her about rising to the rank of a young lieutenant who was as surprised as his fellow Rebel soldiers by his fighting prowess.

He told her about leading guerrilla raids behind enemy lines, killing Union officers and couriers and sabotaging munitions dumps and railroads. He told it all flatly, without bragging, because he didn't think it was anything to brag about. It was something he'd been ordered to do, so he'd done it, and that was that.

In fact, he was a little ashamed to have found himself — an orphan without a real home to speak of — so at home in the war and in the shoes of an efficient warrior.

Finally, while Celina stood rapt at the range, her back to him, making gravy from the elk loin she was roasting, he told her about joining the frontier cavalry after the travesty of Appomattox, about nearly being killed by Apaches, and about being discovered badly wounded and having had the good fortune of getting nursed back to health by an old, Arizona desert rat and his beautiful granddaughter, Jewel.

Then he told her about the drunken soldiers who'd come into the old prospector's camp when Sartain, well on his way back to health, had been off buying supplies in Benson. The soldiers had been part of a larger contingent who'd been scouring the desert for the missing soldier.

Instead, these men, who'd gotten drunk earlier in Benson, had found the beautiful Jewel. They'd raped and murdered her after they'd murdered her defenseless old grandfather and stole his gold cache.

Sartain left out the part about also finding his and Jewel's miscarried child lying dead beside Jewel's body. He hadn't withheld that part because he thought Celina might be too sensitive to hear about it. He'd withheld it because he hadn't wanted to evoke that image in his head again.

It evoked itself enough times without his conscious help.

"And now what do you, Mr. Sartain?" Celina asked as she set the bowls and platters of food — way too much food for two people — onto the table. Like the coffee earlier, the aromas were intoxicating. The steam fogged the windows that were turning whiter and whiter.

Sartain hesitated.

She looked at him almost as though she

could see him, though, like most blind people he'd known, she appeared to be staring right through him. Then she chuckled and wiped her hands on her apron.

"Come on, Mr. Sartain — after all you've already told me, do you expect me to be shocked that you didn't enter the priesthood?"

Sartain laughed.

Then he told her that he killed people who needed killing, for those who couldn't kill such folks themselves.

She stared at him from across the table. It was the first time she'd really seemed to be looking at him instead of through him. Her cheeks were flushed slightly, her lips parted.

Then she smiled, removed the apron she'd been wearing over her jeans and belt buckle, and hung it on a hook. "Well, then, *señor,*" she said as she moved carefully around the table and sat in her chair. "I am most fortunate to have a man such as yourself show up at my *casa* at such an opportune time."

She smiled. It was almost a beatific smile.

She rested her hands in her lap and bowed her head. "Shall I say grace?"

Chapter Sixteen

After the delicious and filling supper, Sartain went outside to look around. The snow fell steadily, whipped by a light wind, but it didn't seem to be getting any heavier. Several inches lay on the ground, but he could make out the moon's glow through a thin patch of clouds.

The squall would likely blow on out by morning.

He checked on Boss, who appeared content, and then kicked his way back through the fresh snow to the house.

"How does it look out there?" Celina asked. She was standing with her back to the fire, staring in his general direction. She'd pinned her hair into a loose chignon behind her head, with several strands fluttering down along her cheeks.

She'd also exchanged her red shirt for a light cotton blouse that, while buttoned at the throat, outlined her breasts. She had a round, curvy, alluring figure.

"I think the storm will be gone by morning. Not much of a storm, really."

"At least, not down here. I bet Papa and that outlaw, Beacham, are pinned down pretty good on the other side of High Canyon." She rubbed her arms and shook her head. "So frustrating. He's not ten miles away, but he could be a hundred. He took his coat and wool hat and gloves, thank god. And he strapped his blanket roll to his saddle before he rode out with . . . that man."

She wrinkled her nostrils in disgust.

Sartain hung his coat on a peg by the door. "He'll be all right. It's not that cold." He kicked out of his snowy boots and walked over to her. "I'll head out after him at first light tomorrow."

"I'm going with you."

"No, you're . . ." He let his voice trail off. Had he underestimated her again? "How?"

"Their sign will be wiped out by the snow, but I know the trail. I've been on it many times, and Papa has described it to me. You can call out the landmarks, and I'll point out the direction you need to take. I want to be there when you find them, Mike. Papa might need me."

"I don't think it's a good idea, Celina. I'm

going to be worried about you. I know you're stronger than I first thought you were, but you're still blind. My concern for you could distract me when the chips are down."

She turned down her mouth corners, and nodded. "All right, Mike. I see your point."

They'd agreed over supper to start using each other's first names.

"Good." Sartain smiled as he gazed down at her. "Say, you're a right special gal, Celina."

"And you're a special man, Mike."

He yawned. "This warm fire is makin' me tired. I reckon I'll turn in. Can I throw down right here on the floor?"

"Only if I can throw down with you."

Sartain studied her skeptically. Had he heard her right?

She stepped up close to him and placed her hands on his face. She started reading him again with her fingers. "What's the matter — does my blindness repel you?"

Sartain glanced down at her bosom rising and falling slowly beneath the tight blouse.

"Not at all. It's just that . . ."

"Am I being too forward?" Celina's hands continued to move on his face, her fingers occasionally pressing deeper as though to more easily read the lines forming his expression.

She smiled. "You're blushing, Mike."

She leaned forward to kiss his chin. "I've found that if I do not make the first move, no move will be made. Men seem hesitant to try to seduce me. Oh, there was one — a neighbor boy, a Basque shepherd named Rico — but that was a long time ago. I have made love since — mostly with men who worked for Papa. But there have not been many in recent years. I am lonely, Mike. I want to make love with you on the floor here by the fire."

She lowered one of her hands to his crotch, and pressed it against his staff, which was beginning to swell behind his denims. "I'm sorry if it sounds impersonal, but I don't want to let this opportunity slip through my fingers." She smiled coquettishly as she rubbed him, appearing to stare at his chin, and tucked her lower lip under her two small front teeth. "And I am beginning to sense — or to feel — that you might not want to let this opportunity slip through my fingers, either."

"Nah," Sartain grunted. "No, I don't."

He drew her to him gently and kissed her. It was a soft, sweet kiss at first.

Gradually, however, he could feel the body of the woman in his arms soften and grow warmer. She kissed him more hungrily, probing his mouth with her tongue. As she did, she kept her hand pressed against his crotch, by turns squeezing and massaging him through his denims.

After a time, Sartain pulled his mouth off of hers. His heart was thudding heavily. He unbuttoned her blouse and slid it off her shoulders. She wore a simple undershirt beneath it. Through the thin, wash-worn garment, he could see her nipples jutting. He lifted the shirt to reveal her breasts, pale, upturned, and swollen.

He lowered his head and suckled each nipple in turn until she threw her head back, groaning.

After a time, she stepped away, removed a bearskin blanket thrown over the back of a rocking chair, and spread it on the floor. She knelt on it, and hooked her finger at him. He moved forward, feeling as though each foot weighed ten pounds. She unbuttoned his pants, worked her small hand through the fly, and gently eased out his manhood, caressing it before she sucked him until she could sense he was near his peak.

"No, no," she said, wagging a finger at him. "Not yet, *amigo.* The night is young."

He knelt before her, laid her back on the

bearskin, and slowly undressed her while she continued to caress him, smiling beguilingly at the ceiling. When she lay sprawled naked before him, her body plump and creamy, the dark-brown nest between her legs glistening in the firelight, he undressed himself while she continued to smile at the ceiling.

Naked, he knelt between her legs, which he spread with his hands.

"No," she said, pushing up onto her knees, shaking her head. "Not yet. I want to *see* you first."

She pushed him down onto the bearskin. She built up the fire, adjusting the log with a poker, and then began slowly running her hands across the Cajun's body. She "read" every inch of him carefully, lifting his arms and caressing his sides as though he were trying to hide something from her. He was fascinated by the expressions that played across her face as she explored him — his nose, lips, eyelids . . . his hair, his chest, belly, crotch, thighs, even his toes.

"You are much man, Mike," she concluded, as she gained her knees again, and slowly straddled him.

He cupped her jostling breasts in his hands.

"Much, much man," she repeated.

"Ah, hell," he quipped, grinning up at her as she lowered herself onto him with a long, slow sigh through parted lips, squeezing her eyes closed and smiling as though she'd just seen heaven.

As Sartain had suspected it would, the snow stopped sometime during the night.

The next day dawned bright, clear, and cold, though it warmed up fast as the sun rose. He had breakfast with Celina and then kissed her goodbye, slid his Henry into his saddle scabbard, and rode off along the base of the ridge flanking the Otero ranch yard.

Celina had told him he'd find High Canyon out this way. Once he crossed it, he climbed another ridge via a switchback trail and then dropped down into a little, high mountain park in which the old Basque shepherd's cabin supposedly sat.

Sartain just hoped it was there that Miguel Otero had stowed the loot. Otherwise, he was on a wild goose chase, and who knew what would become of the old Mexican rancher? The Revenger had promised Celina he'd bring her father back safely. He didn't want to disappoint her.

The creek came storming down from the northern ridge about two miles away from the ranch. The snow was melting fast. In fact, the ground was already bare in places, snake-like tendrils of fog replacing the snow that had recently melted. The creek, roughly a hundred feet wide, was sheathed in pines and aspens, and its bed was lined with boulders.

Sartain cursed as he watched the white water thunder down from the higher reaches. Though the rain and snow of the day before had stopped, the snow was melting and filling the cavity through which the creek flowed. Sartain probably should have waited a couple of more hours, giving the snow time to melt and run off down the creek bed, but he'd thought there was a chance he could cross by midmorning, which it now was.

He looked around.

Maybe there still was a chance.

He turned Boss off the main trail and into the aspens, riding along the raging water until he dipped down a steep slope and came to a relatively flat area. Here the water wasn't running as violently as it had been up above. There was only one, small rapids. It still slid along its gravelly bed at a fast clip, but the Cajun decided to try it.

He urged the sure-footed horse forward. Boss lowered his head to sniff the water, as though he himself was gauging its speed and force. He rippled his withers, shook his head, and plunged into the creek.

The water rose a little higher than Boss's knees. He high-stepped through it. When he was about ten yards from the opposite bank, his right hoof slipped on a stone, and the horse lunged to that side.

Sartain's left leg dropped into the icy water, soaking his pants to the knee. His calf went numb. He grabbed the saddle horn, leaned hard to his right, and held on for dear life. If he plunged into the frigid snowmelt, he'd be a goner before he could thaw himself out.

With a shrill, angry whinny, Boss heaved himself back to all four hooves, lunged forward, and stormed out of the creek and up the opposite bank like a grizzly with a buckshot-peppered ass. His hooves clattered on the stones. When he got to the edge of the forest, he shook so hard that he nearly threw his saddle and rider.

"Ah, quit actin' like a sissy!" the Cajun admonished the mount. "You oughta be able to ford a creek twice that gnarly."

He grinned, relieved that they'd made it, and patted the horse's damp neck.

He put Boss up the switchback that rose on up through the forest on which tufts of melting snow occasionally rained down from overburdened branches, thudding on the damp ground. Birds sang and squirrels chittered angrily at the interloper. Fog snaked up from the warming ground. The smell of mushrooms and pine was so strong, rising from the spongy forest duff, that it nearly took the Cajun's breath away.

He crested the ridge at a windy pass so bright it stung his eyes. There were larger patches of snow up here where it was cooler, but the sun was fast melting those, as well.

He stared down into the canyon park Celina had described via her father's eyes. It was a heavenly place ringed with low, rocky ridges. Granite boulders lay strewn like the toys of a giant child. The park slanted off to Sartain's left, where a pond of flawless turquoise and ringed with spindly, bare aspens flashed in the sun.

Sartain looked around for the Basque shepherd's shack. Celina had said it would be in the park. Where, exactly, she hadn't indicated. Not having seen it, maybe she hadn't known. Sartain thought he'd find it easily enough.

He started down the slope, meandering around boulders.

From somewhere in the park below, a pistol cracked, echoing flatly.

So much for the serenity of the view . . .

CHAPTER SEVENTEEN

Sartain drew sharply back on Boss's reins and automatically reached for his rifle.

As he shucked the Henry from the scabbard and cocked it, another shot flatted out, its echo dwindling quickly. A man shouted something from too far away to be clearly heard.

The shout was followed by another pistol shot.

The shooter couldn't have been shooting at Sartain. Not with a pistol from so far away. Still, the Cajun swung down from the saddle, ground-reined Boss, and strode down the slope, continuing to weave around the boulders that had obviously tumbled from the far ridge, which was a massive chunk of jutting granite.

As he stepped around another boulder, he stopped and dropped to a knee.

On the far side of the park, roughly a hundred yards away, lay the remains of the shepherd's hut. It could have been mistaken for just another pile of rocks that had fallen down from the crag, but this pile roughly took the shape of a small house.

Most of the rear wall still stood. The other three walls had badly disintegrated. But what caught the brunt of the Cajun's attention were the two men standing out in front of the place. Miguel Otero stood farther away from the cabin than Chick Beacham. The men were separated by about twenty feet. They faced each other. Beacham was staggering around with a bottle in one hand, a pistol in the other hand. His left foot was still wrapped.

"Dance! I told you goddamnit, you chili-chompin' old bastard!"

Beacham leveled the pistol. Flames lapped from the barrel. The bullet plumed dust around Otero's mule-eared boots. The pistol's crack reached the Cajun's ears a wink after he'd seen the gun's orange blossom.

Otero stood still, stoically facing Beacham.

"Shit!" the Revenger raked out.

He looked around carefully, then moved to his right, circling around behind the old stone house and Beacham. When he'd gone about fifty yards to his right, he dropped down the slope. There were no covering boulders near the house, so he had to crouch, keeping the ruin between himself and the obviously drunk outlaw.

Otero probably had him in sight by now. If so, the Cajun hoped the old man wouldn't inadvertently give away his position.

As he worked his way toward the stone shack's nearest rear corner, Sartain saw a box on the ground to the left of the shack, near the front and where Beacham was trying to get Otero to dance.

The strongbox. The lid was open. The pale shapes of coin sacks shone humping up above the box. One sack lay on the ground, the sunlight glinting on the gold spilling from the sack's open mouth.

When Sartain had reached the shack's rear wall, Beacham laughed loudly and then stifled his laughter to shout, "Come on, you damn greaser son of a bitch — I'm celebratin'! I'm a rich man! And, as a rich man, I order you to dance, you peon!"

The pistol barked again. The bullet spanged shrilly off a rock.

"Please, *Señor* Beacham," implored Otero, holding his hands out, palms up, "I beseech you to stop this. There is your gold. You promised that when I took you to the gold, you would let me return to my ranch and my daughter. She needs me badly, *señor*.

I'm sure she is very worried."

"I'm gonna let you go, I'm gonna let you go," Beacham said as Sartain moved slowly, keeping his head low, along the shack's left wall. "Just as soon as you dance a little Mescin jig for me."

He took another swig from the bottle and stumbled around drunkenly on his bad foot. Then his voice rose with rage. "If you don't dance for me, goddamnit, I'm gonna blow your goddamn head off!"

Sartain stopped at the shack's front corner and loudly racked a cartridge into the Henry's breech. Standing straight and tall, he leveled the rifle on Beacham, who stood twenty feet away from him, and slightly to his right.

"Hold it, Beacham! Drop that pistol or I'll blow one through your ear!"

Beacham had frozen, pistol aimed at Otero. He glanced at Sartain. He started to lower the pistol, but then raised it again, again taking aim at the Mexican as he said, "No, no. You drop that Henry, Mr. Revenger, sir. Or you're gonna have an awful time scoopin' this bean-eater's brains out of the grass."

Sartain cursed himself for not shooting the man in the back, before Beacham had known he was here. Live and learn. He just hoped he didn't learn that lesson at Otero's expense.

Beacham shook his head with mock sadness. "Sure would be a shame, me havin' to kill that poor blind girl's old man. Who'd take care of her, then?"

"*Señor,* please!" said Otero in frustration, stomping one foot.

"What led you here, Beacham?" Sartain wanted to know.

Beacham chuckled, easing his weight off his bad foot. "Process of elimination, mostly. Besides, the Mex here seemed to be the only one *not* looking for the gold. Which meant he must have knowed where it was. You gonna make me shoot him?"

"All right," Sartain said, depressing the Henry's hammer. "I'm gonna set it down."

Beacham glanced over his shoulder at Sartain, who leaned forward to set the rifle on the ground.

"Look!" screamed Otero suddenly. "I am going to dance a jig for you now, *Señor* Beacham!"

Laughing and whooping as though he'd gone insane, Otero jumped up and down, stomping his feet and waving his arms. It was the distraction Sartain needed. He raised the Henry once more, racked a shell into the chamber again, and fired three times quickly from his hip.

Beacham had turned his head forward again. As the bullets punched into his back and his left side, under his arm, he triggered his revolver wildly, and stumbled forward and sideways, cursing. He got his bad foot tangled up with the good one, and hit the ground in a patch of melting snow.

"Ah, shit!" the outlaw intoned, writhing on his back. "I just knew I was never gonna live to spend that gold." He looked up at Sartain. He was dying fast, blood turning the snow to pink slush. "How do you suppose I knew that?"

Sartain lowered the Henry and stared down at the outlaw. "I don't know, Chick. Maybe you're smarter than you look."

Beacham almost smiled at that. Then he grunted, and his head sank back against the snow. He lay still, staring up at the cobalt sky between half-closed lids.

Sartain looked at Otero.

"Let's get you back to your ranch, *señor.* Your daughter is worried sick about you."

Otero's and Beacham's horses were tied in a natural rock shelter behind the shack, where they'd been tucked away from last night's snowstorm. There was a mule there, too — the big Missouri mule the outlaws had originally used to haul the gold.

Sartain and Otero rigged up all three mounts. Then they wrestled the heavy strongbox onto the mule's back and into the wooden, cradle-like packsaddle. They strapped it fast with rawhide and rope.

When they reached the creek, it was still rushing and roaring down its steep bed, but not with as much violence as before. Still, they forded the stream where Sartain had crossed earlier, having an easier time of it now that much of the snow had melted in the higher reaches, and headed on back to the ranch.

The Cajun led the big, lumbering mule by its lead rope.

They rode into the yard from the backside, angling away from the flanking ridge. The mule brayed, probably smelling the hay and oats in the barn. Boss whinnied his own anticipation at a hearty meal. The calls echoed in the thin, high-altitude air.

It was late in the afternoon, the long shadows angling out from the stone and wood cabin and outbuildings turning velvet. There was a wintery bite to the fresh, clean mountain air.

As they rode around to the front of the cabin, Sartain saw several horses in the corral. They hadn't been there when he'd ridden out earlier. He didn't recognize the mounts from Otero's cavvy — a steel dust, a skewbald paint, and a sleek cream.

Wait a minute — he *did* recognize the cream. That was Dixie's horse. And the paint belonged to Dewey Dade.

Before he could fully wrap his mind around the thought, Otero said sharply, *"Mierda!"*

Sartain followed the Mexican's horrified gaze toward the cabin. The Cajun's heart lurched and hammered.

Celina stood on a chair on the gallery. There was a rope around her neck. The rope was tied to a beam about a foot above her head. A red bandanna had been tied over her mouth. Her sightless eyes stared into the yard, lines of terror cutting across her forehead.

Raucous laughter bellowed from the big bear of a man standing beside her, in front of the cabin's open door. He must have stood a good six and a half feet tall. He wore a long bear robe and a long, tangled, salt-and-pepper beard. He had two big Colt pistols holstered around his waist. The flaps of his heavy coat had been tucked back behind them.

On his head was a ragged fur muskrat hat. He had a pipe wedged in the corner of his mouth, and a Henry rifle much like Sartain's own in his big, gloved hands.

He threw his head back, laughing. It was a deep-throated, hearty explosion that echoed loudly around the yard.

"You two done look like you come home to find the three bears in your beds!"

The man laughed even louder.

Then the laughter was cut off abruptly, and his face with its hard, gray eyes clouded up and appeared about to storm, his rugged cheeks above the beard turning dark red. "If you don't throw down your guns, I'm gonna give this chair here a little nudge with my foot."

He stepped sideways and kicked a leg of the chair, causing it to bark as it scraped a few inches sideways. Celina cried out behind the bandanna as she desperately repositioned her feet on the chair.

"Like that — see?" said the big man, laughing again.

"Please, Señor Hadley . . . !" cried Otero, quickly shucking his pistol and tossing it onto the ground. "Do not hurt her! I beseech you!"

"Hadley," Sartain muttered. "Rench Hadley . . ."

"Before your eyes, Sartain." Hadley hardened his eyes again. "Your turn. Step down from your horse and very slowly toss all your guns onto the ground, then my assistants will gather them up and put them somewhere they can't cause any trouble."

A figure materialized in the doorway behind Hadley. A female shape. Then Dixie McKee stepped out of the cabin, holding a carbine in her gloved hands. Dewey Dade walked out behind her, his right arm in a sling. He held his Spencer in his right hand.

Dixie did not meet Sartain's gaze. The kid did, though his eyes owned a sheepish cast.

"Figures," Sartain said as he lightened himself of his LeMat and Henry.

Dixie came down the steps, picked up the rifle and the big pistol, and stepped back. She looked at Sartain, but she did not say anything.

"You disappoint me, girl," the Revenger said.

She drew a breath, then let it out slowly. "Gold makes a person do crazy things, Mike."

She glanced at Miguel Otero, who had swung down from his horse to stand looking worriedly at his daughter and holding his horse's reins. "I'm sorry, Miguel. I saw you and Mike talking, and . . . something told me you'd told him about the gold. Since you know everything that goes on in this neck of these mountains, I figured you probably knew about the gold, too."

Sartain said, "How did you come to throw in with Hadley?"

"He rode into Hard Winter yesterday. Wanted me to show him the way out here. Promised me and Dewey here a cut of the gold if we helped him."

"You see," Hadley said, "when I was last here, I was in little condition to pay close attention to where I was. All I knew was that I'd left the gold with the bean-eater."

"You break out of jail?" Sartain asked.

"Ain't never been a jail could hold Rench Hadley." The big outlaw looked at Otero. "We'll be enjoyin' your hospitality tonight, *señor.* Tomorrow, we'll be pullin' out — the girl an' me, anyways." He glanced at Dewey Dade. "There's no room on my trail for a snot-nosed kid. Dixie . . . well, she's another story."

Dixie lowered her eyes, cheeks coloring slightly with shame.

"You do disappoint me, girl," Sartain said slowly, meaning it, feeling the disenchantment in every bone.

Otero strode forward. "Please, *señor* — my daughter!"

"Go ahead and cut her down," Hadley said. "She's got work to do. Kitchen work.

I'm so hungry, my belly's thinkin' my throat's been cut."

As Otero cut Celina down from the roof beam, Dewey Dade came up behind Dixie and stood before Sartain. "I do apologize, Mr. Sartain. You saved my life. But that doesn't give you the right to take all that gold for yourself."

Hadley laughed. "Sartain, you have gone from a very rich man to a very poor one very quickly. How do you like that?"

"He was not taking the gold for himself, *señor,*" Otero told the big bear-like outlaw as he removed the rope from around Celina's neck. "He was taking it back to its rightful owners. You must let him do this. The gold is evil! Everyone who becomes involved with it dies! It is a curse on these mountains!"

"Ah, shut up with your bean-eater superstitions," Hadley snarled. "Get on inside here, Sartain. I promised Dixie I wouldn't kill you. That's why you ain't dead. But you try anything, all bets are off. We're gonna tie you and Otero up so we can all dine comfortably this evenin'."

He glanced at Dewey. "Kid, get that gold over to the barn. Unsaddle these horses and tend 'em. A man's gotta tend to horses . . . even the horse of his enemies."

He smiled at that and stepped aside, wagging his rifle toward the open doorway. Sartain glanced once more at Dixie and then started forward. When he'd reached the bottom of the gallery steps, Dixie said, "Wait, Mike."

Sartain stopped. He tensed. He knew what was coming.

Dixie pressed the barrel of her rifle against his back. "The derringer, too."

Sartain sighed, and shook his head. He reached into his vest pockets, pulling out the watch and then the derringer. He removed the pearl-gripped hideout pistol from its chain and handed it back to the girl.

Hadley slapped his thigh, laughing. "You're damn lucky you're still alive, Sartain. The only reason you are is because of her. I promised. And I'll be damned if this old outlaw don't keep his promises."

He shook his head as though it were a severe inner weakness.

"Go on inside, Mike," Dixie said, giving him a shove with her rifle.

Chapter Eighteen

Sartain stepped through the cabin door. Celina was making coffee in her steady, methodical way.

"You all right, sweetheart?" the Cajun asked her.

She turned her face slightly toward him, and feigned a reassuring smile. "I am all right, Mike. I'm sorry I couldn't warn you."

"Ain't that all just sweet?" said Hadley, moving around Dixie and shoving Sartain into the cabin. "Sweetheart, eh? You two musta got to know each other real well. Don't mind 'em blind, eh, Sartain? Well, maybe later I'll give her a try myself!"

Sartain turned to him, bunching his lips and clenching his fists at his sides. Fury burned behind his eyeballs.

Hadley stood by the table, staring back at him, sizing him up. "You wanna make a play for me, do you?" He leaned his rifle against the wall. "Well, go ahead."

Hope lightened the Revenger's heart. Had he stumbled upon his chance to get him and the Oteros out of this mess?

If he could hammer the big outlaw unconscious, he might be able to do just that. The man was a little bigger than he was, but he'd kicked the shit out of both ends of men bigger than Hadley, who also appeared at least ten years older and weighed down with extra tallow around his middle.

"Sure," Sartain said, curling his upper lip and spreading his feet aggressively. "Why the hell not? You wanna take it outside?"

"Yeah," Hadley said, nodding slowly. "Yeah, why don't we just do that?"

"Get the humps out of your necks, both of you!" Dixie scolded, standing by the door and holding her carbine across her belly. "There's no point in doing anything to risk losing that gold, Rench."

Hadley scowled at her, deep lines cutting across his forehead. "What? You think I can't take him?"

Dixie glared at him in frustration. Then she let the muscles in her face relax, knowing that the way you got a man like Rench Hadley to back down was not by challenging him further.

"Rench . . . honey," she said, though the "honey" had come out a bit like a prune pit, "let's not make this any more complicated than it needs to be, all right?" She faced him, smiling winningly, a tad sexily. "All we want is the gold."

Sartain laughed. "She doesn't think you can take me, Hadley. You know what? I think she's right."

Hadley lurched toward him. Dixie stepped in front of the big man, holding her rifle across his chest. "Rench, no! Don't fall for it, honey — you're smarter than — !"

She whipped around as Sartain made his move, bulling toward her and Hadley, hoping to get his hands on her rifle. He stopped dead in his tracks as she faced him now, aiming her carbine at his belly and loudly racking a cartridge into the chamber.

"I'll do it, Mike. I'll shoot you." Dixie shook her head slowly. "I've been dirt poor all my life. Rench has promised me ten thousand dollars — more if I ride with him. That's far from what I was hoping for, but it's enough for me to start another life."

"Whorin' yourself to him, huh?" Again, the Cajun shook his head.

"Like I said," Dixie said. "I've been dirt poor all my life." She glanced at Hadley. "See what he's doing? He's trying to distract us both from our purpose here, Rench."

Hadley stretched his lips back from his

large, yellow teeth. "Shoot him, sugar. Just go ahead and shoot him. Then we won't have to worry about him . . . or listen to him no more."

Dixie spoke to Hadley while keeping her gaze and her rifle on Sartain. "No, Rench. You promised. No killing. And you leave Celina alone."

Hadley glanced at her, lust causing his eyelids to grow heavy. "I will as long as I got me another option."

"You do. That's what I promised. If you follow through with your promise, I'll follow through with mine."

"All right," Hadley said. "Let's stop all this palaver. You tie him and the bean-eater up good and tight."

Otero stood beside Sartain. He and Celina had both frozen in fear to watch as the Cajun and the big outlaw had faced off. Now Sartain thought he could hear them both give a collective, albeit silent, sigh of relief that the storm had blown over.

As Hadley sat down at the table and told Celina to get back to work, Dixie ordered Sartain and Otero to sit on the floor with their backs to separate ceiling support posts. She didn't have her rifle now. She'd wisely leaned it against the wall by the door.

Sartain looked at Hadley. The outlaw sat

in a chair at the table, smiling at the Revenger. Reading his mind. The outlaw held his own Henry barrel-up on his knee, flicking his thumb against the hammer.

His eyes told Sartain that he wanted him to try something. Anything. So he could justify shooting him to Dixie.

Sartain returned the outlaw's grin as Dixie ordered him to snake his hands back around the post. Boots thumped on the gallery, and Dewey Dade came in. He started to doff his hat when Hadley growled, "Get out there!"

"What for?" the kid asked indignantly. "I done took care of the hosses and mule."

"Don't you challenge me, bucko! I said get out there! Never know who else might be after my . . . uh . . . *our* . . . gold." Hadley chuckled. "You'll spend the night on the porch, keepin' watch."

Dewey Dade chuffed his consternation, glanced at Dixie, and then turned and stepped back out, closing the door behind him.

Silently, Celina made a stew from the elk hanging in the keeper shed. She also made a couple of loaves of bread, and set the fresh bread and a bowl of butter on the table.

She also made coffee. Hadley added a

goodly portion of the busthead he hauled out of his saddlebags to the coffee, and stirred it with a spoon.

Dixie brought a plate out to Dewey Dade. When she came back in, she looked down at Sartain and Otero. "Can I feed them?" she asked Hadley.

"You'd have to untie 'em."

"How 'bout if I untie 'em and hold a rifle on 'em while they eat?"

Hadley was shoveling the stew into his mouth, mindless of the mess he was leaving in his beard. He eyed her, grinning with half his filled mouth. "How bad you want 'em to eat?"

"Rench, they have to eat."

Hadley's lusty grin broadened. "How bad?"

Dixie only shook her head in disgust and filled two bowls with Celina's stew. Hadley chuckled again lustily. Dixie set a slice of the steaming bread into the bowls, as well, and she and Celina untied Otero and Sartain. Dixie sat in the rocking chair six feet away from the Cajun's extended legs, holding her carbine across her thighs, watching him and Otero down their stew.

Sartain ate in frustration, despite the succulence of the stew. He had no idea how he was going to get himself and the Oteros out of this whipsaw. At least, he didn't know *yet.* He wasn't going to give up. They still had a long night ahead.

Something told him that was about all the time he and the Oteros had. He had a feeling Rench Hadley was a man accustomed to getting his way. After he'd satisfied his itch with Dixie upstairs tonight, he might not be so amenable to keeping Sartain alive.

If he killed Sartain, he'd likely go ahead and kill Celina and her father, as well. To keep them quiet about his presence here, if for no other reason. He might also kill Dixie and Dewey Dade. There were other nights ahead. Other women. He likely wasn't a man fond of sharing his plunder when he didn't have to.

Rench Hadley wasn't a man who needed many reasons to kill.

When Sartain and Otero had finished eating, Dixie retied them while Hadley held his rifle on Sartain with the same challenging grin as before. Then Dixie sat at the table across from the silent Celina, and ate a bowl of stew.

Finished with his own meal, Hadley poured more whiskey into his coffee cup, got up from the table, and sat in the rocking chair parked by the fire. He rocked, holding his rifle across his thighs, and gave

Sartain the stink eye.

He did that for a long time before he took a sip of the whiskey, swallowed, and said, "Big man, ain't ya, Sartain? Big, tough fellow. The Revenger, they call you. Yeah, I've heard of you."

"You have me at a disadvantage, then, Rench. I wouldn't know you from Adam's off ox. But, then, you never hear too much about the little men workin' the wrong side of the law. Little men who swipe old schoolmarms' beaded reticules, an' such."

Dixie shot Rench a warning look. "Don't listen to him, Rench. He's at it again." She turned to Sartain. "Shut up, Mike!"

"Don't worry, don't worry, sugar," Rench said. "He ain't gonna crawl my hump. He knows who stole that gold out there in the barn." He chuckled. "Sure as hell wasn't no hind-tit calf of no penny-ante outlaw. Hah!"

"It couldn't have been all that hard," said Sartain. "I mean, you had enough men. Until you got 'em all killed, that is. Even with all them boys backin' your play, you sure have had a damned hard time keeping your hands on the loot."

Hadley's cheeks colored above his beard. "Yeah, well, I was double-crossed."

"By Chick Beacham? Pshaw! I left him dead just over the next pass. He wasn't nothin' to take down. And anyone —"

"Don't listen to him, Rench!"

"— and anyone with half the sense God gave him could see the man wasn't to be trusted." Sartain chuckled. "You must be new to the business, Hadley. Shit, I think young Dewey Dade out there could have pulled off that job without getting horn-swoggled and whipsawed by the likes of Chick Beacham!"

Dixie got up and strode over to Sartain, glaring down at him. She held her rifle across her thighs. "Mike, if you don't shut up, I'm going to let him shoot you."

Sartain looked up at her, smiling. "He's not man enough for you, sugar. Can't you see that? He's old and stove up. Why, he's a fool, to boot. He'll get himself . . . and you . . . killed!"

"Old and stove up, am I?" Hadley said, gaining his feet. "How 'bout if I come over there and kick you to a bloody pulp? Then you'll see how old and stove up I am."

"Please, do not do this!" Celina shrieked, covering her ears with her hands. She was standing near the range. Sartain hated scaring her like this, but he saw few other options in trying to save her life.

Miguel Otero sucked air through his teeth and shook his head in consternation.

Sartain kept prodding the big outlaw, who'd gained his feet and stood glaring down at the Revenger, big fists balled at his sides. "You'd kick a man when he's down and tied? Now, you see there, sugar? You really wanna throw in with a yellow mutt like that? Coward, is what he is."

"Mike, goddamnit!" Dixie swung around toward Hadley. "Rench, stop listening to him."

"I tell you what, Hadley," Sartain said. "If you can beat me straight up at arm wrestling — no fisticuffs or any of that nonsense, just a good, harmless arm wrestling match — I'll shut up."

"Arm wrestlin'?" Hadley said with a skeptical cast to his gaze.

"Yeah. Arm wrestling. But let's put a little bet on it."

"What kind of bet?"

"Rench, he's up to somethin'."

"I am up to somethin' — I'll admit it," Sartain said. "I'm jealous, Dixie. You and I had us a fine time together back in Hard Winter. I just hate to see you throw in with this stove-up old outlaw for a little gold. I say if I can beat him at arm wrestling, he don't take you upstairs tonight."

"And if you can't?" Hadley said, while Dixie just stared down at Sartain as though trying to figure his angle.

"If I can't — well, then, she's yours. May the stronger man win her body if not her heart."

"If you win, you take her upstairs?" Hadley said.

"You got it. I don't care nothin' about no gold. This is just about you an' me an' Dixie. I don't wanna have to sit down here tonight and hear you two goin' at it like a coupla horny polecats. Not if there's somethin' I can do to stop it."

"Rench!"

"What do you say, Rench? Gonna be a long night. Long, borin' night. Let's make it interesting, shall we?"

Hadley's cheeks and nose were bright red. The Cajun hadn't accomplished his first task of getting the man's blood up. Now, he just had to hope he could beat him at arm wrestling.

Hadley turned to Dixie. "Untie him."

"Rench, you're walking right into his trap!"

"Hell, it ain't no trap. I'll beat him fair and square and make him sit down here, tied up, listening to me make you groan like a mare in season!" Hadley laughed and slapped his thigh. "By damn, I think it's a damn fine idea."

He grabbed his Henry off the table, cocked it, and aimed it at Dixie. "Untie him. Now! Do as I say, or you won't get a lick of that gold!"

"Rench, honey," Dixie said with that ingratiating smile again. "Let's leave him tied up, and you an' me go upstairs right now. Wouldn't you like that?"

Hadley grinned, then slid his hard-eyed gaze to Sartain. "I'd love it a whole lot better after I've whipped this tough-talkin' son of a bitch at arm wrestlin'. So he can sit down here and chew his arm off. Hah!"

He scowled at her, hard-jawed. "Untie him!"

Chapter Nineteen

Dixie untied Sartain, telling him, "You try anything, I'm going to shoot you. I promise I will."

"Don't doubt it a bit," said the Cajun.

He was beginning to think she would.

He glanced at Otero. The Mexican was looking up at him through his customarily slitted lids. Celina had rolled and lit a cigarette for him, and he puffed it now, smoke billowing around his head where he sat with his back to the ceiling support post.

Sartain offered a reassuring smile. Then he turned to Celina, who sat in the rocking chair near the popping fire, gazing at Sartain, head canted slightly to one side, frowning, as though she were trying to understand all that was going on around her.

"Get over here," Hadley said, pounding the oilcloth-covered table. He sat with his back to the range, facing the front of the cabin. "By God, I'm gonna teach you to mind your manners, Sartain. And then I'm gonna take her upstairs and give her the time of her life!"

"Talk's cheap," Dixie muttered.

Hadley looked at her sharply. Then he looked at Sartain and laughed. "By God, I like her. She's got pluck. I like that in a girl . . . when they're fun to look at. I think I'm gonna keep her. We'll have a good ole time of it, her an' me."

Dixie didn't say anything. She just sank into a chair at the end of the table, and held her rifle on Sartain, who slacked into a chair across from Hadley, his back to the door.

The door opened. Dewey Dade poked his head into the cabin, frowning curiously. "What's goin' on?"

"Get back out there and keep an eye on that gold!" Hadley roared at him.

Dewey cussed as he pulled his head back outside and closed the door.

Hadley rolled up his right shirtsleeve. "For Dixie."

"For Dixie," the Revenger said, rolling up his own sleeve.

"How flattering you fellas are," Dixie said dryly.

Hadley leaned forward, placing his elbow in the middle of the table. Sartain did the same. They locked hands.

Hadley glanced at Dixie. "Say go."

"Oh, shit . . . just go, for chrissakes!"

Hadley's hand tightened around Sartain's and he began thrusting the Revenger's own paw toward the table. Sartain tensed his arm and grunted, forcing Hadley's hand back up.

The man was strong. Sartain could tell that right away. And he had a powerful grip. He didn't think he was any stronger than Sartain himself, but he could tell it was going to be a battle. Sartain's arm had been angled behind his back for the past hour, the wrists tightly tied, impeding his blood flow. He hadn't yet gotten all the feeling back into his hands.

Nor the strength.

As he and Hadley bunched their lips and grunted and shifted around in their creaking chairs, Sartain was vaguely aware of Celina standing and moving slowly, tensely, about the kitchen, tending to her post-supper chores. The girl was frightened, and she was trying to busy herself to keep her mind off the chaos and violence around her.

Otero smoked on the floor, staring dubiously toward the two arm wrestlers.

Sartain was hoping to somehow get his hands on a rifle. He couldn't have done that with both hands tied, but now he had a chance. Somehow, he either had to take advantage of Hadley's absorption in the match and pull one of the man's two pistols from their holsters strapped to his waist, or lunge for Dixie's rifle.

He thought she'd probably hesitate before shooting him, giving him a chance at the Winchester. He'd hoped she'd stand or sit a little closer to him, but she hadn't. He had to play with the cards he'd been dealt.

To snag one of Hadley's revolvers, he'd first have to pull the big man toward his side of the table, and make a long, fast reach. Long odds, but there they were. Sitting on the floor with his hands tied had been getting him nowhere but closer to the void.

He looked at his hand wrapped around the outlaw's. His knuckles were white. He drove Hadley's hand down to his left a ways. Hadley grunted, gritted his teeth, and smiled at Sartain as he funneled more strength into his arm, shoving the Revenger's hand back up and over toward the table.

"Got me a feelin' we're almost done here tonight, Sartain," Hadley spat through gritted teeth. He glanced toward Dixie. "Best start prettyin' yourself up, sugar."

"Like I said," Dixie said, "talk is cheap."

Sartain grunted and heaved his hand back

up over the outlaw's. "You can say that again," he said, driving Hadley's hand down toward the table, both hands jerking as they fought.

Sartain thought that when he had the outlaw's hand down flat on the table, he'd punch him hard with his left fist, pull him toward himself, and reach for his pistol. He could do it now, but his own consarned pride compelled him to beat the man first. Hadley would be distracted enough by the loss that Sartain's plan just might work.

Might . . .

Sartain drove Hadley's hand farther . . . and farther . . . and farther down.

Hadley's eyes were blazing and haunted as he stared at the two clenched fists, Sartain's now shoving his within six inches of the oilcloth.

Sartain glanced at Dixie. She was smiling at him, her rifle aimed at his head. Shit, he thought. She'd read his mind. She knew what he was going to do, and she was ready for him.

Shit, shit, shit . . .

Hadley cursed loudly. He drove his hand up, forcing Sartain's back.

"Oh, hell," the Cajun grunted, changing his strategy and easing the tension in his arm.

Hadley laughed and slammed the Revenger's hand down on the table.

"There you go, you sonofabitch!"

Dixie lowered the rifle slightly, frowning, puzzled.

"Ah, shit!" Sartain said, holding onto Hadley's hand.

Hadley looked at the two hands still locked together. Then he looked at Sartain.

Sartain drew Hadley's hand toward him. The man's head jerked toward him, as well. Sartain slammed his left fist against the man's nose, feeling the flesh give beneath his knuckles. Dixie had been caught off guard. As Sartain released Hadley's hand, he grabbed the table and slid it sideways, slamming it into Dixie just as she leveled the rifle on Sartain's belly.

The girl screamed. The Winchester roared, the slug plunking into the ceiling over Sartain's head.

"Oh, you bastard!" Hadley roared.

Sartain threw himself across the table, bulling into Hadley and clawing for his the pistol holstered on his right hip. He got to it too late. The gun was already in the man's hand. Hadley was raising it, clicking the hammer back as the two fell together onto the floor by the range.

Sartain winced, steeling himself for the

bullet that would likely blow his guts out.

But it didn't come.

The pistol dropped from Hadley's hand. Sartain felt a warm substance spurt against him. To his left, he saw Dixie gain her feet, screaming and racking another cartridge into her Winchester's breech.

Automatically, Sartain kicked her legs out from under her.

Again, she drilled another round into the ceiling a quarter-second before she hit the floor with a *boom!* The rifle clattered to the floor, as well. Sartain crawled over to it, shoved the cursing Dixie away from it, grabbed it, and rose to his feet, racking a round into the chamber and turning toward where Hadley lay on the floor by the range.

Sartain frowned.

Hadley lay quivering, blood spurting from the paring knife sticking out of the left side of his neck. The outlaw cupped his hands to the wound and stared in shock and horror at the ceiling.

Celina stood with her back to the range, eyes wide as she gazed blankly toward Sartain, turning her head slightly to listen. Her cheeks were pale, lips trembling.

Sartain turned to Dixie. She was gaining her feet, looking at him through her mussed hair jostling about her flushed cheeks. She looked at the rifle in his hands. She didn't say anything. She just turned her mouth corners down and shook her head.

"So close," she said. "I was so close." She looked at Hadley, scowling incredulously. "What the hell? Who . . . ?"

She let her voice trail off as she looked at Celina, on whose lips a slight smile grew.

Dixie turned to Miguel Otero, who smiled up at Sartain, the butt of his cigarette poking out from between his leathery lips.

"You were right — weren't you, Miguel?" Dixie said. "You were right all along. That gold really was a curse."

"Oh, it still is," the Mexican said.

He drew the cigarette into his mouth, dousing it, and then spat it out onto the floor, still smiling.

Outside, hooves thundered. A mule brayed. It brayed again as the hoof thuds dwindled into the distance.

Sartain stepped outside. Dewey Dade was nowhere in sight.

In the distance, the mule brayed again. And then the hoof thuds fell silent.

Dixie came out to stand beside Sartain, looking in the direction that Dewey Dade had ridden off with the gold. Celina came out a minute later, followed by her father. They all stood staring into the distance.

Sartain sighed as he pulled his makings sack out of his shirt pocket.

Dixie looked up at Sartain. "Can you forgive me, Mike?"

Sartain hiked a shoulder as he rolled a quirley in the light angling through the open door. "I reckon. Like you said, gold does strange things to people. I'm just glad we're rid of it."

He looked at Otero and Celina. "You two all right?"

"Sí," said Otero, wrapping an arm around Celina's shoulders, drawing his daughter against him. She turned to her old man and wrapped her arms tightly around him, kissing his cheek.

"Sí," said Celina. "I am fine now, too. I am glad to have my papa back."

"That was some neat trick," Sartain told her. "You likely saved us all."

Celina shrugged. "I honestly didn't know I was going to do that until I did it."

Otero sighed. "It is the boy I am worried about."

Sartain folded his cigarette closed and stared once more into the night alive now with only twinkling starlight and a single, yammering coyote.

"Go with God, kid," he said, and poked the quirley into his mouth, sealing it. "But I got a strong hunch the devil's gonna be the one doggin' your heels."

ABOUT THE AUTHOR

Western novelist **Peter Brandvold** was born and raised in North Dakota. He has penned over 100 fast-action westerns under his own name and his penname, **Frank Leslie.** He is the author of the ever-popular .45-Caliber books featuring Cuno Massey as well as the Lou Prophet and Yakima Henry novels. The Ben Stillman books are a long-running series with previous volumes available as ebooks. Brandvold/Leslie's novels are also published in hardcover editions as well as large print editions, by Five Star Press/Thorndike. Head honcho at "Mean Pete Publishing," publisher of lightning-fast western ebooks, he has lived all over the American West but currently lives in western Minnesota. Follow him at Amazon.com and follow his blog at: www.peterbrandvold.blogspot.com.

The employees of Thorndike Press hope you have enjoyed this Large Print book. All our Thorndike, Wheeler, and Kennebec Large Print titles are designed for easy reading, and all our books are made to last. Other Thorndike Press Large Print books are available at your library, through selected bookstores, or directly from us.

For information about titles, please call:
(800) 223-1244

or visit our Web site at:
http://gale.com/thorndike

To share your comments, please write:

Publisher
Thorndike Press
10 Water St., Suite 310
Waterville, ME 04901